D1465192

BY ADAM CHRISTOPHER

The Empire State
Empire State
The Age Atomic

The Spider Wars
The Burning Dark
Cold War
The Machine Awakes

The Ray Electromatic Mysteries
Brisk Money
Made to Kill
Standard Hollywood Depravity
Killing Is My Business
I Only Killed Him Once

Elementary
The Ghost Line
Blood and Ink

Dishonored
The Corroded Man
The Return of Daud
The Veiled Terror

Seven Wonders
Hang Wire

DARKNESS ON THE EDGE OF TOWN

STRANGER THINGS

Fiction

Suspicious Minds: The First Official Novel

Non-Fiction

*Worlds Turned Upside Down: The Official
Behind-The-Scenes Companion*
Visions from the Upside Down: A Stranger Things Art Book

DARKNESS ON THE EDGE OF TOWN

ADAM CHRISTOPHER

arrow books

Arrow Books
20 Vauxhall Bridge Road
London SW1V 2SA

Arrow Books is part of the Penguin Random House group of companies
whose addresses can be found at global.penguinrandomhouse.com.

Penguin
Random House
UK

Stranger Things: Darkness on the Edge of Town is a work of
fiction. Names, places and incidents either are products of the author's
imagination or are used fictitiously. Any resemblance to actual events,
places, locales, or persons, living or dead, is entirely coincidental.

First published in Great Britain by Century in 2019
First published in paperback by Arrow Books in 2020

www.penguin.co.uk

A CIP catalogue record for this book is available from the British Library

ISBN 9781787466555

Book design by Elizabeth A. D. Eno

Printed and bound in Great Britain by Clays Ltd, Eclograf S.p.A.

MIX
Paper from
responsible sources
FSC
www.fsc.org   FSC® C018179

Penguin Random House is committed to a sustain-
able future for our business, our readers and our
planet. This book is made from Forest Stewardship
Council® certified paper.

For Sandra, always.
And for Aubrey, because.

DARKNESS ON THE EDGE OF TOWN

HOPPER'S CABIN
HAWKINS, INDIANA

Jim Hopper tried to kill the smile he felt spreading across his face as he stood by the sink, arms immersed in hot, soapy water, watching through the kitchen window as the snow fell outside in huge, fist-sized clumps.

Christmas wasn't a good time, not for him, not since . . . well, not for a long time. Not since Sara. He knew this, he accepted this, and for the six years—going on seven, now—he'd spent back in Hawkins, he had resigned himself to the growing feeling of misery and loss that steadily grew stronger and stronger as the holiday season approached.

Resigned himself? No, that wasn't it, not quite. In truth, he had *welcomed* the feeling, allowing himself to be overwhelmed by it, because it was . . . easy. Comfortable.

And, strangely, safe.

At the same time, he hated himself for it, for giving in, for letting the seed of despair in his mind grow each and every year until it fully blossomed. And his hatred did nothing but drive him deeper into the darkness, and the whole cycle went on, and on, and on.

But not anymore. Not now.

Not this year.

This was the first year, really, where things were different. His life had changed, and that change had let him see how far he had fallen, to see what he had become.

All because of her. Jane, his adopted daughter. Legally, officially, his family.

Jane Hopper.

Eleven.

El.

Hopper felt the smile grow again, pulling insistently at the corners of his mouth. This time, he didn't try to stop it.

Of course, having El around didn't mean he had to forget the past—far from it. But it did mean he had new responsibilities. Once more, he had a daughter to raise. And that meant moving on. His past wasn't gone, but, finally, he could let it sleep in the back of his mind.

Outside the snow continued to fall, the trees that surrounded the cabin now embedded a good two feet up their trunks in the soft white blanket. The radio had said it wasn't a storm and there were no weather warnings, but the forecast Hopper had caught earlier in the afternoon now seemed a little optimistic. A generous dumping had been predicted over the whole county, but right now Hopper wondered if it had all landed in the few acres around his grandfather's old cabin. If you had to travel, the weather report had said, just . . . don't. Stay inside. Keep warm. Finish off the eggnog.

And that suited Hopper just fine.

El, on the other hand . . .

"Water's cold."

Hopper blinked out of his reverie and found El suddenly by his side at the sink. He looked down at her, her expression so intense, so interested, so *concerned* that he had been standing at the sink doing the dishes for so long that the water had gone cold. Then he looked down at his hands, lifting them from the dying foam. His fingertips had turned to prunes, and the stack of dishes from their post-Christmas leftover feast hadn't gotten much smaller.

"Everything okay?"

Hopper glanced down at El again. Her eyes were wide, expectant. He found that smile growing again. Dammit, he just couldn't help it.

"Yeah, everything's okay," he said. He reached over to ruffle her mop of dark curls, but she retreated with a grimace at the touch of his foam-covered hand. Hopper laughed, pulling his hand back and slipping the towel off the counter next to him. Drying his hands, he nodded back toward the den.

"You manage to raise Mike yet?"

El sighed—with perhaps a little too much drama, Hopper thought . . . but, then again, everything for her was still new and often, it seemed, a challenge. He watched as she headed back to the couch and picked up the hefty rectangle of her new walkie-talkie, holding it out to him, like he could somehow conjure up her friends out of the ether.

They looked at each other, then after a few moments El waggled the walkie-talkie impatiently.

"What am I supposed to do?" asked Hopper, slinging the kitchen towel over one shoulder. "Is it not working?" He took the device, and turned it over in his hands. "Can't need a new battery already?"

"Nobody there." El sighed again, her shoulders slumped.

"Oh, yeah, I remember," said Hopper, recalling now that Mike, Dustin, Lucas, and Will were all out seeing extended family today; the whole gang was well out of range of El's new walkie-talkie. El took the device back and fiddled with the controls, clicking the volume knob on and off, on and off, short bursts of static emanating from the speaker with each turn of the control.

"Careful," said Hopper. "That was a very nice gift they got you." Then he winced, realizing that his own efforts in that department—Hungry Hungry Hippos, of all things, a game *far* too young for El, the realization hitting him like a sledgehammer as soon as she had pulled the paper off it yesterday—paled in comparison to the walkie-talkie that the boys had pitched in together to buy.

It seemed he was well out of practice at fatherhood. He bought the game almost without thinking, because Sara had loved the game, and—

And El wasn't Sara.

But El didn't notice Hopper's discomfort now, so intent was her focus on the device. Hopper walked back to the sink and turned the hot tap on, stirring the water in the sink with one hand. "And you had a nice time yesterday, right?" He glanced over his shoulder. "Right?"

El nodded, and stopped clicking the walkie-talkie.

"Right," said Hopper. "And they'll all be home tomorrow. In fact," he said, turning the tap off, "you'll probably be able to raise them on that thing later tonight."

With the sink refilled, Hopper resumed his dish duty. Behind him, he heard El pad back into the kitchen. He glanced down as she appeared at his side again.

"Hey," he said, submerging a dish from the pile, "I know you're bored, but bored is good, trust me."

El frowned. "Bored is good?"

Hopper paused, hoping he was heading in the right direction with this piece of ad-lib parental wisdom. "Sure it is. Because when you're bored, you're safe. And when you're bored, that's when you get *ideas*. And ideas are good. You can never have enough ideas."

"Ideas are good," said El. It wasn't a question, it was a statement. Hopper looked at her again. He could almost see the cogs turning in her mind.

"Right," he said. "And ideas lead to questions. Questions are also good." Hopper looked out the window, hiding his frown from his daughter. *Questions are also good?* What the hell was he talking about? He wasn't sure if he'd had too much leftover eggnog, or not enough.

El slinked out of the kitchen; a moment later Hopper heard the click of the TV. Glancing over his shoulder, he saw she was sitting on the couch, the TV well out of her reach but the channels cycling through in rapid succession anyway, the screen flickering from one wash of multicolored static to another.

"Yeah, it's the weather. Sorry, the TV won't be working for a while, I think. Hey, you want another game of Hungry Hungry Hippos?"

Hopper's question was met with silence. He looked back over his shoulder again to see El twisted around on the couch, giving him a look that could only be described as . . . *unamused*.

Hopper laughed. "Just a suggestion. Go read a book, maybe."

Hopper finished the dishes and pulled the plug from the sink. As the dishwater drained away, he dried his hands and looked up at the kitchen window. In the reflection, Hopper could see the couch and the still-on TV, with no sign of El.

Good, he thought. He couldn't help the weather, but maybe it wasn't so bad, being stuck in the cabin. They'd had a busy few days over Christmas, El spending time with her friends and Hopper taking the opportunity to spend some time with Joyce. She seemed to be holding up, and had enjoyed his company. Jonathan too.

Hopper turned and headed over to the red square table that sat against the wall on the other side of the kitchen counter, where the open Hungry Hungry Hippos box sat. Idly wondering if you could play against yourself, he pulled out a chair just as El reappeared from her bedroom. She looked at him, her expression so serious Hopper felt himself freeze, one hand still on the back of the chair.

"Ah . . . everything okay?"

El tilted her head, like a dog listening for a sound far beyond the range of human hearing, her eyes still fixed on Hopper.

"What is it?" asked Hopper.

"Why are you a cop?"

Hopper blinked, and let out a deep breath. The question had come out of the blue.

Where is she going with this?

"Well," he said, running a still-damp hand through his hair, "that's an interesting question—"

"You said questions were good."

"Ah . . . yes, I did. And they are."

"So?"

Hopper chuckled, and leaned on the back of the chair with his elbows.

"Sure. I mean, it's a good question . . . I'm just not sure there's a simple answer."

"I don't know about you," said El. "You know about me."

Hopper nodded. "That's . . . actually, that's true."

Hopper swung around the chair and sat at the table. El pulled out the chair opposite and sat, leaning forward on her elbows.

Hopper considered. "I'm not sure I really *wanted* to be a cop," he said. "It just seemed like a good idea at the time."

"Why?"

"Ah, well." Hopper paused. He straightened his back a little and rubbed his unshaven chin with one hand. "Well, I didn't really know what to do with myself. I'd just come back from . . ." He paused again.

Ah, no, not yet. That's a topic for another time.

He waved his hand dismissively in the air. "I wanted to do something. Change something. Help people, I guess. And I had some skills and experience I figured could be useful. So I became a cop."

"And?"

Hopper frowned. "And what?"

"Did you change something?"

"Well—"

"Did you help people?"

"Hey, I helped you, didn't I?"

El smiled. "Where were you?"

Hopper shook his head. "I'm not sure you're ready for that story yet." He suddenly felt a little tight in the chest, a small surge of adrenaline combining with the lingering effects of the last of the eggnog making him feel a touch of nausea.

Now it was El's turn to shake her head. "Questions are good," she repeated.

She was right, of course. He had taken her in, helped her, protected her. Together they had been through things people couldn't even imagine, and now they were legally family . . . and yet, he realized that he was as much a mystery to her as she had been to him that night at Joyce's house after he had found her and the boys in the scrapyard.

El lowered her chin and looked at him, her head tilted, a response clearly required by the young girl.

"Listen, kid, there are some things you're not ready to hear, and some things I'm not ready to tell you about."

El's brow knitted in concentration. Hopper found himself watching her in fascination, wondering where her train of thought would take her next. "Vietnam?" she asked, sounding out the word as though she had never spoken it out loud.

Hopper raised an eyebrow. "Vietnam? Where did you hear that?"

El shook her head. "I read it."

"You *read* it?"

"On a box. Under the floor."

"Under the . . ." Hopper laughed. "You went exploring?"

El nodded.

"Okay, well, yes, you're right. I'd come back from Vietnam. It's another country, a long way from here."

El pulled herself up to the table.

"But . . ." Hopper paused. "Actually, no, this isn't a good idea."

"What?"

"Telling you about Vietnam."

"Why not?"

Hopper sighed. Now *there* was a question.

But what was the answer?

The truth was, Hopper realized, that he didn't want to talk about Vietnam, not because it was a trauma or a personal demon, but because it was ancient history—but more than that, it felt like part of some other person's life. Although he hadn't really stopped to consider it properly, he was aware of how he had compartmentalized his past in his own mind. So, yes, Vietnam had been difficult, and he had come back changed—as most people did, of course—but it just wasn't relevant, not anymore. That wasn't him, not now.

Because he had come to accept that there were really only two parts to his life.

Before Sara. After Sara.

And nothing else really mattered. Vietnam included.

He just wasn't quite sure how he was going to explain that to El.

"Because," said Hopper with a smile, "Vietnam was a long time ago. I mean, a *really* long time ago. And I'm not that person now." He leaned forward on the table, resting on his elbows. "Look, I'm sorry, really. I can understand that you are curious. And I understand you want to know more about me. I'm your—"

He paused. El raised an eyebrow, cocked her chin again, waiting for the response.

Hopper sighed, happily.

"I'm your dad, now. And yes, there is a lot you don't know about me. Vietnam included. One day I'll tell you about it, when you're older."

El frowned. Hopper held up a hand, deflecting the retort he knew was coming.

"You'll just have to trust me on this one," said Hopper. "You'll be ready one day, and so will I. But for the moment, we'll have to take a pass. Okay, kid?"

El pursed her lips; then, finally, she gave a nod.

"Okay, good," said Hopper. "Look, you're bored, I know, and you have questions. That's good. So maybe we can find something else to talk about, okay? Just let me get some coffee on."

Hopper stood and headed into the kitchen and got to work on the coffee machine, a relic he had found in one of the cabinets that, remarkably, seemed to work just fine. As he began filling the reservoir with water, there was a heavy thud behind him.

El stood by the red table, dusting her hands on her jeans. On the table itself sat a large file box. On the side of the box were written two words:

NEW YORK

Hopper hadn't seen that box for years, but he knew what it contained. He moved back to the table and pulled it toward him, then he looked at El.

"You know, I'm not sure—"

"You said find something else," said El. She pointed at the box. "Something else."

Hopper knew from the look in her eye, the tone in her voice, that she was not going to back down, not this time.

Okay. New York, New York. Hopper sat at the table and

looked at the box. It was at least something a little more recent.

Was she ready for this?

Or, for that matter, was he?

As El sat across the table, Hopper flipped the lid open. Inside was a mess of files and documents, on top of which sat a fat manila folder, bound with two sets of red elastic bands.

Oh.

He reached in and, without taking the folder out, slid the bands off and opened the cover. A large black-and-white photograph now faced him—a picture of a dead body lying on a bed, the white shirt soaked to black with blood.

Hopper closed the folder, then closed the box, then sat back in his chair. He looked at El.

"This is not a good idea."

"New York."

"Look, El—"

That was when the lid of the file box flipped open all by itself. Hopper blinked, then looked at El. Her expression was firm, unmoving, determined.

Hopper rolled his neck. "Okay, fine. You want New York, you got New York."

He pulled the box closer still, but this time he ignored the manila folder and pulled out the object underneath. It was a large white card, sealed inside a plastic bag, stapled at the corner to a single sheet of paper recording the particulars.

Hopper stared at the card—it was featureless—then turned it over, folding the paper sheet back around. On the reverse of the card was a single symbol, apparently hand-drawn in thick black ink: a hollow, five-pointed star.

"What's that?"

Hopper looked up. El had stood, and was leaning over the box to get a look. Hopper pushed the box out of the way and held the card up.

"It's just a card from a stupid game," he said, laughing. Then the laugh died in his throat, and he looked back at the symbol. "Actually, it's a game I think you'd be pretty good at."

El sat back down. She looked at Hopper, and when he looked at her he saw a light in her eyes.

"A game?"

"We'll get back to that," said Hopper. He placed the card down in front of him, then lifted the file box and set it down on the floor next to his chair. Still ignoring the folder on top, he pulled out another pile of documents. The topmost form was a letter of commendation from the *Chief of Detectives, NYPD.*

Hopper read the date at the top: *Wednesday, July 20, 1977.*

He took a deep breath, then he looked up at El.

"Before I was chief of Hawkins police, I used to be a cop in New York City—a detective, working homicide."

El mouthed the unfamiliar word.

"Ah, yeah," said Hopper. "'Homicide' means murder."

El's eyes went wide.

Hopper sighed, wondering if he really had just opened Pandora's box.

"Anyway, in the summer of 1977, something very strange happened . . ."

CHAPTER ONE

THE BIRTHDAY PARTY

JULY 4, 1977
BROOKLYN, NEW YORK

The hallway was white. Walls, floor, ceiling. The works. White on white on white and it did nothing for Hopper except make him feel slightly dizzy. Snow blindness in the inner city. Imagine that.

A whole house that was white, top to bottom, every room, every level. Outside it was a Brooklyn brownstone. Inside it was an art installation. Clutching his glass of red wine by the bowl, Hopper was terrified of spilling even a drop.

Only rich people could live in a house like this, he thought, because only rich people could afford the army of cleaners it must need to keep it just so. Rich people who thought they were Andy Warhol. Rich people who were *friends* with Andy Warhol, or at least knew his decorator.

And they had kids, too. Two of them—twins, who, even now, were celebrating with a joint birthday party in the vast kitchen at the rear of the house, a kitchen that opened onto a lush garden surrounded by high walls, an impossible oasis hidden in the spaces between row houses, the greenery somehow surviving the baking summer heat that was turning the rest of New York into a dust bowl. The noise of the party reverberated down the spartan hallway in which Hopper had sought solace, at least for a short while, with his ill-chosen drink.

He lifted the glass and peered at the contents. Red wine at a kids' birthday party.

Yes, the Palmers were that kind of people.

Hopper sighed and took a sip. This wasn't how he had planned to spend the Fourth of July, but he knew he shouldn't judge. The children—all thirty of them, nearly the whole of Sara's elementary school class—were having a great time, being entertained by a team of professionals hired just for the occasion by the Palmers, and being fed and watered—and *sugared*—by a catering crew that were probably being paid more for this one gig than Hopper earned in a whole month.

It wasn't just the children who were being entertained. The adults were too. Somewhere down the white hall, through one of the many white doors, the parents—minus Hopper—were all gathered around a show put on just for them. Some kind of magic act, someone had said. Diane had tried to persuade Hopper to come along—had even tried dragging him by one arm—but . . . a magic act?

No, he was fine right where he was. Alone. In the hallway of infinite white. With his wine.

A roar of laughter came from the kitchen, matched by an almost simultaneous roar from the other end of the hallway. Hopper looked one way, then the other, wondering which act to catch. Then, with a shake of the head as he chided himself for being a party pooper, he headed for the parents. As he opened the door at the end of the hall, he half expected to find beyond a white room with a white grand piano in the center, John Lennon at the keys, Yoko Ono draped over the top.

What he found was another reception room, one of several within the brownstone, this one perhaps slightly less stark than the rest of the house, the white walls at least broken up by the warm brown of ornate, probably original, bookcases.

Hopper clicked the door closed behind him and nodded in polite greeting to the other parents standing nearby. They were, Hopper noted, mostly the men, while around the large circular table that occupied most of the room sat the mothers and aunts, their attention fixed on the woman who sat at the "head" of the table, directly opposite the door. The woman was young and wore a red patterned scarf over her head, and sitting on the table in front of her was nothing but a goddamn crystal ball.

Hopper's jaw tightened, but he resisted the urge to check his watch. He felt uncomfortable and out of place, apparently the only man present who hadn't taken an invitation to a child's birthday party as an opportunity to dress up. The other fathers were clad mostly in wide-lapel sports jackets in varying earthen shades, with ties to match.

Ah, yes, the Model T jacket and tie. Any color you like so long as it's brown.

Suddenly Hopper didn't feel quite so bad in his red plaid shirt and blue jeans. At least he was comfortable. Polyester in this heat was not a wise decision—as some of the men around him seemed to have discovered, given the red faces and sheen of sweat on several of them.

Hopper hid his grin in his wineglass as he drained it, and turned his attention to the scene unfolding in the middle of the room, where Diane sat with the other women—most clad in long, flowing cotton dresses that looked a lot more breathable than the men's fashion choices—leaning in to listen as the fortune-teller stared into the crystal ball and pretended to read the future of . . . was it Cindy, Tom's mother?

Hopper had lost track. Suddenly he felt like another glass of wine.

The fortune-teller droned on. She was younger than Hopper would have expected, although he wasn't really sure what age group fortune-tellers were supposed to be. Weren't they meant to be old women? Not that it mattered—this was an act, nothing more.

Hopper told himself to relax, enjoy the show, stop being such a jerk.

The round of applause that came next snapped Hopper out of his reverie. He looked around the room, and saw that the women at the table were shuffling themselves along, so the next subject was now sitting opposite the fortune-teller.

It was Diane. She laughed at something her neighbor said, then glanced over her shoulder. Her eyes lit up when she saw Hopper, and she waved at him to come over.

With a sheepish look to his fellow fathers, Hopper moved forward to stand behind Diane's chair. His wife held her hand out and he squeezed it, then she looked back up at him with a smile.

He grinned back. "Hey, what are you looking at me for? Madame Mystique here is going to see your future."

At that, the fortune-teller laughed. She pushed back her scarf a little and looked at Hopper. "The past, the present, the future—all ways, all paths are open to me!" She waved her hands over the crystal ball.

Diane grinned and, taking a deep breath, straightened in her chair and closed her eyes. She let her breath out slowly through her nose.

"Okay," she said. "Lay it on me."

The room cheered and the fortune-teller, fighting to hold back her own laughter, rolled her neck and stared intently into the crystal ball, her palms flat on the table either side of it.

The fortune-teller didn't speak. Hopper watched as her gaze narrowed, her brows knitting together as she appeared to concentrate. There were some murmurs from the back of the room as some of the men lost interest.

And then—

"I . . . Oh!"

The fortune-teller jerked back from the crystal ball. Hopper laid his hand on his wife's shoulder, and felt her hand rest on his.

The fortune-teller closed her eyes, her features twisted as though she was in pain. Hopper felt Diane's grip tighten around his hand. Hopper started to feel a little uneasy. This was an act, and none of it was real, but something in the room had changed, the lighthearted feeling of fun suddenly evaporating.

He cleared his throat.

The fortune-teller opened her eyes and tilted her head as she looked into the crystal.

"I see . . . I see . . ." Then she shook her head and closed her eyes, screwing them shut tight. "There's . . . darkness. A cloud . . . no, it's like a wave, spreading out, sweeping over . . . sweeping over."

Diane shifted in her chair and looked up at Hopper.

"Light . . . There's . . ." The fortune-teller grimaced, like she'd just bitten into a lemon. "There's . . . No, it's not light, it's an . . . absence. A void. Dark, a cloud, like a wave, coming in, sweeping over . . . over . . ."

The fortune-teller gasped. Diane jumped in fright, along with half of the people in the room.

Hopper shook his head. "Hey, if this is some kind of joke . . ."

The fortune-teller shook her head again, and again, and again. "A darkness. There is nothing but darkness, a great cloud, serpent black . . ."

"I think that's enough," said Hopper.

"The darkness is coming. A night with no end. A day with no dawn. The day of the—"

"I said that's *enough*!" Hopper thumped the table with his

hand. The fortune-teller's eyes snapped open and she gulped a lungful of air. She blinked several times as she looked around the faces in the room, her own expression one of surprise, like she had just woken from a deep sleep.

Then everyone started talking at once. The women started to leave their seats, quickly, suddenly embarrassed at having taken part in the game, while their husbands muttered to one another at the back. Diane stood. Hopper put an arm around her shoulders.

"You okay?"

Diane nodded, rubbing her forehead. "Yeah, I'm fine." She turned and gave him a weak smile.

Hopper turned back to the fortune-teller. "Look, I don't know what this is supposed to be, but this is a kids' birthday party, for Christ's sake. You want to scare people, maybe you should save it for Halloween."

The fortune-teller looked up at Hopper, her face still blank, her eyes narrowed like she was trying very hard to follow what he was saying. Around them, the other parents were filtering out of the room. Hopper turned to follow.

"Are you okay?" asked Diane. Hopper looked around but found she wasn't talking to him; she was talking to the fortune-teller, who was massaging her temples.

"Ah, yeah, listen," she said, "I'm sorry about that. Really I am. I'm not sure what came over me."

"Yeah, I'm sure," said Hopper. He pulled Diane's shoulder, moving her away from the table toward the door. Just before they left the room, Hopper looked back. The woman left sitting at the table suddenly looked even younger than before, the big red scarf and crystal ball suddenly ridiculous. "I'll be talking to Susan and Bill about this," said Hopper.

"Jim, just leave it," said Diane, shaking her head.

Hopper frowned, exhaled hotly through his nose, then left the room. As soon as they entered the hallway, he found his anger abating as Sara came barreling toward them with the other children, a white paper bag with red stripes clutched in one hand, and in the other, a brown cardboard box with square holes cut in the side, the top folded to form a sturdy handle, which she squeezed until her knuckles went whiter.

"Hey, kid, what've you got there?" said Hopper as he knelt down to pick up his six-year-old daughter.

"Birthday cake! And a pet rock! Everyone got one. It's called Molly."

"Okay," said Hopper slowly, tilting the box containing the pet rock with his fingers as Sara held it up for him to have a look. "Do you think Molly will want some birthday cake?"

"Don't be silly, Daddy. Molly only drinks lemonade."

"Of course she does."

Hopper turned to Diane, his mouth in an open O of surprise, eyebrows high. "Hey, that means more cake for us!"

Diane laughed, and tugged at his elbow. "Come on, let's go," she said, and turned to follow the other parents and children as they filed toward the front door. Waiting for them in the entrance hall were two entertainers from the children's group, both dressed as Uncle Sam for Independence Day. They were handing out little American flags on short sticks, at the end of which was tied a small paper bag of candy, one to each child as they went past. Sara thrust her pet rock box at her dad, freeing her hand to grab the offered bag.

"What do you say, Sara?" asked Diane.

"Thank you, Mr. Clown!"

Together, the trio walked down the steps leading to the sidewalk, the other party guests disappearing into the fleet of cars that had taken up nearly all the space available in the street.

For the Hoppers, they could walk. Home was not far, and no sooner had they taken a few paces down the street than Hopper felt Sara tugging on his hand. He let her go, happy to have her burn off some excess energy as they headed for their own apartment just a few blocks away.

Diane linked her arm through her husband's, and leaned her head against his shoulder as they slowly walked.

"Great party," she said.

"Yeah, great party," said Hopper. "I spent the whole time terrified I was going to spill red wine over something I couldn't possibly pay for, then we get a prediction of a coming apocalypse from a prophet of doom." He lifted the box. "Oh, and we have a new and unexpected addition to the family. Yeah, great party. I can't wait for next year."

Diane laughed and pulled away from Hopper, playfully punching the shoulder she had just been leaning against. "Oh, come on, it wasn't that bad. Lisa just got . . ." She tailed off, her hands rolling in the air as she tried to come up with an explanation.

"Lisa?"

"Lisa Sargeson, the fortune-teller. She's actually one of the parents, and does magic as a kind of side business."

"Fortune-telling is magic?"

"Well, it wasn't just fortune-telling. Actually she did some pretty good escapology tricks with locks and chains—Janice McGann volunteered and got locked up in cuffs, and she nearly had a heart attack when Lisa said she didn't have the key!"

At this Hopper smiled. "So what was with the fortune-telling anyway? Lisa Sargeson just got, what, carried away?"

Diane shrugged. "Lost in the moment."

Hopper gave a low whistle. "Some moment."

"Some party."

"You can say that again. I mean, Sara's whole class was there, with all the parents, but I swear the hired help outnumbered us all. And entertainment for the adults, too? Now, tell me Susan and Bill weren't just showing off."

"Well," said Diane, "I had a good time, even if you didn't."

"No, I didn't say that."

"You didn't have to. I saw the way you were."

"I told you, I was afraid of making a mess."

"Yeah, right."

"Yeah, right!"

"James Hopper," said Diane, once again linking her arm through her husband's. "You were tense the whole time. You need to learn how to relax."

Hopper opened his mouth to speak, then closed it. He shrugged, only to find his shoulders refused to come down again. "It's just . . ."

"Just what?"

"I mean, that house. *Those* people. Okay, the Palmers are a nice family. But . . . they're not like us. They're not like any of the parents. I mean, they only didn't have the party out at their place in the Hamptons because they knew nobody would be able to afford the gas just to get out there."

"That's not true," said Diane, with a smirk.

"Yeah, well," said Hopper, finally getting his shoulders to relax. "Maybe not. But really. That house? Come on, normal people don't live like that. And they have so much money, why do they send the twins to public school?"

"Hey, that school is just fine. I wouldn't teach there—certainly wouldn't let Sara go there—if it wasn't."

"I know, I know," said Hopper, "but there must be dozens of fancy private places they could send their kids to. I mean . . . wouldn't you, if you could afford it? Sara's school may be just fine, but come on, this is the New York public school system we're talking about."

"And if I didn't think the New York public school system works, I certainly wouldn't be giving it my blood, sweat, and tears, now would I?" Diane looked up at Hopper. "You're not the only one trying to make a difference here, Jim. I didn't come to this city just to cheer you on from the sidelines. Sometimes you need to remember that."

Hopper nodded, and drew his wife back to his side as they walked on. Sure, NYC had problems, but Sara's school *was* a good one. Hopper knew how lucky Diane was to have been placed there, given the current state of education in the city. She'd told him about other schools, where she'd heard the teachers sometimes didn't even show up for class, how kids as young as twelve might pass a bottle of wine around between them while the teacher sat at the front, unwilling to intervene, knowing any attempt to assert authority would be ignored—if it wasn't met with violence. And sure, those were extreme examples, but there were times when the whole city felt like an extreme example. Virtually bankrupt, with public services crumbling alongside the infrastructure.

Welcome to New York City, 1977.

Not that Hopper regretted their decision to move there. Far from it. For him, it was precisely the right thing to do, at precisely the right time. Coming back from Vietnam, returning to Hawkins, Indiana, had been like stepping into some kind of parallel universe. He'd given his blood and his sweat and, he sometimes thought, a part of his sanity to fighting a war that didn't seem to end, that was being fought for no kind of reason he could really understand, and meanwhile life in Smalltown, U.S.A., had entered some kind of loop in time, changing not one iota by the time he got back.

Hopper wondered if it really ever would, or even could.

He'd been restless, and he hadn't tried to hide it. Diane's arrival in '69 had been a welcome distraction; the romance that soon blossomed was followed by the birth of their daughter, Sara, in '71. And that helped.

For a while, anyway. But Hawkins, Indiana, was still Hawkins, Indiana. Domestic bliss could last only so long. Hopper needed . . . something else. Something bigger.

Some*where* bigger.

Somewhere like New York City.

Truth be told, Diane had taken some persuading, and occasionally Hopper still felt a pang of guilt. As much as she supported him and wanted him to do what he felt he needed to do, moving from Hawkins to New York was a big move, in more ways than one. Hawkins was small and soporific, but they'd made a home there, a family. It was safe, and it was comfortable. And, with the memories of Vietnam fast receding, it was . . . easy.

Perhaps that was the problem. Safe and comfortable and easy was just great, but Hopper soon realized that wasn't what he wanted. Two tours of Vietnam had changed him, and he'd come back and found himself sinking into suburban oblivion.

He had seen the signs early—so had Diane—and for that, he was grateful. He leaned on her support, without which . . . well, he didn't know what might have happened. He'd seen what had happened to others who had gone out and come back and then not been able to cope.

Hopper needed a change. So they made one. They moved to New York. A big city, a city in trouble, a city in need of help.

Hopper knew he could do it. He knew it would be hard, a baptism of fire in a city that some people had started calling a hell on earth, even then, before the proverbial had *really* hit the fan.

But . . . it was what he wanted. What he *needed*.

So, in the spring of 1972, Diane said yes. She agreed with his arguments—now was the time to do it, while they were still young and capable of forging a new path through life. It would be good for all of them.

Hopper's record stood him in good stead. He'd joined the Hawkins PD when he'd returned from service. Three and half years of solid police work and a handful of commendations combined with his military experience to earn him a place in a fast-track recruitment program in the understaffed New York City Police Department, turning beat cops with special experience straight into much-needed detectives. After a few short months of uniform work to learn as much about the city and the department as he could, Hopper found himself with a shield in his pocket and a desk to call his own. He put in the work, put in the hours, and it didn't go unnoticed. As budget cuts and personnel reductions swept through the department, he was promoted again, this time to homicide.

Hopper had never been happier.

True, they didn't have much—and that was what had really grated so badly at the Palmers', that gratuitous display of wealth—but . . . they were happy. They had an apartment in a Brooklyn neighborhood that wasn't so bad, not really. A place-ment for Diane at an elementary school that was fine, really—middling, could be better, could be worse. Sara was a capable kid and although she had only just started first grade, she was doing well—and Diane was there, not to hand-hold, but . . . just to keep an eye out.

This *was* New York City, after all.

Hopper felt a sharp tug on his leg, breaking him out of his daydream. Looking down, he saw Sara pulling with all her might on his knee. Their building was just a few doors away.

"Come on, come *on*!" said Sarah. "It's time for more cake, Daddy!"

"Yes, because if there is one thing this young lady needs, it's another overdose of sugar," said Hopper, laughing as he lifted his daughter onto his hip while Diane walked ahead and un-locked the front door. He was about to follow her in, but in-stead bumped into her back as she paused.

"What is it?"

Diane looked at her husband. "Is that the telephone?"

Hopper listened. She was right, there was a telephone ring-ing from somewhere above them—from their apartment, which occupied the second level.

"Here," said Hopper, swinging his body around so he could pass Sara over to Diane. "I'll see if I can get it. It could be im-portant."

Daughter safely in her mother's arms, Hopper took the stairs two at a time.

"Hello?"

"Hop, you are a hard man to track down," said a female voice. It was fairly deep and had a smoker's rasp. Hopper knew that voice well.

"I should hope so too, Delgado," he said. "It's Independence Day and the only duty I had today was taking Sara to a birthday party."

"Yeah, well, I need to invite you to a different kind of party altogether."

Hopper felt his pulse quicken. If Detective Rosario Delgado, his partner of six weeks, had been trying to call him on his day off, then he knew she had a damn good reason.

And, standing by the telephone on the wall next to the refrigerator, he had a feeling he knew just what that reason was. Behind him he heard Diane and Sara enter the apartment. As the pair walked into the kitchenette, Diane looked expectantly at her husband. He met her eye, and gave a small nod of the head.

"Hey, Mission Control to Detective James Hopper, come in please."

He pulled the telephone mouthpiece back around. "Sorry." He paused. "It's another one, isn't it?"

"You should get down here, soon as you can fix it."

Hopper nodded. "I'm already on my way. What's the address?" He turned around, looking for a pen and paper, only to find Diane had fetched from the counter the small pad they used for grocery lists and was holding it and a pen out for him. He mouthed his thanks at her, then turned and held the notepad against the wall near the phone. Delgado gave him the details and he jotted them down.

"Okay, got it," he said. "I'll be right there."

"I'll have the red carpet waiting," said Delgado. Then the line clicked off.

Hopper put the phone back on the cradle. He felt Diane's hands on his shoulders. He reached up and took them, and turned around in a tight circle.

"Ah, listen—" he began.

Diane nodded. "You have to go."

"I have to go. I'm sorry."

Diane smiled. "Do not apologize," she said. "Never apologize for doing your job."

"I'll make it up to you."

"I'll hold you to that."

Slipping out of her embrace, Hopper headed for the door. He opened it, and turned around, his hand still on the doorknob. "I'll call and let you know where I am," he said, then he looked over at Sara, who was already busy with her cake at the kitchenette's small dining table. "Hey, leave some for me, kid!"

Sara looked up at him and smiled, her face covered in red and blue icing.

Diane gave Hopper a kiss on the cheek.

"Stay safe."

Hopper kissed her on the lips.

"That's the plan," he said, and then he left, closing the door behind him.

CHAPTER TWO

THE THIRD VICTIM

JULY 4, 1977
BROOKLYN, NEW YORK

"What a mess, what a mess."

Hopper glanced at the uniformed officer, unsure whether the offered opinion was regarding the state of the apartment or the nature of the crime. *Both*, he thought as he stepped cautiously down the hallway, keeping his hands curled into fists, careful not to touch anything or get in the way of the small army of cops who seemed to fill the place. He looked around, taking mental snapshots, as he did with every crime scene. Sure, there would be photographs taken from every conceivable angle, and someone would draw a layout, and someone else would measure everything and mark every item of interest with a little yellow flag, but nothing would beat the time actually spent at the scene, in person, seeing the place with your own eyes, getting a feel for the location, the layout, the setting. The relationships between one room and another, one object and another.

But the cop was right. The place was a mess. The hallway was lined with bags of junk, none of which looked like they had moved in a while, and as Hopper glanced into the adjoining rooms as he moved down the hallway toward the actual scene of the crime, he saw more of the same, the entire place seemingly filled with trash. There was no particular smell that Hopper could discern, other than the general staleness that came with hot air trapped inside a closed apartment in a heat wave.

That changed the closer he got to the crime scene. The characteristic rancid butcher's block smell of death made itself known soon enough. Given the heat, Hopper was surprised it wasn't worse.

"Detective Hopper, so nice of you to drop by."

Hopper turned to see his partner, Detective Rosario Delgado, standing in one of the doorways he had just passed, her hands on her hips. She was wearing blue bell-bottom jeans with a six-inch-wide brown belt and a lighter blue polo shirt opened as far as it would go, her detective's medallion hanging on a chain around her neck, the gold badge bouncing on the lowest button of her top. Seeing the badge reminded Hopper of his own, which he pulled from his back pocket and clipped onto the front of his own belt. Delgado watched him, a smirk growing on her olive features.

"Nice shirt," she said. "Don't tell me, the party was fancy dress and you went as a lumberjack."

Hopper glanced down, suddenly self-conscious in his straight jeans, red checkered shirt, and Cuban-heel Chelsea boots.

"What can I say, I like plaid."

"And I bet it drives all the girls wild."

He gestured at her own clothes. "Talking of dress code . . ."

Delgado shrugged. "I was on my way to Studio 54 when we got the call."

"Really?"

"Hell no. It's hot, what am I supposed to do? Come on." She led the way down the hall. Hopper followed.

The hall ended in another pair of doors, guarded by two more uniformed officers. Delgado entered first, Hopper close behind.

He looked around the room first—not so he didn't have to face the horror show in the middle of it, but again, to take it all in. The room. The décor. The dimensions. The relationships.

The *scene*.

It was a bedroom, the walls done out in a brown striped wallpaper that didn't look old and didn't look new. There was a rectangular window with green striped curtains that let in a decent amount of light. The floor was carpeted in a busy blue and red floral pattern. There was a set of drawers in a brown wood that didn't match the hue of the walls, and there was a circular shaving mirror on top. There was no chair in the room, but there was a single bed. It looked like it had been slept in and then the bedclothes roughly put back into place without much care or interest. The room was relatively free of trash, "relatively" being the operative word.

Only then did Hopper allow his attention to be taken by the object on the bed, the thing that made this crummy apartment a crime scene.

The body of the latest victim.

Delgado pointed to the bed. "Okay, so, same old same old. Victim is male, late thirties, in good shape, apart from most of his blood being on the outside of his body."

Hopper stepped closer as Delgado took one step back to give him some room. The victim was lying faceup on the bed, and he was dressed: blue dress trousers, white shirt with the sleeves rolled up. His feet dangled off the end of the bed and they were clad in black socks and black shoes that had a good polish on them. His head had fallen just short of the pillow. The bedspread was a heavy brown material that had turned almost black around the victim's torso where it had soaked up the blood.

The man's chest was a mess. His white shirt was torn open and Hopper could see a familiar pattern of darker stripes on the skin.

He took a deep breath and folded one arm around his middle, his hand cradling his elbow as he stroked his chin. He shook his head.

"Same as the others," he said.

"Same as the others," said Delgado. "Stabbed five times, then slashed between the entry wounds to form—"

"A five-pointed star," said Hopper. "A goddamn five-pointed star." He glanced at his partner. "Everything else the same?"

She nodded. "Yes," she said. "No signs of forced entry. No signs of struggle. No reports about noise or anything suspicious from the neighbors."

Hopper looked around the room again. He walked over to the window and carefully peered between the partially drawn curtains. "So who found him?"

"That would be the building super," said Delgado. "Apparently someone complained about the smell so he let himself in."

"We get a statement?"

"We did. He's being very cooperative."

Hopper nodded and turned back to the window. Outside was a Brooklyn street like any other. There were some cars parked on the curb. Another car cruised down the lane, engine purring. An older man wearing a white vest and black fedora walked on by, while in the other direction a younger woman led a young girl by the hand, the high-necked floral print dresses of both billowing like sails in what little breeze there was.

A street like any other.

A street like his, the one where he and Diane and Sara made their home. And okay, their apartment was a step or two above this place, but did that make any difference, really? Someone's private space had been invaded here. Someone had been killed in their own home. That made everything equal, didn't matter who you were or where you lived.

He didn't know who the man on the bed was—but he could have.

What if it had been Diane?

Hopper pushed the thoughts out of his mind. Being a cop was one of those jobs where everyone told you that you couldn't let it get personal, where every textbook and manual and training program said that you had to come to it with a certain detachment, otherwise it would tear you apart. Which was true. Hopper knew that.

But he also knew that if it *wasn't* personal, then . . . then why the hell would he do it?

The trick—the answer—was to control it, before it controlled him.

He looked down at the street. Outside, the world went on as usual. Inside was another story, but he took a breath and cleared his head and got back to the job.

"So, for those of us keeping score at home," said Delgado, somewhere behind him, "that's the third victim. The crime scene is identical, the method of killing is identical, everything is identical."

Hopper closed his eyes and pinched the bridge of his nose. "I don't need to ask if another one was left, do I?"

"No, you do not."

He turned around. Delgado was already holding the evidence bag out to him. He looked at it for a moment, then took it and turned it over in his hands.

Inside the clear plastic bag was a card. It was rectangular, but larger than a playing card—maybe twice as big. One side was blank, white.

Hopper turned it over in his hand, knowing exactly what was going to be on the other side. He was not disappointed.

The card had a shape on it—three short, wavy lines, running in tight parallel across the narrow width of the card, neatly drawn by hand with a thick brush in heavy black ink. The symbol was different from those on the cards found at the previous crime scenes—but it was clearly part of the same set.

"Add one to the collection," said Delgado. She reached behind her neck and lifted her wavy black hair up, trying to get some respite from the stuffiness of the room. "I suggest we leave it to the professionals now. This heat is starting to get to me."

Hopper nodded, handing the card back. Delgado took it and handed it to a crime scene technician who was standing by the doorway. Then she walked out. Hopper hung back a moment, taking another look at the body and then at the scene.

Hopper held his breath.

Three victims. Each stabbed five times, the wounds joined together as the killer carved a star into the bodies.

Three victims. Same MO. That settled that.

Brooklyn had its very own serial killer, dispatching his victims in some kind of ritualistic way.

Hopper let out his breath and left the scene.

As if New York City didn't have enough on its plate.

DECEMBER 26, 1984

HOPPER'S CABIN
HAWKINS, INDIANA

"The *third*?"

Hopper looked down into his coffee mug. It was empty already. One mug drained and he'd only just gotten started. He was going to have to pace himself.

Across the table from him, El shook her head, her mouth a lopsided curl of confusion. Hopper stood and headed toward the coffeepot in the kitchen.

"Yeah, that was the third one," said Hopper, topping himself off. "We'd been working the case for almost two months at that point. Two murders the same, that forms a pattern, and clearly we're looking for the same person. But three murders turns it into something else—that was when we really knew we had a serial killer to catch."

El's eyes narrowed in concentration. "Like . . . breakfast?" she asked, drawing the word out, uncertain.

Hopper dropped back into his chair. "Oh, no, not 'cereal.' *Serial*." He spelled it out for her. "A serial killer is . . . well, it's someone who kills a lot of people."

"Like Papa?" she asked.

Papa?

Then it dawned on him. She meant Brenner—*Doctor* Brenner, the monster responsible for her laboratory-bound upbringing.

Ah, crap.

"No, this is different. *He* was different. It's . . . complicated. Listen . . ."

He paused, and drank some coffee. Was he really doing this? Suddenly it seemed like a very bad idea. El was, in many ways, younger than her physical age, and now he was telling her about New York in the 1970s and that time he faced off against a serial killer?

That was too much. He sighed and rubbed his face.

"I'm not sure this is a good idea, really. I mean . . ."

El sat bolt upright. "Don't stop now."

Hopper sighed. Again. "You're really sure about this? Because—"

"But what happened?"

"Because I don't want to be giving you nightmares for the next year, okay?"

El looked at Hopper with her customary intensity. The silence stretched between them before El finally spoke.

"Go back to the start."

"The start? The story is long enough as it is. And the first two murders were the same. Like I said, it was on the third one that things began to happen."

El looked at the table. Hopper looked at her from over the rim of his mug. She didn't speak, and Hopper lowered his coffee.

"Now what?" he asked.

"Beginning, middle, end," said El, not lifting her eyes from the table. "That's a story. Beginning, middle, end."

"That's true."

El looked up at Hopper. "Start with Delgado."

"Delgado? Now *that* question, I can answer."

Hopper sipped his coffee and started at the beginning.

CHAPTER THREE

SONNY AND CHER

MAY 17, 1977
BROOKLYN, NEW YORK

The detectives' bull pen of Brooklyn's 65th Precinct wasn't exactly a hive of activity at eight in the morning, but Hopper blamed the lethargy on the damned heat. New York was being slowly roasted alive and summer hadn't even arrived yet. If the weather kept up like this, Hopper was already making plans to drag his desk up in the service elevator and out onto the roof. At least up there, there was a breeze. Down in the bull pen, the only thing moving the air were three virtually derelict standing fans that Sergeant McGuigan had unearthed from a long-lost supply cupboard. Of course the AC wasn't working. Hopper couldn't remember if it ever had, and he didn't hold much hope for it being fixed anytime this decade, not with the current level of budget cuts being inflicted on the New York City Police Department.

Exhibit A, the desk opposite his. Like all the others driven by the squad of six homicide detectives in the precinct—no, make that *five*, now—it was made of metal and had seen better days, but this one was bare, the drawers empty, not even a blotter or telephone on it. It had been like that for weeks now, the last round of departmental redundancies hitting the 65th with particular viciousness, culling their squad of one detective and leaving Hopper without a partner.

In a way, Hopper understood the need to make efficiencies. The city was out of money and the federal government wasn't lifting a finger, so cuts had to be made. That didn't make it *right*—you could only slice so much fat off before you began to draw blood—but at least he understood the math.

And he also understood that he was damned lucky. In the first half of 1977—so far, anyway—there had been nearly six hundred homicides across the city. But the rate was not evenly distributed across the five boroughs. The 65th oversaw a relatively quiet patch of Brooklyn, with each of the five remaining homicide detectives handling no more than three ongoing investigations at one time. That was still too many, but Hopper knew it could get much, much worse than that, and for the moment, even without a partner, he was thankful for his assignment. It was the captain he felt sorry for—Bobby LaVorgna, a big, heavyset Italian with a thick walrus mustache and twenty-five years of experience who juggled case assignments between his detectives like an old master. But these days he seemed to spend more time locked in his office, filling the air with cigarette smoke as he argued on the phone with the higher-ups, pleading for more resources, for more money, for more men. Life as a New York City homicide detective was no cakewalk, but at least, Hopper thought, he wasn't stuck behind a desk all day, pushing paper and shouting at the moon.

"Hey, you heard what happened yesterday?"

Hopper looked up from the case file he had been reviewing

and swung his legs off his desk as Detective Symonds approached from the direction of the breakroom, steaming mug of coffee in one hand and a copy of the morning's *New York Times* in the other. He handed Hopper the paper, then perched himself on the corner of the empty desk, hitching up the trousers of his powder blue suit to get more comfortable. Hopper glanced up from the newspaper and watched as Symonds ran a finger under the collar of his shirt and flapped his short, wide tie, the color of which matched his suit perfectly.

"You ever thought about some natural fibers, Symonds?"

Symonds sniffed, then drank some more coffee. "It's called style, James Hopper. I start wanting fashion advice from Mr. Country Fair here, I need to find a better shrink."

Hopper shook his head in amusement, then returned his attention to the newspaper. Front and center was a photograph of a wrecked helicopter.

"You know that thing came down on Madison Avenue? My wife was on Madison Avenue. Jesus." Symonds drank some more and shook his head.

Hopper read the headline: 5 KILLED AS COPTER ON PAN AM BUILDING THROWS ROTOR BLADE.

Hopper *had* heard about it last night on the late news, but the article in the *Times* gave him a better picture of what had happened when the landing gear of the idling New York Airways helicopter gave way, toppling the vehicle over onto the deck just after 5:30 yesterday evening. The blade killed four people on the roof before shearing off and tumbling over the side of the building, bouncing off a window and flying into Madison Avenue, where it killed a pedestrian.

"My God," said Hopper. "Is Jacqueline okay?"

"She is, thank Christ, she is, but she saw it happen. She's shook up—I told her to take the day off today but she said she'd rather be back at work, you know?" Symonds shook his head again. "But I tell you, it's something." He gestured to the newspaper with his coffee mug, like that explained everything. "You don't know when your time is up, you know? You just don't know."

Hopper nodded, the muscles at the back of his jaw tensing up. Symonds was right—when your number was up, it was up. As a cop—as a *veteran*—Hopper perhaps knew that more than a lot of people, but it wasn't something he thought about much. He couldn't. You started worrying about things like that and soon enough you'd feel the walls closing in around you. Hopper had seen that happen to too many people who had come back from the exact same place he had.

There was a bang from the other side of the room, breaking Hopper's reverie. He handed the paper back to Symonds, who slipped off the desk and looked across the bull pen. Hopper turned in his chair and followed his colleague's gaze, toward the big windows that looked in on the captain's office.

Within, LaVorgna was pacing up and down, having slammed his door shut with all his might. Eight in the morning and the first battle of the day had already been fought and lost, it appeared. Hopper watched as the captain paced, phone pressed in the crook of his neck as he tried to light his next cigarette while gesticulating wildly, his hands moving the fog in his office around in eddies big enough for Hopper to see from his desk. Hopper watched the captain's mouth moving as he railed against whatever the latest decree from on high was. The windowed partition was a surprisingly effective sound barrier, rendering the captain's actions into mime.

Then, it happened. LaVorgna was a stickler for regulation, and despite the heat he still wore his full uniform, although he had at least consigned the heavy wool jacket to the back of his chair. But now, as he listened to the telephone and shook his head, his cigarette firmly in place, he loosened his tie and unbuttoned the collar of his crisp white shirt.

That was never a good sign.

Symonds slinked over to his desk and Hopper returned his attention to his own work, but no sooner had he opened the case file again than there was another bang from the captain's office. LaVorgna was now stalking across the bull pen, the office door still swinging behind him after bouncing off the frame. He vanished through the main doors leading to the elevator lobby.

Around the bull pen, the other detectives got back to work, the morning's entertainment now officially over, the three standing fans buzzing as the quiet murmur of police work resumed.

Hopper turned slowly in his chair. After a year at the 65th, he still hadn't clicked as much as he would have liked with the four other detectives in Sergeant McGuigan's shift—Symonds and Harris were perhaps the two he might have been comfortable enough to call, at a push, work friends, but Marnie and Hunt were a pair of macho assholes whom Hopper was happy to keep at a distance. And besides, he knew before he arrived that it was going to be difficult—he was the new boy, the country boy, the Midwestern hick who thought he could steam in and save the city the others had called home their entire lives. Hawkins, Indiana, may as well have been Timbuktu, as far as the others were concerned. His fast track to homicide probably hadn't helped any, either. Maybe the others saw it as favoritism, although from whom, Hopper had no idea. But they resented his quick promotion, at least a little.

Symonds and, to a lesser extent, Harris had softened to him over time, but Hopper didn't let it get to him. Yes, he had come here with a job to do and . . . well, perhaps they were right, he was also here with a mission, of sorts. But it wasn't to save the city. It wasn't about being a hero. The city didn't need heroes. It needed cops—good cops—who could do their job.

Cops like Hopper.

But while Captain LaVorgna was on his side like any captain should be, he was still bound by protocol and the combined peer pressure of his other detectives. As the newbie, Hopper had accepted his assigned partner without question— orders is orders—but he knew he'd been palmed off on Joe Stafford, an elder detective whose career was clearly in terminal decline. Reluctant to leave his desk, Stafford still didn't seem to be able to handle his paperwork. More than once Hopper found him poring obsessively over Yankees box scores rather than looking at the case files steadily growing on his desk until, having survived at least two rounds of redundancies, his number finally came up and the NYPD gave him and his cream leisure suits an early retirement.

The main doors flew open and Captain LaVorgna reappeared, cigarette burned down to the filter, the big man wiping the sweat from his forehead as he marched back to his office, the door behind him once again rattling in the frame. If the captain carried on like that today, the AC wasn't going to be the only thing in the precinct that needed repair.

Hopper glanced across the aisle at the nearest occupied desk, where Detective Harris was scribbling something in a file while he absentmindedly tossed and caught an old baseball in his other hand.

"Harris, any idea what's going on?"

Harris shrugged but didn't look up. "Hell do I know, Hopper?"

Hopper swung back around to get on with his work. A moment later there was a wolf whistle from the desk behind his. Hopper looked up, noticing that the bull pen had once again fallen silent, and then there was a sudden blur of blue and a thud as someone dumped a large cardboard box on the empty desk in front of him.

"And you can shut the hell up too," said the newcomer.

She stood with her hands on her hips beside the empty desk. Clad in a pair of dark blue bell-bottom slacks and a white shirt with frills down the front, underneath a tight waistcoat. She looked about thirty, and had shoulder-length black hair with a distinct wave in it. She was frowning at Hopper, one eyebrow slightly raised.

Hopper glanced around, saw the rest of the bull pen watching them in silence. Some of the detectives were grinning, and down at the far end, Hunt and Marnie—the pair dressed in nearly identical light gray suits over multicolored shirts unbuttoned almost down to their middles—exchanged hushed words that almost doubled Marnie over with laughter, the mop of his tight blond perm shaking around his ears as he struggled to contain his amusement.

Hopper ignored them, and turned back to the newcomer.

"Ah . . ."

She jerked her chin at him. "You Hopper?"

He looked down at his desk, just for a moment, and without meaning to, but it was enough.

"What, you looking for your badge to check now?"

Hopper blinked, and looked back up at the woman.

"Yes, I'm Jim Hopper," he said. "Ah . . . and you are?"

The woman held out her hand, her frown changing into a smile that looked more than a little forced. Hopper took it, and found his fingers crushed in her strong grip.

"Your new partner, Detective Rosario Delgado."

"My new . . . *partner*?"

Delgado withdrew her hand and moved back around the empty desk. She pulled the cardboard box toward her and peered into it before starting to pull out bits and pieces. A stapler. Some paperwork. A mug full of pens that had a flag of some kind printed on one side and something written in Spanish underneath it.

Hopper glanced around the bull pen. The grins from the others had vanished. Harris was watching them, the baseball now squeezed firmly in one hand, his eyes narrow.

Hopper turned back to Delgado. "Sorry, did you say, my new *partner*?"

She didn't look up as she continued unpacking. "Ten out of

ten for aural comprehension, Detective. I bet you got a certificate from the academy and everything."

Hopper stared at her. Around them, the other detectives moved closer, the Marnie-Hunt double-act now leaning on opposite sides of the support column in the middle of the room, their arms folded, their grins firmly back in place as they looked Delgado up and down. Marnie caught Hopper's eye and lifted both his eyebrows.

Hopper ignored him. He turned back around in his chair. "Okay, listen, Ms. Delgado—"

"*Detective* Delgado, Detective Hopper," she said. She'd finished unpacking her belongings from the cardboard box, and placed it on the floor beside her desk. Then she stood tall with her hands on her hips again and looked at Hopper from underneath her dark bangs. "Don't tell me: using your amazing police powers, you've deduced I'm a woman. Congratulations. I'll be sure to put you in for a commendation."

Hopper opened his mouth to speak, but was saved by the appearance of Captain LaVorgna. The boss stood, sweating, by their desks, and began the process of rolling his sleeves up his tree-trunk-like arms, the glowing end of his ever-present cigarette pulsing in time with his breaths.

"I see you two have already met," he said. "Detective Delgado has joined our precinct from the 117th in Queens. She's a new homicide detective and she's your new partner, so if you have any problems with that, I suggest you keep them to yourself, and if you have any questions, I don't want to hear them." He adjusted the folded cuff of one shirtsleeve just below the elbow. "Do I make myself clear?"

Hopper straightened up in his chair. "Perfectly clear, sir." He paused. "It's just, ah . . ."

Delgado grinned. "What Detective Hopper is trying to say, sir, is that his new partner appears to be a woman."

LaVorgna sighed heavily, killed his cigarette in the already overflowing ashtray on Hopper's desk, then turned to address the entire shift.

"All right, listen up. We are proud to be part of a new initiative, spearheaded by the commissioner himself. From this month, female detectives can be assigned to homicide. Detective Delgado is one of the first nine assigned to precincts all over the five boroughs. She will have the same duties as the rest of you, will work the same cases as the rest of you, and probably be as much a pain in the ass as the rest of you. She's the replacement detective for the dearly departed Detective Stafford." He stabbed a finger at Hopper. "You've been waiting for a new partner for too long, so merry Christmas."

Detective Marnie barked a short laugh. LaVorgna glared at him.

"Problem, detective?"

Marnie's jaw clicked as he chewed on some gum. "Well, I guess we did need someone to make the coffee," he said. Hunt chuckled unpleasantly again.

"Laugh it up, Detective," said LaVorgna. "This city needs cops and it needs good ones, and they can come from the rings of Saturn for all I care, so long as cases are solved and the board gets cleared. Now, everybody get back to work."

LaVorgna headed back to his office and the other detectives slowly returned to their desks. Harris, who hadn't moved, was still looking at Delgado. Delgado stared back at him, until finally Harris dropped his baseball onto his desk and, grabbing his mug, went in search of coffee.

"Friendly crowd," said Delgado, pulling her own chair out and sitting down at her new desk. "The seedy underworld of Brooklyn must be quaking in fear with us on the case."

Hopper smiled. "New York City's Finest."

Delgado shook her head. "God help us all." She shuffled a few papers, dumped a handful of pens in a desk drawer, then looked at Hopper. "So what's your story, partner?"

Hopper lifted an eyebrow. "My story?"

"Yes, story. Just skip the part about star signs and favorite color, because I give precisely squat." She eyed the ashtray. "I see you smoke?"

"Doesn't everybody?"

"Not me," said Delgado. "But my dad said to never trust a man who doesn't smoke, so we're good. You don't look like you belong here. You don't sound it, either."

"That's true," said Hopper. "I'm from the Midwest. Indiana."

"My condolences."

Hopper leaned back in his chair and looked at Delgado.

She shrugged.

"What?"

Hopper pointed at the mug on her desk. "Is that a Cuban flag?"

"He has geography, too. The Indiana education board does it again."

"Are you from Cuba?"

"No, Queens."

"Oh."

"My parents are from Cuba. They escaped to Miami, then escaped to New York before I was born."

"So what does that mean?"

Delgado cocked her head. "What does what mean?"

Hopper leaned forward, his sprung chair pushing him to the upright. He tapped the side of her mug with his pen. Underneath the Cuban flag was a line of Spanish.

"That."

Delgado smiled. "But he speaks no Spanish. It says, *Eres la mejor mamá del mundo*."

"Okay . . ."

"You're the best mom in the world."

Hopper grinned. "You have kids?"

"No," said Delgado, "I just liked the mug. What about you?"

"One daughter, Sara. She's six."

"Six years old in New York City," said Delgado. "That's tough."

Hopper shrugged. "We do okay."

"Where did you say you were from?"

"Indiana. Town called Hawkins."

"They have cops in Hawkins, Indiana?"

"They do. Electricity and running water too."

"Hey, you learn something. So what, the glitz and glamor of the big city draw you here, or do you have some kind of death wish?"

Hopper laughed. "Not at all. It was just the right move to make at the right time."

Delgado leaned forward. "There's a right time to move to New York? Being a cop in Hawkings—"

"*Hawkins.*"

"Hawkins, whatever. But being a cop there is not like being a cop here." She tapped her desk with a fingernail. "I don't get it."

Hopper pursed his lips. "You're right, it's different. But I needed a change. Before I was a cop, I was in the army. Signed up out of high school, did four years all over the country. Then one day I found myself in a jungle on the other side of the world."

Delgado hissed between her teeth. "You volunteered for that shit? You don't seem like the Uncle Sam type."

"And I'm not, but it seemed like a good way to get the hell out of Indiana. And it was—and I even enjoyed it, at first." Hopper licked his lips. "Did two tours, '62 to '68, then was back in Hawkins, Indiana, with a Bronze Star and nothing to do."

"So you became a cop?"

Hopper spread his hands and gave a tight smile. "And here we are. What about you?"

Delgado laughed. "Oh, that's easy. Joined the NYPD. Worked the beat, did my time. Became a detective. And here we are."

Hopper raised an eyebrow. "You always wanted to work homicide?"

"Hell yes. Homicide is the top of the tree for a detective. And let me tell you, I never gave up, either. Welcome to the Swinging Seventies, detective. Now pass me a file and let me see what mysteries of the universe you clowns are trying to find the answers to."

Hopper laughed and passed her a stack of files from his desk, then watched as his new partner flipped open the top folder and began to read. She sat with her head bent over the desk, and after a moment she reached for a pencil and began to follow along underneath each line of the file as she read.

Hopper had known his new partner for all of five minutes, and already his head was spinning. She was smart, and fast, and full of . . . well, attitude.

Then he and Delgado looked up as LaVorgna's large frame cast a shadow across their desks for the second time that morning.

"Great, you're settled in, you'll be a fine team, have each other's backs, you're a regular Sonny and Cher," said the captain. "Wonderful. I'm so happy for you."

Hopper raised an eyebrow and exchanged a look with Delgado, who was smiling. "Something we can do for you, Captain?"

"You can solve a murder for me is what you can do," he said, tossing a new file onto Delgado's desk.

Delgado pulled the file toward her and flipped it open. Hopper leaned forward to see. On the top was a large crime scene photograph. It was black-and-white, and looked like a series of abstract shapes before he figured out he was looking at a body.

"Jesus," he whispered. "What the hell happened?"

"The usual, Detective," said LaVorgna. "Somebody was killed and it's your job to find out who did it."

As she read the file, Delgado was shaking her head. "This is some weird shit."

Hopper looked at her, then at the captain, his eyes widening expectantly.

"Weird is right," said LaVorgna. "Medical examiner is on-scene. He's expecting you two about five minutes ago."

Hopper stood and grabbed his jacket from the back of his chair. Delgado rose more slowly, her eyes lingering over the file before she closed the folder and handed it to her partner.

"You ready?" asked Hopper.

"Always ready."

Hopper took the folder, gave Delgado a nod, and the pair headed out to investigate their first case together.

```
HOPPER'S CABIN
HAWKINS, INDIANA
```

Hopper could see a question coming, so he stopped talking and sat back, and wrapped his hands around his coffee mug, holding it against his chest.

"So . . . ," El began, then stopped.

Hopper raised an eyebrow. "So?"

El cocked her head and crinkled her nose. "They didn't like her."

"Delgado?"

"Everyone looked at her," said El, "and they were mean. . . . Made her angry."

Oh. Boy.

"Well," said Hopper, then he stopped. How was he going to explain this? He took a searing gulp of coffee and exhaled hotly, and decided to go straight in. "Well, they didn't like her because she was a woman, and she was Hispanic."

"Hispanic?" El sounded out the word slowly, imitating Hopper as best she could.

"Someone with Spanish heritage. Truth is, they were afraid of her."

El shook her head. "Afraid?"

"They were afraid of what she could do—that she would be better at the job than they were, and they didn't like that. They felt threatened by her. Intimidated. I mean, this was all new, back then. They thought this was their domain, and suddenly a woman comes in, and she's full of attitude, and she's ready to push back against them. They thought she was invading their world, and they thought she belonged somewhere else and that she should stay there. The NYPD had never had female homicide detectives until that day. She'd had to fight just for the simple right to walk through that door as one of us. Some of the others didn't like that."

El frowned. "That's not right."

"Nope."

"She was a detective."

"Yep."

"Like you."

"Yes, like me."

"Did you want her there?"

"Me? Well, I was surprised, sure. But I like to think I was a little more open-minded. And like you just said, Delgado was a homicide detective, just the same as I was. I needed a partner, and I was given one, and we got to work. But you also have to remember, this was a long time ago, and things were different then."

"Is it fixed?"

"Ah, well . . ."

"Is it fixed?"

Hopper shook his head. He was already regretting this conversation—as necessary as it was.

"No, it's not . . . fixed. But it's better now. Sort of."

El nodded. "I would be angry too."

Hopper grinned. "I'll bet. But Delgado knew how to handle it. She didn't let it get to her." Then he laughed. "She was one tough cop, that's for sure. And as it turned out, she *was* better than the other detectives. Myself included."

El smiled. "The case was the start."

Hopper's own smile faded. He leaned forward, resting his arms on the table. "Yes, that was the start. The captain gave us that case on Delgado's first day."

El nodded. "Weird stuff," she said, pronouncing the words slowly, like they were important and official. Hopper's smile returned—of course, those hadn't been Delgado's words, but El didn't need to know that. His story was going to feature murders, violence, and danger, and he was doing his best to temper those elements as best he could. He didn't have any problem with bad language himself, but he was at least trying to set some kind of example for El.

Hopper sipped his coffee and resumed the story in the "present"—the Fourth of July, 1977.

CHAPTER FOUR

JUST ANOTHER
DAY AT THE OFFICE

JULY 4, 1977
BROOKLYN, NEW YORK

It was nearly midnight by the time Hopper slipped the key into the lock of his front door, turned it quietly, and entered the apartment, not wanting to wake his wife or daughter.

He need not have worried about the former. There was a light on in the living room, and as Hopper clicked the door closed behind him, he heard the shuffling of papers over the low-key funk of Alan O'Day's "Undercover Angel," and a gentle, distinctive tap—the sound of Diane placing a coffee mug down on one of the cow-shaped souvenir ceramic coasters they'd picked up on a trip upstate last year.

He put his keys on the kitchen counter and as he padded into the other room, Diane looked up from her work.

"Hey," she said.

Hopper walked around the table and kissed Diane on the top of her head. "Sorry," he said, "I was trying to be quiet."

"Oh, don't worry, I'm nearly done here."

Hopper cast his gaze over the table, which was covered with stacks of paper, at the center of which was a wide calendar sheet, already covered with Diane's neat handwriting. By her elbow was a large notebook. He didn't quite follow what she had been doing, but he knew lesson planning when he saw it.

"How's it all going?"

Diane dropped her pen into the notebook and sat back. "Pretty good, actually." She pointed at the calendar. "I've re-worked the class schedule for next year. I think this works really well now." She laughed. "Of course, Derek is going to throw a fit when he sees it."

Hopper grinned. Derek Osterman—the school's vice principal and a stick-in-the-mud who didn't like Diane's ideas, simply because he didn't have the imagination to come up with them himself—was a not uncommon topic of Diane's after-work conversations.

"Well, one day you'll have his job, and will have your own out-of-town upstart to wrestle with."

Diane laughed, and stood up from the table. She moved to the turntable on the sideboard and returned the stylus to its cradle, then moved over to embrace her husband. She held the hug for a few seconds, then pulled back a little.

"You been drinking?"

"Just one. It was a tough night," he said, then: "Sara okay?"

Diane smiled. "Molly the rock took up all her attention most of the afternoon, so you'r off the hook," she said. "Then I let her stay up and watch the fireworks on TV with me, but she was tired from the party and all that cake, and went to bed without a fuss."

"You read her—"

Diane nodded. "To the end of chapter five, although I'm not

sure how much she heard, she was out like a light. I didn't realize at first and just kept reading."

Hopper grinned. "Well, it is a good book." Then his grin faded and he sighed. He gently let his wife's arms trail off him as he entered the kitchen. He opened the fridge and eyed the last of the six-pack of beer that sat on the top shelf by the light. Then, changing his mind, he closed the door and began opening the top cupboards of the kitchen, making his way around the small space.

Behind him, Diane folded her arms, her mouth creasing into a frown.

"Tough night, huh?"

"Sure was," said Hopper, still going through the cupboards. Kitchen orbit completed, he frowned and shook his head. "I'll need to be in tomorrow, too."

"Happy Independence Day," said Diane, as she nudged a bottom cupboard with a slippered foot. Hopper paused, then bent down and opened the cupboard, extracting from within a half-dead bottle of scotch.

Diane watched him as he grabbed a glass and poured himself a generous measure. "Seems a lot of nights are tough nights," she said. "And some of the days, too."

Hopper paused, looked at her, then took a hot mouthful of scotch. He held it for a moment, enjoying the pleasant burn as it filled his mouth, then swallowed, allowing the fiery sensation to spread out across the chest.

Oh yes, he needed that.

"Well, my dear," said Hopper, pouring a second time, "New York is a tough city, and being a New York City cop is a tough job."

Capping the bottle, he drained the glass and turned to lean against the counter, facing Diane. She tightened the fold of her arms and watched her husband.

His shoulders slumped. "I'm sorry," he said. "Really, I'm sorry." He put the glass down and pushed himself away from the counter, moving toward his wife, holding one hand out. She resisted at first, but then lifted her own hand and let it be taken by her husband.

She shook her head, then moved closer, wrapping her arms around his shoulders again and turning her head to rest it against his chest. He wrapped his own arms around her.

"It's okay," said Diane. "You wanted this job and you're doing your best and you never have to apologize for that."

Hopper rested his cheek on the top of Diane's head. "Nobody said it would be easy."

Diane laughed, quietly. "We wanted a challenge. It seems like we got one."

"That we did," said Hopper. He exhaled loudly. "You ever want to go back to Hawkins?"

Diane pulled away and looked up at her husband. She grimaced. "Are you kidding me, James Hopper?"

He smiled. "Well, you know what I mean," he said. "Did we make the right decision, coming here? To New York? I mean, Jesus, the place is falling apart around us."

"Maybe we're just suckers for punishment," said Diane. "But I believe in you."

"Hey, I believe in you too."

"No, listen. I believe in you—and that means I believe in what you want to *do*." Diane shook her head. "We couldn't stay in Hawkins. I know that and you know that. Not after everything you went through. You wanted to turn that into something that would help others, and as much as the Hawkins PD needed you, you needed something bigger. That was what you said. I believed you then, and I believe you now. And look— I needed something bigger too. This is good, for the both of us. We did the right thing—we're *doing* the right thing."

Hopper embraced his wife. She was right, that was *exactly* what he had said. It had sounded so damned corny at the time, when he thought back on it—and think back on it he did, probably more often than was good for him.

Hopper drew his wife in for a kiss, deeper this time. He felt the warmth of her body through his plaid shirt, felt the quickening of her pulse under his hands as they roved around her neck.

Yes, it had been a long day, and this—*this*—was what he needed, more than the booze, more than another round of wondering whether they'd made the right decision in coming here. Hell, they'd been in the city for nearly five years now. If the place was really so bad—if they really had made the wrong decision—then why were they still even here?

Breaking off from their embrace, Diane looked up at Hopper and smiled. He smiled back, looking deep into her eyes.

"Have I mentioned lately," said Hopper, "that I love you?"

Diane frowned. "Hmm, let me see. You've mentioned it now and again, when I think about it." Then she grinned. "Come to bed."

She turned and, hand in hand, they left the kitchen and headed toward the bedroom.

CHAPTER FIVE

INVASION OF THE G-MEN

JULY 5, 1977
BROOKLYN, NEW YORK

Hopper was only vaguely aware of Delgado's arrival, but the heavy thud of her bag as it hit her desk brought him back to the room after being lost in casework for who knew how long. He looked up as his partner, still standing behind her desk, unbuttoned the top three buttons of her green blouse and began fanning herself with a manila folder. Not even eight and it was already pushing ninety outside; inside, the mercury felt like it was at least ten degrees higher still.

"You're in early," said Delgado.

"You're telling me you can sleep in this heat?"

"I'm from Cuba, this is nothing."

"No, you're from Queens, and even for Queens, this is something."

Delgado laughed and put the folder down, picking up her mug. "Coffee?"

"Now you really are joking."

Delgado put one hand on her hip. "One, you should know me well enough by now to know I don't make any attempts at humor before lunch; and two, you look like you need to inject it into a vein rather than drink it; and three, it's hot and—"

"And you like to torture yourself to prove your self-worth and your right to be a homicide detective?"

One of Detective Delgado's eyebrows went up, along with one corner of her mouth.

"You are the king of the jackasses, you know that, right?"

Hopper leaned back. "It has been mentioned upon occasion." He smiled, and after a moment Delgado sighed and shook her head.

Six weeks of being partners and they'd fallen into a routine that, he had to admit, he loved. He hadn't realized what he'd been missing for so long. While Stafford had technically been his partner, they'd never hit it off. Stafford may have been a good cop once, but Hopper suspected that had probably been around the time Paul Revere had ridden to warn that the British were coming.

Rosario Delgado was a *real* partner. Dedicated, capable, and someone he could trust—with his life.

"It's hot . . . and?" he asked.

"And," said Delgado, "drinking a hot drink in hot weather will cool you right down."

Hopper frowned. "I'm not sure that's true."

"Hey, listen to Mr. Indiana Education, here. I might be from Queens but I know a thing or two about Cuba and coffee."

Hopper stood. Delgado waved him away. "Sit down, I can get the damn coffee and still be a homicide detective. Besides, you were deep in thought and I know how long it takes to warm up those brain cells of yours."

Hopper handed his mug over and Delgado stalked off to the coffee room without another word. Hopper watched her for a moment, then sat and returned his attention to the files laid out on the desk.

They were a series of crime scene photos—three large prints, all black-and-white, laid out side by side across the center of his desk. Around them were smaller prints, showing the same scenes from different angles. Across the bottom, Hopper had lined up three plastic evidence bags corresponding to each scene.

Three scenes, three bags.

Three white rectangular cards, blank on one side, a different symbol drawn on each in black on the other side.

Victim one: Jonathan Schnetzer. White, male, twenty-two. Hollow circle.

Victim two: Sam Barrett. White, male, fifty. Cross.

And from yesterday, victim three: Jacob Hoeler. White, male, thirty. Three wavy lines.

Hopper rolled his neck and began adjusting the layout of the cards and photographs on his desk, shuffling them a little but keeping everything aligned while he let his brain work on the problem.

One thing was for sure: when Captain LaVorgna handed the first case to him and Delgado—on Delgado's first day as a homicide detective, no less—he'd been right when he'd said it was weird. One ritual killing had turned into two, had turned into three.

There was no connection between the victims that he or Delgado had been able to find. All seemed like average citizens, whatever "average" meant in New York City. About the only thing they did have in common was that none of them had families or partners—at least, none that the detectives had been able to trace.

That, and, of course, the manner of their deaths. Each one stabbed with a blade of four to six inches in length, as measured at autopsy, and each one stabbed five times in a distinctive, and deliberate, pattern. Any one of the wounds would have been enough to cause death, and while five was certainly overkill, it was actually relatively restrained. In his time as an NYC cop, Hopper had seen victims stabbed thirty, fifty, a hundred times, the attacker driven into a frenzy by drugs or desperation or mental illness or a combination thereof.

Here, there was a precision, not least of all because the wounds were carefully positioned to form the distinctive shape of an inverted five-pointed star.

"Coffee," said Delgado, placing Hopper's mug on the edge of his desk. "I can't make any promises for the flavor, but I can promise you it's hot." She moved around to stand beside her partner, looking down at the spread of photos as she sipped from her own mug. "This really is something else, right?"

Hopper rubbed his jaw and reached for his coffee. "Ain't that the truth."

"No leaks yet?"

He shook his head.

"Well, that's something," said Delgado, and she was right. The previous summer, two Bronx teens, Donna Lauria and Jody Valenti, had been shot as they sat in Jody's car; Jody survived, Donna did not. Since then, five more victims had been claimed—the most recent less than two weeks ago—with the killer writing to not only an NYPD captain, but, just a few weeks ago, to the *Daily News*, signing off both letters with a bizarre nom de plume.

Despite himself, Hopper felt his gaze drawn over to Harris's desk. The detective hadn't yet returned, and the homemade sign he'd made was clearly visible, sitting beside his old Smith-Corona typewriter. It was a macabre—but perhaps necessary— reminder of the evil that still lurked in the city.

IT HAS BEEN 9 DAYS SINCE
THE SON OF SAM LAST STRUCK

Since the first murders, New York had become obsessed with its very own serial killer, Son of Sam dominating the news for weeks, months—at least when the media wasn't wrestling with the city's ongoing monetary problems or the chaotic free-for-all that was the race for the mayor's job. The election, perhaps the most important for a generation of New Yorkers, loomed just four short months away.

And now, with Son of Sam no closer to being caught, it seemed there was another serial killer at work. Right from the discovery of the first victim, Hopper and Delgado had both come to the same conclusion: this case had to be kept under wraps, for now at least. Captain LaVorgna had readily agreed. Son of Sam was enough. There was no telling how the public would react if a second serial killer was added to the six o'clock news.

"At least it doesn't look like we've got a copycat," said Hopper. "Our perp is not taking any cues from Son of Sam. He hasn't tried to contact the authorities." He leaned over the photographs. "And the ritualistic nature of the killings is different."

"Obviously," said Delgado, sitting at her desk and drinking her coffee.

"No, I mean they're not doing it for publicity, or for the attention. In fact, I'm not even sure they're doing it for the murders."

Delgado frowned. "That coffee too hot for your brain, Detective? You kill someone with a knife, you tend to be doing it for the murders. He sure as hell ain't robbing the victims."

"But that's just it," said Hopper. "Hear me out. They're not robberies. They're homicides, yes, but maybe that's not what's driving him."

"I don't follow this."

Hopper picked up one of the crime scene photographs and passed it to his partner. "Look at the scenes. These are ritualistic murders, the victims killed in a very specific way, each scene then marked with a symbol. Nothing else is touched. That has a meaning in and of itself—so what if the killer isn't doing it for attention? He hasn't read about Son of Sam and thinks he can do one better. He's following his own purpose. Attention and publicity is an irrelevance."

Delgado put the photograph down and looked at Hopper as she leaned back in her chair. She swung her feet up onto the corner of her desk, showing Hopper the soles of her square-heeled boots.

"So you're saying the cards he's leaving, they're not for us? He's not trying to give us a message?"

Hopper shook his head. "Nope. The pattern of the stab wounds, the cutting, the cards. They have meaning, but they're not designed to tell us anything."

"So what? It's a nice theory, but it doesn't help us much. So he's not trying to leave us a message. So he's a friggin' mental case. Tell me something I don't know."

Hopper sighed. He looked across the evidence bags at the cards. His eyes settled on the one they had found yesterday— three wavy lines.

"These mean something to the killer. If we can figure out *what*, maybe we can figure out the why."

"Leading us to the *who*," said Delgado. "But these cards have given us nothing, Hopper. No fingerprints. White cards you can buy anywhere. Acrylic ink you can buy in relatively fewer places, if you count every single art supply store in the city as relatively fewer."

That was when Captain LaVorgna emerged from his office. Hopper saw him out of the corner of his eye, and turned to look only when it was clear something was up. LaVorgna stood in the doorway of his office, one hand on the doorknob, his eyes darting left and right as he scanned the bull pen.

"What's with the captain?" asked Delgado. "Heatstroke, maybe?"

"Hopper!" LaVorgna jabbed a meaty finger in Hopper's direction before ducking back into his office and sitting behind his desk, the door left open.

"Why do I have a bad feeling about this?" Hopper asked, before standing and heading over to the office. He stopped at the door and the captain waved him in immediately.

"Close the door," said LaVorgna, clasping his hands in his lap and staring intently at the blotter on his desk, rather than at his detective.

Hopper hesitated, wary of the captain's mood, then complied with the request.

"Take a seat, Detective," said LaVorgna. Again not looking up.

Hopper moved to stand behind one of the two chairs that were positioned in front of the captain's desk. He laid his hands on the fuzzy blue fabric, his fingers sticky with sweat.

"This news I need to sit down for?"

LaVorgna looked up. "I don't have time for games, Detective. Take a seat or stand, I don't care, and I don't have time to care, not yesterday, not tomorrow, and most certainly not today."

Hopper bit his bottom lip, then swung around the chair and sat down. "Is this something about the case? Delgado and I were just—"

LaVorgna closed his eyes and slowly shook his massive head from side to side. Hopper stopped talking.

"Ah, okay, I—"

"You say 'I' a lot, Detective."

"Well, I . . . I mean . . ."

The captain held up a hand. "There is no case, Detective. Not anymore."

Hopper blinked. He took a breath in, held it, and looked around the office. Had he missed something? Had there been a breakthrough? New information? New evidence? Something found at the third crime scene? Had someone been caught? Confessed?

These and a hundred other questions began to circulate

around his head. Hopper let his breath out slowly, readjusted himself in the chair, suddenly aware of how his shirt was plastered against the small of his back with sweat.

He eventually settled for the most obvious question that came to mind.

"What?"

"No case, Detective. As of now, the card homicides are off our board."

Hopper adjusted his seating again. "What happened? Did we get new information? Somebody get a break?"

LaVorgna said nothing. He just looked at Hopper and once again slowly turned his head, left to right, left to right, all the while not taking his eyes off the detective.

Hopper opened his mouth to say something else, but that was when the office door was opened, without a knock. Hopper turned in his seat, expecting to see Delgado joining them. She may have been a junior detective, but this was her case too.

What he saw instead was a uniformed officer holding the door open as a man in a dark blue suit stepped swiftly inside. The uniform raised her eyebrow at LaVorgna, but the captain just sighed and waved her away. She retreated, pulling the door closed.

The man in the blue suit placed his briefcase down flat on the captain's desk and, not even acknowledging the presence of either police officer, began to thumb the revolving combination locks on the latches.

Hopper watched him, his jaw hanging. He looked at the captain, who merely met his eye and shook his head, once more, with exaggerated slowness.

Hopper watched the man fuss with the briefcase. He was average in just about every way—perhaps a touch on the lean side—and had one of those faces whose age was impossible to tell, outside of a rough estimate of forty to fifty. He was clean-shaven, and his hair was very short and very dark and was plastered down with tonic and parted in the middle, the trails of a fine-tooth comb evident with almost mathematical geometry. He had thin lips that were pressed into a white line of concentration as he worked on the combination locks. His suit was narrow and full of square edges, the trousers straight, like the ensemble was fresh off the rack—1967, not 1977.

Hopper had seen his type before. He was a lawyer, or some other kind of official from the district attorney's office, perhaps even from the state. A man who kept his office tidy to the point where you weren't sure anyone actually worked there. Hopper could imagine the row of mechanical pencils and ballpoint pens lined up along the man's desk next to the correction fluid, because the man in the blue suit looked exactly like the kind of automaton who would devote all his energy to making his reports true and accurate and without typo or blemish. A desk jockey—a *career* desk jockey—and proud of it. Someone whose sole purpose was to make the lives of New York City's Finest a lot harder than they really should be.

Hopper disliked him already and the man hadn't even spoken. "You need a little help there?" he asked, nodding at the briefcase. "You tried one-one-one yet?"

At that, the latches of the briefcase snapped open with a sound that echoed around the office like a gunshot. Apparently satisfied, the man in the blue suit stood tall and gave a tight smile, although it was clear it was intended for his own enjoyment and nobody else's. "Gentlemen," he said, giving a curt nod to the captain and then to Hopper.

"Ah, excuse me," said Hopper, "but who the hell are you?"

The man turned his tight smile on Hopper. He had blue eyes that matched his suit, and there was a faint trail of sweat on his upper lip.

Ah, so he was human after all.

LaVorgna cleared his throat and gestured to the newcomer. "This is Special Agent Gallup. He is here to oversee the transition of your case to his department."

Hopper frowned deeply and nodded in mocking appreciation. "Ah, okay, right, good, good." He looked up at Agent Gallup. "And what department would that be, Special Agent Gallup?"

Gallup's smile tightened, if that were possible. "That information is on a need-to-know basis, Officer."

Hopper gave the man a tight smile of his own. *"Detective."*

"I apologize," said Gallup. He turned to LaVorgna. "The ins and outs of the police department," he said, and then he shrugged, like he really, truly, did not care at all.

Hopper felt his temperature rising, and not just because of the clammy heat of the office. He stood, pushing himself up on the arms of the chair. He took a step closer to Gallup. He was nearly a head taller than the agent.

"Listen, *friend*," said Hopper. "I don't know who you are, or what gives you the right to just waltz into our precinct and into my captain's office, but you're treading on some thin ice here."

Gallup looked up at Hopper, the smile firmly plastered on his face. Hopper watched the pulse in the man's temple.

"We've been working this case for six weeks now," Hopper continued. "We're making progress. We can handle it. So I'm sorry, *Special Agent*, but I'm not going to let some G-man in a fancy suit just come in and take over."

Gallup licked his lips. Hopper continued to stare down at him, but it was having no effect. Gallup would not be intimidated; his calm, almost placid exterior remained entirely unrippled.

Finally he nodded. "I understand your concerns, Detective, but the case is no longer yours." He glanced at LaVorgna, who hadn't moved a single muscle as he sat behind his desk. "Nor is it the concern of anybody employed by the New York City Police Department. We are taking this case from you." He paused and looked back up at Hopper. "You can wipe it off that blackboard of yours." He glanced at LaVorgna again. "Actually, that blackboard is a good idea, the way you list cases and detectives. I might borrow that. It could be useful back at the office."

"And which office might that be?" asked Hopper.

"I am not at liberty to say, Mr. Hopper—"

"*Detective* Hopper."

"Sorry, Detective Hopper." Gallup looked at the captain again. "Sorry, I'm terrible at titles, your organization is so . . ." He waved his hands in the air. "Hierarchical."

Hopper sighed and turned to the captain. He leaned over the desk, elbows locked. "Captain, what is going on here? This is bullshit."

LaVorgna sighed and rubbed his face. After a moment of apparent thought, he loosened his tie at the collar and undid the top button of his uniform shirt. This time, however, the action made Hopper smile. He stood back and folded his arms.

Here we go.

"Special Agent Gallup," said the captain. "I understand why you are here, and my superiors have ordered me to give you the fullest cooperation, which I am happy to provide. But perhaps if you could give us just a little more information, we might be able to expedite things for you just a little."

Gallup nodded. "Of course." He opened the briefcase. Hopper got a quick look inside, but all he could see was a single brown manila folder, which Gallup pulled out and handed to him. Hopper took it, and looked at the blank cover. Gallup sat down, then gestured to the other chair. "Please."

Hopper sighed again and sat down. He opened the folder.

Inside was a thin sheaf of papers, stapled at the corner. On the top was a form of some kind—in the top right corner was a photocopied picture of a man that was such bad quality it took Hopper a few seconds to recognize before he read the name underneath.

It was the third victim, Jacob Hoeler, the form adding the middle initial *T*. The address matched the crime scene. The rest of the sheet seemed to be some kind of official record of service, but half of the text had been redacted underneath thick black lines. Hopper turned the sheet over, and saw more of the same. There were a few lines of text readable, but, with no context, about the only thing that made sense was another address.

Special Agent Gallup neatly arranged his hands on his lap as he crossed one knee over another.

"Your third victim was one Jacob Hoeler," he said.

"We know," said Hopper.

"What you *don't* know, Detective, is that Jacob Hoeler is one of ours—*Special Agent* Jacob Hoeler. He was working on assignment, and the fact that he was killed in the course of his duties is of primary concern to my department. Therefore, we need to be sure that a most thorough investigation is carried out. In order to ensure that happens, we will be taking the case in-house."

Hopper shook his head. "That's not how it works," he said. "If you work for federal law enforcement, you can submit a formal request. Or you can just ask nicely and we can cooperate. But what you can't do is just come in here and tell us to stop work. I don't care who you work for. That's not how it works."

Gallup's smile returned, tightened by several degrees. He looked at Hopper, then turned to LaVorgna.

"Do all your detectives have such a chip on their shoulder?"

"Only the good ones," said the captain.

Gallup adjusted himself in his chair, swapping one crossed leg for another as he half-turned to face Hopper.

"In point of fact, I have full authority to just walk in here and take a case away from you. I have the legal power to order the NYPD to surrender any and all case files and documentation pertaining to the case in question, and furthermore, I have the authority to disbar the NYPD from any further action on said case. And further to *that*, I have the ability to lay

charges as I see fit, which may include obstruction of justice."
He lifted one wrist and adjusted the square cufflink so it was
lined up exactly parallel to the edge of the shirt cuff. Then he
looked back at Hopper. "Do we have an understanding, *Detective* Hopper?"

Hopper ran his fingers through his hair. He looked at the
captain, but LaVorgna just shook his head again.

"My hands are tied, Hopper. This comes from the chief of
detectives himself. When I got the call, Special Agent Gallup
and his men were already on their way." He sat back in his
chair and spread his hands. "There's nothing we can do. This
case is no longer ours."

Hopper frowned. "'Men'?"

The office door flew open and Delgado burst in. She took
one look at the trio, then her gaze settled on the captain.

"What the hell is going on, sir? They're taking everything."

Hopper jumped to his feet and moved to the office windows.
Looking out across the bull pen, he saw two men in dark suits
busy loading casework from his and Delgado's twin desks into
large file boxes, while a third agent seemed to be having a very
one-sided conversation with Sergeant McGuigan, in that McGuigan was yelling at him and the agent wasn't saying a thing.

"You got to be kidding me," said Hopper. He left the office,
Delgado close behind. As he got to his desk, the agent being
given an earful by McGuigan looked over at him. The sergeant
stopped midstream and turned around.

"Hopper, what's going on, man? These bozos won't say
nothin'. And who's that with the captain?"

Hopper turned as LaVorgna approached, Special Agent
Gallup at his elbow. Behind them stood Delgado, fuming, her
arms folded.

"That'll do, Sergeant," said the captain. Gallup smiled and
Hopper had to dampen his sudden and urgent desire to wipe
the expression from the man's face.

The special agent glanced sideways at LaVorgna. "This another one of your good ones, Captain?"

LaVorgna ignored him. He stepped between Sergeant McGuigan and the other agent. Around them, the other detectives in the bull pen watched. The captain moved around his sergeant to address the room.

"Nothing we can do, everybody. Best to just let them get on with it and get out. In the meantime we still have police work to do, so I suggest we do it."

Murmuring, the other detectives returned to their desks, although Hopper could see that few were really returning to their work. Delgado stormed over to her desk, removing her coffee mug before the agent clearing her desk swept it up into his carton.

"Case files, idiot," she muttered.

LaVorgna tapped Hopper on the arm. "Go get some coffee and come back in five. They'll be done by then."

"And then what? They'll have cleaned us out."

"What do you want me to do, Detective? Call Beame at City Hall and ask for a favor? Trust me, he's busy. We all are. Or maybe you've forgotten the other cases on the board with your name next to them?" He paused, and sighed. "Maybe this is for the best. Maybe the card homicides were too big for this precinct to handle. Maybe I would have called in the feds anyway."

With that, the captain stalked off, back to his office. He closed the door behind him.

Hopper turned back to watch the agents continuing their packing. They were slow, methodical, and—Delgado's coffee mug aside—they did seem to be checking the files before they loaded them into their boxes, making sure they took the card homicide material and nothing else. Standing nearby, the attaché case swinging in one hand, Special Agent Gallup conferred with the third agent.

Hopper turned and headed toward the coffee room. As he passed Delgado, she tapped his elbow. He glanced at her and she gestured with a nod of her head in the direction he was already facing. Holding her mug, she walked ahead of him.

Once they were in the coffee room, Hopper closed the door behind him as Delgado moved to the window and looked back down the hallway toward the bull pen. In the corner of the room sat a fourteen-inch black-and-white television set, on, but with the sound muted; Hopper twisted the volume control just as Vicki Lawrence began extolling the virtues of Carnation instant milk. Happy that they now wouldn't be overheard, Hopper turned to his partner.

"You okay, Delgado?"

"This is bullshit," she said.

Hopper nodded. "Sure is."

"But," said Delgado, turning around to face her partner. "I have an idea."

CHAPTER SIX

PLAN OF ATTACK

JULY 5, 1977
BROOKLYN, NEW YORK

"*All news, all the time—this is WINS. You give us twenty-two minutes, we'll give you the world!*"

Hopper sank back behind the wheel of a precinct pool car and turned the radio down as the tinny xylophone music of the 1010 WINS news break filled the vehicle's interior. The car was a huge white Pontiac Catalina that might have been a nice ride when new but now rocked and rolled on worn shocks like a boat in a stormy sea, thanks to the budget-saving increase in the intervals between services.

It was, however, still relatively comfortable, especially for someone as tall as Hopper. And after an hour of waiting in the underground parking garage, angled low in the driver's seat, he was grateful for what lower back support the seat still offered.

"*Good evening, it's seventy-five degrees at seven o'clock, I'm*

Stan Z. Burns, and here's what's happening. Mayor Beame urges talks resume between the city and unions, but he says the unions have to give in a bit . . ."

The underground garage occupied two levels underneath the 65th, and the Pontiac was on the lower level, right in the back, the interior in perpetual shade thanks to the unfortunate angles of the garage lighting. Perhaps he was overdoing it, but the pool of vehicles was in regular use by the precinct, and the fewer officers who saw him, the better. If things got difficult later, he didn't want anyone else forced to admit they'd seen him and Delgado down in the garage on the night Special Agent Gallup had taken the card homicide case off them.

Or . . . thought he had.

The garage was at least relatively cool, certainly compared to the city streets above, if the radio was anything to go by. Hopper kept the windows rolled down—not just to keep the temperature comfortable, but so he could hear as well as see everything that happened in the garage.

He just hoped she came soon. He hadn't called Diane to let her know he'd be late—it was a common enough occurrence that he knew she wouldn't be worried, but he hated the fact that, this time at least, his lack of communication was deliberate.

Delgado appeared a few minutes later, walking down the main ramp that led to the upper level of the garage. She paused at the bottom, scanning the cars. Hopper turned the key to start the battery, and flicked the lights once. She headed toward him and got in on the passenger side.

"This is crazy," she said.

"Call it caution."

"Call it paranoia." She turned toward him, then glanced down at the radio and frowned before reaching for the knob and turning it off.

Hopper smirked. "You don't like Stan Z. Burns?"

"I prefer Mellow 92 myself. But look, when I said to meet later, I didn't expect the cloak-and-dagger routine."

Hopper's smile vanished as he leaned in toward his partner. "Hey, I'm on your side, but I think we need to be careful. We go where we're going, I get the feeling it's a one-way trip. We will win or we will lose, and losing will be bad. So, yes, I'm taking precautions."

Delgado looked at him. She was an experienced cop, but still a new detective—one apparently willing to bend the rules of the job if the greater good demanded it.

So here they were, hiding in a pool car, disobeying direct orders.

Because they were not going to give up the case so easily.

Back in the coffee room, Hopper had listened as Delgado explained her plan. At first, a tiny seed of doubt began to grow in his mind, but as she continued he saw the commitment in her face and heard the determination in her words, and quickly dismissed his fears.

Because she had been right. He had listened as she talked about how they had a job to do, a city to protect. How this was their neighborhood and there were people depending on them, and they couldn't just let the case go. That they had a duty to protect the people they'd sworn to protect, and how Gallup had no right to take the case off them and—

And he had agreed. He had listened, and he had taken it in. It was a crazy idea but it was a good one—one that Hopper knew, there and then, that they had to enact.

A few minutes later they returned to the bull pen and . . .

Well, Hopper had started a fight. He had walked up to Gallup, gotten in the man's face, and started yelling.

His outburst had the desired effect. The other agents and detectives gathered round, and LaVorgna had rushed out of his office to intervene. Behind them all, Hopper saw Delgado slip into the captain's office. A few moments later, she was out again. She gave him a nod, and Hopper made a show of giving up his argument.

Before getting back to work, Captain LaVorgna had given

Hopper an earful of his own. Hopper gave his apology—a genuine one, at that—and life went on in the 65th. Hopper buried himself in another case, and he and Delgado spent the rest of the shift avoiding each other. That was part of the plan too: Hopper's outburst was a bad example to set for his junior partner, so it was reasonable to assume they would both be embarrassed by it, and give each other some space for the rest of the day—which they did, save for a brief hallway encounter in which Hopper gave his partner the time and place for their secret rendezvous.

"Anyway, sorry I'm late," said Delgado. "I had to finish some stuff off. But, mission accomplished."

She opened her bag and pulled out the thin file belonging to Jacob Hoeler, the same file that was supposed to be sitting pretty inside the folder on Captain LaVorgna's desk. "And before you say it, yes, I saw it too."

Hopper took the file and flipped over the top page. On the back, swimming in the sea of black lines, was the second address.

"Dikeman Street," said Hopper. "A building and apartment number, but no cross street or zip code."

Delgado nodded, and opened the car's glove compartment. From within she extracted a greasy spiral-bound street atlas. Flipping to the index, she frowned at the page before reaching up and turning the car's inside light on. Now able to see, she traced a finger down the densely printed list of street names before finding the avenue in question. Turning back through the pages, she found the area in question.

"Only one Dikeman Street, so this must be it." She tapped the page. Hopper took the book and squinted at it. "So what do you want to do?" asked Delgado. "Go check it out?"

Hopper nodded. "Yeah, I think we should." Then he looked at his partner. "Are you sure you're okay with this? There's still time to pull out and deny everything."

Delgado shook her head. "I wouldn't have suggested a stunt

like this in the first place if I wasn't okay with it. I don't like it when agents, special or otherwise, mess with my stuff, and I certainly didn't fight to become a homicide detective for my first case to be taken off me just like that."

"You know what could happen to us if we're caught, right?" asked Hopper. Although he agreed with his partner's plan of action, he was still the senior detective, and he felt obliged to point out the reality of the situation they were about to enter, whether she wanted to hear it or not. "We screw this up, you won't be a homicide detective much longer. There's a lot riding on what happens next and—"

Delgado held up her hand. "Trust me, I get it. But we have work to do and we're going to do it." She adjusted her position in the seat to better face Hopper. "So let me ask, are *you* in?"

Hopper grinned. "Oh, I'm in, Detective."

"Okay, good," said Delgado. "So, let's go check out Dikeman Street."

"Actually," said Hopper, "I want you to go back to the apartment."

Delgado's brow knitted in confusion. "The crime scene apartment?"

"Yes. I want you to go in and take another look. See if there is anything we missed. We know more about the victim now than we did before, maybe you can shake something out."

"Okay," said Delgado. "Meet back here later?"

Hopper checked the time again, and winced. "Actually, no, I'll need to get home." He looked at his partner. "You do the same. We'll talk tomorrow."

"Got it." Delgado clicked the door of the pool car open. "Happy hunting, Detective," she said, then got out, closed the door, and disappeared back up the parking garage ramp.

Hopper waited a few more minutes to give her time to get clear, then he started the car up and headed out toward Dikeman Street and the mystery apartment.

CHAPTER SEVEN

HOUSE OF SECRETS

JULY 5, 1977
BROOKLYN, NEW YORK

Hopper parked the pool car a couple of blocks away from Dikeman Street, took the police-issue flashlight from behind the passenger seat, and went the rest of the way on foot. He had no idea what he would find at the apartment, but he told himself to remain optimistic. There was something funky going on with the case—the case he wasn't even supposed to be working—and he felt that little tug of adrenaline somewhere deep in his chest as he told himself over and over that he was doing the right thing.

Wasn't he?

Dikeman Street was in a mixed-use neighborhood, the residential block rubbing shoulders with a good number of local stores—bodegas and bottle stores, furniture stores, hair and nail salons. It wasn't the best area in town, but, given the state of the city, Hopper was quite comfortable walking down the streets washed yellow under sodium lamps. Despite the hour, the bodegas and bottle stores were doing a brisk trade and Hopper was far from the only person out.

Jacob Hoeler's mystery apartment was on the second floor of a walk-up with an open front door. One short flight of stairs later and Hopper found himself in a wide hallway with linoleum on the floor and pairs of brass lights along the walls. Half of the lights were dead; the linoleum was worn and shiny as Hopper's shoes scuffed along.

Hopper read the numbers off the doors as he walked down the hallway, and soon came to the apartment of interest at the end, where there was a large window and, beyond, the iron lattice of a fire escape.

He stood by the window and checked the hallway, but he was alone. The window glass was thin and did nothing to muffle the sound of traffic in the street outside, and the indecipherable chatter of several television sets echoed loud and clear from the other apartments.

Almost indecipherable. As Hopper looked back down the hallway, someone in a close apartment turned their set up, the theme from *M*A*S*H* cutting in abruptly.

As Hawkeye and Colonel Potter debated who went to hell in the neighbor's living room, Hopper pulled a clean checkered handkerchief out of the inside pocket of his jacket, and draped it over the apartment's doorknob before giving it a turn. His hand slid around on the cold metal, the knob refusing to move.

Locked, as expected.

Looking over his shoulder again, he fished a thin leather wallet from another pocket and opened it, pulling a set of picklocks from the holder. Gripping the wallet's edge in his teeth, he crouched down and got to work.

Thirty seconds later, he was inside the apartment. He swung the door closed, careful to keep his handkerchief between his hand and the doorknob. He was operating strictly off the books, and the last thing he wanted to do was leave his prints all over the place.

Pulling the bulky flashlight from where he had jammed it in the waistband of his pants at the small of his back, he activated the light and kept it low, wary of advertising his unauthorized presence to anyone in the street outside.

It took a moment for Hopper to process what the pool of light was showing him. He wasn't sure what he had been expecting to find, but it sure as hell wasn't this.

The apartment was empty. Or at least the room in which he stood was. The place was tiny, the front door opening directly into the living area. To Hopper's immediate left was a galley-style kitchenette. Playing the flashlight around, he saw a door on the left, a window dead ahead, and a blank wall on the right—the exterior wall of the apartment building.

The living space wasn't just empty, it was *bare*. The floor was bare boards. The walls were also bare, remnants of wallpaper clinging in patches, the edges ragged and revealing decades of layers. In the center of the ceiling was an ornate plaster rose, another relic from a time when this part of the city had been somewhat more desirable. From the rose hung a thick braided wire, ending in a bare bulb. Satisfied that he was alone, and the curtains were drawn across the window opposite, Hopper found the light switch with his cloth-covered hand. The naked bulb buzzed in protest, but lit all the same. Hopper turned off the flashlight and replaced it at the small of his back.

He stepped into the room, slowly, aware of how the wooden floor would act as a soundboard. He did a circuit of the room, and learned precisely nothing. The place was empty. Abandoned. It appeared that nobody had lived here for years.

Or had they?

Hopper paused. A shut-up apartment would be dusty, especially in a building as old as this, with exposed walls and crumbling plasterwork. But the place was clean—not *cleaned*—but not dirty. Whatever dust had gathered over the years had been disturbed by the movements of someone using the apartment.

That someone being Jacob Hoeler.

But what had he been using it for? The living room was clearly a wash, unless there was something under the floorboards. Hopper paced a few lengths, but the boards were as solid as iron, having been installed maybe a hundred years earlier and left untouched. Then he moved to the kitchenette, examining the cupboards with his cloth-covered hand. They were all empty. There was a refrigerator in the corner that might have been something to look at in the mid-1950s, but it was turned off, and empty inside.

Finding nothing of interest, Hopper moved to the only other door he could see. It opened freely, and showed him a truncated hallway, with an open door on his left leading to a bathroom, and a closed door—probably to a bedroom—on the right. Hopper took his flashlight out again and shone it into the bathroom. There was a bath and no shower, a toilet, and a cabinet mounted on the wall above, a mirror set into the door. Hopper blinked as his light was thrown back at him by the mirror, then decided to look in the bedroom.

Bingo.

The bedroom was devoid of a bed or other furniture, but it was far from empty. There was a camp stretcher in the middle of the room, with blanket, sheet, and pillow arranged roughly in place. There was a wooden folding table standing next to the stretcher, on which was a sprung desk lamp more suited to an office than a bedroom. Next to the lamp was a thick hardback novel: *The Shining*, by Stephen King. Hopper hadn't read that one yet.

Hopper turned, shining the flashlight around the small room.

Then he saw them.

Lined up along the baseboard of the wall housing the bedroom door were a set of file boxes, all identical, made of heavy black cardboard with a white label on the spine. On the labels were written long numbers in a neat hand using a fat felt-tipped pen. Below each number was a large machine-printed label:

U.S. DEPARTMENT OF DEFENSE
WITHDRAWAL FORBIDDEN

Hopper stepped back, moving the flashlight along the row. There were fifteen boxes in total. Hopper stood, deep in thought.

There was something very strange going on. He turned on his heel, shining his light over the camp stretcher.

What the hell was Special Agent Hoeler doing here? That he was using the crummy apartment as a base of operations was obvious. What was less clear was why—and how—he had a bunch of federal files with him. Did Gallup know about the files? He knew about the apartment, but the files—WITHDRAWAL FORBIDDEN—were still here.

Hopper shook his head, and turned back to the files. He had to find out what was in them. He dropped to his haunches and reached for the first box.

That was when he heard it. A creak, faint but unmistakable, the same sound he had made just minutes earlier as he had crossed the floor of the main room.

Someone else had entered the apartment.

Hopper froze. It must be one of Gallup's agents—of course, the apartment would have been under surveillance, and perhaps the files had been left deliberately as . . .

Bait.

Hopper had walked right into a trap.

He stood and killed the flashlight, then pushed himself flat against the wall next to the bedroom door. Getting arrested by a federal agent was not what he had in mind. He strained his ears to listen. He was in luck—it sounded like only one person.

Maybe, just maybe, Hopper could get away.

He controlled his breathing, calming himself, focusing on the sounds from the other room. After a minute, his patience paid off. The creaking footsteps of the intruder got louder as they stepped into the short hallway outside the bedroom. A moment later and the doorknob began to turn, slowly.

Hopper took the presented opportunity. He stepped away from the wall, moved in front of the door, and reached for the doorknob. As the doorknob began to turn, Hopper grabbed it and yanked the door open.

The intruder was pulled into the room, and into Hopper. Hopper was ready and pushed him away and to the side, giving himself a clear run for the door. Hopper got a glimpse of a black ski mask and his hands slipped on the man's leather jacket.

This was no agent.

That moment of hesitation was all the intruder needed. He regained his balance and pushed back against Hopper with surprising strength. Hopper lost his footing and hit the floor, and the intruder fled.

"Son of a *bitch*," Hopper breathed as he got to his feet and ran into the main room—just in time to see the apartment door bang shut, the sound of heavy footfalls receding as the intruder hotfooted it down the hallway.

Hopper swore again and burst through the main door, not pausing as he powered down the hallway in pursuit. There was no visible sign of the intruder, but he could still be heard as he raced down the stairs.

Hopper sprinted after him, swinging into the stairwell and taking the steps down two at a time, almost overbalancing at the first landing, holding his hands out in front of himself as he bounced off the wall. Using the momentum, he pushed back and continued down the second set of stairs.

The building's front door was still swinging shut as Hopper arrived in the lobby. Hopper burst after his quarry, pausing only once in the street to determine the direction.

It wasn't difficult. The sidewalk was not empty and the subject of his pursuit had pushed his way through the gaggle of young men who were hanging outside the bodega on the corner. There were four of them, all topless, their shirts tied loosely around their waists, their dark skin slick with sweat as they waved beer cans in the air, cheering at the fast-disappearing form of Hopper's target.

Hopper set off, the quartet of youths now clapping for him as he shot through the middle of the group. Ahead, the intruder had crossed the street and was sprinting for the next corner. Hopper had to catch him, and soon, or he would be lost in the unfamiliar crisscross maze of streets.

Soft-soled loafers pounding on the street, Hopper hoofed it to the other side, his flashlight digging painfully into his back as he ran. As he reached the corner of the next street he could already feel himself beginning to flag as the initial surge of adrenaline began to fade, replaced now with a stitch in his side. He'd jarred his right knee on the stair landing, and now it began to signal with bright flashes of pain that he wouldn't be able to keep this up.

Catching his breath, Hopper turned the corner. His quarry was still running, his arms pumping like an Olympic sprinter as he tore down the middle of the street. There were fewer pedestrians here, but they all stopped and turned to watch.

Hopper kept after him, but the gap was increasing between them with every stride. Eventually, Hopper came to a stop—he had to, or he was going to be sick. He stopped in the center of the street and bent over, hands on knees, as he whooped for breath. There was a sharp honk from behind him and he half turned, blinking into a set of car headlights. The invisible driver leaned on the horn again. Hopper waved an acknowledgment and dragged himself off the street and onto the sidewalk. The car passed, the driver offering a colorful opinion through his open window. As the taillights receded, Hopper looked down the street.

The intruder was long gone. And there was no point in calling it in, either. Hopper had no description of the intruder apart from the fact he'd been wearing a black ski mask and black leather jacket. And besides, Hopper wasn't even supposed to be at the apartment, and he didn't feel like explaining himself to someone like Gallup.

But he had been right. The apartment was important.

Hopper retraced his steps, slowly, feeling the stitch in his side as he walked back to Dikeman Street.

Who had the intruder been? Not an agent—Hopper couldn't be sure of that, of course, but there was just something about his clothing, and certainly something about his behavior, the way he had run off.

Was he Hoeler's killer? Had Hopper just tussled with the Brooklyn serial killer himself? And why had he been in the apartment—had he seen Hopper come in, or was it just coincidence that they'd both shown up at the same time? But if the intruder hadn't been there for Hopper, he had been there for another reason.

For the files?

Hopper broke into a jog as he got within sight of the apartment building. The youths outside the bodega had moved on and the street was now empty.

Hopper entered the building and made his way back up the stairs. The apartment door was still open. Hopper listened outside, just for a moment, just to be sure there was nobody inside, but out in the hallway the neighbor's TV was too loud, canned laughter bouncing around the hallway. Hopper closed his eyes, trying to concentrate, but gave up. The only thing he had been able to deduce was that *M*A*S*H* had finished.

Just how long was I gone?

He stepped inside the apartment. The main bulb was still on but there was now light spilling from the other door. Moving through, Hopper found the desk lamp in the bedroom was on.

Hopper turned around.

"Shit!"

The files were gone. All fifteen boxes.

Gone.

Hopper looked around, not quite believing what he was seeing. He did a circuit of the room, like that would reveal anything. Then he went into the microscopic bathroom, taking all of three seconds to confirm there was nothing in there.

He returned to the bedroom and sat down heavily on the camp bed. The rolled mattress was thin, and the flimsy folding metal frame gave a squeal in protest.

Hopper stared at the wall against which the files had been arranged. How long had he been gone? He checked his watch, and was surprised to see it was nearly ten. His pursuit of the intruder, and subsequent slow return to the apartment, had taken more than a half hour. More than enough time for someone—probably more than one—to come in and take the files away.

Hopper rolled his neck, then stretched out his right leg so his heel was against the floor. He began massaging his sore knee while he mulled events in his mind.

That was when he saw it. Flexing his knee back to ninety degrees, he reached under the mattress and pulled out a notebook, the edge of which had become visible only after Hopper's weight had shifted the bed under him.

The notebook was spiral-bound, with most of the pages torn out. The few that remained were all blank. Hopper flipped through them, then sighed and tossed the open notebook onto the table. He rubbed his face and resisted the urge to scream at the top of his lungs.

He opened his eyes, and glanced again at the notebook.

The top sheet was not blank. The way the desk lamp was angled, the way the notebook was tilted slightly against the lamp's base, revealed a secret.

Hopper pulled the lamp around, blinking at the sudden increase in brightness, then picked up the notebook and held the page under the bulb, tilting it this way and that to get the best angle.

The indentations were clear, a ghosted shadow of what someone—he assumed Hoeler—had written on the page immediately prior to this one. Hopper squinted, unable to quite make anything out clearly—the words were small, although the way they were arranged suggested it was a list.

But one word was clear—written on the other side of the sheet in large, bold letters that had been circled multiple times.

Hopper frowned. He turned the notepad over in his hands again, studying both sides of it, lifting each of the last sheets, holding each one up against the light to see if anything else could be revealed. But that was it. Only one sheet showed the indentations.

Hopper pocketed the notebook, that one single word reverberating through his mind.

Vipers.

CHAPTER EIGHT

THE LIST

Delgado stood with her hands on her hips as she looked around Jacob Hoeler's other apartment, the one in which the special agent had met his unfortunate end. When she'd arrived, she'd found the place still sealed with police tape and a uniform on duty in the hallway, reading a newspaper tightly folded to the sports section, transistor radio on the floor next to him blaring something Delgado thought she recognized as "Sir Duke" by Stevie Wonder. Delgado berated him for breaking protocol—knowing that she couldn't quote the relevant sections if he asked, but also fairly sure that he wouldn't—then ordered the bored officer to let her in and then go get a coffee and leave her to it. He left with a sigh, slapping the paper into Delgado's hand, like she didn't have anything better to do than check the baseball scores. She watched him walk down the hallway before kneeling down to turn off the radio.

"Sorry, Stevie," she said, then scooped up the radio and went inside, dumping it and the newspaper on the kitchen counter before getting to work.

Delgado had been searching for what felt like hours, and had come up with nothing. The bedroom had been stripped and the bed itself was gone, carted off to the crime lab for analysis, along with a large square of carpet that had been unevenly cut out, leaving a tattered section of underlay in its place. All of the loose trash had been collected from the whole apartment and, again, was likely sitting in bags in the lab, waiting for someone to sift through it all.

Delgado thought they'd have better luck than she would.

The bedroom had a closet and a set of drawers. Delgado had searched them all, but found nothing out of the ordinary, nothing hidden, and nothing in the pockets of any of the jackets or pants, nothing hidden inside socks or folded inside the underwear.

The living room was also a wash. With the trash cleared out, the place was sparse, with only a threadbare lounge suite and sticky coffee table. Delgado turned the cushions over, felt them, but found nothing.

She had better luck in the kitchen. The cops, or perhaps Gallup's agents, had turned it over, and the counters were crowded with pots and pans and crockery, the cupboards themselves left standing open and empty. Delgado poked around, not hopeful of anything, and was about to leave when she saw the edge of a corkboard on the back wall, near the fridge, mostly hidden behind a stack of pots.

Surely they couldn't have missed it?

Delgado moved the pots, one by one, until she had clear access. The corkboard was studded with pushpins, holding a dozen pieces of paper to the board. They were mostly receipts, but one larger sheet caught her eye.

Delgado unpinned the note. It was a list of addresses—five in total, spread out across Queens, Brooklyn, and Manhattan. She turned it over in her hands, but that was all that was on it.

Setting the note side, she began pulling the receipts off the board, hopeful they would provide more clues.

"Hey, what's going on here?"

Delgado turned around as a large man appeared in the kitchen doorway. He was middle-aged and balding, a ring of curly brown hair surrounding a scalp shining with sweat. He wore large square glasses and was dressed in tracksuit bottoms and a wifebeater.

Delgado held up the medallion around her neck. The man leaned forward to see, holding his glasses a little out from his face as he concentrated. Then he nodded and stood back.

"Oh, sorry, Officer, I didn't realize you folks would be coming back. I mean, there was a guy standing outside but he left, so, y'know, I thought maybe you were all done finally." He cleared his throat, and there was a clunk from behind him.

Delgado raised an eyebrow and the man cleared his throat again and sheepishly brought out the baseball bat he had been hiding behind his leg. He shrugged.

"Hey, I didn't know you were a cop, okay? But do you blame me? Huh? Do you blame me? Town like this, I need to take precautions, right?" He nodded. "Precautions . . . ah, *ma'am*," the afterthought added before he glanced at the floor, clearly embarrassed at having been caught with the improvised weapon.

"I'm Detective Delgado." She narrowed her eyes at the man, recognizing him from her previous visit. "You're the super, right?"

"Ah, yes I am," said the man. He held out his hand. "Richardson. Tony. Tony Richardson."

Delgado looked at the man's hand. It was slick with sweat. He noticed, and dropped his hand, wiping the palm on his sweatpants.

"Sorry," he said. He laughed, nervously. "I must look a mess, right? This damn heat. AC is out in the whole building and I haven't had a chance to do any laundry yet, so this is all I got."

He looked at the floor again. Delgado laughed.

"Tell me about it," she said. "I've been breaking department dress code for two weeks, but hell if anyone is going to tell me what to wear in this weather."

Tony looked up and smiled, clearly relieved—she imagined his encounters with the NYPD were, in general, somewhat less friendly.

"Tell you the truth," he said, "it's kinda . . . exciting. Right?"

Delgado frowned. "Exciting?"

"Yeah, you know. An apartment under my watch is a crime scene. Murder, right? Real Son of Sam stuff. I tell you, not much happens around here, so this is, y'know, exciting. I'm excited."

Delgado's frown deepened. Richardson looked at her, his eyes slowly widening. He cleared his throat again.

"I mean, I'm excited to help, is all," he said, mostly to the floor. "You know, keeping the city safe, doin' my civic duty, that kind of thing."

"Uh-huh," said Delgado. She returned to the corkboard and started pulling the receipts off it again.

"Sorry to give you the whole third degree," said the super, swinging the bat in one hand. "But you know, you gotta understand my position here. All this," he said, swinging the bat and indicating the apartment in general with the business end of it. "All this is my responsibility. I gotta look after it and I gotta watch who comes and goes, what with the cops trampling everywhere. Right? I have to look after it. So, y'know, don't mind me if I check up on who's in and who's out, you get me?"

"I get you," said Delgado. "Just do me a favor and lose the bat, huh?"

"Oh, yeah, sorry. Ah, *ma'am*," said Richardson. He lifted the bat and placed it gently on the kitchen counter, and picked up the discarded newspaper. "But you know, what am I supposed to do?" he asked, waving the paper as a fan with one hand as he turned on the small radio with his other.

"*. . . and that was Thelma Houston with 'Don't Leave Me This Way,' the song that hit the top of the Billboard back in April and is keeping the disco dancefloors moving this summer . . .*"

Richardson leaned over to the radio and turned the dial before Delgado clicked it back to the off position.

"Do you mind?"

The super held his hands up. "Hey, sorry, just seeing if I can get me some sports." He lifted the newspaper to read.

"Of course I thought you were the others," he said, continuing with his earlier train of thought. "You know, sniffing around again."

"The cops?"

The super slapped the folded newspaper with the back of his free hand. "Ah, geez Louise, will you get outta town? Three–one? How many times are the Mets going to lose to the Phillies? I mean, come on. This is killing me here." Richardson looked up. "Oh, I mean, no offense. Ma'am."

The detective raised an eyebrow. "Do you mean there were cops here, or someone else?"

"Oh no, not the cops. The others. Kinda hinky they were too. Didn't like the look of them."

Delgado paused. He must have been talking about Gallup's agents, although "hinky" was an odd way to describe them. She turned back to the super.

"Men in suits?"

Richardson pushed his big glasses up his nose with a thumb. "Suits?"

"The men who came by?"

"Oh, yeah," said the super. "I mean, no, they weren't wearing no suits. No, these guys, they were . . . I don't know. Guys." He shrugged.

"Tell me about them."

"Ah, well, lemme see, lemme see." The super pushed his glasses up again and dropped the paper back onto the counter. "There was the three of them. I didn't see them come in, but I heard the banging. I was downstairs—ah, the super's apartment is the one right below this one, ah, *ma'am*. Anyways, it was . . . oh, afternoon. Or was it evening? Not late, anyway. So I heard this banging, see, *thud thud thud*, like they was really trying to bust the door down. They were shouting for Jacob, too, but of course he never did answer."

Delgado shook her head. "Wait, when was this?"

"Oh, two days ago? No, three. Last week. Before, y'know, everything. Anyways, they were calling for him and *thud thud thud* on the door, so I came up to take a look at what the whole racket was, tell them to clear off. The neighbors, you see, they don't like no disturbances, and who gets it in the ear when this happens? Me, that's who. I tell you, I get lines forming outside my office like it's a damn peep show in Times Square." The super took off his glasses, rubbed at the nose rest, then put them back on. "So anyways, I came up to them and I told them to stop beating on the door and start beating on the stairs. You know, to scram." He paused, like he was expecting confirmation from Delgado that she was still awake and listening.

All she did was lift an eyebrow. The super took this as the sign he was looking for, and continued.

"So anyways, they stop beating on the door and they all look at me, and I'm ready to go get my bat, just in case, y'know. But strike me, if the guy doing the thumping didn't just stand there and smile and say he was sorry. Nicest bunch of punks I ever did see."

"Punks?"

"Ah, well, okay, maybe not punks. But, y'know. Kids. Well, maybe not kids. Older. Well, older than you, younger than me. Kinda rough'n'tumble, you know? And those jackets? I swear I would have baked from the inside out wearing those things."

"What kind of jackets?"

"You know, green jackets. Kinda like, you know, is it khaki? Maybe it's khaki. You know. Army jackets. Not like uniforms, unless flared jeans are uniforms these days. Maybe they are, what the hell do I know?"

Delgado narrowed her eyes as she tried to pick out the relevant parts of the super's story. "What happened next?"

"Ah, well, you know, they says they're looking for Jacob, and I say he's not home. And of course that's when I noticed it."

"It?"

"Oh yeah, it. The *smell*. I mean, the neighbor next door—that's number fourteen—she said something the day before, but she's always saying something. But up here I could really get a nose of it, you know? At first I thought it was the three guys in those army jackets, but when they were gone the smell was still there. So I knocked on the door. I mean, I don't know why I did it because unless he'd climbed in through the second-floor window in the last minute then Jacob still wasn't at home. So I left it there but then number fourteen, a couple of days later she pokes her head into my office and gives me what for about the smell, and she won't leave me alone until I go check, so I get the master keys and take a look and . . . well, you know the rest."

Delgado nodded. She'd read Richardson's statement a few times, but it only began with the complaints of the smell from the neighbor. Everything else he'd just related was new to her.

"You left a hell of a lot out of your statement, Tony."

At that, the super raised his hands defensively. "Oh hey, listen, what am I supposed to do? The cops, they're not interested, are they? None of them asked a damn thing, only how did I find the body. And look—" He paused and picked up the baseball bat. Delgado tensed, but he only lifted it and held it out to her, like he was showing it off. "Sometimes you just gotta look after yourself. Listen, the cops cleared out, they left one on the door, but that was it. I asked what was happening and did they tell me? Did they hell. What am I supposed to do? I'm the super, I got responsibilities and duties, and now I got this place to watch."

Delgado nodded. The super had a point. The cops—the uniformed ones, anyway—would have been in and out as fast as possible, all responsibility for the scene handed over to homicide. They hadn't told Richardson anything because there was nothing to tell, it just wasn't their department. And with her and Hopper taken off the case, it sounded like Gallup had yet to send his own agents in to take over. The super had been left in the dark.

"Listen," said Delgado, "you've been a big help today, really."

The super grinned and pushed his glasses up his nose. "Oh hey, anytime. I'm just downstairs. Come by anytime, glad to help. I wish there were more cops like you, you know what I mean?"

Delgado, unfortunately, knew exactly what he meant. She began gathering up the pieces of paper from the corkboard, shuffling them in her hand. From the pile she pulled a narrow strip of card and looked at it. Richardson appeared at her side, adjusting his glasses, and read the card.

"Frank Sinatra tickets!"

Delgado frowned and moved to one side a little, giving herself more personal space. The super tapped the card in her hand.

"Forest Hills Stadium, July 16," he said, then he gave a tuneless blow through pursed lips, which Delgado thought was probably supposed to be a whistle.

"Man alive, what I would do to have tickets to Frank Sinatra. I tell you what, now, that'll be some concert, some concert indeed. Oh, yes."

He looked at Delgado. He adjusted his glasses. Delgado held his gaze, watching the super's magnified eyes blink behind his square lenses.

The super shrugged, then tapped the ticket again. "Because he's not going to be going, is he? Mr. Hoeler. I mean, you ever hear of a dead man going to a concert?"

Delgado felt the smile grow on her face. "Can't say that I have," she said, her tongue planted firmly in one cheek.

Richardson nodded. "That's right, that's right!"

Delgado bit her bottom lip to stop herself from laughing. "Well, I guess I could just leave the ticket here on the counter. If anything were to happen to it, I wouldn't hold anyone responsible."

The super narrowed his eyes as he processed Delgado's words, then he grinned and nodded. Delgado placed the ticket on the counter, Richardson's eyes glued to it, then shuffled through the remaining collection of notes and papers pulled from the board. Pulling out the largest sheet, the list of addresses, she turned it right way up and slid it onto the top of the pile.

"Wait, that Reid and Andrew?"

"What?"

The super reached for the list and plucked it from the pile. He straightened it out, then straightened his glasses, then stabbed a finger at the list.

"Here. Reid and Andrew Streets—65 Reid. That's, ah, Dixon's. Dixon's Boxing."

Delgado took the paper from him. "A boxing club?"

"Yeah," said Richardson. "Well, not just a boxing club. I mean, yes, it's a boxing club, but they got space there, you can hire it and such. You know, for meetings and the like. Friends of Bill W."

Delgado looked at the super, recognizing the euphemism. "The AA?"

The super held his hands up again. "Hey, not me. For my cousin. I've been taking him there, oh, six months now."

"To Dixon's?"

"Yes ma'am. It's really working for him too."

Delgado held the list out to the super again. "You recognize any of these other addresses?"

The super took the paper and held it near his nose, lifting his glasses with his other hand again and moving the note back and forth to get a better focus.

"No, none of the others." He handed the paper back. "Guess they might all be AA meetings?" He shrugged. "You don't have to keep going to the same one. Some people do because they like it, because, y'know, it's supposed to be anonymous, but it ain't really, not once you start to get to know people. Others, they like to keep to the *A* part of the AA, and move between meetings. That's fine. So long as you're going, you're going."

"How often do you go?"

"With my cousin? Weekly. Dixon's is just two subway stops. Nice and easy, and he likes going over to the big island, as he calls it. Manhattan, you know."

"You ever see Jacob Hoeler there?"

The super made a gesture like he was running his fingers through his hair, although he was really running them through nothing but thin air.

"Never. Never once. Never saw him. Never knew he was going. Hell, I hardly ever spoke to the guy as it is. Only been living here a few months, you know. But if he was going to Dixon's, I never saw him."

"Do they hold meetings there more than weekly?"

"The AA? Sure, I guess. We always go Tuesdays. I think they run one Fridays. Maybe Jacob was a Friday guy. Or maybe he was boxing."

Richardson looked at Delgado with wide eyes, like he'd just discovered a major clue. Delgado smiled at him.

"You never know," she said. "Thanks for your help. Enjoy the concert."

The super did a mock salute. "Hey, thanks, and anything to help, anything to help."

Delgado led the way out of the apartment. The uniform had not yet returned, and Delgado wondered if he would.

"I'll lock up," Richardson said, as Delgado headed down the hall. "Hey," he called over his shoulder, "any idea when this will all be cleared up? I gotta fix up the apartment and get it back out there, you know what I'm saying?"

"I'll see if I can get someone to give you a call," she said. "I'm sure it won't be long now."

"Yeah, *you're* sure!" said the super, but Delgado was already gone.

CHAPTER NINE

THE INFORMANT

JULY 6, 1977
BROOKLYN, NEW YORK

Delgado was at her desk sipping coffee when Hopper arrived at the 65th the next morning. As Hopper nodded a greeting, Delgado immediately stood and motioned for them to move into the hallway leading to the coffee room. But their plan for a clandestine exchange of information was thwarted when Captain LaVorgna called out for Hopper to join him in his office.

Hopper sighed. "Straight after," he said. Delgado nodded and returned to her desk while Hopper walked across the bull pen toward LaVorgna, who stood leaning in the doorway of his office, watching the detective approach. He gestured for Hopper to take a seat, then closed the door.

"Too damn hot again," said Hopper.

LaVorgna grunted as he moved around behind his desk. "They say it's going to hit a hundred before the end of the week."

"Any word on getting the AC fixed?"

"I've got more chance of landing one of my detectives on the moon than getting the AC fixed," said the captain, before pulling himself toward his desk so his stomach hugged it. Hopper knew what this meant: it was time to cut the chat and get down to work. "I have a new case for you."

Hopper sighed. "Even killers aren't taking a break in this heat."

LaVorgna shook his head, and stroked the underside of his mustache with an index finger as he looked at his detective. "Not a homicide. We've got a guy down in holding. Says he has information and he wants to exchange it for protection."

Hopper frowned. "Protection from what?"

"That's what I want you to find out, Detective."

Hopper shook his head. "I'm not sure, sir. I work in homicide, not vice, and—"

"I'm well aware of which department I command, Detective," said LaVorgna, raising his voice. "And if I say I'm giving you this case then I'm giving you this case, got it? You may not have noticed, but it's not just this squad whose resources are being stretched. We're short of people and money all over the precinct. So sometimes I may ask you to help out with another department, and you will thank me for the opportunity to expand your horizons."

Hopper sighed and ran a hand through his hair. Then he let his hand fall to his thigh with a slap. "Yes, sir. Sorry, sir." He rubbed his face again. "I'll see what I can shake out."

LaVorgna gave a big smile. Hopper wasn't entirely sure he liked it.

"See, that's why I like you, Hopper."

Hopper frowned again. "Sir?"

"The fact that you do what you're told and you don't give me grief."

Hopper felt the muscles at the back of his jaw tighten.

Yes, Captain, about that . . .

He raised a thumb over one shoulder. "You squared it with Delgado?"

"You let me worry about her assignment, Detective. Now I suggest you get to work. They're expecting you downstairs."

"Aye-aye, sir," said Hopper. He stood and gave a mock salute, but the captain's attention was already on the paperwork in front of him.

"What was that about?" asked Delgado, as Hopper arrived back at his desk.

"Oh, didn't you hear? Turns out I don't work for homicide anymore."

Delgado nearly choked on her coffee. "What?"

Hopper held up a hand. "Relax. It's only temporary. Looks like I'm seconded to vice. They've had someone come in, wanting protection in exchange for information, I don't know. Probably just some drugged-out lowlife."

Delgado ran her tongue between her teeth. "You think the captain is trying to keep us apart?"

Delgado had a point. "Maybe," said Hopper. He glanced toward the captain's office. "You think he knows we're still digging at the case?"

Delgado followed Hopper's gaze. "I don't see how. But listen, we need to talk."

Hopper nodded as he stood. "Yes, we do. Come on, I need a coffee before I go downstairs."

The coffee room was empty, Sergeant McGuigan leaving just as they arrived. Hopper and Delgado said good morning, then waited until the sergeant had returned to his desk, his back to the hallway. Then Hopper closed the door and moved to the coffee machine.

Delgado held out her mug as Hopper filled it from the pot. "What did you find at Dikeman Street?" she asked.

"Something interesting," he said, now filling his own mug. He took a sip, winced at the temperature and bitterness of it, then filled his partner in on his adventure of the previous night—the empty apartment, the file boxes marked government property, his failed pursuit of the intruder, and the subsequent disappearance of the files.

Delgado listened, nodding slowly as she absorbed the information, her eyes darting between Hopper and the coffee room door as she kept watch.

"I knew it. Something funky going on."

Hopper nodded and sipped his drink. "Something funky is right. Here." He reached into the breast pocket of his shirt and took out the top sheet of notepaper from the Dikeman Street apartment. "See what you can make of this while I'm downstairs."

Delgado took the sheet and slipped it down the front of her polo shirt.

"Anything from the crime scene?" asked Hopper.

Delgado nodded, and told him about the three men who had come looking for Hoeler, and described the list of addresses she'd found. Hopper frowned into his coffee as he listened.

"They were wearing army jackets?" he asked.

Delgado shrugged. "That's what the super said. I mean, you can get jackets like that from any army surplus, I'm not sure it's useful. Why?"

"I have a jacket like that," said Hopper. "I kept it from the army."

Delgado lifted an eyebrow. "You mean they could have been veterans?"

"The super said that Dixon's was used for the AA?"

"Yes."

"So maybe it was also used by others as well—like a veterans' support group."

"There's such a thing?"

Hopper nodded. "There is. A lot of people came back from Vietnam needing help, you know."

"Hey, I don't doubt it. I'll dig into Dixon's, check out the other addresses, get a list of groups together. You'd better get downstairs."

Hopper checked his watch and nodded. The coffee room door opened and Harris appeared. He stopped when he saw the two of them, and grinned.

"Oh, our two lovebirds having a secret meeting, eh?"

With a sigh, Hopper left, leaving Harris to wither under the death stare of his partner.

The man had been taken into an interview room by the time Hopper got downstairs. He walked in, nodding in acknowledgment to the uniformed officer who was standing with his arms folded in the corner of the room. The officer pushed himself away from the wall, shaking his head. "Good luck with this one," he said, tipping the brim of his cap with a finger before sauntering out of the room, thumbs hooked through his utility belt.

Hopper closed the door, the sinking feeling growing in his stomach. This was going to be a waste of time. He set his coffee and the file he'd been handed on the table and regarded the person he was supposed to talk to.

The interviewee was a young man—maybe even still a teenager, going by the look of him. He was wearing a thin leather vest over a button-up baseball shirt, the long sleeves bunched at the elbows. Seated at the table, he had crossed his arms in front of him and was resting his head in their cradle, his face turned away from the door, as though he was asleep. His hair was trimmed into a neat, round Afro.

The behavior of the informant—although Hopper was hesitant in thinking of him as such, given he had yet to provide any actual information—was nothing new, of course. People acted in all kinds of ways when they were in custody, and Hopper had seen it all. In this case, he thought the informant was probably sleeping something off, either drink or drugs. As he sat opposite, Hopper could smell something sweet wafting off the young man, and settled on the latter option.

Hopper sipped his coffee and checked his watch, then sighed and knocked on the table with his knuckles. The informant jumped in his chair, licking his lips and blinking as he looked at the detective.

"Sorry to disturb you," said Hopper, tightly. "I guess you should have asked reception for a wake-up call before you checked in."

The man continued to lick his lips, his forehead creased in confusion as he looked at Hopper.

"What?" he asked eventually.

Hopper sniffed and picked up his pen. "Never mind." He flipped open the folder and ran his pen down the partially completed form. "Okay, you are Mr. Washington Leroy."

"No, no, no," said the man, waving his hand over the form. Hopper glanced up, and the man stared intently at him. His eyes were bloodshot, but without a flashlight Hopper couldn't see the state of his pupils. He thought they were probably pretty well dilated. "Leroy Washington. *Leroy*. You got the names around backwards, my man." He whistled and slumped back in his seat. "Leroy Washington."

"My mistake," said Hopper, crossing the names out and switching them on the form. "Leroy Washington."

"Who are you, anyhow?"

Hopper didn't look up from the form. With one hand he reached into the top pocket of his shirt, pulled out a card, and handed it over. The young man took it and held it close to his face.

"Detective James Hopper . . ." Leroy looked up. "Homicide?"

Hopper ignored the question as he looked across the table. "You say you've got some information."

At this, Leroy's expression lit up. "Information, yeah! Yeah, that's right." He looked at Hopper, but his gaze was unfocused.

Hopper shrugged. "Okay, let's hear it."

Leroy nodded and licked his lips, then laid his hands out palms-down on the table. Hopper glanced at them and saw the nails were ragged and grimy. Leroy had a variety of bracelets around both wrists, a mix of what looked like twisted colored hair ties on his left, and on his right a wide leather strap with a silver buckle bigger than the one Hopper had on the belt around his middle.

"Okay, man, listen," said Leroy, tapping the table with a cracked fingernail. "There's something big coming, man, and I mean *big*." He sat back in his chair and sculpted the air in front of him with both hands. "Big, man. He's been planning it, oh, a long time now. Months, man, months. Maybe years."

Leroy shook his head, then leaned forward on the table on his elbows and, staring intently at Hopper, tapped his temple with a finger. "You don't know the Saint, man, you just don't know. Dude got it all up here. All of it."

Hopper pursed his lips as he looked at Leroy. "Okay, something big is coming?" he asked.

Leroy nodded and sat back heavily.

Hopper watched him a moment longer, then sniffed. "Look, I'm going to need something more than that," he said. "If you want protection, if you're in danger, then we need something tangible."

Leroy frowned. "Tangible?"

"Yes, tangible," said Hopper. "Names, places, dates, times. We need to know specifics. If you need protection, then we can arrange that, but you have to give us something we can act on, something that will lead directly to the prevention of a crime, or to the apprehension of a criminal. We don't just give protection to anyone who walks in off the street."

Leroy shook his head and tapped the table again.

"Yeah, but I told you, dude, I *told* you. I gave you a name—the Saint. He's got it *all* planned."

Hopper sighed. "Has *what* planned, Leroy?"

Leroy didn't seem to be listening. He had closed his eyes and tilted his head up, toward the ceiling.

The guy was off his nut on something. Hopper sighed yet again, and was about to stand, but then stopped right where he was as Leroy spoke again.

"It's coming. The darkness, the night, serpent black." Leroy didn't open his eyes, but he grimaced. "He's coming, here and now, here and now. The throne of flame is prepared and the Serpent shall take His throne and He shall rule all with His fire and His might and His cloak of shadows shall sweep over the city."

Yep. High as the proverbial. Hopper could see it, clear as day. The NYPD had enough to do without humoring drug-addled cranks who wanted to tell them the world was about to end. Hopper flipped the folder open in his hands, double-checking he'd signed the right part, and was ready to go ask a uniform to throw Leroy back out onto the street when the young man jerked suddenly on his chair. He opened his eyes, blinked, then began feeling around his pockets.

"Wait," he said. "You want something, man, I got something, I got something." He pulled an object out of the inside pocket of his leather vest.

Hopper's heart kicked up a notch. He lowered himself back into his chair, his eyes fixed on the thing that Leroy Washington placed on the table in front of him.

It was a white card, larger than a playing card. On the front there was a symbol, neatly drawn by hand in thick acrylic ink: a hollow five-pointed star. Hopper hadn't seen that particular symbol before, but the card was clearly part of a set he knew very well indeed.

He stared at the card for what felt like a thousand years.

Leroy was saying something, but Hopper couldn't hear him over the roaring in his own ears.

Then Leroy began to hyperventilate, taking in big whoops of breath, his sudden change breaking Hopper's trance.

"Where did you get that card?"

Leroy wasn't listening. His eyes were closed again and he spoke between gulps of air.

"The day of darkness shall come . . . and day will be night and the night will be serpent black and the throne will be made ready for His arrival . . . so says the Saint . . . so says the Saint."

Then Leroy regained control of his breathing and slumped back in his chair, and then he started to laugh, his chin bouncing against his chest, his eyes still closed.

"Hey," said Hopper. Leroy ignored him.

Hopper slammed his hand down on the table. *"Hey!"*

Leroy jerked back, blinking like he'd come out of a deep sleep. He looked at Hopper.

"Where did you get this card?" Hopper yelled the question, his raised voice bouncing off the walls of the small room.

Leroy didn't appear to notice the change in Hopper's mood. He just sat and smacked his lips and looked around the interview room, then back at Hopper. "You got a smoke, man? My throat is on fire, man. I need something, something." He wiped his mouth with the back of his hand.

Hopper couldn't stop himself. He reached forward, grabbing Leroy by the wrist. Leroy yelped in fright as Hopper pulled his arm forward.

"You say you have information, and I want to hear it. Is it something to do with this card? Do you know where it comes from? Do you know who made it? If you know anything about the murders, you need to tell me, and you need to tell me *right now*."

Leroy pulled back against Hopper's grip, and Hopper relented. Leroy fell back against his chair. "It's all part of the plan. That's what he said. All part of the plan."

"Who said? What plan?"

"The Saint."

"Who is the Saint? Leroy, *who is the Saint*?"

"Saint John. He's come to save us all, to set the throne in place, to make ready for His arrival."

"What? Arrival?" Hopper rubbed his face. "Whose arrival?"

"No, man, I can't say His name, I can't say His name."

Hopper was on his feet. He leaned over the table, his pulse pounding in his temples. "What are you talking about, Leroy? Whose arrival?"

Leroy looked up at him. He shook his head, and there were tears forming in his eyes. His lips moved as he tried to find the words.

"Satan, man," he said, his voice a low whisper. "Satan is coming and New York will be His throne."

CHAPTER TEN

THE CARD

JULY 6, 1977
BROOKLYN, NEW YORK

In the bathroom stall, Hopper sat with his elbows on his knees. He rubbed his face. He'd been sitting in the stall for twenty minutes. He wasn't hiding, but he wanted total privacy with his thoughts, and the old bathroom in a back corner of the precinct was the lowest-traffic area of the building he could think of.

He stared at the blank white of the stall door, the card in the breast pocket of his shirt feeling as heavy as lead.

He'd been shaken by Leroy, and for that he chastised himself. Yes, the appearance of the card was a surprise, but he was a cop, for God's sake. He'd let his temper get away from him again—it was a character flaw he was well aware of.

But the card was good news.

Because the card was a lead.

Leroy Washington knew something. Maybe he was even involved—although he probably wasn't the killer himself, the way he had come offering information in exchange for protection. In his addled state he had offered little apart from the card, but he knew something, and that knowledge had apparently put him in danger.

Perhaps put him in the crosshairs of the killer.

And that other stuff? Satan coming to New York, the city in flames and darkness? Nothing you couldn't hear about from any number of cranks on the street corners around Times Square. *The end is nigh.* Sure it is, pal, this is New York City. The world is always ending for someone.

There was a bang as the bathroom door opened. Hopper looked up, his reverie broken. Someone entered the stall next to his and slammed the door shut.

Hopper left his stall. He took a long, hard look at himself in the mirror over the sinks. He looked like crap, and he felt like crap, and that was that. Not enough sleep, too much coffee, and the fact that he was acting against his captain's orders was stressing him more than he thought it would.

Telling himself to get a goddamn grip, Hopper left the bathroom and headed back upstairs.

As Hopper walked back into the homicide bull pen, he saw Delgado standing in the doorway of one of the file rooms. At the sight of his partner, he instantly felt better, whatever cloud had settled over him lifting suddenly, completely.

Seeing Delgado was a reminder that he was not in this alone.

As he headed toward his desk, she intercepted him, leading them to the coffee room.

"You sure took your time," she said. "But listen, I got something."

The coffee room was empty. Once inside, Delgado closed the door, turned the TV up, then moved to the big table in the middle of the room. She laid out the sheet of notepaper Hopper had given her earlier.

"We can thank our late friend Jacob Hoeler for having a heavy hand," she said. She pointed to the paper, which was now covered in blocks shaded in light gray pencil. "It's pretty simple. We used to do this kind of thing at school."

The imprinted writing was now clearly visible, as well as the word *VIPERS* in large bold printing with a box drawn around it. The rest of the text was indeed a list. Hopper read it aloud.

"*Savage Slits. Killer Kings. Bronx 45s. East Village Legion. Fulton Furies. Mercy Nation.*" He looked at Delgado. "They're all gangs."

Delgado nodded. "Yes. But not just any gangs. I checked. This list covers all five boroughs. All of the gangs except the Vipers are well known to both the NYPD and the feds, and all of them have one thing in common—except the Vipers."

Hopper stroked his chin in thought. "Which is?"

Delgado tapped the paper. "They're all gone. Vanished. None of these gangs exist anymore, as far as we know. Wiped out, or disbanded, or moved out of town, who knows."

"Except the Vipers?"

"Except the Vipers," said Delgado. "We haven't heard of them before. Nobody has." She shrugged. "That's assuming they *are* a gang."

"The name fits," said Hopper. "Could be a new group. Gangs must form and disband all the time."

"But listen, Hopper, you know what this means, right?"

Hopper glanced up at his partner as she continued.

"The third of our victims, Jacob Hoeler, was a federal agent with a secret hideout. He had a list of gangs, including this new one. He gets killed in the line of duty, then Special Agent Gallup shows up on our doorstep and takes the case out of our hands. It makes perfect sense. They might not want to tell us what's going on, but it doesn't take a degree in rocket science to figure it out."

"Jacob Hoeler was part of a federal gang task force."

"Exactly. They're FBI, maybe ATF, maybe both. It explains a whole lot. Special Agent Gallup may have a stick up his ass, but he's protecting a lot more than just his job."

Hopper nodded. "If he's leading the task force, then he's got agents out there in the city, most likely embedded in these gangs, deep undercover. The task force may have been operating for months. Years, even." Hopper pointed to the paper. "Perhaps that's where those gangs went. They've been working to disband them, from the inside."

"Right," said Delgado. "Then one of their undercover plants gets himself killed, the NYPD comes in and risks screwing up their operation. So Gallup has to come in and take over. He needs to protect his agents, no matter what. So he has to take the whole thing in-house. He has no choice."

Hopper shook his head. Things were starting to come together. He pulled the symbol card from his shirt pocket and showed Delgado. His partner's eyes widened at the sight of it.

"Where the hell did that come from?"

Hopper tossed it onto the table. "The kid I was supposed to interview, the one asking for protection. He gave me a load of nonsense about the end of the world—"

"He did what now?"

Hopper shook his head. "The guy was out of his gourd on something. But he had this card, said it was proof he had information we would be interested in."

"So what was the information?"

"He didn't give it. We'll have a better shot once he sobers up, but it must be connected to the card murders." Hopper pointed to the card. "There's a *gang* connection to them. The kid—Leroy Washington—he didn't say he was in a gang, but he fit the bill well enough. He could be in with these Vipers."

Delgado rubbed her temples as she considered. "Ritual killings aren't usually gang style," she said, but Hopper shrugged.

"I agree. But there's no way this is coincidence. Jacob Hoeler is proof of that. So is Leroy Washington."

"Where is he now?"

"I had him put back into a cell. He needs to come down from wherever he is before he can give up his information." He looked at his partner. "But you know what this means, right?"

Delgado sighed. "It's over."

Hopper nodded. She was right—the case was over. They'd walked into the middle of something much, much bigger than they had anticipated, a federal operation that, if interfered with, could place the lives of who knew how many other agents in jeopardy.

"But our work isn't wasted," said Hopper. "We'll take everything to the captain, let him pass it on up the chain to Gallup and the feds. With a bit of luck, they'll overlook our involvement."

Delgado didn't say anything, but she nodded in agreement. The two detectives sat at the table. The TV's speaker warbled, the volume loud enough to rattle the cheap plastic casing of the set, as a news broadcast replayed mayoral candidate Ed Koch's latest impassioned speech about crime. Delgado frowned at her partner.

"What?" he asked.

"You look terrible."

Hopper laughed, weakly. "Tell me something I don't know."

But she shook her head. "Go home, Hop. Take an early afternoon. Spend some time with Diane. Take her to the movies or something. I'll cover with the captain and we can take all this to him tomorrow. Sounds like your informant isn't going to be in any fit state until tomorrow anyway. This can wait until then."

Hopper looked at Delgado for a long while, then finally he sighed.

"Okay. Thanks."

"Anytime, Detective, anytime."

The dusk gathered outside along with the snow as Hopper busied himself in the kitchen. He'd been talking a long time, and he and El both needed a break. She'd protested when he stopped the story, but her eyes had lit up at the mention of her favorite snack—no, favorite *food*, period.

It was time for Eggos.

"Serpent . . . black."

Hopper glanced over his shoulder. Stretching her legs, El had moved back to the den, and was now sitting cross-legged on the floor, facing him.

"What does it mean?"

Hopper gathered the prepared Eggos onto a plate and, pouring a fresh mug of coffee, headed back to the table. El stood and made her way over.

"Who's telling this story?" he asked, placing the big plate of waffles in the middle of the table before returning to the kitchen to fetch smaller plates. When he came back, El had already gotten started on her first one. He slid the small plate underneath her hands.

"Questions are good," said El, through her mouthful.

"Hey, manners, young lady." Hopper slid a hot waffle onto his own plate. "And yes, questions are good. But so is patience."

"Leroy said it." El frowned. "And Lisa."

Hopper picked up his fork, then paused as he looked across the table.

"You want to do this now?"

El looked at him, but said nothing. Instead she just narrowed her eyes a little.

Hopper put his cutlery down. "Okay, yes, they both said it. And actually, I did notice when Leroy said it in the interview, but once we figured out the thing about the task force, it didn't seem that important. I told Delgado about Lisa at the birthday party, and what Leroy had said, and she thought it might have been a lyric from a song, or something from TV. It's like sometimes when you hear a new word for what you think is the first time, and then suddenly you hear it everywhere."

El just continued to look at him, her jaw moving as she chewed her food. Hopper sighed.

Okay, bad example.

"Anyway," said Hopper, returning his attention to the hot waffle in front of him. "Yes, I did notice it, but we didn't put it all together until later."

El stopped chewing. She swallowed, then let her jaw hang open.

Hopper frowned. "What?"

"Until *later*?"

"Well . . ."

"A serpent is a snake?"

Hopper nodded.

"A viper is a snake too."

"That's right."

"Serpent . . . viper . . . snakes!" El waved her hands, her eyes wide.

Hopper only lifted an eyebrow.

El sighed again in deep frustration. "They all go together."

"Who?"

"Leroy, Lisa, Vipers . . . the third one."

"Third one? You mean Special Agent Jacob Hoeler."

El nodded eagerly.

Hopper took another quick bite and drank some coffee. He reached over and plucked a napkin from the open packet on the side of the table, and cleaned his hands.

El almost seemed excited. Was El taking the story in? Did she understand what had really happened, all those years ago? It was a difficult question and Hopper wasn't sure he had the answer. El was smart, and would certainly grow up into a capable woman. Of that, he had no doubt.

But her upbringing in the care—if you could call it that—of Dr. Brenner had introduced some . . . well, wrinkles. In some ways El was old beyond her years. In others, she was less mature than other girls her age.

Not that Hopper had much experience with that.

"Yes, Jacob Hoeler," he said again, emphasizing the name, unsure if it was important that he should. But there was a danger here of trivializing the story. This was no fantasy, no bedtime fairy tale.

It was the truth—at least as far as he knew it.

"Just be patient, and you'll find out," he said.

El frowned and narrowed her eyes, but didn't delay in getting started on Eggo number three.

The pair ate in silence for a few minutes.

"It was strange," said El.

"What was?"

"The captain knew . . ." She looked up. ". . . the card."

Hopper smiled. He gestured to El with his fork.

"That's good, kid. Good attention to detail. Yes, the captain did know about the card—Leroy had been waving it around as soon as he came into the precinct. The officer who called the captain mentioned it, so the captain picked me. He didn't tell me why, not even in private, because he knew he had to keep himself out of it. He didn't like the case being taken away from the department any more than we did, but in his position, he couldn't say anything. And remember, he didn't know anything about the task force either, not until Delgado and I had figured it out. But he filled me in later with what had happened."

El nodded, apparently satisfied, and went on eating.

Then she asked, "Is your job dangerous?"

Hopper frowned. "It can be, yes."

"You stop people . . . murders."

"Stopping people before they commit a murder is difficult. Normally the job is to find out who committed the murder after it happened." Hopper shrugged. "Not always. The card homicides were a special case—when you have what they call a serial killer, there's a chance they will keep on killing until they are stopped. So yes, in those cases you're trying to stop them from killing again. But those cases are rare. Most detectives never have a case like that."

"You look for bad people."

"Absolutely."

"Bad people hurt you." El looked at him like she was expecting more.

Hopper wasn't sure he had anything more. Her question was so simple, but the answer was . . . complicated. He sighed.

"Yes," he said, "being a cop means dealing with bad people and dangerous situations. It's part of the job, but it's not the only part. I help people too. You know that. I helped *you*."

He paused, the realization dawning that . . . Was this the first time El had really stopped to consider his life? His job?

More important: how those two things involved her. Not just in the past, dealing with the Demogorgon and the Mind Flayer. But *now*, going forward, how his job and his life would impact her in the future they would share together.

The future we will share together.

Hopper blinked a tear out of his eye as he looked at his adopted daughter, whose whole life had been, until recently, ruled by fear and pain.

El lifted the empty glass by her plate and held it out to Hopper. He smiled, took the glass without a word, and got up and went back to the kitchen. A few moments later he returned to the table with the glass full of Kool-Aid.

El took a drink, then set the glass down. "Dangerous job . . ."

Hopper lifted his eyebrows, watching as El slowly pieced together the logic of her next question. It was remarkable, to see her figure out what should have been simple concepts for a girl of her age but which she had never before had to wrap her head around. Not for the first time, Hopper silently cursed Brenner, but . . . she was getting better. Hopper could see that. And while he was doing his best to teach her, he knew her improvement would be even more profound once she was properly integrated back into the real world.

But that was something to worry about some other time. Right now, El winced, like she was in pain, as she searched for the right words.

El shook her head. "Wanted to be a cop . . ." she said, trying to come at the problem from a different angle.

Then it clicked for Hopper. It was like one of those word games, linking two different statements together to come up with a third logical conclusion. He smiled and sat back.

"So if being a cop is dangerous," he said, "and I wanted to be a cop, why would I want a job that was dangerous?"

At that, El nodded and relaxed, her confusion—her *frustration*—evaporating in an instant. She had another sip of drink, her whole demeanor calm and collected as she waited for an answer. Of course, danger wasn't something that fazed her at all—Hopper knew that, and he also knew her response to danger was partly due to her upbringing and partly because she could . . . well, protect herself.

But perhaps now, with this story, she was beginning to understand that other people sometimes had to put themselves in danger, deliberately.

She's learning, she's learning.

"Well, yeah," said Hopper, "the job can be dangerous, but I didn't choose to become a cop *because* it was dangerous. I chose to become a cop so I could help people. Protect people. Sure, there are bad people out there, but remember, there are good people too. And good people can do good things if they really want to. Even if that means getting into a little bit of danger. But that's why I knew I wanted to be a cop. Because I had the experience and the skills to handle that danger while I did as much good as I could."

El looked into his eyes as the seconds stretched on. Then she nodded and finished her drink.

"And remember," he said. "The story ends okay. I'm here, right? So I was okay. Now, are *you* okay? Do you want me to keep going?"

El smiled, and nodded, and this time, pushed her empty plate forward.

Hopper grinned.

"Coming right up."

CHAPTER ELEVEN

MR. REBEL

"I mean, come on, when that big spaceship thing came in over the top? Seriously, I swear the walls of the theater were shaking!"

Hopper lifted his hands, formed them into a wide V, and then, starting over his own head, mimed the movement of the spaceship in question as it swept in toward his wife, sitting opposite across the high diner table.

"Bmwawwwwwwwmmmmmmmmvvvvvffffff!"

Diane was laughing so hard that tears began to stream down her cheeks as her husband continued his one-man re-enactment of the movie they'd come out of not a half hour ago. He sat straight on his stool, hunched his shoulders, and cupped his hands in front of his face, using the echo to put on the most dramatic wheezing breath he could possibly muster.

"Jim!" Almost gasping for breath, Diane waved a hand at her husband and glanced around the tiny diner, but nobody was paying attention. Hopper brought his hands down and made gun shapes with his fingers.

"*Pew pew, pew pew!*"

"Sorry," said Diane, finally getting her breath back. "*How* old is my husband supposed to be? Thirty-five going on thirteen?"

Hopper dropped the act and laughed. Between them on the table was a single large egg cream in a huge, old-fashioned vessel that was more like a flower vase than a glass. As Hopper leaned in, taking the straw on his side in his mouth, Diane did the same, taking a quick draw on the chocolate concoction before letting the straw go and giving her husband a peck on his nose.

"Well, I'm glad you enjoyed it," she said, sitting back. "Hey, do you think Luke and Leia will, y'know . . ."

Hopper nearly choked on the egg cream. "Will what, exactly?"

"Y'know," said Diane, her laughter making its return. "Get it *on*."

Hopper grinned. "That's your takeaway from the greatest movie you've seen in your life, and you were calling *me* a teenage boy?"

"The greatest movie *I've* seen in my life?"

"Come on, admit it. It was pretty great, right?"

Diane wiped the dampness from her cheeks. "Okay, fine, I admit it, it was pretty great." She reached for her straw and probed the drink. "I think Sara would like it. Maybe we can bring her next time."

Hopper leaned on the table with his elbows. "You don't think she might like *Annie* a little better?"

"That new musical that's just opened at the . . . where was it?"

"The Alvin, I think. Fifty-Second Street or something."

Diane shrugged. "Maybe, but I saw the ticket prices for that in the newspaper."

Hopper winced. "That bad, huh?"

"Let's just say another night at the movies is the more fiscally responsible option."

Hopper nodded. "Hey, this is New York City, I'm all for fiscal responsibility. And now that it has the mom and dad seal of approval, sure." He sat back and smiled. "See?"

Diane shook her head. "See what?"

"You thought it was so great you want to see it again, and you're using our beloved daughter as the weakest excuse I've ever heard."

Diane gasped in mock indignation. "Objection!"

Hopper went in for more egg cream. "Maybe you hadn't noticed," he said, after a mouthful, "but I'm a cop, not a lawyer, so that trick doesn't work on me."

"Well, *Detective*, you're still pretty good at evading difficult and important questions."

Hopper used his straw to stir the drink. "What was the question?"

"Luke and Leia. Yes or no?"

"Oh. No."

"No?"

"Girls like the rebellious guy, always."

"Oh, is that a fact, Mr. Rebel?"

"Sure," said Hopper. "It'll be Han. No question."

Diane shrugged, pulling the drink away from Hopper, tilting the glass as she mixed it with her straw. After a moment of concentration, she looked up to find Hopper staring at her.

"What?" she asked.

The corner of Hopper's mouth lifted. "I love you, Diane Hopper."

Diane leaned on the table with her elbows. "And I love you, Mr. Rebel. You seem happy."

Hopper's smile froze. Diane, apparently seeing the confusion on his face, reached over and grabbed his hand.

"Hey! Relax! You seem happy. That's all. You're more relaxed now than you have been in weeks. It can't just be down to a movie and an egg cream."

Hopper considered, and actually . . . he *was* relaxed—happy, even.

She was right. (And she always was.)

Diane cocked her head. "So, what is it? Something happen at work?"

Hopper folded his arms loosely on the top of the high table. "Actually, something did happen." He lowered his voice. "You know that case, the . . . ah, multiple homicides?"

Diane leaned in. "What, did you get a breakthrough?"

"No, not at all," said Hopper. "In fact, it's not even our case now. It was taken off us."

"What? And that makes you happy?" Diane leaned back, frowning deeply.

"Oh no, don't get me wrong. That's a case we wanted to solve. But the feds have come in and taken it over. Turns out there's a gang connection, and they've been running a special task force. They need to handle that themselves, without the NYPD getting in the way, so they took it off us."

"Okay," said Diane, nodding. "How does that make you feel?"

Hopper blew out his cheeks. "Well, I mean . . . sure, we wanted to be the ones who caught him, but this is bigger than us. Bigger than me. I'm happy to leave this one to the feds. And . . ."

Hopper paused, considered.

Diane cocked her head. "And . . . ?"

"And yes, okay, I'm happier. It was a tough case. Part of me wanted to solve it—but the other part of me is glad I'm not involved anymore. Plenty more cases for Detectives Delgado and Hopper to solve."

Then he smiled.

"Now what?" asked Diane.

Hopper slipped off his stool. "*Now* what I really want are some fries. I'll be back in a minute."

Hopper went to the counter, leaving his wife to laugh into the remnants of the egg cream.

The evening was warm. Hopper held the door of the diner open for Diane, and was already regretting putting his jacket back on. As his wife zipped up her bag and waited, Hopper slipped his jacket off and slung it over one shoulder. As he did, a large card, almost glowing white under the streetlights, drifted to the sidewalk.

Diane bent down to pick it up. "What's this?"

"Oh!" said Hopper. "I'm not even supposed to have that." He held his hand out. "That needs to go back to the precinct with me, first thing."

Diane didn't hand it back immediately. As she stood, she held it in front of her.

"It's a Zener card."

Hopper blinked, his hand still outstretched.

"A what card?"

Diane handed it back to him. "A Zener card."

Hopper took the card and looked at it, turning it over in his hands like he hadn't studied the damn thing for hours already.

"You know what this is?"

Diane shrugged. "Well, not really. Only that they're used in psychic tests, or something." She pointed at the card. "There's a whole set of them."

Hopper licked his lips, then took a step closer to his wife. Diane looked up at him, concern playing over her face.

"Jim? What is it?"

"One of these has been left at all three of the ritual homicides that we were investigating, before the feds took over," he said quietly. "All handmade, each one with a different symbol drawn on it in acrylic ink. Clearly they have some meaning to the killer, but if he's trying to send a message, we sure as hell aren't getting it."

Diane worked her jaw for a moment. "You mean you don't know what the cards are?"

Hopper shook his head. "Nope. These cards have had us stumped for weeks." He paused. "How do you even know what they are?"

"You remember Lisa Sargeson, from the birthday party on Sunday?"

"The fortune-teller. How could I forget."

Diane gave a smirk. "Right, well, I think she uses them for something, as part of her act. She didn't use them on Sunday, but she gave a little talk about her work, and she had them with the rest of her stuff." She paused. "I *think* she said they were Zener cards. I might have misheard."

Hopper frowned. "What, and they're like some kind of tarot card, used for fortune-telling?"

"I don't know," said Diane, with a shrug. "Look, I really don't know much about them at all. She mentioned psychic experiments, but I thought that was just part of her spiel. You know, make out like her act was a mix of actual science and magic, rather than just stagecraft."

Hopper shook his head in disbelief.

"Jim?"

He sighed, then slid the card back into the pocket of his shirt. He took Diane by the hand, and they walked off in the direction of the subway.

"All this time we've been trying to figure those cards out, when a cuckoo magician at a kid's birthday party could have told us."

He stopped, pulling Diane to a halt. She looked at him, one eyebrow raised.

"You think you could do me a favor?" Hopper asked.

"What? Of course."

"You think Lisa could tell us more about the Zener cards? About what they mean?"

"Ah, yeah, I guess. But didn't you say you're not on the case anymore?"

Hopper nodded. "I did, but this card came from an informant who came into the precinct. Seems like he has gang affiliations, so we were going to hand him over to the federal agents tomorrow. If we can hand over a little more information at the same time, that's got to be of some help to them. Do you have her number? You said Lisa was one of the parents."

"Yeah, I do. I can call her in the morning, if you like."

Hopper winced. "Actually . . . maybe you could call her to-night?"

"It's getting pretty late, Jim."

"I wouldn't ask if it wasn't important."

Diane sighed. "Okay, sure."

The apartment was quiet when they got home—Sara was fast asleep, and Rachel, the babysitter, reported that all was well as Hopper forked some cash out of his wallet and handed it over. The teenager's eyes lit up as she checked the amount. "Thanks, Mr. Hopper!" She waved them both a good night, and as soon as she was out the door, Hopper headed for the kitchen. He stood by the telephone, waiting for his wife.

"A little patience, Detective."

He smiled. "Sorry."

Diane deposited her bag on the counter and opened it, pulling out a slim, leather-bound address book. She leafed through the pages, then went to the phone on the wall by the fridge. Balancing the receiver in the crook of her neck, she read the number in the book and dialed it. Then she turned to Hopper. They both stood in silence, waiting.

After what felt like an eternity, Diane shook her head and turned to hang the phone up when Hopper heard the click, and the faint muffled sound of someone picking up.

Diane ducked her head down.

"Hi, Lisa? Hi, it's Diane . . . Oh yes, no, nothing's wrong. Sorry to call so late . . . Okay." She laughed, and Hopper relaxed. He leaned back against the kitchen counter, his arms folded, and waited.

Diane explained that her husband wanted to ask something, and—after reassuring Lisa it had nothing to do with the birthday party—she handed the phone over to Hopper.

"All yours, chief," she said, before disappearing into the other room, giving him a kiss on the cheek as she left.

Hopper moved over to the counter, unwinding the tangled cord of the telephone receiver as he leaned on his elbows.

"Miss Sargeson? Hi, James. Listen, ah, thanks for agreeing to talk." He rubbed his forehead. "And, ah, listen, about Sunday, I really need to apologize.

"But I wonder if I could ask you a few questions."

HOPPER'S CABIN
HAWKINS, INDIANA

"Well? Are you going to try it or not?"

"Where is the egg?"

Hopper shook his head.

"Nope. No egg."

"No cream?"

"Correct."

El's gaze fell back to the tall glass that stood on the kitchen counter between her and Hopper. Hopper hadn't been able to find the right kind of vessel, but the egg cream he'd just made didn't look too bad. It was a nice light brown, and he'd even managed to get something of a head of foam on it.

El closed one eye, peering at the glass with the other, clearly not trusting Hopper and his weird, old-fashioned concoction.

"Milk, chocolate syrup . . ."

"Lots of chocolate syrup," said Hopper.

"And seltzer?" El wrinkled her nose as she slowly pronounced the unfamiliar word.

Hopper nodded. "Yes, water with lots of bubbles." He leaned down on the counter, folding his arms and resting his chin on them so he was at more or less the same level as El. "So are you going to try it? You wanted me to make it."

El opened her closed eye, and tilted her head this way and that.

"Why 'egg cream'?"

"Ah, well, that's a long story—"

"Sounds gross."

Hopper stood tall. "Are you kidding me? It's delicious. Look." He picked up the glass and one of the two straws lying on the counter next to it. He plunged the straw through the drink's creamy head, and took a deep draw.

"*Mmmmmm!*" He held the glass out at arm's length, and looked at it like he was considering the properties of a fine vintage wine. "Let me tell you something, kid. This is good. It's a Brooklyn classic, you'll love it." He placed the glass back on the counter. El leaned in, looking down into the frothy drink.

"Go on," said Hopper, "try it."

El didn't say anything. Hopper picked up the other straw and offered it to her.

Then she hopped off the stool. "No," she said, and walked back to the table.

"Well, fine then," Hopper replied as he lifted the glass and followed her.

"More for me."

CHAPTER TWELVE

BIRDS AND CAGES,
CATS AND BAGS

JULY 7, 1977
BROOKLYN, NEW YORK

Hopper slunk across the precinct bull pen with just one
thought on his mind.

Coffee.

It had been a late night. He hadn't kept Lisa Sargeson on
the telephone for long; in fact, their conversation had been
very brief indeed—Lisa had herself only just gotten back
home and had an early start in the morning, so Hopper's request to ask a few questions had ended with an arrangement
for him to go over and see her later the next day. But he had
spent the next few hours lying awake in bed while Diane slept
beside him, blissfully unaware of her husband's insomnia as
he rolled recent events around in his mind, over and over and
over.

But he'd come up with a course of action, one he was happy

with and which was simple and free of complication. He would talk to Leroy Washington again—Hopper was hopeful he would be a little more coherent, now that he'd had a chance to sleep off whatever it was he was on the previous day—get whatever information Lisa could offer about the nature of the Zener cards, and present everything to Captain LaVorgna. The captain would probably make a show of being angry, just to add a little good old-fashioned plausible deniability, but Hopper already suspected that his superior had known Leroy was in possession of a card. There was no way his assignment to talk to Leroy had been a coincidence.

Hopper slipped his jacket onto the back of his chair and unbuttoned his shirt cuffs, rolling up his sleeves as he headed toward the coffee room. For once, it wasn't quite so hot in the office this early, and for that he was grateful, as he was for the full pot of coffee left waiting for him by some kindly soul. Alongside the pot was a box of donuts, and there were even a couple left inside.

God bless the night shift and all who sail in her.

Hopper poured himself a mug. The coffee was burnt and oily, but he knew he needed the caffeine. He picked up a donut and took a bite, if just to get the taste of the coffee out of his mouth. Walking back to his desk, he gave the customary morning nod of greeting to Detective Harris and Sergeant McGuigan, the eyes of both lighting up as they saw what he was eating.

Hopper sat at his desk, happy to have arrived a fraction earlier than his colleagues, happy also to avoid the battle royale that was about to take place between Harris and McGuigan.

Checking the time, he finished his donut and brushed sugar off his hands and onto his pants, then picked up the telephone. The desk sergeant downstairs picked up immediately, making Hopper almost choke on a sip of coffee before answering himself.

"Ah, sorry! Good morning, Sergeant. It's Detective Jim Hopper from the sixth floor. Yeah, hi. Listen, that subject I was questioning yesterday, Leroy Washington, can you have him brought up to an interview room for me?"

What the desk sergeant said next woke Hopper up more than the coffee in his system. Unable to stop himself, he stood up, gripping the mouthpiece of the telephone like a vise.

"What do you mean, he's been released?"

Hopper listened, then screwed his eyes closed, his free hand massaging his forehead. When the sergeant was finished, Hopper shook his head, his eyes still closed.

"Yeah, well, thanks, that's a great help."

He slammed the telephone into the cradle. Detective Harris emerged from the hallway leading to the coffee room, donut and coffee in hand, a sullen-looking Sergeant McGuigan behind him with only one of those items in his.

Harris used the donut to point at Hopper. "Hey, you start slamming phones down before eight in the morning, you're in for a rough day. That's how it works."

Hopper almost fell back into his chair. "Yeah, well, tell me about it."

Harris took a bite of donut and sip of coffee at the same time. When he spoke it was with a full mouth that made Hopper grimace. "So what's up?"

"That kid who came in yesterday? The teenage gangster offering information?"

"Yeah," said Harris. "He wanted protection or something. Did he come through with the goods?"

Hopper shook his head in frustration. "That was what I was hoping to find out today," he said. "But some jackass released him this morning."

Harris swore. "Say what?"

Hopper gestured to his desk, like the answer lay upon it. "Yesterday I told them to keep him in holding, but some uniform saw the state he was in and threw him in the drunk tank with all the other bums instead. Then, five a.m., the tank is cleared out."

"Huh. That's some weird way of offering a kid protection."

"You're telling me."

"You want me to go down there and bust some balls? I know the desk sergeant. He owes me a favor or two."

Hopper shook his head. "No, but thanks," he said, pushing himself up off his chair. "I'll need to talk to the captain about this."

LaVorgna had been no help, but took Hopper angrily storming into his office unannounced rather well, considering he had only just arrived at work himself. Leroy Washington's release was as much a surprise and disappointment to him as it was to Hopper, and before Hopper had even left the office, the captain was already shouting into the phone at someone downstairs.

As Hopper headed back to his desk, his own telephone started to ring. With no sign yet of Delgado, he hurried over and picked it up, expecting it to be his partner.

"Hopper, homicide."

The telephone roared in his ear like a distant ocean, and then the noise quieted down, replaced by quick, shallow breathing. Then the roar came again, and went, and Hopper realized whoever was on the line was moving a cheek of stubble against the mouthpiece.

Hopper sat down. He listened to the breathing for a moment longer and was about to put the phone down—crank calls to the cops were an occupational hazard—when the caller finally spoke.

"Detective Hopper? It's me, man, it's me," said the voice, barely a whisper.

Hopper blinked. He looked around the bull pen, but nobody was watching. Hopper turned around in his chair anyway, so he was facing the wall.

"*Leroy?*"

The caller exhaled loudly, and the relief in his voice was evident when he next spoke.

"Oh man, Detective! Thank shit you picked up, man."

Hopper closed his eyes. "Where the hell are you? The desk sergeant said they let you go last night."

"Let me go? Man, they grabbed me by the ass and damn well *threw* me out into the street!"

Hopper sighed and rubbed his forehead. "Okay, fine, but listen—"

"Detective, you've got to help me, man. Please. I'm asking for help here. For real."

The rustling sound came again. Hopper could imagine Leroy huddled in a telephone booth, the phone pressed tight against his mouth as he spoke, then him turning his head, left and right, left and right, keeping watch, waiting for his number to be up. At least he sounded better—far more lucid, more in command of his faculties, his voice quiet but clear.

"Where are you?" asked Hopper.

"Please, man, please!" repeated Leroy, apparently not listening. Then Hopper heard something else in his voice.

Fear.

"Listen," said Leroy, "Saint John is planning something, man, something very big, something that's gonna hit this city like a tidal wave. I'm serious here. Saint John is the real deal, okay? He's dangerous, he's got all these ideas about the devil and the end of the world, man. Maybe you don't believe all that, and maybe I don't either, but *he* does, man, he really does. So, look, I gotta get away, and I really need your help on that. I can't do it on my own. It's like . . . it's like you can't even get *near* him or he takes hold, like . . . like . . ."

Hopper narrowed his eyes as he focused on Leroy's voice.

"Like what? Leroy?"

Leroy sighed over the phone. "Like, I don't know—it's weird, it's like he's got some kind of power. I mean, *real* power. Like he can read your goddamn mind, like he can know what you're going to do before you even know yourself. I said he was dangerous. You have to believe me. And you have to help me, man. I need a way out, and fast, man."

"Yes, okay, I can help you," said Hopper. "Tell me where you are and I'll come and get you."

"And my sister, too."

"Your sister?"

"Yes, my sister. She's in it too—Saint John, he's got his claws into her deep, man. You have to help me get her out too. Before the shit comes down on us all, man, on the whole city."

"Okay, listen, Leroy—"

"Did you hear what I said, Detective? Are you listening to me? This is bad, man, very bad."

"LEROY!"

Hopper glanced up. McGuigan and Marnie, standing nearby, having a conference, glanced over at him, but he ignored them. He pulled the mouthpiece close to his mouth. Over the phone, he heard the ragged breathing of a man terrified.

"Tell me where you are, and I'll come and get you, right now. We can talk and you can tell me about Saint John and your sister. Okay? You can tell me all about it and we can make a plan, okay?"

The only sound Hopper could hear over the phone was a shivering, fearful breath, the rubbing of Leroy's unshaven chin against the telephone mouthpiece as he checked to see if the coast was clear again.

"Leroy, are you listening to me?"

"Yes, I hear you. Come get me, please. Soon as you can, man, soon as you can."

Leroy finally gave an address, then the phone quickly went dead. Hopper spun on his chair, replacing the telephone and jotting the rendezvous location on the notepad. He tore the paper off, then wrote another note, this one for Delgado. He stood, reached over and placed the note under her coffee mug, then yanked his jacket off his chair and ran for the door.

CHAPTER THIRTEEN

THE DROP

JULY 7, 1977
BROOKLYN, NEW YORK

The location Leroy had given for the pickup was down in Sunset Park, a neighborhood of shipping yards and warehouses with a crime rate that Hopper didn't really want to think about. When he left the precinct, he made sure to take his gun, checking the shoulder holster four or five times as he made his way into the precinct parking garage and collected a Catalina that didn't look anywhere near as inconspicuous as he would have liked for a place like the one he was going to. As he got near the rendezvous, he parked near a packing warehouse, the place busy with workers who, he hoped, might even do something if they saw someone trying to jack his vehicle. Hopper continued the rest of the way on foot, sticking to the main arteries.

The address Leroy had given was actually just an intersection. As Hopper approached, he saw the whole block was defined by a huge rail yard, sunken below street level like some vast archaeological dig. The vast openness of the space was surprising but not unwelcome. If trouble was on the way, he'd at least be able to see it coming.

The rail yard was bustling with activity. Boxcars, freight cars, and engines were all in motion, most of it slow as they clanked and thudded over rail junctions, while workers in dirty, grease-covered blue and brown jackets and overalls and hard hats worked around and between them. As Hopper surveyed the area from street level, he saw every available surface was covered with graffiti—and that included the sides and roofs of every single piece of train, carriage, container, and car that was either moving or stationary down in the yard. To his right and left, the multitude of tracks vanished on both sides into tunnels lit only vaguely by the yellowish glow of service lights.

The rail yard was, Hopper thought, the perfect place to hide, because despite the workers there was a lot of machinery and equipment that was both enormous and quite still, plenty to provide cover. And as he watched, Hopper saw movement from the tunnel entrance on his left; as an engine lumbered into the open, a group of three people, as dirt-caked as the workers, darted back into the tunnel, two of them dragging a sack of something behind them. Homeless people, most likely—it was a dangerous place to live, but Hopper had no doubt there would be more people hiding in the dark of the tunnels.

Of Leroy Washington, there was so far no sign.

Hopper looked up the street. On the next corner was a store selling cigarettes and adult magazines, and next to it a lunch stand that most likely existed only to serve the rail yard workers. Both establishments were little more than booths, with no actual way inside for customers—just a counter behind which stood the proprietors with, most likely, a weapon or two within easy reach. Outside the corner store was the shell of a tele-phone booth. The rest of the surrounding block looked indus-trial, just flat, tall buildings, featureless in themselves, covered completely with graffiti that would have been a multicolored riot when fresh but was now a sea of dull, faded grays and browns.

Hopper waited some more. No Leroy. Glancing around to get his bearings, Hopper decided to make a circuit of the rail yard.

Hopper's orbit took a full fifteen minutes—he kept it slow, kept his eyes open, and stopped at intervals, looking down into the rail yard from different angles, trying to see if Leroy was indeed hiding down there. The concrete around Hopper was already being baked by the morning sun and it wasn't even noon. As he came back around to his starting point, Hopper glanced at the store and the lunch bar. There were people at both now, but none of them were Leroy, who was, by now, a complete no-show.

Reaching into his pocket, Hopper found he was down to his last cigarette. With a sigh, he took one more look around, then turned and headed across the street to the store. Hopper bought a new pack from the man at the counter, and while he waited for his change, he glanced down at the magazine racks. Next to an image of a bikini-clad model hugging a giant bal-loon shaped like a bunny's head, Hopper was surprised to see a copy of *Time* magazine, the cover proudly announcing HERE COMES SUMMER in huge block letters.

"Someone needs to send them the message, right?" said Hopper, gesturing at the magazine as the proprietor handed some greasy dollar bills back. But the man was apparently in no mood to talk, finishing the transaction with just a frown.

Hopper said thanks anyway, and back at the curb, pocketed the new pack and slid the last cigarette out from the old one. He walked over to the telephone booth, Zippo at the ready. A stiff breeze had picked up, bringing with it just more of the summer heat, and he slipped behind the booth for shelter, cradling the cigarette in his hand as he lit it. Then he stood tall and drew in a deep lungful of smoke.

He'd waited long enough. He was at the right place. Leroy wasn't. Perhaps he'd gotten spooked, pulled out. Perhaps he'd gotten caught by the Vipers, the very gang he was trying to escape from?

Or perhaps it had all been some kind of, what, gag? A street gang of devil worshippers? A man called Saint John trying to summon Satan Himself to the city? Zener card aside, Leroy's entire story was ridiculous, wasn't it?

Hopper enjoyed his cigarette and contemplated his next move. Even without Leroy's information, they had enough to hand over to the captain, especially—assuming she read his note—once Delgado had gotten back from seeing Lisa Sargeson about the Zener cards.

It was a long way back to the precinct, so Hopper decided to call in to the office, see if Delgado was back yet and had anything to report. It also occurred to him that Leroy might have called again, perhaps with a new place and time for a pickup. A man on the run, that was entirely within the bounds of possibility.

There came the roar of an engine from down the street. Hopper glanced up and saw the sun glinting off the silvered sides of a boxy delivery truck as it powered through the intersection ahead. It was the United States Postal Service, and Hopper didn't blame them for making their rounds in a hurry in this neighborhood.

Hopper went around to the other side of the telephone booth, ready to make his call, only to discover some punks had ripped out the phone itself, leaving nothing but a graffiti-painted shell littered with cigarette butts and old newspaper. Hopper dragged on his own cigarette; behind him, the sound of the truck got louder; the vehicle ground gears, then there was the sound of screeching tires and the smell of hot diesel exhaust and smoking rubber that Hopper noticed even over his cigarette.

He turned just in time to see the van mount the curb at an angle, right outside the store. The vehicle was big, all square angles and silver, with the familiar blue eagle and red bars of the USPS logo emblazoned on the side. Engine still running, five figures leaped from the truck. Hopper took all this in, and then the cigarette dropped from his lips and the empty pack dropped from his hand as he backed away, stumbling over his own feet.

Hopper was not a small man but each of the five approaching him were built like football players. They wore an odd collection of sportswear—gray jogging pants, a blue tracksuit jacket, a red tracksuit jacket, a yellow T-shirt pulled tight over well-developed muscles. But it was the ski masks that drove a dagger of fear into Hopper's heart. Black, smooth, featureless, no holes for nose or mouth, just five pairs of eyes beading out at him through circular portholes.

Hopper turned on his heel, the air suddenly too thick, the sidewalk suddenly too slippery. He felt hands on his shoulders; this was fine, as with a slight duck and a twist of his arms he let the first assailant pull his jacket clean off, aiding his flight. But the angle of his escape was wrong, and Hopper tipped forward. He braced his fingers against the sidewalk, and used his overbalanced forward motion to propel himself like a sprinter from a start gate.

But he'd lost too much time already. He flailed his left arm behind him to get balance, but he was grabbed below the elbow and yanked backward, the sudden change in direction almost dislocating his shoulder. Hopper gritted his teeth and swung around, using the grip on his arm as an anchor as he balled his other fist and sent it flying toward his assailant. He caught the man on the right side of his chest, but it was like punching a tree. Hopper felt his knuckles slide, pain shooting up his wrist as it bent too far in the wrong direction. He tried to pull himself fully upright, but this merely exposed his stomach to a hammer blow from one of the others, a fist seemingly the size of a Christmas ham exploding the air from Hopper's lungs. He felt his throat fill with bile and he spat, hot and acidic, the pain now blooming in his abdomen, radiating out like he'd been touched with a live electric cable from down in the rail yard.

Hopper slumped forward, his strength gone. He kicked once, twice, three times, but all that did was raise his legs up high enough for them to be grabbed by his assailants. Another blow, this time to the back of his neck, sent black stars swimming into his vision, and the last thing he saw as the men dragged him into the back of the silver truck was the guy standing behind the counter of the corner store, a frown on his face, his arms folded, happy to watch, unprepared to do a single thing about it.

CHAPTER FOURTEEN

THE SECRET HISTORY OF
LISA SARGESON

JULY 7, 1977
BROOKLYN, NEW YORK

Delgado stood in the middle of the living room, casting her eye around the décor as Lisa Sargeson told her to make herself at home.

"Thanks," said Delgado, moving over to one of the book-cases that lined almost every available piece of wall the small apartment had to offer. "I'm sorry to bother you, but I hope this won't take too long." She turned her head sideways to read the spines of the nearly identical leather-bound tomes that occupied most of this particular shelf. *The Journal of the American Academy of Psychiatry and the Law,* volumes one through four, 1973 to 1976, took up a full yard of shelf.

Talk about light bedtime reading.

The sound of laughter echoed from elsewhere in the apartment.

"No, please, I'm the one who has to apologize!" Lisa called out. "I've just got in myself—my last job ran over and I need to make sure I'm on time for my next appointment."

Delgado stood tall and looked at the next shelf up. There, instead of a row of uniform spines, the books were a tightly packed collection of what looked like textbooks—*Modern Psychiatry: Fifth Edition; Principles of Clinical Psychology; Practical Assessments for Case Analyses: Part II; Inside the Human Mind*. Delgado ran a finger along the shelf, counting another dozen or so volumes. Looking around the apartment, the rest of the shelves had more of the same—more bound journal collections, more academic texts. With such a heavy, serious collection on display, it was almost a relief to Delgado to see a shelf of novels by Arthur C. Clarke and Ursula K. Le Guin tucked away closer to the sofa that occupied the large bay window at the other end of the room. Also on the shelf, in front of the books, was a set of handcuffs and a multicolored feather boa, rolled into a ball. Two more of Lisa's magic props, Delgado thought.

The detective walked over to the window, enjoying the sun that was streaming in. "Well, like I said, I hope this won't take too long—"

"I'm happy to help!" Lisa reappeared through the door, having changed from the magician's top hat and tights she had greeted Delgado in to a yellow and red floral dress and knee-high brown leather boots. As she squeezed what looked like a large gold mood ring onto one finger, she saw Delgado look her up and down, and laughed again.

"Quite the transformation, I know," she said. "But it would be weird to show up in fishnets." She moved around the apartment, sweeping her dress under her legs as she sat down in the armchair to the left of the bay window. "Please, take a seat."

Delgado smiled and followed the invitation. As she did, she looked again at the bookshelves.

"I gotta say, this wasn't what I expected," she said.

Lisa laughed. "I'm not sure what your partner told you, but telling fortunes and doing illusions isn't really much of a career these days."

Delgado cocked her head. "So, what exactly *do* you do? When you're not pulling rabbits out of hats." She pointed at the shelves. "You've got more books in here than my local branch of the New York Public Library."

"Well, believe it or not, Detective, I am actually a fully qualified and legally registered clinical psychologist."

At that, she twisted in her chair, arching her back so she could reach the shelf behind her. From it she pulled another leather-bound volume, then offered it to the detective.

Delgado took it, unsure quite what she was looking at. The leather was black and hard, and the writing on the spine and front cover embossed in silver.

"Sociological challenges to readjustment psychology: Patterns of societal reintegration—an historical meta-analysis and practical methodology," Delgado read from the cover. *"Doctoral thesis, Lisa Sargeson, Department of Psychology, Miskatonic University, Massachusetts."* She looked up at Lisa. "You're a doctor of psychology?"

"Doctor of *philosophy*, clinical and criminal psychology. MU, 1974."

Delgado nodded and flipped through the book. Despite the double-spacing, the text looked dense, and there were pages of charts and graphs. "You know, I got a gold swimming certificate when I was in ninth grade," said Delgado, closing the thesis and handing it back to Lisa. "Seems a long way from criminal psychology to street magic," she said, gesturing at the top hat, which stood on the coffee table where Lisa had left it.

Lisa shrugged. "I guess it's one of those things," she said. "You think you know what you want to do, and you spend a lot of time working toward it, only . . ."

Delgado raised an eyebrow. "Only?"

Lisa smiled. "Only once you get there, it's not quite what you expected."

"You didn't enjoy the academic life?"

"Not for me, I'm afraid. I'd spent so long there already, by the time I was done writing this thing"—she hefted the thesis—"I couldn't wait to get out."

"What brought you to New York?"

"A job," said Lisa. "There was a place called the Rookwood Institute. It was a rehabilitation center for federal prisoners who were due for imminent release. I mean, we're not talking felons from supermax here, but those who had done their time and were being released soon. I mean, can you believe it? Someone in the Federal Bureau of Prisons actually realized that maybe these people shouldn't just be thrown out onto the streets, maybe they need to actually be rehabilitated—you know, given assistance to get them reintegrated into society. Because if you just let these people out, without giving them any kind of help? What are they going to do? They're going to just go back to what got them into prison in the first place. So you give them help, you teach them how to live normal lives, to live with other people, then that recidivism rate drops like *that*." Lisa clicked her fingers.

Delgado nodded. "That makes perfect sense."

"Right? And it was a good fit for me—I mean, I only did my doctorate on that same subject! The bureau did their homework when setting the institute up, too—my thesis was used as part of their own research, and they offered me a job."

"Wow," said Delgado. Then she paused, and frowned. "But that's not where you work now, is it?"

Lisa shook her head. "Nope. The Rookwood has been closed a year now. And . . . maybe that was my fault, although I think the end was in sight."

"What happened? Why did they close it?"

Lisa laughed. "This is New York City, why do you think?

Money! But, you know, things weren't going well anyway. When they hired me, they said I was joining an ongoing program. But when I showed up, there was nothing. Seriously, not a thing. I was expected to set the whole thing up and get it running."

"You're kidding!"

Lisa shook her head. "I mean, don't get me wrong, I was more than up to the job, and there was a good team at the institute, but it soon became clear that the one thing I needed the most was the one thing I didn't have—finances. Setting something up like the Rookwood, getting it to actually *work*, takes time and it takes money." Lisa shrugged. "I don't know what they really expected. I managed to get a pilot program up and running, but it soon became clear that I couldn't deliver what they'd hired me to. So I quit."

"You . . . quit?"

Lisa waved her hand. "Walked right out the door. I mean, by then I'd at least gotten an understanding of what was happening—what *is* happening—in this city. The Rookwood was a great idea but there was no way it could do what it was supposed to do. I was wasting my time—time I could better spend out *there*, doing something real to help people in the city."

Delgado allowed herself a small smile. "By becoming a magician?"

Lisa laughed. "Street magician and rehabilitation counselor, please!" She reached forward and picked up the top hat, bouncing it from hand to elbow with theatrical aplomb before setting it back down on its crown. "*This* is the sideline. Back when I was at university I landed myself a part-time job as a magician's apprentice—no, really, it was great. It paid the bills and was a lot more fun than flipping burgers. Turns out people really like a good magic trick. Here."

Lisa reached down to the floor beside the sofa and lifted a magazine, folded back to an interior page, that had been sitting out of Delgado's sight. She turned it over in her hands before passing it to the detective.

"Middle column, halfway down."

Delgado took the magazine and peered at the dense type of the classified ads.

"Magic," she read aloud. "Magician . . . all occasions . . . reasonable rates. Lisa." There followed a telephone number. Delgado flipped the pages over to the front and found she was holding a copy of *New York* magazine, the cover showing a photograph of a middle-aged man in a suit pouring champagne over the heads of three other middle-aged men in suits, the quartet apparently delighted by the situation as two of the men pumped their fists and the one in the middle clutched a large wooden trophy with a gold model of a car on the top.

Delgado just shook her head as she handed the magazine back.

"Anyway," Lisa continued, "when the Rookwood went south, I set myself up again so I could keep doing the real work."

"Which is?"

Lisa rolled the magazine and put it into the upturned top hat. "Like I said, rehabilitation counseling—actually more or less what I wanted to do at the Rookwood. When I left, I was going to set something up by myself, but then I found a charity organization with much the same aims, so I offered my services. Their setup is perfect for me, but the catch is they only pay a basic stipend. So I still get to wear a top hat or wave my hand over a crystal ball, depending on who hires me!"

"But wasn't the problem with the Rookwood a lack of money?"

"Yes it was," said Lisa, "but the Rookwood was different— it's one cog in a giant federal machine. Sure, it had potential, but even to get the smallest result it needed a disproportionate amount of funding. That just seems to be the way central government works. The charity is different—fewer people, fewer resources, but it can reach out across the whole city. Sure, the scope is smaller—as are the aims—but, I don't know, it feels like we can actually do something . . . get something done for these people." She sat back in her chair. "And hey, so far, so good. We've had good results, and it really feels like we're making a difference. It may be smaller, but it's more effective. More targeted, if that makes sense."

Delgado found herself nodding in agreement.

Lisa leaned back to check the clock on the wall. "Okay, sorry, I really am starting to push it now."

Delgado nodded and opened her bag, pulling out a fat manila folder from within. Setting it on her lap, she opened it and took out a series of large photographs. They were black-and-white, glossy, each showing one of the strange cards found at the three murder scenes she and her partner had, until just recently, been investigating. Each image also featured a ruler along one edge, showing the scale of the cards.

"We were hoping you might tell use more about these? I believe they're called Zener cards?"

Delgado laid the photographs out on the table—the hollow circle, the cross, the three wavy lines.

Lisa nodded and picked up the photo of the circle card.

"That's right." She looked at the other two images over the top of the photo she was holding. "Well, you have three of them. It's a set of five in total."

Delgado nodded and took out her notebook. "We have another—a five-pointed star."

Lisa looked closer at the photograph in her hand. "Are these handmade?"

"We believe so," said Delgado. "All handmade; all made, apparently, by the same person, who didn't leave any fingerprints. We're assuming they were left for a specific reason, but we'd like to know more about them. That's where we hoped you would come in."

Lisa raised an eyebrow. "Are you saying these cards were left at crime scenes? What kind of crime scenes?"

"That I'm afraid I can't tell you." Delgado pointed at the photographs before taking her notebook out of her bag. "But if you can help us with the cards, that would be a big help."

Lisa sat back. "Well, sure. Zener cards are used—or were used, anyway—for experiments in clairvoyance."

Delgado's pen stopped on the page.

"Clairvoyance?"

Lisa nodded.

"Like, what . . . telepathy? Mind reading?"

"Well, it's usually called 'extrasensory perception' in scientific circles."

Delgado put her pen down. "*Scientific* circles? Are you serious?"

"Absolutely," said Lisa. "I mean, we're talking a long time ago now—at least forty years. They were created by a psychologist, Karl Zener, back in the 1930s. The idea was that you took a deck of twenty-five cards—five of each symbol—shuffled them, then showed the back of each one to a subject, who had to say which symbol is on the card."

Delgado resumed taking notes. "And that's it?"

Lisa shrugged. "It was supposed to be simple. Problem is, it's too simple. Zener published some work which claimed to show there was an extrasensory effect, but nobody was ever able to replicate the experiments. And there's lots of confounding factors—like, bad shuffling made the cards easy to guess, or the subject could even see the reflection of the card in the eyes of the tester. Once things like that were accounted for, the effect disappeared."

Delgado glanced at the cards. "But the cards still exist? I mean, people still use them?"

"Oh yes," said Lisa. "In parapsychology—"

"*Para* . . . psychology?" Delgado looked up from her notes.

Lisa nodded. "Parapsychology. Psychology beyond the normal scope of the science."

"Like telepathy?"

"Like telepathy. But, point is, whether or not any of that really exists, some psychologists think that how people behave and react in relation to things like that is just as important to study as the phenomenon itself." Lisa turned her photograph around so Delgado could see the image. "Hence, the Zener cards. Some people still use them."

"Did you ever use them? At university?"

Lisa shook her head. "No—criminal psychology is the study of the *ab*normal, not the paranormal. But there were some in the department who ran a little parapsychology club with a few grad students, just for fun—I mean, the equipment was all there. I did help them out, sometimes. We ran some Zener card experiments sometimes, but never very seriously."

"Okay," said Delgado, finishing off her notes. She pointed again at the photographs with the end of her pen. "So these don't have any other meaning outside of the Zener experiment? The symbols don't indicate anything in particular?"

"Nope, that's all they're for. The symbols were designed to be simple enough but distinct enough for them to be easily recognized. Probably a key consideration when you're trying to read somebody's mind."

Delgado nodded. "And you said there were five symbols?"

"Right. These three, the star you mentioned, and the fifth will be a square. Hang on a minute."

Lisa uncurled herself from the armchair and went over to the bookcase opposite Delgado. From the bottom shelf she pulled out a file box labeled with the crest of Miskatonic University and put it on the coffee table. Flipping it open, she shuffled through the stack of papers within until she uncovered a stack of small cards, held together by two rubber bands.

Lisa slid the bands off and shuffled the cards. "I knew I'd kept this. Circle, star, cross, lines, and . . . here we go." She picked one out and offered it to Delgado. "Square."

Delgado took the card. It was larger than a playing card, and made of stiff glossy paper with rounded edges. On the front was a black outline of a square. Turning it over, she saw the name of the manufacturer and their location—*Cincinnati, Ohio*—printed in tiny letters along the bottom.

Delgado held the card up. "They're manufactured commercially?"

Lisa stood, closing the file box and returning it to the bookcase. "Oh, sure. Like I said, the Zener cards are still used. There are a few stores in New York that would sell you a pack like that. Although the ones you have were homemade."

"Yes. And the number of stores in New York that sell the same kind of card and the same kind of acrylic ink is a little more than a couple."

Lisa checked her watch.

"Okay, I'm sorry, but . . ."

Delgado nodded, and packed her notebook and pen in her bag. She held Lisa's card up. "Can I keep this?"

"Please! It's been in that box for three years. I'm not likely to start running my own Zener experiments now."

"Thanks," said Delgado, standing. "And thanks for the information."

"You think it will do any good?"

Delgado frowned. "That I don't know. But hey, I know more now than I did when I came in, so I call that a win." She paused. "Where do you need to be? I could give you a lift. I've kept you long enough as it is."

"Hey, I won't say no to that!" Lisa led the way to the door. As she locked the apartment after Delgado, she gave her the address, then started off down the hallway.

Delgado didn't move from the door. She was too busy processing the address that Lisa had just given her.

Down the hall, Lisa stopped and turned.

"Is that okay?"

"Ah, yeah, of course," said Delgado. "No problem."

Lisa smiled and turned back around. Delgado followed, her mind racing as she ran the address over and over and over again.

18 Dupuis Street. An old Methodist church hall. Used for all kinds of community groups and small events—including, it seemed, the counseling sessions run by Lisa.

And second on the list of addresses written by the late Special Agent Jacob Hoeler.

DECEMBER 26, 1984

"Delgado got a card?"

Hopper stopped, midflow.

"Ah, well, not one of *the* cards, but Lisa gave her the Zener card with the symbol we were missing, yes."

El clutched her curly hair with both hands.

"She's next."

"Whoa there, no!" Hopper held his hands out to El, willing her to calm down. "She didn't get the same kind of card. Don't go jumping to those kind of conclusions. I haven't finished the story yet."

El's breathing slowed, and she let go of her hair, letting her arms fall to the table.

"Delgado's okay?"

Hopper laughed. "What, suddenly you're worried about Delgado getting a card but not about me getting kidnapped in broad daylight?"

"You're here," said El. "You're okay. Is Delgado okay?"

"She was just fine. Trust me."

"Is she okay *now*?"

"She sure is," said Hopper, rubbing his chin, a smile playing over his face. "Actually, she's alive and well and living in Washington, D.C."

"Washington?"

"Yeah. She was a great cop, but an even better agent. About a year after this all went down, Gallup tapped her for a job at his agency. Believe me, she couldn't get out of the precinct fast enough. She's still there, too. They both are, I think. I haven't heard from her in a while, but I used to get Christmas cards."

El shook her head, her eyes narrowing at Hopper. Her lips formed the start of a question, but she didn't speak, as if she couldn't figure out what to ask first.

Hopper laughed. "You know, you remind me of her, in a weird kind of way."

El let out a breath . . . and then she smiled, just a little.

"Anyway, speaking of Special Agent Gallup," said Hopper, "I'd better tell you what happened next."

CHAPTER FIFTEEN

THE OFFER

JULY 7, 1977
BROOKLYN, NEW YORK

Hopper's journey was short, but not particularly sweet. Once they'd put him in the back of the truck, they bound his hands and put a heavy sack of pale beige canvas that was scratchy as all hell over his head. He was unable to support himself with his hands tied tightly behind his back, and the men—still with him in the back of the truck—seemed quite happy to let him bounce all over the interior as the vehicle moved at some speed, each corner sending Hopper crashing against the side, every sudden stop throwing him forward, every pump of the brakes tossing him against the rear doors.

It was an old technique, but an effective one. Hopper had seen the NYPD do it. How to rough a prisoner up without laying a finger on him in one easy step . . .

But that had been . . . what, an hour ago? Maybe longer?

Now Hopper sat on a cold cement floor, his world still a musty canvas nowhere. He had given up on shouting. He was alone in the room, and all he was doing was shredding his voice.

So he decided to save his strength. He sat and contemplated his situation, occasionally shifting his legs to stop them from going to sleep. They would come to him eventually. He was patient.

He could wait.

No sooner had he thought it than someone *did* come in. There was a heavy metallic *clunk* as a door was opened, and the footsteps echoed; Hopper listened carefully—he was somewhere in an industrial area, maybe a warehouse, maybe even somewhere around the rail yard.

There was a scuffling sound—somebody started to say something, but their conversation was stopped before it even began as Hopper heard the unmistakable sound of a fist being applied to a body. There was a *whoop* of air from whoever had been on the receiving end, and a moment later Hopper felt a body collide with him, knocking him sideways on the floor, as another prisoner was thrown into the room.

Hopper rolled over as the heavy door banged shut. Beside him, he felt the other person kick out, scrambling as they got themselves upright, hitting Hopper in the process.

"Hey!"

The other person stopped moving for a second, then Hopper heard them roll around and then stand up. Hopper got himself back upright, wincing as he freed his pinned hands from underneath himself.

And then the sack was yanked off his head.

Hopper blinked, coughing as canvas dust swam in the air around his face.

"So they got you too, man."

Leroy Washington stood over him. He was unbound and smiling, his lower lip fresh with bright red blood.

Hopper stared at him. "Leroy? What the hell is going on?"

He shifted on his behind, moving his bound wrists so Leroy could see. "Untie me and let's get the hell out of here."

"Man, I have no idea what's going on," said Leroy, kneeling down. He got to work on Hopper's bonds. "Don't know where we are. Don't know who *they* are. All I know is that I was waiting for you like I said and I even saw you, man. I was watching, just, you know, making sure the coast was clear. And I thought it was, but then they got you. There wasn't nothing I could do about it, neither. And then . . ."

With a jerk, Hopper's hands were free. Leroy stood back, a stretch of yellow canvas rope in his hands. Hopper rubbed his wrists and stood. He looked at Leroy.

"And then what?"

Leroy's smile flickered and went out. He played with the rope in his hands, then tossed it to one side. "I guess they were watching me like they were watching you. I turned around and, *bam!* There they were. And here we are."

Hopper nodded. It was possible that Leroy was lying—that this was some kind of setup—but something nagged at him, a gut feeling that the young gangster was telling the truth. He remembered how he'd sounded on the telephone. The fear in his voice, primal, electric.

Still rubbing his wrists, Hopper began pacing the room, looking around for any clues as to where they might be.

It didn't take much deduction. The room was square and fairly small, maybe twenty feet by twenty. The door was heavy and green, with an industrial locking mechanism consisting of horizontal and vertical bars that looked more complicated than it probably needed to be. From the ceiling hung fluorescent strip lights.

But it was the bags that gave it away. They were long canvas sacks, almost like punching bags, leaning in stacks against the rear wall. Most were full and tied at the top with more of the yellow canvas rope, threaded through big metal loops. Turning in a circle, Hopper saw stacks of empty folded sacks sitting in a metal feeder-frame by the door. All of the sacks were the same, and all had the same blue eagle and red bar logo that had been on the side of the truck that brought Hopper here.

That was when the levered locking mechanism of the door sprang into motion; Hopper and Leroy both backed away as two burly men squeezed into suits entered—they weren't wearing ski masks and running outfits now, but Hopper felt he recognized them from the altercation outside the corner store.

Backed against the mail sacks, Hopper felt Leroy tense beside him. He glanced sideways, and saw the young man trembling with nerves.

The two large men moved to one side and stood impassively with their hands clasped in front. A moment later a third man entered. He was wearing a blue suit and was positively dwarfed by the bulk of his two minions.

Hopper felt almost every muscle in his body tense as Special Agent Gallup turned on his regulation smile for his prisoners. "Detective Hopper, Mr. Washington, so glad you could join us."

"Son of a—"

Hopper couldn't help it. Fists bunched, he launched himself at the G-man, spittle flying from his lips as his anger, for just a moment, took over. It was a useless gesture, and he knew that, but when one suited goon caught him under the arms and dragged him backward, away from the boss, he still struggled as hard as he could. It was like trying to wrestle with an oak tree. The goon then shoved Hopper back against a stack of mailbags and stood over him, ready to go again if the prisoner hadn't already got the message.

Hopper caught his breath, and wiped his mouth with the back of one hand, the strength of the enemy now soundly tested. "You know," he said, "when you said you worked for a federal agency, I didn't expect it to be the postal service. No wonder you wouldn't say."

Gallup's smile grew wider, but only for a moment. Then he

shrugged. "The agency I work for is still on a need-to-know basis," he said, "but it really is amazing what facilities the USPS can be persuaded to make available to those with the right authority."

Hopper pulled himself to his feet, then looked sideways at Leroy. "So he's not the postman then."

Leroy looked at him, his eyes wide with fright. Hopper frowned, but the gangster's reaction confirmed his earlier instinct, that Leroy was as much a prisoner as he was, and his story was a true one. The fact that he'd been picked up moments after Hopper meant that the feds had known about the meet—which suggested that Hopper's phone at the precinct had been bugged. Delgado's too, most likely. No wonder the agents had taken so long to pack up the case files.

Hopper turned back to Gallup. "Okay, listen, *Special Agent*," he said, spitting the man's title like an insult, "I am a detective of the New York City Police Department, 65th Precinct. And you are in some very deep shit. You've just kidnapped a police officer and"—he hooked a thumb over his shoulder at Leroy— "a witness who is under our protection. Now, I don't know what kind of authority you think you have, but I'll give you a choice. You can either let us both go, right now, and leave us the hell alone, or you can answer to the police commissioner and the chief of detectives. Do I make myself clear?"

Silence reigned in the mail storeroom. Gallup's two agents had their eyes on Hopper, but they didn't move or make a sound. Hopper could hear Leroy fidgeting near the mail sacks behind him. And in front, Special Agent Gallup was looking down, busy adjusting his shirt cuffs. Then he flapped the lapel of his jacket and looked around the ceiling.

"Boy, it's hot in here, isn't it? I guess the mail doesn't need air-conditioning."

Hopper risked taking a step closer to Gallup. At this, the goon who had laid hands on him before did it again, pushing a meaty palm into Hopper's chest. Hopper pressed himself against it, but the man's strength was immense.

"I said, do I make myself *clear*?"

Gallup smiled his infuriating smile again and looked at Hopper. Seconds passed. Hopper felt the heat rise in his face, felt the sweat drip down the small of his back.

Then Gallup jerked his head like he'd just gotten an electric shock.

"Oh, I'm sorry, have you finished, or is there more of the tough New York City cop thing coming?"

Hopper felt his temper rise again, and he couldn't resist pushing a little harder against the hand on his chest. This time, perhaps the agent's arm moved, but only a little.

"You're right, of course," said Gallup.

Hopper shook his head. "Right about what?"

"You *don't* know what kind of authority I have." Gallup looked at Hopper, then he looked at Leroy. "Good," he said, finally. "Now, gentlemen, seeing as we have all that settled, I suggest we get down to business. It does indeed seem, Detective, that we have a little misunderstanding to clear up, because I distinctly remember paying you and your captain a little visit . . . when was it? Only Monday?" He glanced at his besuited goons. "I tell you, this has been a long week. Anyway, I also recall giving you explicit instructions that you were not to work on the card homicides, and that the case was now under the jurisdiction of the federal authorities, under my direct control."

Hopper didn't flinch from Gallup's unrelenting gaze. Gallup took a step closer, and folded his arms.

"Now," he continued, "I know you New York City cops like to think you're some kind of special breed. And, actually, maybe you are. It takes a lot of guts and determination to walk these mean streets. That, I admire. Guts and determination. That's good. And then you get a serial killer in your own neighborhood—well, correct me if I'm wrong, Detective, but that's probably the worst kind of homicide case there is, isn't it? This is no drug deal gone wrong, no turf war between gangs, no violent assault or armed robbery turned fatal. This is a madman on the loose. And all the while, you're trying to investigate the case *and* keep it out of the public eye, because the city is busy obsessing over this so-called Son of Sam." Gallup whistled low. "*Two* serial killers at work." Then he shrugged. "I'm from Vermont. More trees than people, which is how I like it."

"Good for you," said Hopper.

"Actually, I think you'd like it. My hometown is a little bit like Hawkins, Indiana." Gallup tapped a finger against his lips. "Oh, wait, no, maybe you wouldn't like it, because it's a little like Hawkins, Indiana. Because small-town life isn't for you, is it? You were missing something in your life—after Vietnam, right? What did you serve? Two tours, right? And you volunteered. Wrong age for the draft, of course, but you still wanted to make a contribution to the cause." Gallup cocked his head. "Funny, I don't see you as particularly . . . patriotic? Apple pie, sure, but the Stars and Stripes?" He clicked his tongue. "No, don't see it."

"You've done your homework," said Hopper, quietly.

Gallup gave a tiny nod of acknowledgment. "I like to think I'm thorough. Anyway, as much as I'd love to chat about the old days, I suggest we get down to the matter at hand."

Hopper sighed and took a step backward, away from Gallup's minion, the big agent lowering his hand and resuming his neutral stance.

Of course, Hopper was in the wrong—and he knew it. He'd continued to look at the card homicides—they both had, he and Delgado, with his partner stealing Hoeler's file and Hopper going to the second apartment. Leroy's involvement may or may not have been a coincidence, but ultimately he and Delgado had agreed to give up and hand everything over to the feds. It had been the right decision, but maybe one they had made too late.

"Okay, look," said Hopper. "Yes, we thought we could continue with the case—I mean, you said it yourself. This is *our* neighborhood. Our people we're trying to protect. We stepped over the line and we shouldn't have, but we going to bring it all to you. We found out some more information which we thought would be useful for your task force."

Hopper held his breath. Gallup was watching him, his infuriating placid smile fixed in place. Hopper risked stepping closer again. This time the big agent didn't move, but he did turn his head to look down on the detective.

"But, look. We can *help* each other. Before Agent Hoeler got himself killed, me and my partner had been working this case for weeks. Now, I know that Hoeler was one of yours, and I know this is all now tangled in your gang task force, and that changes everything. I get that. But I can help. You may not think much of the NYPD, but I'm good at my job, and so is my partner. So let us help you."

Hopper licked his lips and looked at Gallup with his eyebrows raised. If he could just get through to the agent, maybe, just maybe—

"Yes," said Gallup.

Hopper blinked. "What?"

"Why do you think I brought you here? Yes, you are going to help me, Detective Hopper. Mr. Washington, too. You both are."

Gallup paused. "And," he continued, "you have absolutely no choice in the matter whatsoever."

Hopper looked at Leroy, who was watching the conversation in wide-eyed wonder.

Then Hopper turned back to Gallup.

"What are you talking about?"

Gallup's smile vanished, instantly. Hopper hadn't liked it, but he liked the agent's new, hardened expression even less.

"Let me make myself perfectly clear," he said. "You will help me. Or you will never see Diane and Sara, or anyone else for that matter, ever again."

CHAPTER SIXTEEN

THE LOST AFTERNOON

JULY 7, 1977
BROOKLYN, NEW YORK

Detective Delgado put the phone down, and checked her watch. So far today she'd had precisely zero luck in tracking down Hopper, and she knew that trying to find him was starting to become a distraction from her actual work. Because as much as she wanted to bounce ideas off her partner, she was a detective in her own right, and was more than capable of carrying out her side of the investigation on her own.

On her own—and without raising Captain LaVorgna's suspicions. Luckily for her, he had been out most of the day at some meeting of the higher-ups, so Delgado was largely free to follow up on new leads, while keeping her other, assigned cases floating around her desk.

New leads like Lisa Sargeson, who just happened to be running her charity rehabilitation workshops from one of the addresses on the late Special Agent Jacob Hoeler's list.

On the face of it, there wasn't anything suspicious about that. Delgado had gone into the building, an old Methodist church hall, with Lisa, and had scanned the crowded noticeboard in the building's lobby. Lisa's group was one of many. Indeed, it seemed that the hall was never *not* in use by one organization or another, let alone the church itself.

After that, Delgado had watched Lisa for a minute or so through the windows of the door that led into the hall itself. Lisa had stood at the front, while about a dozen men sat on hard chairs in front of her. It looked like a class, and Delgado supposed that was what it really was.

On the drive back to the precinct, Delgado allowed herself to zone out, letting her brain get on with it on its own. It was all part of her process, various theories and ideas—the mundane and the outlandish alike—whirling around inside her head, her subconscious hard at work on the problem. Delgado had found that if she focused too hard on something, that particular thought, that avenue of investigation, would grow and dominate, forming a preconception that her brain would try to fit theories and evidence into, no matter what.

A dangerous habit for a detective.

So instead, the key—for her, anyway—was to let it all go, at least for a while. With any luck, something a little more rational would shake itself loose while Delgado got on with her other investigations.

Back at the precinct, she found that Lisa Sargeson was still at the forefront of her mind. There was something there, she was sure of it. *Something.*

A lot of good that was. "Something"? Gee, great. How about a big fat coincidence? And then she had spent the rest of the afternoon staring at the list from Hoeler's apartment, and wondering where the hell Hopper was.

That was when Captain LaVorgna arrived back at the precinct, the doors at the end of the bull pen banging against the frame as he stormed through them and into his office, slamming his own door behind him. Through the windows, Delgado saw the captain take off his jacket and yank his tie off. Then he stood in the middle of his office and shook his head, before glancing out into the bull pen while rummaging through his pockets, likely looking for a cigarette.

Delgado froze, feeling—ridiculously, given there was no way LaVorgna could see what was on her desk—like she'd been caught red-handed, working on a case she wasn't supposed to. But then the captain just frowned and snapped the blinds closed.

Oh boy.

Delgado slipped Hoeler's list under a folder, and turned her attention to another case. But all the while, just one name kept rolling around in her mind.

Lisa Sargeson.

CHAPTER SEVENTEEN

THE OP

JULY 7, 1977
BROOKLYN, NEW YORK

Hopper paused at the far end of the table, then started what must have been his fifth lap as he paced the length of the meeting room buried somewhere deep in the warren of USPS offices. At the table sat Special Agent Gallup and Leroy Washington and a half-empty silver carafe of coffee, next to an empty one the trio had finished what felt like hours ago.

Gallup watched Hopper pace. "Are you done yet, Detective?"

Hopper stopped to run his hands through his hair. He turned to face the agent. "Am I done? You asked me if I'm *done*?"

"I did, yes. Because the sooner you realize the gravity of the situation you've gotten yourself in, the sooner we can get to work."

Hopper shook his head. "This is insane."

"No, it isn't," said Gallup. "And you know that. I can run through it again, if you like. Maybe this time you can take some notes, because you seem to be having a hard time comprehending just what I can do to you and your friends and your family if you don't cooperate."

"This is crazy." Hopper resumed pacing.

"Because I will ruin their lives, and yours, if you don't cooperate. And it won't be my fault, it will be yours. Because the choice is entirely up to you."

Hopper stopped in the middle of the room. He closed his eyes. Behind his lids, red shadows danced.

"You go undercover for me," Gallup continued from somewhere a million miles away, "or you disappear. Diane loses her job. The IRS goes after them. She loses the apartment. Same for Detective Delgado. And that'll just be the start, believe me."

"You can't do that," said Hopper. He opened his eyes. "You can't do any of that. Nobody can."

Gallup looked at Leroy. "What am I doing wrong here, Leroy?" He gestured to Hopper. "Does your detective friend not speak English anymore? Did my agents hit him too hard on the head?" He turned back to Hopper. "I'll try one more time. You will rot in whatever hole I put you in, and everyone you know will wish they were in there with you. Do you understand *that*, Detective?"

Hopper placed his hands on the table and leaned toward the agent. "And you can't do *any* of that!"

Gallup shook his head. "I have the power to do precisely what I please. The choice is entirely yours."

Hopper and the agent locked gazes; Hopper held it for a good few seconds, then he sighed and paced the room again.

Leroy's eyes followed Hopper as he walked from one end of the room to the other and back again.

"Hopper, come on, *listen*. If this is a chance to get my sister out and to stop Saint John, then maybe it's the only plan we got. Will you just sit down and listen to him?"

Hopper sighed and closed his eyes, willing his temper to calm. When he opened his eyes, he moved back to his seat and sat heavily in it. He looked at Gallup.

"So what if I said yes?"

Gallup linked his fingers together on the table. "You'll cooperate?"

"No, I asked a question. And Saint John? How do we stop him? We don't even know what he's planning, do we? Apart from summoning the devil, that is."

"Well," said Gallup. "We're assuming this devil worship that Mr. Washington has talked about is really a cover for something far more real and far more serious. Something I'm hoping that you'll be able to find out. That *is* the whole reason I'm proposing this course of action."

Hopper leaned back in his chair and shook his head in disbelief.

Gallup unlinked his hands and turned his attention to his shirt cuffs, adjusting them so they were just *so*.

"Our task force has been watching the Vipers for some time, Detective. They're a new gang—New York is full of gangs, of course, but so far our intel suggests that the Vipers are something different. We believe their leader, the man who identifies himself as Saint John, has been gathering not only new recruits, but matériel. The recruits we think have come from other gangs. Somehow Saint John has done what few gang leaders have been able to do, uniting different factions and gangs, organizing them together under his own umbrella, as it were. Combining gangs also combines resources, and we know he has accumulated a lot of money and weapons. But it seems he's recruiting from elsewhere, too—he's forming a sort of inner circle, somehow finding people with particular expertise. What that expertise is, we don't know. What he wants them for, we don't know either. But we believe he's planning something big, something that will pose a severe and significant threat to this city and its people."

At this, Leroy nodded, rocking back on his chair. "Something big, man. I told you then, I'm telling you now. Things are going to get crazy. Day of the Serpent, that's when it is."

Hopper glanced at the gangster, then looked back at Gallup.

"Except we don't *know* when that is. And all this talk of devil worship and summoning Satan. You think that's just window dressing?"

Gallup pursed his lips. "You know as well as I do how the gangs of New York can be . . . colorful, shall we say. Each one carves out its own niche and identity. Saint John, whoever he is, seems to have been cultivating something of a cult of personality. We suspect that's how he has been able to get other gangs to join him so readily. A charismatic leader, talking about the end-times and how his gang is not only going to summon the devil but serve him in the coming apocalypse, his words reinforced by ordering a series of ritual killings? It's pure fantasy, but in a town like this, people can be drawn in, probably more easily than you would imagine, whether they really believe in it or not."

Hopper rubbed his face, then dropped his hands to the table. "Seems like you have a lot of intel already."

"Mr. Washington here has been most helpful," said Gallup. "Plus—as you rightly suspected—we have other informants who have been able to feed us information. Agent Hoeler was one such informant."

"One such informant who got himself caught and killed," said Hopper.

Gallup nodded, but didn't say anything.

Hopper shook his head again. "So why do you even need me? Why not just throw me in jail for obstructing your investigation? You already have informants, you already have intel, why not just go in, take Saint John and his gang out?"

But Gallup was already shaking his head. "We can't risk precipitous action. If we start this, we need to know we can end it. We need to know what Saint John is planning. We need details, plans, times, dates, people. Everything. If we go in now, we might hurt the Vipers, but we might trigger Saint John's plan—or a contingency plan. It's too much of a risk. We need something concrete we can act on, and as soon as possible. *That* is why we need you."

"But why *me*?"

"Because you're not just any homicide detective. You're a decorated veteran. You have the experience and you have the ability. You can handle yourself under the most extreme circumstances—your record speaks for itself. And . . ."

Gallup smiled. Hopper didn't like the expression at all.

"And?"

"And," Gallup continued, "you *want* to help."

Hopper looked at him. He was in deep—far deeper than he wanted, far deeper than he had any right to be.

But.

Gallup was right. He did want to help. He wanted to stop the card killer. He wanted to catch him, bring him to justice.

More than that, he wanted to protect his neighborhood. Protect his city.

Protect his family.

Special Agent Gallup could read him like a book. Hopper hated him for it. But he also knew that he wouldn't be able to resist. He didn't know if Gallup's threats were genuine, but the man seemed to hold a very powerful, if mysterious, position. It wasn't a risk Hopper wanted to take. He didn't like it and he didn't like people like Special Agent Gallup.

But, even *without* the threats . . . he had to do this.

Had to.

He looked at Leroy, sitting next to him. The young man was drumming his fingers on the table, his knees jiggling underneath it.

"I need to get my sister out, man. Saint John, he's bad. I need to get her out. I need to get *me* out."

Hopper looked at Leroy for a long while, then he turned

back to Gallup. The special agent smiled again and—for the first time—it seemed like a genuine expression.

"We're all working to the same end, Detective Hopper."

Hopper said nothing.

"So there's your choice," said Gallup. "You can say no, and okay, sure, you disappear and your family's life goes to hell"—he waved a hand like it was nothing at all, a minor inconvenience in the grand scheme of things—"and maybe we can get this done without you and everything will just work out fine."

He leaned forward across the table.

"Or maybe it won't. Maybe Saint John and the Vipers will win. Maybe Beelzebub really will erect a throne on top of the Empire State Building and rule over a burning world. Or maybe something much more real and much worse will happen."

Hopper looked at Gallup. He looked at Leroy. The gangster's nostrils flared as he took deep, slow breaths.

"So," said Gallup, "the question is really, are you going to help me save the city, or not?"

Hopper poked his tongue into his cheek. He could feel his heart thudding in his chest.

Then he nodded. Just once.

"Excellent," said Gallup. "Now, the first step, Detective, is to make you disappear."

CHAPTER EIGHTEEN

THE DISAPPEARANCE OF DETECTIVE JAMES HOPPER

JULY 8, 1977
BROOKLYN, NEW YORK

Hopper sat in the pool car on the corner, windows down, enjoying what little breeze there was. There was no need for discretion, no need to slouch down behind the dash as he watched the row of brownstones.

His apartment was in the center of the block. From the car he had a clear view of the stoop and everyone who came and went from the building.

Which, at the moment, was nobody. The brownstone was cut into three apartments: Ms. Schaefer in apartment one, ground floor, was at work. The Van Sabbens, apartment three, were away for a couple of days. And apartment two, the Hoppers, was also empty.

He checked his watch. It was after nine, and Diane and Sara would both be at school. The meeting—if you could call it that—with Gallup and Leroy had run all night, the special agent outlining the details of the plan and answering Hopper's barrage of questions with his implacable, infuriating calm. Gallup had even, it seemed, covered for Hopper, arranging for someone to call Diane and claim to be from the precinct, explaining to his wife that he was in the middle of something important and wouldn't be home. Being away from home for a night wasn't something Hopper often did, but it was not unknown for a homicide detective—but that didn't stop Hopper resenting Gallup for pulling that trick with his family.

Hopper took a deep breath. Just thinking of them set his emotions roiling.

He knew what he was doing was right—that behind the threats, the secrecy, the heavy-handed men-in-black routine, Special Agent Gallup was also just trying to do his job, using whatever means he had at his disposal. And now they had the opportunity, at one fell swoop, to take down the Vipers and stop whatever the hell it was their leader, Saint John, was planning.

Solve the card homicides. Get justice for the city.

Get justice for Sam Barrett. For Jonathan Schnetzer. For Jacob Hoeler.

But somehow, suddenly, that didn't feel like enough for Hopper. Not if it meant hurting his wife and child. Because Special Agent Gallup *had* given him a choice, one where both outcomes would cause pain, fear, uncertainty—one permanently, the other, thankfully, only for a short while.

Because Detective James Hopper was about to disappear. For how long, he didn't know. He was going to quite literally walk out of his normal life and straight into danger. Getting back to his wife and child was only one of several possible outcomes.

He thumped the wheel with the heel of one hand, telling himself to snap the hell out of it. He could do the job. He could handle himself. That was why Gallup wanted him.

Not for the first time, Hopper wondered how much of his army record Gallup had managed to see. Some of it was sealed. Some of it, even Diane didn't know about. But the fact that Gallup was counting so much on Hopper's abilities and experience made him wonder.

Did Gallup know what he'd done in Vietnam?

Hopper cleared his mind. He had to focus.

It didn't work. He drifted back to his family. Part of his brain started rationalizing his actions. Diane would be upset and worried. No doubt about it. But, when it was all over, she would understand. Sara would sense her mother's anxiety, would be upset herself. But she was—thankfully—too young to understand, and there was more than a fair chance she wouldn't even remember what happened. It would become a family story, a great tale told in years to come about how her dad, James Hopper, homicide detective in New York City, had vanished, only to turn up a few days later, having taken out one of the most dangerous gangs around, having saved the city from catastrophe, solving a serial killer case along the way.

Yeah, wouldn't *that* be a story to tell.

If the plan worked. The plan that went like this:

Leroy Washington was still a member of the Vipers, and while he said he wasn't part of Saint John's inner circle, he was someone fairly close to the action. A recruiter, tasked by the gang's mysterious boss to bolster their ranks, picking out potential new pledges with care and attention.

People like Hopper. Whatever Saint John was looking for, he fit the bill—at least according to Leroy. Hopper was a decorated veteran, someone with a proven track record of violence. It was a strange way of looking at it, but Hopper knew it was the truth. The fact that Hopper was also a cop was an interesting wrinkle, one that Leroy thought Saint John would like.

Because Hopper was about to become a *former* cop. He wasn't just going to disappear.

He was going on the run.

Back at the USPS warehouse, Hopper had surrendered his NYPD-issue weapon, a Smith & Wesson Model 10, the old but reliable revolver having then been picked up by one of Gallup's minions, the big agent this time wearing white cotton gloves like a museum curator, and whisked from the room. The gun was the star of his disappearance, the weapon placed at a staged crime scene, implicating Hopper himself as the perp. Hopper would then vanish, and his name would end up on the board back at his own precinct, next to a case number all his own.

Officially on the lam, Hopper would go with Leroy to the Vipers, the disgraced, corrupt, violent cop offering his expertise to Saint John. Once recruited, the job was simple: find out what the grand plan was, and how to stop it. Inside the gang, Hopper and Leroy would be on their own. If they needed extraction, they could contact Gallup's task force, but that would blow the operation sky-high, forcing the feds to take action. Gallup had hammered the fact that, should that be the case, Hopper and Leroy had better have gathered enough intel before hitting eject.

Leroy and Hopper had split up after Gallup released them, Leroy to contact the Vipers and arrange for their new recruit to be brought in, Hopper to handle some personal business of his own. Gallup had advised against it, saying that Hopper needed a clean break from his job, friends, and family, but he hadn't argued too hard. Hopper had given him a piece of his mind about trust, and the special agent had relented.

Hopper and Leroy would meet that night, and the op would begin.

In the meantime, Hopper had a couple of things he wanted to do.

The coast very much clear, Hopper got out of the pool car and made his way toward his building. He moved quickly to the stoop, trotting up the stairs and entering the brownstone without pause, suddenly feeling like the entire neighborhood was watching his every move, despite the street being empty.

In the apartment, Hopper went straight to the master bedroom. First, he needed to take a shower and take a nap. Then he needed to change—it was a little silly, but he felt far too conspicuous in his checkered shirt and slacks. If he was a good cop turned bad, he wanted to look the part, if not for the gang, then for himself. Hopper was well aware that he needed to play a role and play it well—and he needed all the help he could get.

Hopper lay on top of the covers, set the alarm, and drifted off.

BROOKLYN, NEW YORK

"*Apple* green?"

Hopper stood back and, paint roller angled in one hand so it wouldn't drip, tilted his head as he regarded what represented the last hour of work on the bedroom wall. He'd done a good job, and he knew it—painting a wall was hardly the most difficult challenge he'd faced in his life, but he had wanted to get it right and, crucially, he and Diane had agreed to redecorate their new apartment themselves, rather than hire professionals. The move from Hawkins had been easy in the planning but harder in the execution, their bank account absorbing most of the damage. Hopper had only been working his beat a month—having started literally the day after they'd arrived at the start of May—and the couple were very much looking forward to his first paycheck.

But now, as he watched, quite literally, the paint dry on the wall, he wondered if they should have perhaps splashed out a little more on some better paint.

"Hey, how's it going in here?"

Hopper looked over his shoulder as Diane crept in, their fourteen-month-old daughter draped over her shoulder in a deep slumber. Diane carefully stepped around the bunched up ground sheets by the door and joined her husband in the middle of the room. He gave Sara a gentle kiss on the cheek, and his wife a more direct kiss on the mouth, before gesturing to the wall with the roller.

"The tin said apple green."

Diane nodded. Hopper glanced sideways at her.

"Is that frown one of quiet appreciation of my skills as an artisan painter," he asked, "or are you wondering what the hell kind of apples are that kind of color?"

Diane laughed and drew herself closer to her husband, but as she reached one arm around his waist, he held up the paint roller, and she paused.

"Hold on," he said. He ducked over to the paint tray on the floor by the wall, and rested the roller in it, then turned to return to his wife and child when Diane held a hand up. He froze on the spot.

"Oh, Jim!"

"What?"

Diane shook her head and pointed at him. He looked down at his chest, at the yellow Jim Croce T-shirt he'd picked up at a show last year. The folk singer's smiling face was now spattered with green paint.

"Oh, *dammit.*"

Diane retracted her hand to cup her mouth. On her shoulder, Sara began to stir, and Diane instinctively swayed gently from side to side to keep her daughter comfortable.

Hopper looked up, his eyes narrow.

"Are you laughing?"

Diane dropped her hand, her mouth split into a wide grin. "Oh, Jim, you loved that shirt."

He sighed. "I did love this shirt." He watched as his wife's shoulders shook as she tried to control her amusement. "I'm glad one of us finds this funny."

But he couldn't help himself. A moment later his own laughter bubbled up from his chest. As he moved back to join Diane, their noise woke Sara and she shifted on her mother's shoulder.

Hopper moved in to Diane's side, and together they managed a side-by-side embrace that cradled Sara between them. As their daughter yawned and looked around, the two parents regarded Hopper's handiwork again.

"Well, you did say you wanted a change," said Diane. "New city, new start—that was what you said, right?"

"Oh, sure," said Hopper. "New city, new start, new lesson in never to buy paint made by . . . who *did* make this paint, anyway?" He craned his head around, trying to see the discarded pail.

Diane smiled, and twisted around to give Hopper another kiss.

"Well, I think it looks great," she said. "We wanted green and we got green."

Hopper grinned. "We sure did." He looked down at Sara, who yawned again and was now clearly back in the land of the living. "Hey, sweetie, what do you think? Do you like the color, huh? Did your daddy do an excellent job, huh?"

He lifted Sara off Diane's shoulder, and balancing the child on his hip, he took her closer to the wall. Gently squeezing Sara's hand, he bounced her lightly and nodded at the wall.

"Look, this is apparently what apples look like in New York City."

From the middle of the room, Diane laughed. Hopper turned in a circle to face his wife, then, as he adjusted his hold on Sara, he felt her small hands on his face as she balanced herself.

Small . . . *wet* hands.

"Uh-oh," he said, looking down. Sara had found the patches of paint on his T-shirt, and was now busy transferring that paint from his chest to his face—and to her own.

"Apples!" she said, and giggled.

Shaking her head, Diane joined them and carefully extracted Sara from Hopper's custody.

"Okay, how about we leave daddy to it now. He's got a lot of work to do." She glanced at her husband. "And we all know better than to disturb a master at work."

Hopper laughed and waved her away. As Diane and Sara vanished through the bedroom door, he looked down at his chest again, tugging at the edge of his T-shirt, seeing if it was possibly salvageable.

It seemed unlikely.

With a sigh, Hopper picked up the roller and got back to work.

CHAPTER NINETEEN

COFFEE AND CONTEMPLATION

JULY 8, 1977
BROOKLYN, NEW YORK

A couple of hours later Hopper was roused by his alarm clock. He sat up, feeling worse than he had before, disconcerted by the clarity of the dream-memory he had just been wrenched from. Redecorating the apartment . . . *how* many years ago? He couldn't remember. The bedroom walls were still green, the shade thankfully paling once the paint had dried.

Hopper turned the alarm off and ran a shower.

A half hour later, Hopper gave himself a once-over in the mirror. Gone were the sensible pants, shirt, and tie. He wore a pair of old blue jeans he had kept to do yard work in their non-existent yard and the paint-smeared Jim Croce T-shirt that he had unearthed—with the oddest feeling of déjà vu—from the back of a drawer, over which he pulled a leather bomber jacket. His shoes he had replaced with his ancient army boots, another relic kept just in case that yard materialized one day. He had considered digging out his khaki army jacket as well, but he didn't want to over-egg it. He then spent a minute or two with some of Diane's mysterious hair products, until he had found something greasy enough to slick his hair back with.

Relatively happy with his ensemble, Hopper then returned to the closet, diving into the back to access a hidden panel in the rear wall. From within the small space behind it, he took a heavy item wrapped in plastic. Holding the object on the palm of one hand, he unraveled the plastic, revealing a semi-automatic handgun, the Colt M1911 that had been at his side during both tours of Vietnam. He checked the clip, then held the gun up, sighting his own reflection in the mirror. Satisfied, he shoved the gun into the back of his jeans and pulled down the elasticated edge of the bomber jacket, checking to make sure it hid the piece, which it did.

So far, so good.

Hopper replaced the panel, slid a shoe rack back into place, then carefully hung his old pants and shirt up, arranging the other clothes in the closet so nothing looked out of place. Then he looked around the bedroom. Everything looked as it had when he'd walked in.

Including the photograph frame on Diane's dressing table. Hopper paused, reached for it, stopped himself, then gave in and picked it up. The frame was in two halves, hinged in the middle. On one side was a photograph of Hopper and Diane—he in a dark suit, she in a sapphire blue dress, the pair sitting on some rocks in a botanical garden, just a couple of hours after they had gotten married.

Hopper looked at the picture awhile, then at the one opposite. This was a three-shot, the family group—mother, father, daughter. Three pairs of bright eyes staring out at him, all three of them sitting so damn straight that Hopper could almost feel the ache in his back from that hour in the photographer's studio, getting the family portraits done.

Hopper laughed, then put the frame back on the dresser. He adjusted it so it looked right, then stepped backward, not taking his eyes off it until the backs of his knees caught the edge of the bed.

Then he pulled himself away, running his hand through his slicked hair as he headed out of the bedroom.

There was one more thing to do.

In the kitchen, he grabbed the phone by the fridge and dialed. The call was picked up almost immediately.

"Delgado, homicide."

"It's me," said Hopper softly, raising a hand by the phone as though his partner could see the gesture. "Don't say anything else, just listen, okay?"

Hopper could hear Delgado breathing into the phone. He waited.

"Okay?"

"You just told me not to say anything," said Delgado, keeping her voice low.

Hopper couldn't resist a smile. "Okay. Listen, we need to meet." He lifted his wrist and checked his watch. "One hour, Tom's Diner, corner of Washington and Sterling—"

"Yeah, I got it," said Delgado. "That's not close by, Hop."

Hopper nodded. "Then you'd better get moving," he said, and then he hung up.

It was a risk calling her, but he had no choice.

Because while he was on the run, he had a job for her to do.

Tom's Diner had been a fixture of Prospect Heights since the 1930s and, thought Hopper, probably hadn't changed much in all that time. Outside, the diner occupied the ground level of a squat, square building that had no memorable features whatsoever. Inside, the place stank of old grease and cigarettes, but the coffee was remarkably good and the mugs in which the beverage was served seemed clean enough. Hopper nursed his as he sat in a far corner of the place, watching the street through the grimy windows as the chatter of customers in front of the counter and music from the radio behind it blended around him into a pleasant wall of sound.

Delgado arrived about twenty minutes after Hopper—just as the trumpets of "Gonna Fly Now" by Bill Conti blared across the diner. As she walked in, he saw her crane her neck to scan the booths and tables. Hopper looked up and gave her a nod, and she came right over, sliding into the booth and dumping her bag next to her.

"I hated that movie," she said, frowning as she glanced in the direction of the offending music. She caught the attention of a server at the counter, then turned back around and leaned over the table. "So what the hell, Hop?" Then she immediately straightened and smiled as the server came over, her uniform as yellow as her hair.

"I get you a menu?" she asked, before she continued working on the gum in her mouth, her jaw so wide open that Hopper could smell the spearmint over his coffee.

"Just coffee," said Delgado. The server nodded and went back to the counter.

Delgado gave Hopper one of *those* looks, but Hopper only lifted his finger slightly, his eyes following the server as she returned with the jug of coffee and a fresh mug, which she deposited in front of Delgado and filled, before topping off Hopper's.

"Thanks," he said, smiling. The server didn't return the expression but left quick enough.

"Okay," said Delgado. "Now, where was I? Oh yeah. What the hell, Hop? You want to tell me what this cloak-and-dagger is all about? And where have you been since yesterday? I put the captain off a couple times, but your absence isn't making his mood any rosier."

"I'll explain everything," said Hopper, placing his mug on the table in front of him. He cupped both hands around it. It had been another hot day in the city, but for some reason he felt cold. "But I want you to listen and let me finish. You have any questions, you save them for the end, okay?"

Delgado shrugged.

"I'll take that as a yes," said Hopper. "But you have to trust me, okay?"

Delgado just shook her head. "Cut the crap, Hop. You know I trust you. You know you shouldn't even have to ask that."

"Point."

"So what's got you so hot? And what's with the getup?"

Hopper glanced down at his chest. The paint-stained image of Jim Croce looked out across the booth table.

"I'm working for Special Agent Gallup now."

Delgado sipped her coffee and raised an eyebrow. Hopper watched it.

"What, no comment?"

Delgado shook her head. "Plenty. But you told me to wait until the end."

Hopper blew out his cheeks. "Okay, so, that kid who came in, asking for protection . . ."

"Leroy Washington, yes. Only he was let out and vanished into the night."

Hopper shook his head. "Gallup has him, too. In fact, we're working together on this thing. Now, we're going to be gone awhile, and soon enough you're going to start hearing some . . . *stuff* about me." Hopper held out his hand toward his partner, like he was preemptively working to calm her down. "Now, no matter what you hear, it's not real, it's just a cover. Gallup has something arranged that will let me and Leroy get on with the job. So whatever comes up at the precinct, whatever people start saying about me, it's likely to all fall back on you because you're my partner. They'll think you know something about what's going on and where I am, but I just need you to hold your own for a while. You'll need to join in with them. I'll be the enemy. People at the precinct are going to be pissed, believe me, but if this is going to work, I need you to be part of that."

Hopper paused and they drank their coffee in silence, neither one looking away. Delgado's mouth was twisted into an unhappy grimace between mouthfuls.

"It'll get straightened out when I get back," Hopper continued. "Just remember it's all just a nonsense cover and there is nothing to worry about. When the job is done, I'll be back, we can come clean on the whole thing, to everyone."

Delgado gulped the last of her coffee. Hopper waited until she was finished.

"Okay, questions."

Delgado nodded. "Why does the coffee in this place taste like tarmac and why do I want a top-off?"

With that, she lifted her mug and, half rising on the booth's bench seat, she caught the attention of the gum-chewing server. A moment later her coffee was replenished. Delgado took a hot mouthful. Hopper watched as she gasped when she was done, steam puffing out of her mouth.

"Okay," said Delgado. "Why Leroy? Why not me?"

"Leroy is my way in," said Hopper. "And I have another job for you while I'm gone."

Delgado tilted her head. "Way in? You're going to the Vipers, aren't you?"

Hopper drank his coffee and said nothing.

Delgado turned to look out of the window.

"Shit, Hop. How long will you be gone for?"

"I don't know. Just a couple of days, I hope. But as long as it takes. Once we're in, we're in, and there's no way out until it's over."

Delgado continued to stare out the window. "And what's this job you want me to do, apart from being a homicide detective looking for a new partner?"

Hopper pursed his lips. When he didn't answer immediately, Delgado turned to look at him. Her eyes roved over his face, and then she nodded.

"Diane."

Hopper nodded. "And Sara."

"And Sara. I'll keep an eye on them."

Hopper sighed and stared down into his coffee mug. "What comes next will be hard for them. Sara's lucky, she's too young to understand or even remember. But it's Diane." Hopper paused. He felt hot behind his eyes, his chest felt tight, his heart hammering at a million miles an hour.

"Hop?"

Hopper rolled his neck. He closed his eyes, but all he could see was the family photo on the dresser, the three of them, smiling until their faces ached. He opened his eyes.

"Diane is going to hear all the same stuff about me as you will. I need you to be there. I need you to look after them. You got me?"

Delgado nodded. "Don't worry, partner. You can count on me. I'll be there for them."

Hopper sighed. It was weird, but it really did feel like a weight had been lifted from him.

"Thanks, Rosario."

"Oh, hey, now I know things are bad," said his partner, a grin cracking across her face. "You start calling me Rosario and I know we're really in trouble."

Hopper smiled, and drank his coffee.

"But before you go all secret agent on me," said Delgado, "I should fill you in on my own adventures in Crazytown."

Hopper spread his hands. "Anything is useful."

"You remember the list of addresses I found in Jacob Hoeler's apartment?"

"Sure," said Hopper. "One of them was for an AA meeting."

"Right. And another is for a rehabilitation group, a kind of community outreach run by a charity organization. They have a counselor come in twice a week and work with recently released felons, try to help them reintegrate back into civilian life. It's a support group, not big, just like the AA actually. They all help each other, guided by the counselor."

Hopper frowned. "Okay . . . ?"

"And the counselor in question is Lisa Sargeson."

Hopper paused, his coffee halfway to his mouth. He set it back down on the table, and listened as Delgado filled him in on her visit to Lisa's apartment, where she learned about the Zener cards and Lisa's work, past and present.

Hopper stroked his stubbled chin as he listened. "And the other addresses?"

Delgado counted them off on her fingers. "Two church halls, a boxing club, one community center. Each of them used for a variety of groups and clubs—AA, Vietnam vets support groups, some chronic illness support groups, night classes for the unemployed. You name it. A whole bunch of organizations. Lisa's group is just one of several. But . . ."

"When you add in the Zener cards . . ."

Delgado nodded. "There's a link there, Hop. Somewhere, anyway."

Hopper sucked the air through his teeth. "Okay, I think we need—" He stopped, catching himself. "I think *you* need to go talk to Lisa again. Find out more about what she's doing at her community outreach, find out if she knows any of the victims, or the other support groups."

His partner lifted an eyebrow. "So . . . we *are* still working the case?"

At this, Hopper shrugged. "The whole situation has changed. I'm helping Gallup. You're helping me."

Delgado finished her coffee. "Leave it to me."

"Thanks," said Hopper. His coffee mug was getting cold. He checked his watch. "Okay, time's up. You go first. I'll give you time to get clear."

Delgado stood. "Good luck, Hop. Stay safe."

Hopper smiled at her and watched as she left the diner; then, looking through the window, as she crossed the street and vanished from sight.

Hopper waited a few minutes. The server in yellow came by, brandishing her coffeepot.

"You want a refill, hon?"

Hopper shook his head. "No," he said. The server turned, then Hopper changed his mind. "Actually, wait. Yes I do. And you got any apple pie?"

"We do."

"Great. Fresh coffee and apple pie. Actually, make it two slices."

"You want it hot?"

"Yes, please."

"You want cream?"

"Do I ever."

The server only raised an eyebrow, then retreated to the counter to prep Hopper's order. It was a small thing, a simple thing, but he was going to savor this.

He only hoped it wasn't going to be his last meal.

CHAPTER TWENTY

MARTHA

Hopper sat on the front bench seat of the antique station wagon as Leroy rolled it steadily north, crossing off the numbered streets of Manhattan as they headed toward the Viper's nest somewhere in the South Bronx. The windows were down, and for that Hopper was grateful, as the breeze cooled the hot interior of the vehicle, taking with it most of the weed stink that seemed to permeate the very fabric of the vehicle. The car was huge—something more like a hearse than a station wagon, maybe—and in good condition would probably have been worth something to a keen-eyed collector.

"Condition" being the operative word, because the vehicle was a mess. Inside, the bench seat was cracked, the leather painfully stiff, puffs of yellowish foam erupting from the crevices. The ceiling paneling had been removed and Hopper wasn't entirely sure the dashboard dials were working as intended. On the outside, the paintwork had at some point been stripped back to the base metal, then the car had been covered with layer upon layer of spray paint graffiti, the faded tags merging with large islands of rust, so the whole thing had an exterior more typical of your average New York City subway car. The fact that the vehicle moved at all was nothing short of miraculous, given the smoke that periodically belched from the exhaust, and the deathlike rattle that came from the engine every time Leroy applied pressure with his right foot.

Hopper hadn't asked where the car had come from. There were bigger things to worry about right now. He'd just waited at the agreed corner, and gotten into the car as soon as Leroy pulled up, no questions asked.

Leroy drove with his left arm hanging out in the wind, his armpit resting on the frame of the rolled-down window. The car's shifter was on the steering column, and Leroy seemed to like the way the car listed to the left when he let go of the wheel to change gears, happy to leave his free arm flapping outside.

Hopper said nothing. The vehicle had no seatbelts, and Hopper quickly learned to keep ahold of the strap above his door to stop himself sliding into Leroy's lap at almost every turn.

They'd started in Brooklyn, headed north into Queens, then west across to Manhattan, then north again. The traffic had started heavy and gotten thinner as they headed toward the Bronx, and that wasn't the only change. Midtown Manhattan, that monolithic collection of skyscrapers, the streets permanently clogged with yellow cabs, was how it always was; how, Hopper suspected, it always would be. Busy, even as the evening stretched onward. Plenty of people. Plenty of tourists. Plenty of workers.

Advertising billboards stretched across building fronts and around intersections. Most advertised Winston or Salem cigarettes, or one of a half dozen brands of whiskey. The outlier was for a new James Bond movie, *The Spy Who Loved Me*.

Hopper's laugh when he read that one was enough to earn a puzzled look from Leroy, but Hopper waved him off and continued to watch the city go by.

Midtown was midtown and no economic downturn, or financial crisis, or whatever the local news was calling it this week, was going to make much difference there.

Things were different after Forty-Second Street. Markedly so. Hopper knew Times Square was a pit, but he was surprised at how far the cancer-like decay had spread south. It seemed like every second address on either side of them promised the delights of girls without clothes, live on stage, live on film, live within the glossy slick pages of a magazine. Women hung around outside, too, standing in doorways, standing on the curb, all miniskirts and thigh-high boots and puffy fur shoulders, while men dressed in tight polyester lurked in rather less exposed areas. As the car passed through, it picked up discarded newspaper under its front wheels, carrying yesterday's news and crime statistics a few blocks farther up.

Beyond Times Square, the height of the buildings began to fall, and the island of Manhattan undulated like a frozen ocean, the yacht-like station wagon cutting its course across the concrete waves. The street traffic went down and the sidewalk traffic went up, began to gather along with newspapers on street corners, on steps and on stoops. A multitude of people, sweating, swearing, talking. Kids danced under a fire hydrant that cascaded a rainbow-tinged arc of water into the air while their elders talked amongst themselves outside of a furniture store with no furniture and no glass left in the frontage. Cars slept along the curbs and Hopper saw people sleeping alongside, the people of the city worn down and worn out along with the buildings, along with the streets, as the station wagon headed up the island.

Leroy cut left, toward the Hudson, then he pointed the car

north again. Hopper looked past the driver, toward the river, toward the hulking superstructure of the old West Side Elevated Highway. A rusting monument to the failures of a city too poor to dismantle it, too poor to make it good for traffic again, too poor to do anything but leave it beached like some colossal monster of myth along nearly the entire western length of Manhattan. In the winter of 1973, a part of the decaying highway had collapsed, down on Fourteenth Street—Hopper recalled—under the weight of a dump truck carrying asphalt for the highway's own repair. That collapse had closed it for good. That more of the highway hadn't collapsed since was a surprise to everyone; that the empty roadway was still there four years later was a surprise to no one.

The car turned back east and then north, as Leroy followed a route that existed only inside his head. Hopper sat back and watched the city sink into ruin around them.

There was a fire somewhere east, the black smoke rising in an almost vertical column in the still summer air. Looking down the side streets, Hopper saw abandoned cars, abandoned people, abandoned lives. He heard people laughing, people shouting. Kids played street craps out on the sidewalk, wads of greenbacks changing hands, comfortable in the knowledge that there were no cops here to stop them. Old men and old women pushed supermarket trolleys of junk while young men and women pushed junk into their veins on street corners, not bothering to keep their dark business to dark streets and dead buildings.

As they pulled up at a traffic light, somewhere in Harlem, a police cruiser pulled up alongside them, on Hopper's side. Hopper resisted the urge to look. He just sat where he was, staring ahead, watching the lights, all the while feeling the eyes of the cops on him. Then the light changed and the cop car didn't move. Leroy pushed the accelerator and the station wagon heaved forward with a lurch. Only after a few seconds did Hopper look in the rearview, watching as the cruiser finally engaged gears and made a right turn.

Hopper sat more upright, and rolled his neck. Next to him, Leroy clicked his tongue, then spoke.

"You ready for all this, man?"

Hopper turned to Leroy. The young man had his eyes fixed on the road ahead, his free hand turning circles in the air outside as he drove. Another change of gears, the wheel released, the car listing to the left.

Hopper refocused his attention on the road ahead. *Yes, I'm good,* he told himself, and then he told it to himself again before saying it out loud.

Leroy said nothing but hissed between his teeth. Hopper glanced at him, and saw the driver shaking his head softly, his Afro bobbing softly from side to side.

"Are *you* good, Leroy?"

Leroy frowned but didn't answer.

"You have to tell me," said Hopper. "Because I'm good and I need *you* to be good. You know what we're going into. I don't. So I need you to be good, or else this is going to get real difficult real fast."

Leroy's frown continued to deepen.

"Leroy?"

The car began to slow. Leroy nodded ahead, his frown turning into a lick of the lips as his nostrils flared. "We got company," he said.

Hopper looked ahead. Dusk had gathered; the streetlights were flickering on. They were at the top of Manhattan somewhere—Hopper had lost track—but surely there wasn't much farther to go. There wasn't much traffic. In fact, their boat was the only thing on the road.

The way ahead was blocked.

There were only four of them, but that was four too many for Hopper's liking. They stood across the middle of the lane, two black men, one white man, one black woman. The woman stood a little in front, her hands deep in the pockets of a white baseball jacket one size too big, which she wore over a red bikini top, with white jeans tight at the thigh and flared at the calf finishing off the ensemble. Behind her, the men slouched, shoulders angled, like they were posing for a magazine photo shoot with their bare chests underneath sleeveless leather jackets, bandannas tied around their heads.

The woman was smiling. Her companions were not.

Leroy brought the wagon to a halt in front of the group. The woman walked toward them until she could rap a knuckle on the hood, then she moved around to the driver's side window. Leroy retracted his arm into the car for the first time since he had started driving. The woman leaned on the door with an elbow.

"Hey, hey, hey," said Leroy. "What's up, Martha W.?"

Beside him, Hopper shifted a little, and watched Leroy. The young man's demeanor had changed—he wasn't nervous, exactly, but it seemed that meeting the others had given him a new, different kind of energy.

Martha smiled at Leroy, her jaw working on a stick of gum. She was younger than Hopper but older than Leroy, perhaps late twenties, and she had in her posture something that Hopper recognized instantly.

Authority.

Martha looked at Hopper, her gaze lazy, then she turned back to Leroy.

"So where you been, little brother? I was starting to get worried," she said, without an ounce of concern in her voice.

Little brother.

Hopper felt himself tense. He didn't know what he was expecting, but he wasn't sure Leroy's sister was quite it. The way Leroy had talked, his desire to get his sister out of the gang, he'd imagined the woman—Martha—to be as afraid as Leroy.

The woman standing by the car was anything but afraid.

Leroy patted the wheel with both hands.

"Hey, you know, been around, been around," he said, the grin on his face looking perhaps a little too forced for Hopper's liking. But if Martha noticed, she didn't show it. Instead she nodded and turned her gum-chewing grin at Hopper.

"We all good here, Leroy?"

Leroy nodded quickly, patting the wheel again. "Oh yeah, Martha W. Oh yeah, never doubt it, girl, never doubt it. Oh hey, this is the guy I was telling the Saint about. Hopper. Hopper, this is my sister, Martha."

Martha paused in her chewing, but only for a moment. "Right. Okay." Then she stood tall and waved at the others. The trio of men—boys, really, the three of them maybe the same age as Leroy—finished their game of statues and piled into the back of the car. Martha, meanwhile, walked around the front and got into the front passenger side. She pushed against Hopper with her hip, her gum smacking loudly in his ear. Hopper moved toward Leroy. Martha grinned at Hopper, then leaned over and gave Leroy a nod.

"When I heard you were coming back I thought we would meet you, catch a ride, you know."

Leroy put the wagon into gear, and adjusted his grip on the wheel.

"West 207th and Decker," said his sister.

Leroy paused. "What?"

Martha sat back, and put a hand on Hopper's shoulder. She leaned on his side, like it was high school and she was a cheerleader and he was a jock.

"We've got a little job to do before we get home," she said. "And we need to see what our new friend here is made of. You don't mind a little detour, do you, fresh meat?"

Hopper turned his head to face Martha, so close that his nose almost touched hers.

"I don't mind," he said. "And the name is Hopper."

Martha grinned and the trio in the back laughed, one of

them slapping the top of the front bench seat by Hopper's head.

"Oh yeah, let's roll, let's roll!" said the man, and the three in the back hollered as Martha laughed.

Hopper looked at Leroy.

Leroy nodded.

"Oh, I'm good, my brother, I'm all good."

Then he shoved the shift and they headed for their detour.

CHAPTER TWENTY-ONE

CRIMES AND MISDEMEANORS

JULY 8, 1977
UPPER MANHATTAN, NEW YORK

Following Martha's directions, Leroy pulled the station wagon up outside a store with a large plate-glass frontage protected by a grid of heavy metal bars. The three in the back fell quiet as they approached, and for that, Hopper was grateful. En route they had whooped, yelled, and laughed like three teenagers ducking out of school, and Hopper's ears were already ringing. Leroy had stayed quiet, focusing on the driving while his sister had focused on pressing herself against Hopper's side. Hopper sat in the middle, wondering what to expect on this "detour," what they were going to test him on, and weighing up his options, all of which came to round about nothing at all.

Martha had exchanged a few words with the boys in the back, but Hopper still hadn't been introduced to them. A few minutes after they had been collected, there was a flash of orange reflected in the windshield, and the sickly sweet smoke of some very strong marijuana began to fill the car. The boys in the back passed the joint around themselves and then to Martha, who had taken a deep drag before passing it to Hopper.

Hopper had partaken. He had to do whatever he needed to in order to fit in, and, on the face of it, a little weed probably wasn't going to impede him too much. He was careful to hold the harsh smoke in his mouth as long as he could, to give the impression of inhalation as he passed the joint back to Martha.

She took it. "Little brother doesn't need to get some calm?"

Hopper glanced at her, realizing he hadn't offered it the other way to Leroy. But Leroy spoke up, covering for him.

"No, I'm good, Martha W., I'm good."

Now they sat in the station wagon outside the store. It was evening and the store was closed, but from within came the faint glow of a light from somewhere at the back, the workers still on-site, putting the place to bed.

Hopper craned his neck to get a better look out of the windshield. It was an electronics store, and a fairly big one at that. Behind the acre of plate glass and metal bars stood an array of high-end equipment. Huge black speaker stacks, their fronts covered with heavy grilles or the smooth glossy black of horns. There were consoles, small and large, some more like tables, covered with buttons and sliders and dials and gauges. There were other items that looked more familiar—reel-to-reel tape decks, decks that looked like they took eight-track cartridges. A series of turntables on huge silver plinths.

It was AV equipment, but not the kind you would have in your living room. This was industrial, professional-grade studio gear. None of the items on display had price tags because if you needed to know how much they cost, they were most certainly not for you.

One of the boys in the back seat clapped his hands.

"Let's get it on, let's get it on, let's get it *on!*"

They piled out of the back. Leroy exited on his side. Hopper felt Martha's eyes on him as he went to follow, grabbing the steering wheel to pull himself along, but he felt a hand grab his biceps. He stopped and turned to his fellow passenger.

"Something to keep you going," Martha said, pulling a small blue plastic bag from the pocket of her baseball jacket. She rolled down the sides, exposing a multicolored collection of pills, from which she plucked a single circular, white tablet with her long, red-painted nails.

Hopper watched her. She smiled and passed him the pill. He took it without pause and placed it in his mouth, holding it under his tongue. He knew he couldn't afford to show any hesitation, any uncertainty, not now.

The corners of Martha's mouth moved up in a wicked grin, and she pulled herself out of the car. Hopper turned to exit the opposite side, quickly swiping the pill from his mouth. It disintegrated between his fingers, and, feeling around his mouth with his tongue, he felt a chalky residue. He only hoped that the drug was not effective at the tiny dose he had been unable to avoid taking.

Outside the store, the three boys were fidgeting, bouncing on their heels, talking fast and low to each other. Leroy stood to one side, his arms folded as he leaned against the store windows.

One of the boys gave a whoop and started shadowboxing. The others clapped and laughed.

The light inside the store went out. The group stopped, and all turned at once. Their presence had been noticed by whoever was inside.

Then Martha emerged from the rear of the station wagon, a small sledgehammer swinging from one thin arm. One of the boys gave her a wolf whistle as she went up to the front door of the establishment and, without even a break in her step, swung.

The handle and lock mechanism twisted under the blow, embedding themselves farther into the wood. A few more blows from Martha and the whole assembly split away from the body of the door. The lock remained in place, now shattered against the frame, but the three boys were able to push the door open with ease and run inside.

Leroy followed Martha. Hopper followed Leroy.

The store was huge but well packed on the inside, more of the professional sound equipment lined up on platforms between towering stacks of amplifiers and PA system speakers. As the boys ran to the back of the store, they shoved at the speaker towers and mixing desks, sending them tottering to the floor and sliding off their displays. As the main lights flickered on, Hopper watched them carve a path of meaningless destruction as they headed to the back.

Hopper paused, his vision slipping sideways. For a moment there were six boys running, then there were none, and when he blinked again there was an older white man holding a shotgun and shouting something.

The shotgun blast brought Hopper back to his senses and his vision back to stability as plasterwork drifted down around him from where the high warning shot had caught the ceiling. He'd been too slow with the pill, and, combined with the pot he had been unable to prevent inhaling, the effects of both were starting to kick in. He felt light-headed, like he had a buzz from one too many beers, but without the fog of drunkenness.

The screaming snapped him back to reality again. He blinked and looked at the old man. The shotgun was on the floor, along with a fair amount of the old man's blood. Hopper's fist was covered in more of the same. That same fist was curled around the old man's collar, choking him as he pushed him against the back wall of the store, the old man standing on tiptoe as Hopper held him up.

Hopper blinked and shook his head. He didn't remember wrestling the shotgun off the owner. Didn't remember punching him. Didn't remember holding him against the wall. The world started to slide sideways again; the old man whimpered,

Hopper pushed him harder against the wall, and bit the inside of his own cheek.

The pain was small but electric, clearing his mind. Hopper glanced over his shoulder at the commotion behind him.

Leroy and the three boys were stacking up equipment into piles that they could manhandle out of the store as piles. Amplifiers, turntables, boxes of cables, boxes of records, a speaker cabinet the size of a small refrigerator.

There was a sound from somewhere else. Hopper turned the other way and saw a door open to a small back office. Inside, Martha was shoving armfuls of paperwork out of her way as she went through every drawer in the big desk that filled most of the room. Finally, she found what she was looking for—a large steel lockbox. She lifted it and shook, and from within came the distinct sound of paper money and coins. Hopper watched as she fiddled with the lock on the front for a moment before she gave up and, swinging the cash box by the handle, ran out of the office. She stopped behind the counter and ducked down to pick up the owner's discarded shotgun, before heading out of the store.

The store owner made a gurgling sound under the pressure of Hopper's grip. Hopper turned and looked at the man. His eyes were full of tears, and his nose continued to stream blood that was bright red, the color dancing in Hopper's vision.

They locked gazes for a few seconds. Then someone called out for Hopper.

"I'm sorry," Hopper whispered to the man. He released the pressure and stood back. The store owner telescoped downward, collapsing onto the bloodstained carpet. He tried to crawl toward the back office, but gave up after only a few inches and lay there, his body heaving with sobs as he fought for breath.

"I'm sorry," said Hopper again.

Then he wiped his hand on his T-shirt, and ran out of the store.

DECEMBER 26, 1984

HOPPER'S CABIN
HAWKINS, INDIANA

Hopper stood and, under the pretense of having a stretch, moved from the table and did a circuit around the den. In reality, although the break was welcome, the memory of the store robbery the Vipers had forced him into was not a pretty one, and while he had kept the finer detail out of the story for El, there were a few inescapable and unpleasant facts that he knew she would ask about and that he'd had to deal with. He stopped over by the TV and linked his hands behind his head, his back to the red table and the girl still sitting at it.

"It's okay," said El.

Hopper dropped his arms and turned around.

"What?"

El shuffled around in her chair. "Not your fault."

Hopper frowned and shook his head, but El continued.

"They made you . . ." she said, her hands on the top of the chair as she twisted around to look at Hopper. "Papa made me . . . Sometimes . . ."

Hopper moved back to the table and sat down. El righted herself in the chair but kept her eyes on the table.

"Sometimes what, kid?"

"Felt like it . . . wasn't me. Like I was . . . watching." She looked up. "Like the men."

"What men?"

"Behind the mirror."

Hopper's heart fluttered in his chest, and, as he reached over and ruffled El's hair, he felt hot, wet tears gathering under his eyes.

"What happened next?" asked El.

Hopper paused and looked at El, a bit uncertain. She looked up at him expectantly, completely unfazed by the dark memory she'd just shared.

"Well," said Hopper, rubbing his face. "Next, I met the Vipers and their leader."

At this, El's eyes went wide.

"You met Saint John?"

"I did."

"Okay," said El, getting comfortable again. "I'm ready."

CHAPTER TWENTY-TWO

VIPER'S NEST

JULY 8, 1977
SOUTH BRONX, NEW YORK

If anything, the remainder of the journey north was even louder than it had been before. High on adrenaline, the boys in the back of the wagon talked loud and fast about what they'd just done. Hopper couldn't follow any of it, their conversation a mix of street slang that was both foreign and just far too fast for him to even process. He felt nauseous, and cold, and when he moved his head the world seemed to move at a different speed than his own body.

Hopper closed his eyes. He could feel the cracked leather underneath him, Martha's hip against his, Leroy's leg moving as he worked the pedals of the now fully laden station wagon. How they had fit everything in, Hopper didn't know, but the car now sounded as sick and tired as he felt, the motor's death rattle replaced by a deep, hollow growl that surely heralded the end of the road for this particular example of General Motors engineering.

"Hey, look alive, look alive," said Leroy.

Hopper snapped his eyes open and looked at the driver. As the car slowed, Leroy lifted a finger from the wheel and pointed ahead.

They'd crossed into the Bronx seemingly only a few minutes before. Now, they'd come into an alley of sorts. They were surrounded on three sides by flat, high walls. Dead ahead was a featureless expanse with a huge set of double doors set into it. As the headlights of the station wagon crawled up the doors, a smaller, regular-sized portal opened on one side and a couple of men filed out. The one in front gave a wave to the car, then the pair moved to the double doors. Together, they operated the chunky levers of the door's mechanism, then pushed, swinging the doors inward. When there was enough space to pass, Leroy drove forward.

It was a warehouse, the space cavernous and far from empty. The car rolled past containers, some stacked two-high, around which were smaller piles of packing crates, some exposed, others covered under thick tarpaulin. Farther in, Hopper saw a row of angular, almost skeletal motocross motorbikes, parked up along a wall. There were other cars here too, and next to them a large flatbed truck, the rear covered with more tarpaulin, concealing something large and angular beneath.

Leroy stopped the car at the end of the row. Straight ahead, in the corner of the warehouse, a social area of sorts had been established, and was alive with activity. Flames licked out of four oil barrels, and spread around them was a collection of furniture—couches and chairs, some still wrapped in plastic. There were tables, too, beanbags, folding chairs, camp chairs, dining room chairs that could have come from the governor's mansion.

As soon as the vehicle came to a halt, they were surrounded, the doors and trunk opened as the unloading began. The trio in the back hopped out and were welcomed by the others with backslaps and hoots.

In the front of the car, Martha, Hopper, and Leroy sat. Leroy killed the engine.

"Welcome home, welcome home, welcome home," he said. He looked across at Martha. Hopper sat in the middle, looking at both of them, then Martha got out of the car.

Leroy let out a long, slow breath.

"You good, man?" he asked, quietly.

"Ask me later," said Hopper, and he got out of the car.

Immediately, everyone in the warehouse froze. Hopper felt every eye on him and heard nothing but the crackle of the fires. He looked around him, making an effort to meet the cold gaze of everyone as they stared. It might have been Martha's pill, and some of the pot, but he suddenly felt conspicuous, like he'd walked into the middle of the Vipers dressed in his old beat-cop uniform, badge shining proudly on his breast pocket.

Leroy moved next to him and wrapped his arm tightly around Hopper's neck.

"Hey, let me introduce you to some folks, my brother!" he said, very loudly, with a laugh. At this, everyone else seemed to relax, just a notch. The unloading of the stolen goods from the wagon resumed, but people glanced at each other as they worked. Hopper watched as Martha extracted the cash box from the back of the car and stalked off with it under her arm toward the other side of the warehouse, where there was a stack of offices jutting out into the space, an external metal stairwell rising up along one side. There were lights on in the offices. Hopper's eyes followed the stairs up—and then he saw him.

He was standing in the window of the top office, four levels up. The lights were on and bright, rendering the man into nothing but a black silhouette.

Was that Saint John himself?

Hopper felt a wave of vertigo sweeping over him. He closed his eyes and pointed his face at the floor.

"Hey, brother, you feel me?"

Hopper blinked and looked up. There were several gang members milling around, all watching Hopper. Men and women, black, white, Hispanic, Asian. The youngest looked very young—barely teenagers, Hopper thought—and the oldest were a pair of white men, gray and grizzled, both with long beards like they were twins from a forgotten fairy tale. All the faces were hard, expressions set.

And, as Hopper had expected, all wore the same sleeveless leather jackets that Martha's three pals wore. Hopper glanced around, noticing for the first time the red serpent symbol emblazoned on the backs of the men who were shifting the AV equipment from their raid. But apart from the addition of the jackets, it seemed that the others still felt the need to retain the colors of their previous gangs.

"Okay, Smoker, Cookie, Betty, Liz, Jackie O.," said Leroy, pointing to each member of the gang in turn. Hopper gave them a nod, which was returned only by the one called Smoker, a clean-shaven young man with long brown hair in perfect Farrah Fawcett style, the zipped, one-piece light blue jumpsuit underneath the Viper jacket more suited to a night at Studio 54 than the grungy Bronx warehouse.

Next to him, the trio of black women looked at Hopper, their jaws working gum almost in unison as they looked him up and down. The three of them were wearing identical denim overalls over white T-shirts, the legs cut short to show the height of their heavy combat boots. The women leaned on each other's shoulders, the only difference in their outfits being the color of the elasticized ribbons used to hold their high ponytails in place—red for Betty, blue for Liz, white for Jackie O.

Hopper pursed his lips, and Jackie O. popped her gum at

him. Standing beside her, Cookie was the odd one out, clad in tight black jeans and matching T-shirt, his dyed-black hair—which contrasted sharply with the pallor of his skin—cut into a long, soft bob, his bangs hanging at exactly eye level. Hopper wasn't even convinced the man was looking at him.

Leroy guided Hopper around the next grouping. "This here is Bravo, City, and Reuben."

Bravo was a woman with long blond hair, wearing a tight T-shirt with the curled title logo of *Three's Company* flowing across it. The T-shirt was tucked into denim shorts and she had her thumbs looped behind a huge belt buckle shaped like a sheriff's star, which went with the tasseled suede cowboy boots on her feet.

City was a shirtless, rake-thin teenager, his ribs painfully obvious, his hair as long and flowing as Bravo's. He made a clicking sound at the back of his throat, which Hopper realized was a laugh, and nudged Reuben, who stood more than a foot taller, his arms folded, his impassive expression mostly hidden behind a tight black beard only a fraction darker than his skin.

Reuben's attire of striped Mets T-shirt—number 42—and jeans was, at least, approaching somewhere close to normal, thought Hopper.

Whatever normal is these days.

"And Leroy Washington forgets his own again."

Leroy spun around at the voice. Hopper watched a heavyset black man approach, wiping his hands on a greasy cloth. He was wearing the standard jacket over a bare chest slick with sweat, and over one shoulder was slung a pair of heavy-duty gloves. The man's face was smeared with soot and grease, like he'd been working on something mechanical.

"My boy, my boy, my *boy*," said Leroy. *"Damn!"* The two men grabbed each other's hands and drew together for a chest-bumping hug, the big man thumping the much smaller Leroy on the back with the hand holding the rag.

"You were gone too long, Leroy. Too long. People were worried. People were talking."

Leroy pulled away and shook his head. "No, man, we're good, we're good."

At this, the big man stopped smiling. "No, Leroy, people were talking. You feel me? People were *talking*."

Leroy licked his lips and shrugged. "Well, you know, what can I say. I just needed a little time and space, that's all. Hell, this ain't no kindergarten. You know what I'm saying? A man's gotta get some clean air once in a while. You know?"

The big man stared at Leroy, then his face cracked into a wide smile. "I feel you, dude, I feel you," he said, "and I heard you had some good hunting, too." He turned to Hopper. "This the new one?"

"Aye, aye," said Leroy, putting his arm around Hopper's neck again. "This here is my man Hopper. And he's all good, man, all good." He turned to Hopper. "You good, right?"

"Oh yeah, all good," said Hopper.

The big man looked Hopper up and down, then he chewed something and spat it onto the cement floor. Leroy patted Hopper on the chest.

"This here is my main man Lincoln."

Hopper nodded a greeting. Lincoln held out his hand. Hopper took it, only to find Lincoln grabbing his forearm, his vise-like grip tightening around the crook of his elbow. Lincoln pulled Hopper toward him; Hopper tensed, then realized the big man was giving him the same welcome thud on the back as he had with Leroy.

As Lincoln hooked his chin over Hopper's shoulder, Hopper felt his hot breath in his ear.

"You better be real, man," whispered Lincoln.

Hopper pulled away from Lincoln. Lincoln just stared at him.

"Hey, you call this a welcome party?" asked Leroy, slapping

Lincoln on the arm. "I am disappointed, truly I am. Come on, we got to celebrate."

Lincoln raised an eyebrow, then chuckled and shook his head. He turned and headed toward the couches set up in a low orbit around the burning oil drums, Leroy right behind him.

Hopper stayed where he was and looked around. Most of the others had got back to whatever the hell it was they had been doing. The goods from the station wagon had been stacked over on one side of the space, alongside the other crates and boxes.

Hopper looked back toward the office area. There was no sign of Martha, and looking up at the top level, he saw that the man in the window had gone.

"Hey, you need a drink or what?"

Hopper turned and saw Lincoln silhouetted by the fires, holding up a bottle of something.

Hopper took a breath and headed over.

Hopper could hold his own, this he knew, but even so, it was getting ridiculous. There were three empty beer bottles by the dirty recliner on which he sat, and he had nursed the half-full fourth in his lap for who knew how long. The beer had been warm but there was no shortage of it, crates of the stuff stacked up against the far wall. The heat from the oil drum fires wasn't as intense as he had thought, the vast warehouse space soaking up the heat in the air high above their heads. Hopper looked up, and could see now the rusting struts and girders that held the roof in place, some of which had come away from their fittings and hung partway down like broken tree branches.

The others gathered around the motley collection of furniture had long since moved on from beer. Bottles of whiskey, vodka, and other liquors Hopper couldn't place were shared.

Several spliffs had been lit up and passed around, Hopper managing to keep them moving without partaking himself.

To Hopper's surprise, the gang members didn't really seem that interested in him. He sat and listened and watched, nodded and laughed when the others did, even if he couldn't follow most of what was said. As the newcomer, a stranger brought right into the middle of the gang, Hopper knew he needed to play it cool. He was the invited guest, and he knew the hospitality of the Vipers could turn on a dime if they decided that they didn't like him, or that he didn't belong, or that he was here for a reason other than the one Leroy had given them.

He also knew that he was being watched. Lincoln sat opposite, and Hopper felt his eyes on him a lot of the time. No doubt he would be reporting back on the new recruit to Saint John.

Then Martha reappeared, to the hollers of some. She smiled and laughed and headed straight for Hopper. To his surprise, she sat down on the arm of his chair, eliciting a series of wolf whistles and more laughter.

She looked around at the others, then looked down at Hopper. She grabbed the beer from his hand, took a long swig from the bottle, then stood. She held out her hand to him.

"Come with me," she said.

Hopper glanced at the others, then took her hand and let himself be pulled up. The wolf whistles returned; Hopper glanced over his shoulder, and caught Leroy's eye. He gave a slight shake of the head, his expression set, before taking a swig from a bottle of what looked like tequila. Lincoln continued to watch in silence.

Hopper allowed himself to be led by Martha's hand as they left the circle and headed toward the office area.

"Ah, where are we going?"

"The Saint wants to see you."

Hopper stopped where he was. Martha let go of his hand, but kept on walking, glancing once over her shoulder at him before continuing to the stairwell.

Hopper looked behind him. The rest of the group had gotten back to their evening.

Then he turned around and looked up. There, standing in the window on the top level, was the outline of the man again.

Saint John. Leader of the Vipers.

Suddenly sober, clearheaded—and afraid—Hopper followed after Martha.

CHAPTER TWENTY-THREE

BROTHERS IN ARMS

JULY 8, 1977
SOUTH BRONX, NEW YORK

The administrative space of the old warehouse was a warren of corridors and offices that was far bigger than Hopper would have expected. There was no clue what kind of industry had used the building in the first place, and most of the offices he passed had been cleared out of their original contents, and were now mostly being used for storage. As Martha led the way, Hopper glanced through every open door, and saw packing crate after packing crate, all identical, all unmarked.

"So you're a cop?"

Hopper turned his attention back to Martha, who was still walking ahead but glancing over her shoulder at him.

"I *was*."

Martha's eyes flicked over Hopper, then she turned her head back around.

"Is that it?" asked Hopper. "You don't want to know any more?"

"Why, should I know more?"

Hopper didn't respond. He still hadn't quite figured Martha out, and she was the first Viper he'd met who had directly questioned his past. But she couldn't have been the only one to be thinking about it.

Including the leader, Saint John himself.

Martha led him to the top level of the block, and into an office. The space was large, with wraparound windows on two walls that allowed any management executive who occupied the room to look down at the warehouse space. There was a long conference table in the center of the room—Hopper had no idea how on earth it had been brought in—and over on the other side, facing the windows, was a mammoth desk of matching design. Behind the desk were two doors, both closed. Narrow filing cabinets stood against the other wall, next to a set of wider drawers Hopper knew were designed for large-scale documents: plans, blueprints, architectural drawings, and the like.

But it was the man standing in the window that Hopper's attention was drawn to. He had his back to the room as he looked out over his domain. He wore a purple robe, tied at the waist, that stopped mid-thigh, like some kind of martial arts instructor.

"Welcome to the Vipers," he said. Then he turned around.

The man was older than Hopper, his hair razored into a brutal crew cut, a chinstrap beard clinging to his jaw. His nose had at some point been broken, and he wore mirrored aviator glasses. As the man stepped closer, Hopper could see his own reflection loom large in the silver lenses. Underneath the robe he wore a black silk shirt, unbuttoned almost to his middle, the collar turned up. Around his neck was a silver chain, two small rectangular medallions sitting against his bare chest.

A pair of dog tags. Hopper had a pair of just like it, sitting in a drawer at home beside the bed.

Before Saint John could speak again, Hopper took a chance. He nodded, gesturing to the tags.

"What unit?"

Saint John stopped. Behind him, Hopper heard Martha shift position.

"I was First Infantry," said Hopper. "Did two tours." He shook his head. "Saw a lot of shit go down out there, did my job, they gave me a medal shaped like a star and sent me back to the good old U.S. of A."

Saint John smiled, showing a row of big, brilliantly white teeth. He held out his hand, and Hopper took it. The man's grip was strong, but Hopper matched it.

"101st Airborne."

Hopper grinned. "The Screaming Eagles."

"Best goddamn time of my life." Saint John cocked his head. "You were decorated?"

"Bronze Star."

Saint John nodded in quiet appreciation. "How I envy you, soldier. I was seconded for special duties. They kept me out there longer than almost anyone, but what I was doing didn't qualify for any kind of medal, star-shaped or otherwise."

"I didn't ask for mine. I just did my duty."

Saint John's smile tightened. "Oh, we were all just doing our duty, weren't we?"

The two locked gazes for a few seconds, Hopper looking at nothing but his own eyes reflected in the leader's glasses. Then Saint John turned away and moved to the big table. Hopper glanced at Martha, who stood by the door chewing gum and looking bored, then joined the gang leader at the table, the surface of which was covered with a large map of New York

City and what looked like blueprints of some kind. But before he could get a good look, Saint John picked up all the documents, folded them in half, then in half again.

"Leroy tells me you've gotten into a little spot of bother with your own—the NYPD?" said Saint John. He glanced up at Hopper as he aligned the edges of the paper sheets.

Hopper shrugged. "Nothing I can't handle."

Saint John nodded. "Good. Because that's your business, not mine. You bring any of your own trouble here, and you'll find that you're not quite as welcome as you think." He finished fussing with the papers, and then snapped his head up, the mirrored lenses looking right at Hopper. "The Vipers have been welcoming, have they not?"

"Oh yeah, they're a fine bunch, just swell."

Saint John's smile flickered for just a second. Then he turned to the wide file cabinet and, pulling a set of keys from under his robe, unlocked a drawer, opened it, and then slid the papers inside. Drawer closed and relocked, he returned the keys to his pocket.

"The Vipers are not just any common gang of thugs and thieves," said Saint John, his back to the room, his hands resting against the file drawer. "In fact, I don't like that term at all." He turned around, and Hopper once more found himself facing his own reflection. "We are an *organization*. You could even call us a congregation. One that I have devoted my *soul* to. Do you understand that, Mr. Hopper? *Can* you understand that?"

Hopper licked his lips. "Listen, I'm here because I'm looking for somewhere to belong. I came back from that hellhole and was expected to carry on like nothing had ever happened over there. Okay, it was a long time ago. And yes, I was just doing my duty, but I did my job and I did it well, and then they said so long and thanks and here's a medal you put at the back of a drawer and forget about."

Hopper took a step closer to Saint John. He stared at himself reflected in the mirrored glasses, and he saw his stubble, the bags under his eyes, and the blood down his shirt from what he'd done at the AV showroom.

He felt the adrenaline course through his veins and he used it to focus his words, sharpen his mind.

"So, yes, I did my job, like we all did out there. But how are you supposed to come back from that? We went to war for reasons I thought I understood but now I'm not so sure, and I came back to what? To this? One war zone to another, swapping one jungle for another. Only this time there was no job to do, no orders to follow, no country to fight for. So, yes, I'm looking for somewhere to belong. I'm looking for something to fight for. I didn't find it at the NYPD. So maybe I'll find it here." Hopper paused. He glanced down at the dog tags around Saint John's neck, and saw the man's chest moving—he was breathing heavily. "And I think that's why you're here too, right?"

Hopper looked up into the mirrored glasses. Saint John didn't speak. Martha chewed her gum.

Then Saint John laid a hand on Hopper's shoulder.

"Don't worry, my brother, you have come to the right place. You have come not only to your own salvation, but the salvation of all of us, of this whole city, this hell on earth." He nodded, then turned back to the table. He leaned over it, elbows locked. The table was empty, the plans put away, but Hopper found himself following the mirrored gaze of the Viper's leader, as though the mysterious plan that his organization was engaged in would somehow materialize before his eyes.

"The time is coming, Mr. Hopper. Our time."

"The Day of the Serpent?"

Saint John dipped his head as he gave a chuckle.

"I think Leroy has spoken out of turn."

Hopper shook his head. "I'm here, aren't I?"

Saint John looked up at Hopper. He tilted his head, this way, that way.

"There is still much to be done," he said. "The city still has much to give me before I grant it sweet release."

Hopper kept his eyes locked on his own doubled reflection. *Sweet release?* He didn't understand what Saint John was talking about, but one thing was clear. The man was crazy.

No, scratch that. That was unfair, and Hopper knew it. He'd had to dig deep, dragging up long-buried feelings about Vietnam, but it had worked. And it had given him a fast insight into Saint John's mental state.

No, he wasn't crazy.

Saint John was *damaged*. Hopper had seen it plenty of times. War did that to people—Hopper included. The only difference between Hopper and Saint John was that Hopper, despite what he had just said, *had* found a purpose again. He had come back, and had wanted to make a difference, and had found a path that would let him get that work.

Saint John had taken a different path. Hopper wondered where their lives had diverged, whether it could have been as simple as one single decision that took them from a common history to such different places.

Saint John pushed himself up from the table. He nodded at Martha. "Take him downstairs. He can join Leroy and Lincoln's crew." He glanced at Hopper. "I think we will find much work for your idle hands."

And then he walked across the room, back to the big windows. He stood where he had been standing before, hands clasped behind his back, as he looked down at the warehouse.

Hopper glanced at Martha. She had stopped chewing her gum and looked, for the first time since he'd met her . . . different, somehow. Not afraid, or nervous; but some of the authority—the *arrogance*—he had seen had gone. She looked smaller, younger.

Like Leroy had, back at the precinct.

"Serve me, Hopper, and serve the Vipers, and there will be a place prepared for you beside the burning throne."

Hopper looked at the gang leader's back, and then realized that in the reflection of the big windows, Saint John could see the whole room behind him.

Hopper didn't say anything. Then he heard Martha move to the door.

"Come on," she said. "I could use a drink."

CHAPTER TWENTY-FOUR

EMERGENCY BRIEFING

JULY 9, 1977
BROOKLYN, NEW YORK

This was it, it had to be.

Delgado sat in her customary position somewhere in the midpoint of the 65th Precinct's main briefing room while, around her, her fellow detectives filed in and took their own seats. It was a Saturday, and although Delgado's shift had her working anyway, after a few minutes it became very clear that Captain LaVorgna had canceled everybody's weekend. As the detectives filled the available seats, more kept arriving. Delgado recognized members of Sergeant Connelly's night shift, forced to stand at the back and around the edges of the room.

This was it.

Delgado braced herself to hear what her partner had been set up for. She turned in her chair, catching Harris's eye, gesturing like she didn't know why the room was so full. "Maybe they finally caught Sam," Harris said before he buried his nose in his coffee.

Captain LaVorgna's arrival drew the rumble of conversation to a halt. The briefing room had a lectern at the front, which the captain rarely used in his addresses, leaving the more detail-oriented briefings to Sergeant McGuigan. But this morning was different. The captain strode to the lectern, placed a folder on it, then squeezed the sides of the wooden top with both hands. He looked up at the assembled officers, then back down at his file.

"At oh-two-hundred hours this morning, officers from this precinct attended a shooting homicide in South Slope. Two victims were found at the scene, both of whom were informants known to be working with detectives at this precinct. A search of the scene uncovered a discarded weapon identified as police-issue. Ballistics analysis was carried out immediately at the central crime lab, confirming the weapon was the one used to kill the two victims."

Delgado felt her face flush. She sat in place, unmoving, staring at the captain as he gave further details of the crime scene. It felt like any reaction at all would somehow give the game away.

But, boy, this was *bad*.

The captain paused in his summary and glanced across the room. Delgado risked a slight movement, turning a little toward Harris. He was sitting two chairs along, shaking his head. Delgado saw other officers looking at each other.

The captain cleared his throat, regaining the attention of the room.

"The weapon is registered to Detective James Hopper."

At this, a collective gasp filled the room. The captain looked up again as officers began asking questions. He held his hand up, and the room fell quiet.

"Detective Hopper has not reported for duty in more than twenty-four hours, despite being on shift, and we believe he is on the run. As such, James Hopper is currently our prime suspect for the double homicide. All leave is canceled until further notice. Sergeants McGuigan and Connelly will further brief their shifts."

The captain opened his mouth again, then closed it. Then he sighed, and rubbed the bridge of his nose.

"Listen," he said, "I know this looks bad, and believe me, it *is* bad. But we don't know what happened yet. So I suggest we get on with our work and solve this case, no matter what the outcome. We have a duty to this city and I expect each and every one of us to carry out that duty. Do I make myself clear?"

There was a murmur of assent. Delgado didn't join in, and when she looked back at Harris, she noticed that several of the other detectives were now watching her.

"That is all," said the captain. "Sergeant McGuigan, please."

McGuigan peeled off from the wall where he had been standing, and the captain clapped a hand on his shoulder as the two passed each other. Delgado watched the captain leave the briefing room as her sergeant began his own briefing.

"Okay, folks, listen up, and listen good, because none of us are going anywhere until we get this cleared."

As the detectives and uniforms settled in for the extended emergency briefing, Delgado opened her notebook and began to diligently record the sergeant's key points, keeping her head down, her eyes on the paper, and trying very hard to hope her partner really knew what he was doing.

CHAPTER TWENTY-FIVE

SECRET MESSAGES

JULY 9, 1977
BROOKLYN, NEW YORK

As Delgado watched Diane through the two-way mirror, she ran the various options available to her through her mind. In the other room, Diane sat at the interview table with her arms folded and a firm expression on her face as she looked straight ahead at the mirror. Delgado knew she couldn't be seen, but that didn't make her feel any more comfortable.

Bringing Diane in for questioning about her husband's absence—Delgado refused to think of it as a "disappearance," given what she knew—was standard procedure.

Holding her in the interview room, however, was not.

Because Diane wasn't a suspect, or even a witness. A car had been sent to collect her from home, and after arranging to leave Sara with the Van Sabbens upstairs, Diane had been whisked to the 65th Precinct and taken straight to LaVorgna's office, where the captain had informed her of the situation regarding her husband.

Delgado had watched from out in the bull pen—at least until the captain had turned the blinds on his office windows again. While that particular conversation played out in private, Delgado had gone over to Sergeant McGuigan and asked to handle taking Diane's statement. McGuigan had agreed readily—no sooner had the emergency briefing ended than Delgado found herself at the center of a whirlpool of attention, most of her shift and most of the night shift offering their condolences, like they'd just been told Delgado's parents had died. Delgado took them as they came, aware that the only one paying close attention to her reactions was herself. As far as the others were concerned, Hopper was now a bent cop, getting involved in something way beyond what the farm boy from Indiana could handle, with violent results.

Delgado wasn't sure if she was surprised at the speed at which the precinct had turned against Hopper. It seemed that he'd been telling the truth, that he really still was seen as an outsider by many veterans in the department.

Delgado tried not to dwell on how they would have reacted if it had been *her* that Special Agent Gallup had sent into deep cover.

As soon as Diane had emerged from the captain's office, Delgado spirited her away. Diane was clearly pleased to see her, and, while obviously upset, seemed to be taking the captain's news with some resilience.

Now, as she sat in the interview room, Diane looked more annoyed than anything else.

Good on her, thought Delgado. Of course she didn't believe her husband had gotten caught up in a double homicide, let alone been the one to pull the trigger. Delgado wasn't sure how deep the cover went—like, really, were there two bodies cooling in a morgue? Would Gallup have gone that far? Or was it all just an elaborate hoax, one designed to hold together just long enough for Hopper to get into the Vipers and out again?

Delgado didn't have those answers. What she did have was Hopper's wife, secreted away in the interview room. Normally, her interview would have taken place in a meeting room, if not at Delgado's desk. The interview room here was dark and smelly, the ceiling tiles slumping in one corner as damp got to work on the fabric of the building.

The perfect place to scare a suspect.

The perfect place to have a private conversation.

Delgado took a breath and left the observation room. When she entered the interview room, Diane looked up and just shook her head.

"Rosario, just what the hell is going on? I'm really hoping you can give me an explanation here."

Delgado sat opposite. She glanced up at the clock on the wall. Although there was no particular reason *not* to be using the interview room to take Diane's statement, Delgado knew that, sooner or later, someone would come looking for the pair of them. Maybe she was being overcautious, but better that than the opposite.

"We don't really have much time—" Delgado began, before Diane shook her head and lifted her hands from her lap to the table.

"What do you mean?" Diane cocked her head. "Listen, Rosario, there's no way Jim's gotten involved in . . . in whatever the hell this is. Nothing the captain said made any sense."

Diane's face had grown red. She sat back in the chair and rubbed her forehead. Delgado noticed that, despite her bravado, her hand was shaking.

"Listen, Diane, I need to tell you something very important. I want you to listen very carefully, okay? I shouldn't be doing this, but I made a promise to Hopper—"

Diane leaned in. "A promise? Have you spoken to him?"

That was when Delgado heard it—a sound, very faint, from

somewhere behind her. She didn't turn around, but she held Diane's gaze and gave a very small shake of the head. Diane's forehead creased in confusion, but at least Delgado knew she had gotten the message.

Someone was in the observation room. Delgado recognized the sound of the door being closed. It was nothing a suspect would ever notice, and it wouldn't matter if they did, anyway. But one thing was for sure.

Their conversation was no longer private.

Delgado ground her teeth, then reached into her jacket and took out one of her cards and a pen. She quickly flipped the card over, jotted down an address, then slid the card over to Diane, hiding it as best she could under her wrist. Diane, to her credit, followed along, covering the card with her hand and disappearing it under the table.

Just in time.

The interview room door opened, and Captain LaVorgna stepped in.

"Detective Delgado, can I see you in my office please."

Delgado turned in her chair. "Yes, sir, I was just taking Diane's statement—"

"*Now*, if you please, Detective."

With that, the captain stood with one hand on the door handle, the other gesturing for Delgado to leave the room.

Delgado caught Diane's eye, then stood and left the room. Behind her, she heard the captain speaking.

"I'm sorry about this, Mrs. Hopper. I'll have a car take you back home. Thank you for your patience."

Delgado stood with her hands on her hips in front of Captain LaVorgna's desk. The pose was a habit she'd picked up, and most of the time she didn't even know she was doing it.

She did now, though.

The door was closed, as were the blinds. The captain adjusted a few items on his desk, before looking up at his subordinate.

"You can relax, Detective."

"I'm fine how I am, sir. Can you tell me what you wanted to see me about? I've got rather a lot to do now."

The captain nodded. "I can understand your desire to help."

Delgado frowned. "Desire to help? Sir, I'm just doing my job. We've got every detective on this case now, and I would like to go back out there and do my part."

"That won't be necessary."

"Sir, I'm not sure I—"

"A detective partnership is a very special relationship, Delgado. It's a close one, too. There is a lot riding on it, both personally and professionally."

"You don't need to tell me that, sir."

"Actually, Detective, maybe I do, because I'm not sure you're following me." LaVorgna sat back in his chair and tossed a pen onto his desk. "You are too close to this investigation. Not only that, you're still a junior detective, and this is a lot to take in."

Delgado narrowed her eyes, but the captain just sighed.

"Go home, Detective. Take a week's administrative leave, full pay. I won't even record it in the books."

Delgado shook her head. "I really think I can help here, sir."

"And I really think you *can't*, Detective. I want to know that my detectives can work on this case without distraction and without any challenges from others who might think your involvement is inappropriate."

"*Challenges*? Sir, I—"

"Go. Home. That is an order. I'll see you in seven days, and maybe we'll have worked this out by then. I will, of course, call you if anything comes up. Okay?"

Delgado took a deep breath, then nodded.

"Sir."

The captain looked at Delgado, who didn't move.

"You can close the door on your way out, Detective."

Delgado pursed her lips, and left without a word. As she closed the door behind her, she looked over at the clock on the opposite wall of the bull pen.

Then she grabbed her bag from her desk and left the precinct, ignoring the puzzled expressions of the other detectives.

Her destination: Tom's Diner, where she would sit and wait all day if she had to.

She only hoped Diane had understood the message.

CHAPTER TWENTY-SIX

DAY TWO

JULY 9, 1977
SOUTH BRONX, NEW YORK

Hopper's night at the warehouse was hardly comfortable, but he'd suffered worse. After returning to the social area, more beers had been consumed, Martha and Hopper sharing a tattered couch with bad springs. That same couch had ended up as his bed, after the others had finally called a halt to their drinking session and slunk off. Hopper presumed there were other sleeping areas in the warehouse, as when he awoke the main floor was deserted. He had a knot in the muscles in the small of his back.

"Hungry?"

Hopper swung upright, and looked up. Martha had appeared, carrying a pizza box. She dumped it on the table, then fell onto the couch next to Hopper. She flipped open the box and extracted one of two cold slices of pizza. She flopped back and ate it with her mouth wide open.

Cold pizza for breakfast. Hopper sighed, and took the other slice. What he really needed was coffee, and lots of it.

As he ate the stale slice, he looked around, but they were still the only people on the warehouse floor.

"Where is everyone?"

"Working," said Martha. "Which is what we should be doing. You sleep long, my friend. First night, okay. Second night, no way. You want to be in the Vipers, you got to play by the rules."

"Those rules include cold pizza for breakfast?"

Martha laughed. "This is the best I could do. You missed the morning meal in the mess."

Hopper chewed as he thought about this. He turned to Martha, sitting next to him.

"You have a mess?"

Martha shrugged. "Sure. The Saint, he likes things run a certain way. He calls it a mess. I don't know. It's just a room with tables and chairs. We sit in there and we eat out of tins. Army rations or something. Let me tell you, old pizza is a treat compared to that shit."

Hopper nodded. "So where do we sleep?"

"Reminds me, we need to get you set up," said Martha. "You're in Leroy and Lincoln's crew, so you have a spot in with them." With the hard crust of her pizza, she pointed over to a nearby stack of crates. "Go get a roll."

"A roll?"

"Sure."

Hopper pushed himself up and walked over to the crates that Martha had indicated, stretching his arms and legs as he walked after a night on the couch. The stack of crates was partially covered by a tarpaulin. Hopper pulled the covering back, discovering the top crate was without a lid. Inside were large bundles of fabric tied around with canvas straps. Hopper reached in and pulled one out.

It was a bedroll, army-issue, exactly like the ones he'd spent many a night on back in Vietnam. As he turned the bundle over in his hands, he saw that it was the genuine article—musty, but intact. The Vipers must have raided an army surplus store.

"Come on," said Martha. She stood from the couch and headed over toward the office-block section of the warehouse. "We'll get you a spot, then we'll put you to work."

She walked off. Hopper watched her.

The Vipers had a mess. They ate rations. They slept on bedrolls.

They were starting to feel less like a gang, more like a private army.

Hopper hefted his bedroll and followed Martha deeper into the complex.

CHAPTER TWENTY-SEVEN

EXPLANATIONS

JULY 9, 1977
BROOKLYN, NEW YORK

The coffee at Tom's Diner was so bad that Delgado wondered if she was drinking the same pot from yesterday,
but that didn't stop her having three—no, *four*—mugs of the
stuff by the time Diane arrived. She had Sara on her hip, and
Delgado couldn't help but smile as the young girl caught site of
a stack of pancakes and syrup being delivered by one of the
surly waitstaff to a nearby table. As they approached her
booth—coincidentally the same one Delgado had shared with
Hopper just yesterday—Diane was making a deal with Sara
that she could have a pancake if she was a good girl and be-
haved herself while Mommy talked to her friend. Sara nodded
in rapid agreement, and moments later a single pancake and
small metal jug of syrup arrived, along with a coffee for Diane.

A good idea, thought Delgado. The pancake would keep

Sara busy while her mother heard the truth about her husband. But it was Diane who spoke first.

"Listen, Rosario, this better be good, because I need to know what's going on and I need to know what Jim's gotten involved in. I know it wasn't a double homicide, and I could tell the moment I saw you at the precinct that you know what's happening. So cut the—"

Diane paused and glanced at Sara, who was busy dividing her pancake into squares with the side of a fork. Diane leaned in toward Delgado.

"So cut the *crap*," she said, her voice almost a whisper, "and tell me that Jim is okay."

Delgado held her breath. She didn't really know Diane that well—they'd met maybe twice in the six weeks that Delgado had been Hopper's partner—but she knew that Diane was as single-minded and strong as her husband. Honestly, she expected nothing less.

Which was good, because this was going to make things a whole lot easier.

Except . . .

Delgado glanced at the top of the table. In front of her, Diane seemed to sense the shift in mood, and she leaned forward just an inch more.

"What is it?"

Delgado looked up. "I can't answer that question, because I don't know the answer."

Diane sighed, and sat back. "You don't know if my husband is okay? I thought you knew what was going on."

"Hold on, hold on." Delgado held up a hand. "Yes, I know what's going on—not all of it, but enough. And like I said, I made a promise to your husband that I would look out for you. And part of that is setting your mind at rest. Or trying to, anyway."

Diane shook her head. Sara looked up, her chin covered in syrup. She smiled at her mom, and Diane smoothed her daughter's hair back from her forehead. The smile she put on for Sara was nothing like as genuine as her daughter's.

"So if you know what's going on," asked Diane, "then why can't you tell me that Jim is okay?"

"Because I don't know if he is, and that's the truth. I don't even know where he is."

Diane sighed. Delgado could see some of the energy, some of the fight, leave her as she sank a little into the booth's vinyl seat.

She was trying. She was *fighting*. But to say it was a lot for her to handle . . . well, Delgado knew that was the understatement of the century.

"Listen, Diane, I can't be telling you this, and if anyone finds out, we're all going to be in very deep trouble. Your husband is not on the run and I might not know where he is, but he hasn't disappeared. The double homicide is a cover. He's working for a federal task force, who are trying to take down a major criminal gang—one which has a connection to the Zener card serial killings."

Delgado paused. Diane was staring at her. She smiled, and now the tears came.

Sara paused in her demolition of the pancake and looked up.

"What's wrong, Mommy?"

Diane stroked her hair again.

"Nothing for you to worry about, sweetie," she said, then turned back to Delgado and wiped away her tears.

"Tell me everything you know," she said.

Delgado nodded, took a sip of her coffee, and began.

CHAPTER TWENTY-EIGHT

CROSSTOWN INVESTIGATIONS

JULY 10, 1977
MANHATTAN, NEW YORK

It was late Sunday afternoon by the time Delgado reached the last address on Jacob Hoeler's list, a community center in Lower Manhattan, the squat, modern building squeezed between ancient tenements that had been divided into small industrial units.

It was the third location Delgado had been to that day, and in that time she had been to two AA meetings and two support groups for military veterans. She hadn't been sure how well her presence would be tolerated, but, as it happened, she was welcomed warmly at each. Of course, she realized soon enough, everyone was welcome, and nobody was judged. That was the whole point of the groups. Not only that, participation was as voluntary as attendance, so Delgado had been able to quietly sit and observe without drawing any suspicions.

Whether this was the right approach to the investigation, Delgado was less certain. Of the four meetings she'd been to, it was only at one of the support groups—one specifically for Vietnam veterans—that she had found a connection to the card homicides.

And that connection had not even been a direct one. Talking to some of the attendees during a coffee break, Delgado learned that the group she had joined was relatively new, formed from the remnants of an earlier support group. That one had split up suddenly after the facilitator had disappeared.

That facilitator had been Jonathan Schnetzer.

The first victim.

And when Delgado showed the photograph of Jacob Hoeler from the file she had borrowed, two of the group members had recognized him, despite the poor quality of the image. Yes, he'd been to the old meetings a couple of times.

Progress, finally—but while Delgado knew she was on the right track, the task ahead still felt enormous. She'd found a lead, but only at one meeting out of the four she had so far been to, and it was already heading to four o'clock in the afternoon. What she really needed to do was canvass several meetings at once, but that was impossible.

She was on her own, working a case she wasn't even supposed to be on.

As Delgado looked through the front windows of the community center, she saw the notice taped to the glass, almost lost among the similar notices posted so they could be read from the street.

She was at the right place. But was she too late?

The notice read: *Veterans' group 4PM workshop canceled*.

Veterans' group? That had to be the one.

Taking a breath, Delgado entered the community center and found her way to the front desk. The woman behind it pushed her glasses up into her curly hair and looked up at Delgado.

"You looking for something?"

It was time to play it differently. Delgado fished her detective's shield from her bag and held it up. The woman peered at it, dropping her glasses back onto her nose. Then she looked at Delgado over the top of the frames.

"There something wrong?"

"I'm Detective Delgado."

"Uh-huh."

Delgado put the shield away, then pointed at the front window on which was stuck the mass of notices.

"The veterans' group was due to meet at four?"

"Oh, that," said the woman. She stood from her chair and moved over to the window, leaning to make sure she picked the right sheet of paper before peeling it off. "That should have come down already. That group doesn't meet here anymore."

"When was the last time it did?"

The woman returned to her chair. "Well, let me see." Next to her elbow was a large ledger book, already open. She pulled it over and flipped through the pages, scanning the top line of each sheet with a finger before continuing.

"Okay, here we go. Actually, it's been a whole month now. They were booked in twice a week, Wednesday night, Sunday afternoon." The woman frowned, and checked the next page. "That's it. They were paid up for the month, but the last eight sessions didn't happen. I'm sorry, that notice should have been taken down a while ago." She paused, and looked up. "Oh, that's right."

"Do you remember something?"

The woman examined the ledger book again, tapping one line with a finger, then looked back up, lifting her glasses back onto her head.

"The first Wednesday that was missed. The group showed up but their organizer didn't. They were asking where he was. Linda—that's my colleague, she's not here—she tried calling him, but he didn't pick up. It was the same on the Sunday.

Only a couple of people showed up, but again, we tried calling. No reply."

Delgado had a feeling she knew what the answer to her next question was going to be.

"Can you tell me the name of the organizer?"

"Well, Linda's not here. I could look up the number. Although don't you need a warrant or something for that?"

Delgado shook her head. "I'm just after the name."

The woman sniffed, then opened the ledger up again. She traced the lines once more with a finger, then tapped the page.

"Sam Barrett. . . ."

She lifted the book and turned it around so Delgado could read it.

Her guess had been correct. The veterans' group was run by Sam Barrett.

The second victim.

Delgado just had one more question. She took out the photograph of Jacob Hoeler and passed it over.

"Did you ever see this man here?"

Down came the glasses. The woman held the picture close, then far away. She frowned.

"Maybe. I don't know. Hard to tell. This is a bad picture."

Delgado nodded. "If you could think hard."

The woman sighed, like Delgado was really intruding on her day. She looked at the photograph again, then handed it back.

"The Wednesday. He was here on the Wednesday, when the group were all asking where their organizer was. What's this about anyway? We don't want any trouble here."

Delgado returned the image to her bag. "No, no trouble. You've been a big help, thanks." She turned and walked out, and as she went through the doors she could hear the woman at the desk sigh heavily again.

Out on the sidewalk, Delgado paused, and considered what

she had learned about Jonathan Schnetzer, about Sam Barrett, and about Jacob Hoeler.

Then she turned on her heel and headed uptown.

There was one more meeting she wanted to go to. One more person she wanted to talk to.

Dr. Lisa Sargeson.

Delgado checked her watch—if she hurried, she could just make her meeting.

CHAPTER TWENTY-NINE

THE LATE ARRIVAL

JULY 10, 1977
BROOKLYN, NEW YORK

Delgado reached Lisa's workshop with a few minutes to spare, and as she made her way inside, past the gaggle of participants getting ready to sit down, she got the attention of the group coordinator as she walked up to the front of the room.

"Hi, Detective! I didn't expect to see you here." Then she frowned. "Is something up?"

"I was actually wondering if I could ask you a few questions?"

Lisa wrinkled her nose. "Is it important? I'm about to start the workshop."

Delgado opened her bag. "I'm hoping this won't take long." She pulled out the photograph of Jacob Hoeler. "Do you recognize this person?"

But Lisa was already shaking her head. "I don't, sorry. Who is he?"

It was worth a shot.

"His name is Jacob Hoeler," said Delgado. "We have reason to believe he may have been attending several support groups across the city in recent weeks."

Lisa pursed her lips. "Well, this isn't a support group, and the participants are panel-selected. I've never seen him, or heard his name before."

"Okay. Do you know a Jonathan Schnetzer or Sam Barrett?"

Lisa shook her head. "Again, no. Never heard those names before."

Delgado took a breath. "Well, thanks." Her shoulders slumped, but seeing Lisa's puzzled expression, she couldn't resist an exhausted laugh.

"It's fine, really," said Delgado. "I'm just trying to follow up on some leads."

"Well, anything I can do to help, you can call me anytime." Lisa's eyes widened. "It's not to do with the cards, is it?"

"I'm afraid I can't go into that," said Delgado. That was true enough, but this was more butt-covering on her part. If it came out that she'd been looking at the case during the time off the captain had given her, there would be hell to pay. "But thank you for your time." Delgado turned, and saw that all the chairs in the room had been filled, the group participants talking to one another as they waited for the workshop to begin. "I'll let you get on with it. If there are any updates, I'll let you know."

Delgado slipped down the aisle between the chairs and pushed open the double doors at the end of the room. As she stepped out into the main hallway, she walked past a tall man with a military-style crew cut and silver aviator sunglasses, a chinstrap beard outlining his sharp jawline. One of the participants, a late arrival perhaps.

Delgado didn't give him a second thought.

CHAPTER THIRTY

ENTER THE SERPENT

JULY 10, 1977
BROOKLYN, NEW YORK

"That was an excellent meeting, I must congratulate you on your technique."

Lisa continued to pack her satchel. The meeting of the rehabilitation group had just concluded, and one or two of the participants were still hanging around the door, shooting the breeze while their counselor closed the room up.

The man walked up the aisle between the two blocks of tatty old chairs that were arranged to face the front of the old Methodist church hall. As Lisa looked up, he gestured to the chairs, and although his eyes were hidden behind mirrored aviator sunglasses, she got the message.

"Oh, thanks," she said, waving a handful of papers. "And, ah, thanks, I could use a hand. I used to make the group help me pack up at the end of a session, but then I thought I was making it feel too much like school."

The man laughed as he began to stack chairs and move them over to the side of the room, arranging them next to an old upright piano. Lisa watched him, one hand on her hip. As he turned back around to move the next set of chairs, she frowned.

"I'm sorry, but I don't think we've met. You're not part of the group?"

The man paused, then continued with the cleanup. He was tall, with naturally tan skin, close-cropped hair, and a chin-strap beard. As well as the aviators, he wore a purple shirt underneath a black leather jacket, and had a chain around his neck, on which hung two rectangular pendants.

Lisa tensed, suddenly wary of the stranger. While the rehabilitation group was invite only, the participants selected and invited in coordination with the charity directors who ran the program, the Methodist church hall was a public space, the doors always open. The charity had a repeat booking, but it wasn't like Lisa locked the doors at the start of each session. Anyone could come in.

Including this man. He looked, if she was honest, like the others in her group—unlike her time at the Rookwood, the charity didn't have access to prisoners, and instead had to operate slightly differently, helping the rehabilitation of those who had already been released and were trying to make a new, normal life for themselves on the outside. The charity tried to identify at-risk people who had only just come out—the sooner they got to work, the more successful the outcome—so the members of the group, some of them at least, tended to be hard cases, even if they were here voluntarily, recognizing the need to change something in their lives or risk ending up back behind bars.

The men—and they were all men—who joined Lisa's group

were also at high risk of other things, too. Their vulnerability, their uncertainty about life as regular citizens, made them prime targets for gang recruiters, and New York City had more than its fair share of such organizations.

Organizations like the one this stranger belonged to. Because as he stacked his third set of chairs under the pretense of helping her pack up, Lisa saw the patch on the back of his leather jacket—a red snake, curled, forked tongue flicking. Underneath, one word: VIPERS.

Lisa took a breath and stepped up to the man. She'd dealt with his kind before. It took more than a gang patch to rattle her cage.

"Excuse me," she said, moving into the man's personal space as he turned back around. "You need to leave, right now, or I will call the police."

The man held up his hands and nodded; Lisa took an instinctive step backward, trying to keep herself out of his reach. Perhaps she could call out—there would still be some of the group nearby, a few of them usually hung out afterward. That was good, all part of the process, teaching them about friendship, getting them to bond, to form a support group of their own.

Lisa's bag was at the front of the room. Inside she had a can of Mace and a telescopic nightstick. Living in New York City, a woman had to take precautions.

She could handle herself.

She could handle *him*.

"I'm sorry," said the man, "I don't mean to intrude. But I can assure you, I mean you no harm and I do not wish to cause undue concern."

Lisa took another step backward. His manner was strange, the way he spoke hardly like that of a typical street thug. He was educated, intelligent. Different. He kept his hands where she could see them.

"I meant what I said. That you're doing excellent work here.

Remarkable work. Work that is needed to help this city and the people in it. I have to congratulate you. In fact, that's why I came here in the first place."

Lisa cocked her head. "You came here to *congratulate* me?"

The man laughed. "Yes. But also to offer you a job."

Lisa blinked. "I'm sorry, did you just say what I thought you said?"

The man nodded. "I represent an organization—"

"You mean a gang," said Lisa, gesturing to the man. "The Vipers. Did you forget you have it advertised on the back of your jacket?"

The man laughed. "Yes, the Vipers. But, like I said, we're not a gang. We're an organization. True, I did borrow certain elements from other sources, but this is no criminal enterprise. And true, it's not a charity like this one either, but it's aims are similar—to help those who need it. Just like your group. And I want you to join us."

Lisa shook her head and, satisfied the man wasn't going to jump her, moved to the front of the room. She looped the strap of her bag quickly over her head, and grabbed the rest of her materials, shoving them roughly inside.

"I'm sorry, but whatever you're selling, I'm not buying. Good luck with your group, but I'm quite happy here, thank you."

"You happy with that kind of money?"

Lisa paused. "What do you mean?"

The man looked around the room, spreading his arms. "They put you in a dump like this, they pay you hardly anything, and what, you work your ass off, trying to save a dozen souls at a time. Come work for me and you can save hundreds, and you'll be able to pay your rent on time."

She shook her head again. "It's really time to leave now."

The man walked down the length of the room toward her.

"Don't you want to make a difference? Don't you want to do something? Something important? You help people. That's what you do. That's what you were born to do. Come work for me, and together we can help the whole city."

Lisa sighed in frustration. She'd humored this guy long enough, but something still bugged her.

"How do you even know who I am and what I do? You're not part of the group. Do you know someone who is? Have you talked to someone about it?"

"Oh, Dr. Sargeson, I know who you are. I know your work. Your thesis on sociological reintegration methodology was a work of art, if you don't mind me saying. I have studied your work. Yours is a fascinating mind."

Great, so he was some kind of stalker, albeit one who clearly spent his time searching through the public library system instead of peeping through windows.

Lisa took a breath to start another rebuttal, but the man held up his hand.

"Do you have a pen?"

Lisa's jaw clicked shut, then she spoke again. "I . . . a pen?"

The man nodded, and from an inside pocket pulled out a red matchbook. He turned it over in his hands, like he was checking he didn't need it, then reached out an empty hand to her. Lisa frowned, but found herself digging a pen out of her bag and handing it over anyway.

The man moved to the piano and leaned on the top as he wrote on the open flap of the matchbook.

"Here's where we are. Think about it. I have a feeling you'll come around. When you're ready, come and see me. I'll be waiting."

He tore the flap off and handed it over. On the blank side he had written an address, somewhere in the Bronx.

She looked up at him.

"What is—"

"Your pen," he said, offering it back to her. She took it.

Then he turned and walked out. About halfway across the room, he stopped and called out over his shoulder.

"It was nice meeting you again, Dr. Sargeson. I hope you'll come to the right decision."

He left. Lisa was alone in the hall.

She stood, trembling, then looked at the piece of card in her hands.

She sighed, dropped it into her bag, then stopped, realizing that half of the chairs were still not put away.

Dumping her bag on the floor, she got to work on stacking the rest, the image of the strange man at the forefront of her mind.

HOPPER'S CABIN
HAWKINS, INDIANA

Seeing the confused look on El's face, Hopper stopped. He checked his watch. It was getting late, although he suspected he was actually tiring faster than she was.

El formed her mouth into an O.

Hopper raised an eyebrow. "We have a question at the back?"

El folded her arms. "How . . . do you know?"

"How do I know what?"

"Delgado. Lisa," said El. "You weren't there."

"Fair point," said Hopper. "But we—I mean, Delgado and me—we pieced it all together afterward. We had to interview everyone we could, and we put it all into a big official report. Actually, it took way longer to write that thing up than we spent on the investigation itself. We were even flown down to D.C. to present it to a bunch of anonymous suits in some federal building. They grilled us pretty well, too, although I never found out who they all were." He grinned. "Kinda sums the whole thing up, really."

El nodded slowly, but her expression told Hopper she wasn't convinced.

"But sure, I'll admit that some of the information was a bit sketchy, you know? We did our best afterward, but we'll never really have the full picture of what happened and what people were thinking." Hopper leaned forward on the table. "That's another part of being a detective." He swept both hands, palms down, over the tabletop, like he was arranging a set of invisible cards. "You have to take all this different information, statements from interviews, your own information, and figure out how it all fits together. It's not easy, because sometimes a lot of that information doesn't make any kind of sense, and what one person says isn't actually what happened, even if they think they're telling the truth. I mean, I'm telling you this big story, but I can do that now because it's been sitting in the back of my mind for years. Sometimes you need that kind of time, so you can look back and see what really happened."

He sat back, hands in his lap, and gave a shrug. "But yeah, sometimes there are gaps and you have to fill them in as best you can, even if you can't be sure if you are right. But like I said, that's part of the job. A detective has to take what they know and make a case, and hopefully, if they've done their job and been thorough, it will all hang together."

El was looking at the table. Hopper couldn't read her expression, but he wasn't sure he needed to. The story was big and complicated and, hell, it was long—way longer than he had intended.

But it was also pretty dark. He hadn't realized when he'd started, but as much as he was censoring it for El, he now wondered if he'd gone far enough. On the other hand, he had to tell the truth about what happened—for himself as much as for her. These were memories he hadn't had to process in a long time, and El needed—and wanted—to know about his past.

But . . . well, maybe a story about a Satanic cult and a serial killer wasn't the kind of cool adventure he had intended to relate to his young ward. He tried to remember what he had been like at El's age, and how he might have reacted to the same story.

He wasn't sure that gave him any answers.

He leaned forward again.

"Look, kid, it's late. Maybe we'd better pick this up again tomorrow—"

El lifted her head. "No!"

"Um, okay." Hopper tilted his head. "This isn't, you know, too scary for you?"

El paused, like she was considering the question very carefully.

"It's okay," she said, then smiled. "Only . . . halfway scary." The smile went. "It's just . . ."

"Just what?"

"You really were okay?" She narrowed her eyes, like she was figuring out the logic. "You are here . . . so you were okay."

Hopper smiled, then his smile turned into a laugh. El's face lit up and she seemed to relax, quite a lot.

"Yes, El, I came out of it okay. Alive and kicking."

El nodded, apparently satisfied.

"So you want to keep going?"

She smiled.

"Okay then. Where was I?"

As Hopper picked up again from where he'd left off, he thought about El's question, her concern.

Yes, he came out of it okay.

Just.

CHAPTER THIRTY-ONE

DELGADO MAKES THE CALL

JULY 12, 1977
BROOKLYN, NEW YORK

Delgado picked up the telephone, then put it down, then repeated the routine three times before growling at herself and walking a tight circle in the middle of her tiny apartment.

Before she did what she was going to do, she had to make sure it was the right thing. The fact was, she'd been agonizing over it all yesterday, every argument giving rise to a counterargument in her mind.

Because if she was going to make the call, then that was it—there was no going back. She would have to be all-in, and damn the consequences.

So, yes, she had to be sure it was the right thing to do. And if she didn't do something *today,* it was going to be too late.

She paced back to the living room, careful not to slip on any of the dozens of sheets of paper that were scattered over the floor. On the couch was her notebook, where she had spent hours last night distilling her thoughts and theories into something she hoped was coherent.

She picked up that notebook and read through the last page of notes again. At the top of the page were two names, circled, with a line connecting the two bubbles.

Jonathan Schnetzer. Sam Barrett. Both leaders of support groups for Vietnam veterans. Successful groups too—at least until their leaders had suddenly gone missing, forcing the groups to disband.

The third victim, Jacob Hoeler, was the odd one out—but his murder fit into Delgado's theory. Maybe it was a little neat, maybe she was jumping to a conclusion, but . . . it fit. She was sure it did.

Because Jacob Hoeler, special agent, an undercover operative in Gallup's federal task force, had visited each of the locations on his list—specifically, the ones run by Schnetzer and Barrett.

And after each visit, the group leader had been murdered, the group disbanded. Not long after, Hoeler himself had met the same end—murdered by the card killer because he had been *seen* by them. Because the killer had targeted the groups, targeted their leaders—for reasons that were still a mystery to Delgado—and Hoeler had been on his tail.

So he needed to be removed. He became the third victim.

Delgado paused, and shook her head. Did the theory work? Or did she want it to work? Those were two very different things.

And what was Lisa's connection? *Was* there a connection at all? True, she knew what Zener cards were, and she ran a group at one of the locations on Hoeler's list. But as Delgado had seen for herself, there were dozens of organizations that used the Methodist church hall as a meeting venue.

And what had Hoeler been doing? He was investigating the

Vipers, but had he somehow chased down the serial killer? Or was the intersection of his gang investigation and the card homicides pure chance? Had he, in fact, been killed by mistake, the killer thinking he was being trailed when Hoeler was working on something else entirely?

Delgado stared at her notes until her handwriting blurred in front of her. She tossed the notepad down on the couch, did another circuit of the apartment, then made her decision.

Because there was a chance she had uncovered something important. Something useful. Something that might even help her partner, wherever he was.

She went back to the telephone, picked it up, and called the local FBI field office. The call was answered after just a handful of rings.

"My name is Detective Rosario Delgado. I'm from the 65th Precinct.

"I need to speak to Special Agent Gallup, right now."

CHAPTER THIRTY-TWO

DECISION TIME

JULY 13, 1977
BROOKLYN, NEW YORK

"Listen, Jerry, I don't understand. What are you telling me?" Lisa paced her apartment, trailing the long cable of her phone around as she did orbits of the living space, staring at the floor as she tried to understand just what the hell it was that her "boss"—as much as the board chair of the charity that funded her rehabilitation program could truly be called her boss—was telling her.

It didn't make any sense. Not a lick of it.

"I'm sorry, Dr. Sargeson," said Jerry again in her ear. She could imagine him sitting in a small, hot office, somewhere in Lower Manhattan. "But I don't know how else you want me to say it. We are calling a halt to your program, effective immediately. The board has agreed to pay your stipend to the end of the month, but I'm afraid that's as far as the money will go."

Lisa stopped in the middle of her own hallway, and clapped a hand against her forehead.

"I don't understand."

The voice of Jerry sighed over the phone. "I'm sorry, really I am. But we're stretched as it is, and we just can't continue with your pilot."

Lisa's hand tightened around the telephone receiver. Had he just said . . .

"Pilot? Are you kidding me, Jerry? This wasn't a pilot. You committed to funding the group for a year, and at our six-month review, you said the results were excellent. In fact, you said they were better than you could have hoped for. Even the NY-goddamn-PD wrote a letter of commendation. You want me to get it out and read it to you over the phone, Jerry?"

"Dr. Sargeson—Lisa—I understand."

"And I don't."

Jerry sighed again. "Look, I'll be frank. It's the money. We don't have any, not anymore."

"What do you mean, 'anymore'?"

"Take a look out the window, Lisa," said Jerry, a hint of exasperation in his voice. "New York isn't what it used to be. There are people who have given up on it, who think it can't be fixed. And, I'm sorry to say, that includes some of our benefactors. So, I'm sorry, but we can't afford to continue."

Lisa stalked back into her living room and dropped herself onto the sofa in the bay window. She shook her head.

"We can't just leave them, Jerry. The people in the group, they were doing well. We have to keep going. We can't just cancel the meetings. You know what will happen to them."

"I don't think you are giving yourself enough credit, Dr. Sargeson. Or us."

"Excuse me?"

"The board has agreed to help place the program participants in other groups. Yours might have been the best in the city, but you're not the only one trying to help these people.

And your work was excellent. You did help them. Okay, a disruption isn't good, but we'll try to minimize it. They'll manage, and they'll have you to thank for that."

The conversation continued—or at least Jerry's half of it did. Lisa let her mind drift as the board chair droned in her ear.

She couldn't believe it. All that work, all that time, all that effort. Gone. Just like that.

It wasn't the first time she'd been bitten, of course, but at least with the Rookwood Institute she had recognized the sinking ship and gotten herself out. The charity, on the other hand—she was doing so well, and with so little.

She couldn't let that go. Couldn't . . . and wouldn't.

But right now, it didn't seem she had a choice. She ended the call, Jerry offering more apologies, more understandings, more assurances that, actually, she was perfectly good at her job, exemplary even.

It wasn't her, it was them.

Lisa dropped the receiver onto the cradle and leaned back on the sofa, lifting her head and yelling at the ceiling. She closed her eyes, and sat like that for a few minutes.

Then she sat up. She wasn't going to let this stop her. Yes, she was good at her job. Yes, she was helping people.

And maybe she still could.

She stood and almost dived for her bag, sitting on the floor by the other chair. She tore it open and riffled inside until she found what she was looking for—the card—that the man from the Vipers had given her yesterday. She turned it over in her hands; on the front was printed the name of the establishment the matchbook had come from—someplace in the Bronx called Louie's Restaurant—and on the reverse, the dark pen a little hard to read against the red card, the address the man had written.

Was this the right thing to do? Because it was crazy, wasn't it? She had no idea who the man was. He was smart, and well-spoken, but he looked like a gangster and wore a patch, even though he called this group an "organization."

Yeah, right.

But then . . . what if he had been telling the truth? Because it was a pretty strange story to come up with. If he was part of a gang, why would they want to employ her services? Gangs weren't known for their benevolent nature, their concern for their fellow citizens, their desire to help others in need. Quite the opposite, in fact.

So maybe he was telling the truth.

Or maybe he wasn't.

But wasn't it worth finding out? It wasn't like she had any other pressing engagements.

Or job, for that matter, other than magician-for-hire. If the man had been speaking the truth, that he could fund a program of his own, the kind she had been trying to run at the Rookwood and had been running at the charity, but one with adequate funding that would allow her to devote all her time to it . . .

She made her decision. She would go and take a look. Worst case, it was a wasted trip a long way uptown.

But the best case?

Lisa packed the card into her bag, checked she had her Mace and nightstick, and headed for the Bronx.

CHAPTER THIRTY-THREE

HOUSE CALL

JULY 13, 1977
BROOKLYN, NEW YORK

Delgado was still peering at the list of names next to the buzzers when the front door of the brownstone opened. Delgado looked up, and found the person she was there to visit standing in the doorway.

"Detective!" said Diane, her daughter by her side, clutching her mother's hand. "Do you have any news?"

"Oh, no, sorry," said Delgado, straightening up. "Ah . . . I didn't mean to surprise you at home."

But Diane shook her head. "No, it's okay. I've been sitting by the window upstairs all day. I've taken Sara out of school, just for a few days, until this all gets sorted out. But when I saw you walking down the street, I . . . well, I thought something had happened. I didn't mean to ambush you."

"Well, a couple of things have happened—no, I haven't

heard from Hopper—but I thought I'd come down and tell you in person. If nothing else, I thought you might want some company, and I made a promise to your husband that I'd look after you. So that's what I'm doing. Now, you going to ask me in for tea and cookies or not?"

Diane smiled, and held the door open wider.

"Hey, you're more than welcome. I'm going crazy, cooped up in here. Please, come in."

Delgado stepped inside the brownstone. Diane led the way up the stairs.

"This way."

Delgado followed.

CHAPTER THIRTY-FOUR

SAINT JOHN OF
THE SOUTH BRONX

JULY 13, 1977
SOUTH BRONX, NEW YORK

Okay, fine. This was a mistake.

Lisa was big enough to admit that. And, if she was honest with herself, she'd gotten doubts almost as soon as she'd left the apartment. But she'd been angry, and frustrated, and if nothing else she needed time to think. Traveling up to the address on the back of the torn matchbook was a welcome distraction.

And now, walking down a potholed road of an industrial estate, looking around the mix of vast, weed-choked lots surrounded by tall wire fencing and huge, anonymous warehouses the size of aircraft hangars, she knew this wasn't a place to linger. The day was hot, the sky clear and blue, but this wasn't exactly the kind of neighborhood a civilian wanted to be walking around. Even the cab she had taken the last part of the journey had refused to drop her at the exact address, instead dumping her a couple of blocks away, the driver only offering the most halfhearted concern for her safety when she questioned his decision.

Lisa reached the end of the street, the road narrowing until it was almost an alleyway squeezed between two tall warehouses. Ahead was a third; perhaps they were all part of the same connected complex. There was a set of double doors in front of her large enough to drive a big rig through, but no other way forward.

Lisa turned around, getting her bearings. This was stupid. This probably wasn't even the right address, the industrial estate nearly impossible to navigate if you didn't already know where you were and where you were going. She'd walked maybe a mile since the cab had dropped her off, but, if she was right, the main street was actually running parallel to the road on which she stood. If she could cut across one of the empty lots, she'd reach civilization—and another cab—much quicker.

She wrung her hands, then held up her left hand, fingers straight. Her mood ring had turned black, indicating tension, nervousness, or—

Or that the ring was broken.

"Stupid thing," she muttered, stopping her train of thought as she dropped her hands. The ring was old and had long lost its ability to change color, but . . . had it been that dark earlier today?

Telling herself it was her imagination, she set off, her boots knocking loudly on the road, the sound echoing around the tall, flat sides of the warehouses around her. The place was deserted—Lisa had seen not a single person or car or truck or anything—but that didn't make her feel any better. It was . . . well, "eerie" was probably the word for it. It was a mistake coming here, a rash decision born out of anger and frustration, and that was fine, just fine, no problem, she could just go back and go home and drown her sorrows in that little Italian bar just down the street from her apartment.

Maybe she should have gone straight there after her call with Jerry.

As she hit the end of the warehouse block, and went to turn left to cut across the empty lot she had passed walking in, a man stepped out from around the corner of the building.

Lisa gasped in surprise and stopped, then backed away. The man grinned at her, his jaw working on some gum, both thumbs looped through the belt of his greasy jeans. He was wearing a white T-shirt underneath a brown leather vest, and he had a green bandanna coiled into a thick cable and tied around his head.

"You leaving so soon, little lady?" He moved slowly toward her. "Oh, no, no, little lady, we can't have that, no, no. You can't come visit and then not say hello. That's bad manners, that is."

Lisa continued to back away. She pulled her bag around and unzipped it. As she reached inside, the man stopped chewing his gum and shook his head.

"Oh, what you got in there, little lady? You want to play, huh?"

Lisa pulled the collapsible nightstick from her bag and, with a flick of the wrist, extended it out. The man grinned and clapped his hands, three times.

"Oh, nice, little lady. Very nice. Hey, what do you think, Jookie?"

There was a scuffling sound from behind her. Lisa spun around and saw another man, wearing almost identical clothing, peel out from around the corner of the warehouse behind. He kicked at the gravel again, sending a large stone banging against the metal wall of the warehouse, and put a lit cigarette in his mouth.

"I think we're going to have some fun with this one," said the newcomer—Jookie—before tossing the cigarette onto the ground, a gob of spit following the still-glowing butt.

Lisa continued to back away, willing herself to be calm. If she was going to get out of this, she had to control her feelings, focus her mind. Two of them. Okay. Outnumbered, but not outgunned. She was armed, and they weren't as far as she could see, and the nightstick was a formidable weapon in the right hands.

Hands like hers.

She backed away again. The two men approached each other in the alleyway, and slapped each other's hands in apparent greeting, before returning their attention to her. They moved forward and she moved back, keeping the same space between them.

Then she looked up, seeing the warehouses rise on either side of her. She'd gone back too far, and was entering the dead end.

That's when the others appeared, up on the warehouse rooftops. Four on one side, five on the other. Too high to be any danger, but confirming to Lisa how wrong she had been. She wasn't alone—she never had been. She'd walked right into it.

Jookie and his pal laughed, and from up top some of the others clapped and yelled out.

Lisa adjusted her grip on the nightstick. The others didn't matter. If she could get past these two, she could get away.

There was a metallic bang, following by a harsh scraping sound. The men up on the rooftops vanished again, and in front of her Jookie and friend stopped, jumping almost in fright and actually taking a step back.

Lisa risked a look over her shoulder. Behind her a smaller door, one she hadn't noticed, had opened within the larger hangar doors. A man stepped out, his mirrored sunglasses shining in the bright sunshine.

He walked past Lisa to face the other two.

"This is no way to welcome my guest," he said, his voice low and full of menace.

The two men glanced at each other, then back at the other man.

"I will deal with you later," he said, then turned back around. He smiled at Lisa.

"I'm glad you came," he said, then gestured to her nightstick. "And I'm impressed with your preparation. I'm just glad you didn't have to use it. My brothers can sometimes forget themselves."

Lisa shook her head.

"What the hell is this?" she asked. "Why did you ask me to come here? And just who the hell are you, anyway?

"I told you, Dr. Sargeson, I asked you here because I want your help. My name is Saint John, and this is my domain.

"Welcome."

CHAPTER THIRTY-FIVE

FRESH MEAT

JULY 13, 1977
SOMEWHERE IN NEW YORK

Two days of moving crates and unloading trucks, and finally Hopper seemed to have been accepted by the Vipers enough to be trusted with an actual task. Leroy and Lincoln had gone to talk to the boss, and had come back a short while later to lead Hopper to the station wagon. The three of them had piled in and headed out in the early summer evening.

The gymnasium was old, but seemed well equipped. Vaulting horses were stacked against one wall, and ropes and rings hung from the ceiling, tied neatly against the walls. The place was uniformly brown and smelled of old sweat and fresh coffee, two steaming pots of the stuff on a trestle table that had been set up just in front of the stacked horses, their feet resting on the thin carpet that had been laid to protect the hardwood flooring underneath while the gym was used for other purposes.

The three men lingered around the entrance, Leroy and Lincoln now in tight white T-shirts, having ditched their gang colors back at the warehouse. Hopper had kept his bomber jacket on, and had it zipped to the neck to hide the blood on his Jim Croce shirt. It made him warm, but for once the evening air was cool, and the air inside the gym seemed cooler still.

Or maybe that was just his imagination.

Because he had a very, very bad feeling about this.

In the center of the gym, a circle of chairs had been assembled and a few were already occupied, but the other attendees were loitering like Hopper and the two gangsters were, talking to others who had all come here for one very specific purpose.

It was a support meeting. That much was obvious. But this one wasn't the AA, or some other addiction group. It wasn't for chronic pain, or chronic unemployment, or domestic violence. Everyone in the room was male, and all were of a certain age. At least a third of them were wearing old army jackets in varying states of repair, and one man idly held a pair of dog tags, his fingers counting the bubbles of the chain like it was a rosary. Nearly everyone was smoking.

Hopper had read the notice on the door when they'd come inside and . . . yes, that was when his chill had started.

This was a support group for veterans of the Vietnam War.

Hopper knew such groups existed. He knew full well that such groups were needed. That he'd come out of the war unscathed and with his marbles all where they should be was a blessing. Okay, it had changed him, and he wasn't going to pretend that it hadn't been difficult at times. But what the war had done to some people . . . He'd never felt the need to attend a meeting like this himself, but he was glad they were there for those who did feel that need.

As for why he was here now, with Leroy and Lincoln, he

didn't know, but he had to find out. Just being in the room with the other veterans made him feel sick to his stomach. It was a violation, the presence of Vipers—now including himself—an invasion of the safe space that the veterans had come to rely on

Hopper swallowed the bile that was threatening to rise up in his throat, and made his way over to the circle of chairs. He didn't want to be here, didn't want to be doing this, but he also knew he was here for the right reasons. Because he'd managed to gain Saint John's trust, and if he could follow through, then he was just one step away from finding out what Saint John was planning, why his Vipers were targeting groups like this one.

The more he could learn, the sooner he could stop this. All of it.

Within a few minutes, the remaining men sorted themselves out and sat in the circle. Leroy and Lincoln sat opposite each other, at the three and nine o'clock positions, relative to Hopper's six. Directly opposite Hopper sat a man who looked like the others, except for his eyes, which had in them a light not present in the haunted expressions of most of the other veterans. He was wearing a corduroy jacket that looked far too heavy for the weather, and he had a notebook and pen in his hand.

"Welcome, everyone, and thanks for coming," he said. He crossed his legs, the flares of his pants flapping like semaphore, and rested the notepad and pen on one raised knee. "My name is George, and I'm glad to see so many of our regular group here tonight." He cast his gaze around the group, before settling on Hopper. "And I'm glad to see some new faces too." The man smiled and adjusted the notepad on his knee. "So, who would like to start today?"

Hopper heard the roar in his ears. The edges of his vision seemed to spark with white light, and before he even knew what was happening, he had cleared his throat.

"Ah. Hi. My name is Jim."

"Hi, Jim," everybody intoned in unison. Hopper looked up and gave a tight smile, not entirely sure what he was doing—not entirely sure it was really his own voice that he could hear echoing around the gym.

Across their opposite sides of the circle, he saw Leroy and Lincoln exchange a look.

"Ah, hi," said Hopper. "Ah, well, like I said, my name is Jim, and I served in Vietnam."

He leaned forward, resting his elbows on his knees, and he began to talk.

The coffee was passable at best, but Hopper hardly tasted it as he gulped down the lukewarm liquid. After talking for so long, he needed something to soothe his throat. He poured himself another and stood by the table, cup in hand, rolling his neck with his eyes closed. He had no idea what had come over him, that he'd had all of that bottled up inside, but . . .

"It's good, huh?"

Hopper opened his eyes. One of the other attendees was pouring himself a coffee from a fresh pot that had somehow arrived at the table.

Hopper took another sip of his own, and shrugged. "I've tasted worse."

The man applied creamer and sugar to his cup, and moved to stand by Hopper.

"No, I meant the meeting," he said, gesturing with his drink to the circle of chairs.

"Oh," said Hopper, laughing. "Ah . . . yeah, actually, you know what? That did feel good. I feel . . . Actually, I'm not sure how I feel right now."

"I know what you mean," said the other. "Name's Bob, by the way." He held out his hand. "Corporal Devlin, Robert Douglas, US096231777." He looked Hopper in the eye. "I got your back, Jim," he said, repeating what was apparently the mantra of the support group, as Hopper had found out at the end of his talk.

Hopper shook his hand. "Ah . . . yeah, I got your back, Bob. Good to meet you."

The pair sipped their drinks as they leaned against the table, watching the others mill around. Of Leroy and Lincoln, there was no sign.

Hopper licked his lips. "So, you one of the regulars?"

"Yes and no," said Bob. "Regular attendee, yes, just not at this particular meeting."

Hopper nodded. "Yeah, I heard they have these all over the city. You can just go along to any one, right?"

Bob chuckled. "I think you're thinking of the AA. But yes, they are all over, and sure, you can go along to any of them. But they like people to stay regular. It's hard enough coming back to normal life, they say you need stability. You know, an anchor in the storm, that kind of thing."

Hopper smiled over his coffee. "Don't tell me, that one of George's nuggets of wisdom?"

Bob laughed. "I see what you mean," he said, "but no, that was from another group. Good one it was, too, I was a regular there for, oh, couple of years, maybe more. Good group. Good counselor, too. Truth be told, I liked him a little better than George—ah, no offense to George, of course." He took another sip of coffee. "But some people have, I don't know, more of a . . . what is it? A gift. Or is it a skill? I don't know. Or maybe it's just the change. You know, new meeting, new people, takes time to settle in. But that's all on me."

"You move or something?"

"What? Oh, no, that group split up." Bob shrugged. "It happens."

"I'm sure it does."

"Only . . . well, I don't know. It was a real shame, but it was real sudden, you know?"

Hopper cast his eye around the room, but he still couldn't

see Leroy or Lincoln. He turned to face Bob, only half listening. "Sudden?"

"Well, yeah," said Bob. He reached behind him and picked up another sachet of creamer from the table. He tore the corner with his teeth and dumped the white powder into his coffee. "Our counselor stopped coming. I mean, really, he just stopped coming. Never sent a message, never organized a replacement. He just didn't show up. Nobody heard from him again." Bob paused, and shook his head. "Real shame, that. Sam was a good counselor. One of the best, even."

Hopper froze, his cup halfway to his mouth.

"Sam?"

"Oh yeah, Sam Barrett. You know him?"

Hopper gulped his coffee.

Sam Barrett. Support group counselor.

The second victim.

Hopper said nothing.

"Well, I just hope he's okay, wherever he is." Bob shook his head as he finished his coffee. "He was one of us and he suffered just like us, you know what I'm saying? Oh, if you'll excuse me, too much coffee tonight, I need to go visit the facilities."

Hopper gave Bob a nod, and watched as the veteran slid his coffee cup and saucer to the back of the serving table and headed for the restroom.

Sam Barrett.

Of course. Hopper knew that there was a connection between the Vipers, Saint John, and the card homicides, but to hear someone else say the name, someone unconnected with the case or with the gang, made Hopper feel colder than he already was.

That was when Leroy appeared at Hopper's elbow. Hopper set his cup and saucer down with a clatter. He closed his eyes, willing his anger to fade, but it just grew hotter and hotter somewhere inside him.

Enough.

He pushed Leroy to one side, rounding on him and backing him up against the stack of vaulting horses.

"What the hell is this, Leroy?" hissed Hopper, his jaw clenched. "What the hell is Saint John doing? Does he recruit people from places like this? Please tell me I've got that wrong. Because if I'm right, and he's preying on the vulnerable—on people just like him, other veterans—then, I swear, I'll . . ."

Leroy winced and pushed back at Hopper. "Hey, man, take it easy!"

"No, I won't take it easy," said Hopper. "What are the Vipers planning, Leroy? You came to us with information, saying you wanted protection, but as soon as you came down from whatever high you were on, that information seems to have evaporated into thin air."

Leroy adjusted his T-shirt and looked around the room. Nobody was paying them any attention as the veterans all began to regroup at the chairs.

"Hopper, will you cool it, man? You gotta be careful what you say, okay? We're working this together, right? Okay?"

Hopper narrowed his eyes. Leroy looked at him, then looked away.

Hopper could see it a mile away. Years as a cop, he'd seen every kind of tell there was.

"What aren't you telling me, Leroy?"

"We good here?"

Hopper turned as Lincoln approached. Leroy pushed Hopper off.

"We good," he said.

Lincoln looked at them both, then hooked a thumb over his shoulder.

"Got the call. The Saint wants us back uptown."

"What?" asked Leroy. "Why?"

"The Saint don't give me the why, Leroy, and he knows I'm not going to ask it. He wants us to roll so we roll."

He turned and walked away. Hopper spun around to face

Leroy, but Leroy brushed past him as he followed his fellow Viper out.

Hopper left the gym, passing by the counselor, George, as he emerged from the restroom. George stopped in the middle of the hall.

"Hey, Jim, you okay? We're about to start again, if you want to come in and—"

"Sorry, George, I have to run," said Hopper, turning around so he was walking backward toward the main doors. "But thanks. This was a big help, really."

Outside, the car was waiting, Leroy gunning the accelerator. Hopper saw that Lincoln was sitting in the front now. He got in the back, slammed the door, and was pushed back into the seat as Leroy floored it.

DECEMBER 26, 1984

HOPPER'S CABIN
HAWKINS, INDIANA

Hopper stood from the red table and stretched his legs, pacing between the table and the kitchen. He rubbed his face and ran a hand through his hair, and then he stopped, his back to El.

Hiding his expression from her. He rubbed his face again, and glanced at the kitchen window. He could see his own reflection faintly, with El behind him

The Vietnam support group—he'd forgotten about that. No, that wasn't quite it. He couldn't forget, but, over the years, he had learned to compartmentalize, to put memories like that in their own special place at the back of his mind. A place they stay, not forgotten, but sleeping.

Until now. Until tonight, when Hopper's story had arrived

at that point where he visited the support group with Leroy and Lincoln.

Hopper was surprised, as well—surprised at his feelings about that memory, about the *depth* of his feelings. He'd realized, perhaps a little too late, that this part of the story was coming, but he hadn't thought anything of it until he actually began to relate it to El.

He hadn't actually gone into what he had said at the meeting, of course. He knew El's curiosity was piqued when she realized what was happening, but he'd stopped short. He wasn't going to talk about Vietnam. They had already agreed on that. This story was about New York.

The fact that the two stories—the two places—would intersect so much was unexpected, and Hopper felt like a fool. Of course they intersected.

"Are you okay?"

Hopper took a breath and turned back around, leaning on the kitchen counter as he looked over at El, sitting at the table.

"Yeah, I'm okay. How are you doing? This is a really long story, I'm sorry. . . . Remember, we can stop anytime."

El shook her head, then she frowned. "You look tired."

Hopper laughed and rubbed his face again. "Hey, nothing that a little more coffee won't fix."

At that, he slapped the kitchen counter with both hands and turned to start work on a fresh brew. Behind him, El was quiet for a few minutes, until she spoke again.

"I've got your back," she said.

Hopper froze. He turned his head sideways.

"What?"

"What does it mean?"

"Oh." Hopper felt his body relax. "Well, it's an old army expression. Because sometimes, when you're marching along, you can't see behind you. So sometimes you need a buddy to help you and keep you safe. So that's what it means, they've 'got your back.' Sometimes people use it to mean that you can rely on them and trust them to help you when you need it." He paused, and looked over his shoulder again. "That make sense?"

El nodded. She stood from the table and walked around the cabin, stretching her own legs. Hopper watched her for a moment, then got the coffee on.

El appeared by the kitchen counter.

"I've got your back," she said.

He looked at her but said nothing, his eyes searching her face. She was looking at him with chin raised, her expression firm and serious.

"You can . . . rely on me," she said, picking up on his own words. "I've got your back."

Hopper's laugh almost exploded from his throat. El flinched and took a step back, her face creased in confusion.

"Did I say it wrong?"

Hopper shook his head and moved to her, pulling her close in his arms. She wrapped her arms around his waist.

"No, kid, you got it just right."

He felt El nod her head.

"I've got your back."

He ruffled her hair. "And I've got yours, kid. I've got yours."

El pulled away, and sniffed the air. "Coffee. Yuck," she said, her nose wrinkled. Then, like nothing at all had happened, she went back to the red table. "Keep going," she said.

Hopper laughed and poured his coffee.

"Yes, ma'am," he said. He returned to the table and got himself comfortable. Across from him, El linked her hands on the table in front of her and looked up at him.

Hopper scratched his chin. "Okay, where were we . . ."

CHAPTER THIRTY-SIX

POKE A RATTLESNAKE, GET BIT

JULY 13, 1977
SOUTH BRONX, NEW YORK

Hopper had cooled his heels by the time they got back to the warehouse, Leroy rolling the station wagon to a stop in its parking space next to the truck. The support group meeting had rattled him, he realized now, but he couldn't let that throw a wrench in the works. He had to suck it up, and get on with the job Gallup had sent him in to do.

The Vipers were busy, the warehouse now hosting easily double or triple the number of people Hopper had seen earlier. They seemed to be shifting the crates of gear around, teams loading equipment into vehicles. The flatbed truck had been moved a little out from the wall, and a group was working on the thing on the back of it. As Hopper got out of the station wagon, he saw it was a large reel of cable suspended in a mechanical frame, the truck looking as though it had been "acquired" from Con Edison.

Lincoln disappeared farther inside the warehouse. Leroy moved around from the driver's side to stand by Hopper as he watched the gang at work.

"You really got to chill it, man," Leroy whispered.

Hopper nodded. Leroy was right, and he knew it, and there wasn't anything to argue against. Instead he gestured at the truck.

"What's this all for? What is Saint John doing?"

Leroy shrugged, but his expression was tight. "I told you, I don't know."

"They do," said Hopper, nodding at the gang at work. "Someone is giving them orders, instructions. You're just never around when Saint John gives them, right?"

"*Listen*, man," Leroy hissed, checking around to make sure nobody was listening. "This is not my department. Saint John, he's big on organization and rules. Every Viper, they have their place, they have their job, right? So, no, I don't know what they're doing, which is the whole reason why we're standing here, right? What do you want us to do? Just walk up to the Saint and ask him what's going on and what time the devil is going to show for cocktails on the balcony, huh?"

"No," said Hopper, "but it's time we got some answers."

Squaring his shoulders, Hopper pushed himself off the car and walked over to a stack of the packing crates that were being slowly transplanted into the back of one of the other pickup trucks lined up by the row of motorcycles. The crates were long and relatively shallow.

Hopper had a feeling—a very bad one—that he knew what was inside.

With the rest of the gang busy, Hopper took a chance. There was a crowbar on the ground. He picked it up, and was about to start levering the lid off the top crate, when a heavy hand clapped him on the shoulder.

"You looking for something, brother?"

The hand pulled him around. It was Lincoln, and he didn't look happy. His eyes fell to the crowbar in Hopper's hand.

"The hell you doing?"

Lincoln gave Hopper a shove. Hopper landed on the corner of the crate he had wanted to open, the sharp edge digging into the small of his back. He yelped in pain and stumbled, dropping the crowbar and quickly finding himself on his hands and knees. He went to push himself up when he felt a sharp tug on the back of his belt.

"The hell the *hell*?"

Hopper got to his feet, only to find Lincoln standing in front of him, Hopper's concealed handgun now in his grip.

Lincoln looked at the gun, then looked at Hopper. Hopper didn't like his expression much at all.

"Who the hell are you, man? Leroy says you're a cop on the run, and you're hiding your own heat? Shit, man, I gotta wonder, you really on the run, or are you really here looking to be a hero, huh?"

The exchange had caught the attention of the other Vipers. They stopped what they were doing and peeled off, almost one by one, to gather around Hopper and Lincoln.

Hopper looked around at the circle of faces. The gang members were all looking right at him, as was Lincoln. Hopper couldn't see where Leroy was.

Lincoln spat onto the cement floor, cracked his neck from side to side, then weighed Hopper's handgun in the palm of one hand. Hopper took a step forward, then stopped as Lincoln brought the gun up and aimed it right at Hopper's head.

"Thing about heroes," said Lincoln, "is that they don't exist. Heroes are from comic books. You live in a city like this, you know that's a fact. Ain't no capes in New York, and ain't no police in the Vipers."

"We all good?"

Lincoln jerked his head around at the voice. Hopper ground his jaw as he watched the gangsters part to let the newcomer through.

Martha stepped through the circle, moving to Lincoln's side like a catwalk model, one foot in front of the other.

"Martha W., I got this," said Lincoln. He adjusted his grip on the gun, but something had changed. The balance, the weight of the situation, had shifted. He was no longer in charge.

Martha was.

She stepped around Lincoln, ignoring the gun, and moved closer to Hopper. Hopper remained still as she reached down and picked up the crowbar from where it had fallen. Then she moved back to Lincoln, the tool swinging in one hand, the forked end tapping along the warehouse floor.

"Getting a little curious, huh?" she said. She stopped by Lincoln and looked up at him. "Boss wants to see you."

Lincoln rolled his neck. The gun moved up and down a little, but was still pointing at Hopper.

"I said I got this."

"And I said the Saint wants to see you and he doesn't like to be kept waiting."

Lincoln cocked his head, then with a sigh he dropped his gun arm. He gave Martha a look, then handed the piece to her and stalked away, without saying a word.

Hopper watched all this unfold, unwilling to move in case he unbalanced the delicate situation. Martha held the crowbar in one hand and the pistol in the other and lifted her chin at him.

"There's something about you, fresh meat," she said. "Something I don't like. It's like a smell. I got a nose of it when we first met, only I didn't know what it was back then. But I knew I didn't like it."

"I'm here because I want to be," said Hopper. "I'm here to work for Saint John. You go ask him."

"Oh yeah, Saint John told me all about you," said Martha. "But look, fresh meat, I think we're going to do this my way for a change, not his."

With that, she tossed the gun onto the floor, out of range of both herself and Hopper. She hefted the crowbar, then swung it, the tip striking sparks off the floor. Around them, the gang began to re-form their circle. Someone clapped and someone hollered, and within moments Hopper found himself in the center of an arena, facing off against Martha as she began to pace, bar held in one hand like a sword.

Hopper braced himself. He was unarmed, and while Martha was smaller, she was strong—he'd seen the way she swung that sledgehammer to break into the AV store the other night, the way she'd carried the loot out with the rest of them. A life like this, you got tough, or you fell by the wayside.

Just good old-fashioned natural selection.

Survival of the fittest.

Winner takes all.

"You want to be part of this," said Martha, "then you got to prove it."

Swinging the crowbar, she lunged forward.

CHAPTER THIRTY-SEVEN

THE SECRET OF THE WAREHOUSE

JULY 13, 1977
SOUTH BRONX, NEW YORK

The warehouse complex was vast—as Lisa had thought, it wasn't a series of separate, isolated buildings, but one single, interconnected facility. Lisa thought Saint John must have had fairly formidable resources at his disposal to have acquired a headquarters like this.

It wasn't all Saint John commanded. As he led her through the complex, it was clear the Vipers were working hard. He took her through huge rooms filled with people working at long tables, assembling equipment, cleaning equipment, repairing equipment. Men soldered electronic components, screwed together intricate mechanisms, and packed smaller items into storage boxes.

Lisa had no idea what they were all doing, and her guide didn't tell her. But what she did notice was the silence. Not of the work itself—the sound of their industry echoed across the big rooms of the warehouse—but the workers themselves remained unspeaking as they focused on their tasks.

"Why are you showing me all this?" asked Lisa, as they walked past another row of workers. Saint John stopped by the table and turned around.

"Because I want you to understand."

Lisa frowned. "Understand what?" She gestured to the nearby workers. "I don't even know what they're doing."

"I want you to understand that we are doing work here. I said we weren't a gang. We aren't. We are an organization, one dedicated to making New York a better place. To achieve our aims, we must come together with a purpose. We must follow a path, one from which we must not stray, one which we know to be true. To do that requires obedience, and a will to power."

Lisa just shook her head.

Saint John smiled, and clicked his fingers. Immediately the worker closest to them stopped what he was doing, which was attaching the side panels to some kind of device with a long screwdriver.

"Henry-O," said Saint John, "you work for me, don't you?"

"Yes." The man's face was blank, his speech without expression.

"You would do anything for me, wouldn't you?"

"Yes."

Lisa blanched. She didn't understand what was happening, but she didn't like any of it. Around them the others continued to work, their presence completely ignored.

"Thank you, Henry-O," said Saint John. "You have served me well. You know what to do."

At this, the worker lifted the screwdriver in his hand, and held it up to his throat. The end dug into his skin sharply.

Lisa reached for the screwdriver, acting on sheer instinct.

"Stop! What are you doing?"

She pulled on the man's arm, forcing the screwdriver down. Blood trickled from his neck.

Next to her, Saint John laughed. He clicked his fingers again, and Henry-O's arm went slack, Lisa's own hands smacking into the worktable as the resistance was suddenly removed.

Lisa spun around to face Saint John.

"This is sick. You're sick."

"No, it is not sickness," he said. "It is power."

"Give me one good reason why I don't walk out the door and bring the cops down on your head."

"Oh, Dr. Sargeson, I hope I can give you more than one. You want to change the world, don't you? Together, that's exactly what we can do."

He gestured for Lisa to move ahead. Lisa clenched her fists, shaking with anger and fear and a hundred other emotions. At the table, Henry-O was back at work as though nothing had happened.

Then, not quite believing what she was doing, Lisa followed Saint John from the room.

The office was large, its position at the top of a block of four giving it a commanding view of a vast warehouse space through two walls of wraparound windows. Saint John led the way into the room, then moved behind a big desk to a smaller door. He opened it, and gestured inside.

"Please? We have much to discuss."

Lisa stepped through the door and found herself in a small room—a file room, the walls lined with metal shelves, the shelves stacked with books and file boxes. In the middle of the room was a small round table, with two chairs positioned on opposite sides. On the table was a silver knife with an outsized, crossed hilt and handle that made the weapon look more like a crucifix, and a silver goblet filled with something dark.

That was it. Enough was enough.

Lisa turned to leave, but Saint John was standing in the doorway. He closed the door and stepped forward, forcing Lisa to back up until she bumped into one of the chairs.

"Please, take a seat. I will explain what we are doing here and why I asked you to come."

With little other choice, Lisa pulled the chair out and sat down. She glanced around the room, noticing for the first time that the books were all about psychology and psychiatry—academic texts, mostly, nearly all of them familiar to her.

Then she saw them. Among the file boxes were a set of binders, each labeled with a white sticker printed with just two words.

ROOKWOOD INSTITUTE

"What . . . ?" She looked at Saint John, her mouth open in surprise as he sat across the table from her.

"Where did you get those? Who the hell are you?"

Saint John smiled. "You mean you don't remember me? Or you don't recognize me?"

Lisa shook her head in confusion.

"I've been a great admirer of yours," he said. "Your papers on group thinking and the power of suggestion. Fascinating stuff. We even talked about those a little, when we first met."

Lisa narrowed her eyes, her mind racing. Then she looked back at the binders.

The Rookwood Institute. Of course.

The penny dropped. She could see him now—his hair longer, the beard fully covering his face. And no sunglasses, of course.

Saint John nodded, seeing the recognition dawn on her face.

"I was part of the pilot program," he said. "One of the first six prisoners."

"I . . . ," whispered Lisa. "I had no idea. But . . . what are you doing? You said you were running your *own* program? Here?" She gestured to the files. "Are you basing it on my work?"

"I am running a program, yes," he said. "You and your work were just the beginning. When I met you, you rekindled something inside me. Reminded me of a past I had tried to forget. Of work that I had done once, a long, long time ago. You could even call it divine inspiration."

"Divine?"

Saint John ignored the interjection.

"I have been working hard, these last few months. There is so much work to do, to make everything ready. But I've used that time wisely. You're not my first recruit. Far from it. I've spent months sending my brothers out into the city, commanding them to find the lost, the needy. Bringing them here, to me, where I can show them the truth, where I can reveal the plan to them. Where I can put them to work. Where I can put *you* to work."

Lisa shook her head, and went to stand—

But she couldn't move. She looked down, saw her own hands clenched on the arms of the chair, but . . . she couldn't move them. Nor her legs. She was frozen in place.

"The Day of the Serpent comes." Saint John nodded. "You have seen it too, haven't you? I can see it in your eyes. Soon the darkness shall cover the earth, and He shall claim His throne."

Lisa stared at twin reflections of herself in the man's mirrored glasses. She felt . . . faint, but not sleepy—awake, alive, every fiber of her being tingling with electricity. Sitting opposite, Saint John seemed a long way away, too far even to touch. Around her, the metal shelves of the small room seemed to undulate, like waves cresting on a beach.

There was a bang from behind her. She snapped her head up, the room refocusing, Saint John coming into pin-sharp clarity in front of her.

He looked angry.

"Get out," he said, to whoever it was who had burst through the door.

Lisa flexed her fingers, and found she could turn around in the chair. Standing in the doorway was one of Saint John's men.

"There's trouble downstairs," he said.

"Then handle it."

"It's the new guy and Martha. I think you need to come down."

Saint John's nostrils flared in anger and he stood up. He cast one look at Lisa, then stormed out, slamming the door so hard the shelves rattled.

Lisa leaped out of the chair, thankful that she could now move, not knowing if what she'd just experienced had even really happened.

But one thing she was certain of: the door was locked.

She pulled on the doorknob, rattling it, but it was no use.

But a locked door wasn't going to stop her. She pressed her ear to the wood and closed her eyes as she listened, then dropped down onto her knees. Plucking a metal hairpin from her hair, she unfolded it and poked it into the lock, grateful now for her time studying escapology as part of her stage magician's routine—although she'd never thought she would ever use those skills to save her own life.

CHAPTER THIRTY-EIGHT

HIDE AND SEEK

JULY 13, 1977
SOUTH BRONX, NEW YORK

"Enough!"

Hopper and Martha stopped circling each other, both looking toward the unmistakable sound of Saint John's voice. The crowd parted around them once more, allowing the gang leader through to confront the two would-be combatants. He looked at them both from behind his mirrored glasses, then stopped and glanced around at the assembled gangsters.

"Everybody get back to work."

Nobody moved.

Saint John spun on his heel. He swung his arms wide, his purple robe spilling open.

"Get back to work!"

This time, people listened. The gang dispersed, running in every direction to get away from the wrath of their leader.

Saint John moved over to where Hopper and Martha were facing each other, Hopper with his fists raised, Martha with the crowbar in one hand. Saint John ignored Martha, stepping between the two as he faced Hopper.

Behind Saint John, Hopper saw the look Martha gave her beloved leader. It was one of pure, burning hatred.

Hopper found that interesting. Was she angry simply because her sport had been interrupted? Or was her anger part of some deeper animosity toward the gang leader himself?

Saint John addressed Martha, his eyes still fixed on Hopper.

"Martha, you chose this moment to challenge our new friend? You know as well as I that the moment approaches, don't you?"

Then Saint John spun on his heel, rounding on the woman with a swiftness that surprised Hopper. He towered over Martha, who backed away, the crowbar skimming the floor as she stumbled backward.

"Don't you?!"

Martha nodded. "Yes, Saint John, yes."

"Then I suggest you get back to work," he said, cupping her cheek in one hand, giving her a smile that she did not return. Then he dropped his hand and turned back to Hopper, and Hopper saw Martha give that furious look again to her leader's back—confirming to him that, yes, her anger was directed at Saint John himself—then she turned and walked away.

"I can only apologize for the behavior of my . . . *associate*." Saint John cocked his head. "You want to know what we are doing here, I take it?"

Hopper said nothing.

"Maybe it is time. Come, I have things to show you."

Saint John turned and headed back toward the stairs at the far side of the warehouse.

Hopper followed.

"Do you believe in sacrifice, Mr. Hopper?"

Saint John had led Hopper up the gantry stairs and into the second level of the warehouse offices. Again, it was clear the place had been abandoned for years—the offices here were nothing more than empty shells, the brickwork exposed and, for the most part, covered entirely with graffiti. As they moved on, Hopper saw the spaces becoming increasingly filled with crates, the Vipers using the area for additional storage.

Hopper needed to know what was in the crates. As with the ones out in the warehouse proper, they were long but shallow rectangular boxes.

He needed to see for himself.

"It's a difficult question, I understand that."

Hopper looked up, his train of thought broken as he saw that Saint John had stopped in the hallway and turned around to face him. Hopper himself had stopped in front of one of the storage rooms. Saint John had been watching him—watching him look.

"Let me tell you what I think the answer is." Saint John moved closer. Hopper's eyes fell to the dog tags shining on the chain around his neck. "I think the answer is *yes*. I think the answer is that you believe in sacrifice like *I* believe in sacrifice. I think you *understand* it like I understand it. I can see it in your eyes."

Saint John paused. He was so close that Hopper could feel the man's breath on his face.

"They say the eyes are the windows to a man's soul," Saint John continued. "And I think that's true. I think that's very true. And believe me, when I look into your eyes, and I look into your soul, I can see that truth in there. I can see *sacrifice*. I can see *belief*."

You see exactly what you want to see, thought Hopper. *A reflection of yourself, and nothing more.*

"I can see a rare understanding that there is work to be done," the gang leader continued. He nodded. "You and I have been through so much. We have seen so much. And now we are here, ready, waiting, willing. So yes, you understand. Your hands are His hands, hands He will direct as He directs our mission. He will use our hands as His own, wielding us as He wields a tool for a purpose both singular and true. He can see it. He can see the truth of your soul, for that soul is now His. He owns you and He owns me, and for that, we rejoice."

Hopper breathed slowly through his nose. Saint John clearly held him in high regard, apparently because of the simple fact they'd both served in Vietnam.

Was that why Leroy and Lincoln had taken him to the veterans' support group? Saint John placed a lot of weight on military experience.

Of course. The support group—*groups*, plural—were a recruiting ground. Saint John was looking for people. The right kind of people, at least in his mind.

People like Hopper—a veteran with both experience and a burning desire to . . . do something. In Hopper's case, both statements were true, but he'd managed to weave the latter into a fantasy that Saint John had grabbed with both hands, turning him from fresh meat into a favorite.

This close, Hopper could see the engraving on the man's dog tags. The format matched Hopper's own tags in the drawer at home.

SAINT
JOHNATHAN
RA098174174
A POS
CATHOLIC

Hopper looked up into Saint John's—*Johnathan Saint's*—face. His own double reflection loomed large in the convex silver lenses of the man's aviator glasses. The office hallway was well lit and, as Hopper watched, he thought he could see a faint shadow of movement behind the glasses as the gang leader blinked.

"If the eyes are the windows to the soul," said Hopper, "then why do you wear those?"

What are you trying to hide from your followers?

Saint John smiled, then tapped a finger against Hopper's chest. "I knew you were the right one. In the land of the blind there are some who can see, my brother, there are some who can see. You and I, we are the chosen. He sent you to me to do His work—and what glorious work it is."

Saint John turned and headed down the hallway. Then he stopped and turned back around when he realized Hopper wasn't following.

"Who is 'He'?" asked Hopper. He spread his arms. "Who is this all for?"

Saint John smiled.

"We do it for our master."

"*Our* master?"

"*The* master." Saint John stepped closer again. "People know Him by many names, but the one He whispers in my ear is Satan. And soon He will walk among us as we lead Him to His throne of fire."

With that, Saint John walked away.

It took Hopper a few seconds to muster his strength and gather his thoughts and follow, rather than run the other way as fast as he could.

Saint John led the way back into his office on the top level, taking internal staircases now, rather than the metal gantry steps outside. The place was certainly huge, although devoid of activity—at several points, Hopper thought he could hear people at work, with metallic bangs and thuds echoing from somewhere deeper in the complex, as if part of the warehouse was still home to whatever industry had built it in the first place. But by the time Saint John led him to the big office, Hopper still hadn't seen another gang member anywhere.

The office seemed the same as when Hopper had last seen it, but as soon as they crossed the threshold, Saint John marched ahead, rounding the desk and heading to one of the two doors in the wall behind it. The door was now ajar.

"No, *no*!" Saint John hissed under his breath as he threw the door fully open. Hopper joined him. The room beyond was a small file room, lined with shelves and file boxes. In the middle of the room were a small round table and two matching chairs. There was no other door.

Saint John spun around and brushed heavily against Hopper as he rushed out of the small room and into the main office, over to the curved expanse of glass that faced out onto the warehouse proper. He opened a panel in one of the windows, and yelled down to his minions far below.

"Leroy, Lincoln! Come up here! Bring your crews. Now!"

Below, Hopper could see the men spring into life, several jumping up from the old sofas by the oil drum fires and sprinting toward the stairs.

"Something wrong?" asked Hopper.

Saint John turned. Hopper could see the pulse throbbing in the man's neck, echoed in his temple.

"Nothing I can't handle," he said, then he pointed at Hopper. "Nothing *we* can't handle."

Then he went back to the desk. Taking one more look into the empty file room, he turned and pulled open the top drawer of the desk. From his position by the window, Hopper couldn't see what was in it, but the gang leader gave a small nod, then closed the drawer just as the door to his office flew open and Leroy and Lincoln ran in, chests heaving from their run up the stairs. Behind them, several more gangsters gathered.

Saint John looked at them, then went to the long file drawers. Opening the unlocked second drawer, he pulled out a large sheet of paper and swept it through the air, laying it out on the conference table. The others gathered around, Hopper included. Looking down at the sheet, he saw it was a layout of the warehouse and offices. As he had suspected, what he'd seen so far was only a small part of the complex. It looked like the Vipers had taken a couple of the neighboring industrial units as well, the whole block connected by a series of multi-level bridges and walkways.

The gang leader began pointing to different areas on the layout. "Leroy, take your crew and start a sweep of the east side. Divide in two: one group takes the stairs to the top, the other starts at the bottom. Lincoln, do the same, divide up and take the west side. Continue to sweep up and down. Detail some men to cover the exits, north and south sides. If she's still in the building, we can squeeze her into the middle."

Her?

The others nodded, apparently following the boss's instructions without any confusion. Hopper didn't know what was going on, but he thought he could guess.

Someone—a woman, apparently—had been locked in the file room, and had escaped. He wondered who it could be. Surely not Delgado? No, she knew what Hopper was doing, and, more important, she trusted him. There was no way she'd get involved.

So . . . who was it?

Saint John tapped the map again. "Hopper, you take some of Leroy's crew. Start here and work down, covering the central area and offices. Again, if she's in here, we can flush her out into the open."

Hopper looked at the gang leader. "Who are we looking for?"

Saint John stood tall and didn't look at Hopper, his mirrored gaze still directed at the map on the table. "Someone very important. Now go." He waved them out.

The others sprang into life, quickly grouping themselves into small squads of two and three men. Leroy conferred with some of his group, then nodded at Hopper.

"City and Reuben will go with you," he said, as two gang members stepped forward. Hopper recognized them from his earlier round of introductions: City was a young man with a long face and long blond hair held back under a red bandanna, Reuben an older black man with a flattop shaved to mathematical precision. As Leroy and Lincoln left with their teams, Hopper nodded at his two men.

He had an idea. Turning back to the table, he gestured to Saint John.

"Look, I have experience here. I was a cop for years, I know how to organize a grid search. May I?"

Saint John spread his hands and stepped backward to give Hopper room. Hopper moved closer, turning the map around to get his bearings. He traced an area with his finger . . . but his eyes were elsewhere, scanning other sections, trying to imprint the map in his head.

"Okay," he said, after a moment more. "We split up, we can cover more ground." He pointed to the map. "City, take this sector. Reuben, head this way. I'll take the middle. Like the boss said, we act like a pincer. If our target is in the middle, we've got them. If not, we push them out to here or here, and the others should pick them up. Got it?"

The other two nodded in agreement and headed off, City giving Reuben a hearty slap on the back.

Hopper ran his eyes over the map again, then stood up. Saint John was looking at him, his arms folded.

"Good planning, my brother."

Hopper licked his bottom lip, but didn't reply. Instead he gave a nod, then headed out into the complex.

Hopper had two diametrically opposed reactions to the scale of the Vipers' operation. On the one hand, it was remarkable, the gang having apparently claimed a whole block of industrial real estate for their own purposes. He didn't know how many of them there were, but it was clear Saint John needed the space for something.

On the other hand, the fact that they had taken over the warehouse complex so easily was no surprise at all. New York was a city of wild contradictions. At the bottom of Manhattan, the twin towers of the World Trade Center reached for the sky, a testament to the resilience and ambition of a city sliding into the biggest financial crisis of its history. Further up, Midtown continued to boom, while the higher echelons of New York society enjoyed their luxury on the Upper West Side.

How long that would last, Hopper couldn't even guess. Because, as he'd seen himself, other parts of the city were doing far less well. He'd never been a cop in the Bronx, and he'd never had any desire to serve in that borough. He'd heard enough about it even before leaving Hawkins. Different parts of the city of New York had been hit by the mismanagement of its leaders in different ways, but the Bronx was almost like a different planet, one composed of ruined buildings and burned-out shells between empty lots and rows of tenements on the verge of collapse. To find an abandoned industrial complex in this area and co-opt it for their own use wouldn't actually have been that hard for Saint John and his followers. It was the perfect base of operations, too: big enough to grow the gang and turn the place into a full-fledged headquarters, with enough space to gather resources, equipment, matériel; far enough away from existing—and occupied—residential and commercial zones that nobody would bother them, cops included, and yet they'd be able to see anyone coming if they tried; central enough to allow easy access to the city.

All in all, Saint John had done well. He might have been

suffering from some kind of delusion, if not mental illness, but he was clearly an experienced planner and logistician. He'd mentioned being seconded to "special duties" back in Vietnam. Hopper wondered exactly what that meant.

He also wanted to know what it was Saint John was planning, and why.

And now was the perfect opportunity to find out. With the gang searching for the escaped prisoner—Hopper couldn't believe she, whoever she was, was here voluntarily—and Hopper part of that search, he had the freedom he needed to look around, to go digging, without arousing any further suspicion.

Perfect.

He stalked through the empty hallways, trying to picture the layout in his mind. The place was a maze. Initially, Hopper had just assumed that the escapee would have found the exit by now and gotten away, but after a half hour of checking room after room, turning into one corridor after another, Hopper wasn't so sure. He'd lost track of his own location, the map in his mind now long forgotten, but he could hear the others as they searched, apparently happy to be less than stealthy as they tracked their quarry.

Of course, this was just another game to them. More sport.

So far, Hopper's own search of the storerooms hadn't quite revealed what he had expected. This part of the building was mostly used to keep food, it seemed. The old offices and meeting rooms were filled to varying degrees with more crates and boxes, but the ones Hopper had checked had contained tinned ham, packets of powdered milk, canned fruit. There was enough here to feed an army.

Hopper didn't like that thought much.

As for the escapee, there was no sight or sound. Reaching the end of a hallway leading back to a staircase on the west side, Hopper was about ready to head out and try a level down, when he stopped.

There. A sound. As the noise of the search above him reverberated down the west stairs, he was sure he had heard something much closer, on his level—somewhere farther back down the hallway he had just come through.

And there it was again. A creaking door, and the unmistakable sound of a shoe scuffing on the hard cement floor.

The escapee. It had to be. She'd been hiding in an office, waiting for Hopper to leave. Too preoccupied with his own search, he hadn't detected her presence.

Hopper let the stair door swing shut, then ducked back down the hall until he reached the first intersection. He slipped around the corner and pressed himself up against the wall, his head turned toward the sound, and waited.

The footsteps came again. Someone was slowly but surely making their way down the hallway, around the corner.

Toward him.

Hopper braced himself, unsure who or what to expect. But two things came to mind.

First, if he was the one to catch the escapee, then that would earn him more favor with the Vipers. Their leader had already accepted Hopper into his confidence—and rather quickly too, fueled, it seemed, by their shared Vietnam connection. But the others, Leroy aside, were still an unknown quantity. The gang had enjoyed Martha's little sport, and Lincoln certainly didn't like him. Even with Saint John's support, Hopper wasn't sure how firm his standing with the Vipers really was.

But, second, if Hopper could get to the escapee first, he could use that to his advantage in another way. Because while he didn't know who the person was, there was a chance that an enemy of Saint John could be made an ally of his own. Saint John had said the prisoner was someone important—if this was her, perhaps she knew what the gang was up to, what their leader was planning. Perhaps she could provide Hopper with the information he needed to take back to Gallup.

Two more steps, slow and quiet, but in the dead air of the hallway they rang like a bell in Hopper's ears. He strained every sense, trying to form an image in his mind of the person approaching, judge their size, whether they were carrying any weapons. He knew the prisoner was a woman, but that meant nothing, nothing at all. Leroy's sister Martha was half his size but more than capable of taking him on. Hopper could make no assumptions.

If only he could read the person through the solid wall like the symbol on a Zener card.

He tensed, readying himself for action. The person was almost at the corner.

That was when he heard another sound—a door opening, heavy footfalls and loud chatter. It was another search party, entering a nearby corridor. At any moment, they would walk straight into Hopper. The person just around the corner was already spooked by the sound, their own footfalls having stopped.

Hopper had to act, and fast.

He gritted his teeth, and swung himself around the corner.

He caught a flash of red and the look of surprise on the face of the woman with long brown hair, then he stopped, almost midstride.

Lisa Sargeson stared at him, her eyes wide.

Behind Hopper came the sound of the gangsters as they approached. Hopper quickly lifted his finger to his lips, indicating for Lisa to stay silent, then he pointed down the hallway she had just come, and nodded. She got the message immediately, and darted back down the hall and through the closest door.

This office had windows running down one wall, starting at waist height, looking out into the hallway they had just been standing in. Lisa ducked down and slid herself underneath the old desk that was all that remained of the furniture in the room. Hopper went to follow, stopping when he saw there was far from enough room for both of them.

Lisa looked at him, worry etched across her face. He gave

her a silent *okay* hand signal, then moved over to the wall, kneeling down so he was underneath the windows. If the gangsters came in, finding him was less of a problem than finding her.

The Vipers walked down the hallway, their movements a cacophony of noise after Hopper's careful stealth. The office was dark, the hallway was lit; Hopper watched the five shadows move across the office floor and the side of the old desk as the gangsters continued down the hall, moving past them. Hopper lifted himself up, peering over the sill of the office window, watching as the gangsters crossed the intersection of corridors farther along and kept going.

"We clear?"

He turned on his toes as Lisa's face appeared over the edge of the desk. He nodded, waving her over. She moved out from her hiding place but kept herself low.

"What the hell are you doing here?" she whispered.

"Undercover, part of a federal task force. But why are *you* here? Saint John had you locked up in his back office." Hopper checked the corridor again, then turned back to Lisa.

"That's a long story," she said.

"So start talking."

"He offered me a job."

Hopper stared at her. "What? A *job*? Doing what?"

Lisa shrugged. "I'm not sure. But it was just a ruse, anyway. He invited me up here, gave me the tour, but then he locked me in that room." She ran her hands through her hair and shook her head, focusing on the floor rather than Hopper. "He tried to get me to . . ."

Hopper felt his blood run cold. "To what?"

She shook her head again. "Doesn't matter. But listen, this isn't like any kind of street gang I've worked with before. It's weird—it's like, I don't know, a cross between a private army and some kind of cult. Saint John has some kind of hold over these people. He's obsessed with what he calls the Day of the

Serpent—it's some kind of apocalyptic prophecy he believes is about to come true."

Hopper frowned. "You sure you don't believe it too?"

"What do you mean?"

"The party on Independence Day. When you went into a trance, you talked about the darkness coming, a night that is serpent black."

She narrowed her eyes, grimacing in confusion. "I'm sorry, I don't remember any of that." She paused. "Is that *really* what I said? Wow."

"Yeah, wow is right." Hopper shifted on his haunches, getting more comfortable. "You're going to tell me there's no connection between you and the Vipers?"

"Oh, no, there is. I know Saint John."

Hopper felt that familiar pang of adrenaline in his chest. "You *know* him?"

She nodded. "I worked with him before, during an old study I was a part of, at a place called the Rookwood Institute. He was one of the pilot group of felons enrolled in the program. We didn't get very far before it was shut down, but he was in that group."

Lisa filled him in on what she had learned from Saint John while in his company. Hopper listened carefully, processing the information. Then, when she was done, he nodded. "Okay. We need to get you out of here."

"Me? What about you?"

Hopper shook his head. "From what you've just said, the Day of the Serpent is something very big. I need to find out what it is."

"But I can help!"

"Yes, you can. By getting out of here. Go to the 65th Precinct in Brooklyn—to Detective Delgado. Tell her everything you know, and she'll take it to the task force."

"Okay," said Lisa. "But *how* do I get out?"

Hopper rubbed his chin. "I have a contact here, he should

be able to help. But I'll have to find him first. Will you be okay here?"

Lisa nodded.

"Okay, great. Keep the light off, keep out of sight, okay? I'll be as fast as I can."

"Good luck," said Lisa.

Hopper nodded to her, then stood and left, closing the office door behind him with a click.

CHAPTER THIRTY-NINE

DANGEROUS DISCOVERIES

JULY 13, 1977
SOUTH BRONX, NEW YORK

Hopper retraced his steps as best he could, remembering more of the headquarters layout than he realized. It didn't take him long to reach the central block of offices, and, following the sounds of the gang's search, he managed to locate Leroy's team.

"Hey, man, any luck?"

Hopper shook his head, and glanced at the two others standing with his fellow infiltrator. He had to be fast, allowing no room for doubt.

"Someone's seen something over in the west building," said Hopper. He nodded at the two others. "You two, go grab Lincoln and his crew, head over to that side. Me and Leroy will go out into the street, come in from the back. That should corner them."

The other two glanced at each other as they processed Hopper's on-the-fly instructions. It was Leroy who stepped in. He clapped his hands.

"Hey, you heard the dude, let's roll, let's roll!"

This seemed to be enough. The two men slapped Leroy on the shoulder as they passed, picking up the pace as they headed down the hallway. Hopper waited until they were out of sight, then turned to Leroy.

The young man nodded, a wry smile on his face.

"So where is she?" he asked.

Hopper laid a hand on Leroy's shoulder, pulling him in for a close conference.

"Her name is Lisa, and you need to get her out. She's got important information for the feds, okay? She needs to get back to Gallup, safe and sound." He looked Leroy in the eye. "You think you can get her out without being caught?"

"You just leave this to me."

Hopper gave directions back to the old office as best he could, Leroy nodding along, saying he knew where to go. Hopper waved him off, then took a look around, getting his bearings. He was on the ground level of the main office area, Saint John's office four floors above his head.

Perfect.

With Lisa hopefully on her way out to safety, Hopper felt a sense of relief, a weight lifting that gave him new urgency, new energy.

It was time to go take a closer look at the storage rooms.

Now recognizing the hallways of the central block, Hopper ducked into the first empty office he had seen before. The room was filled with the wooden crates, all neatly stacked in piles of six that reached about chest level. Now Hopper noticed that each crate was in fact stamped with some kind of identifying mark, but on every one it had been obliterated with a few haphazard strokes of black spray paint.

Hopper moved to the crate closest. It was nailed shut, and he was going to need a tool to open it, something like the crowbar he'd had back down in the warehouse. Turning around, he saw there was nothing in the office that was going to be of use. Cursing under his breath, Hopper ducked back out in the corridor and tried the next office, then the next.

He got lucky. Like the office he'd left Lisa in, this one still had an old desk in it, pushed into the corner. The top was wooden, but taking a closer look, Hopper saw the drawers on either side of the desk were metal. Pulling one out, he lifted it up to examine the construction. It was four metal plates, held together from the sides by four screws. The base was a flat sheet of metal, and rattled at his touch.

Hopper took the drawer back to the first office. Placing it on the floor, he held the back of the drawer down with the toe of one boot, and grabbed the drawer handle with both hands. Two hard tugs and the drawer buckled—enough for him to pull out the base sheet of metal.

The makeshift tool was better than nothing. Moving now to the stack of crates, he squeezed the corner of the metal sheet under the lip of the crate's lid, alternately levering and sliding the sheet farther in until he had made enough of a gap to get his fingers under. The nails slid out freely after that. Hopper laid the lid against the side of the stack, next to the metal sheet, and looked inside the crate.

It was exactly as he had suspected. Inside, lying on a bed of straw stuffing, was a gun—more precisely, a Kalashnikov assault rifle, also known as an AK-47. Soviet-designed, manufactured somewhere in the Eastern bloc. Largely unchanged in the last thirty years, the AK-47 was surprisingly simple but highly effective, requiring little maintenance and little skill in its use, making it the number one black-market choice for guerilla groups all over the world and the big drug cartels closer to home.

But for a New York gang, it was some seriously heavy metal. Hopper lifted the weapon out, and gave it a cursory once-over. He didn't need to employ much of his firearms knowledge to know he was holding the real deal. Hefting the ugly weapon in one hand, he checked in the crate. It looked like there were five more buried in the straw, making it six rifles per crate. He was standing next to a stack of six identical crates, and there were at least a dozen stacks filling the storage space. Multiply that by the other storage areas, not to mention the stacks of crates down in the warehouse itself, and the scale of Saint John's operation was terrifying.

He wasn't building a gang. He was building an army. An army led by a madman—a Vietnam vet who had gone to war and come back with an idea about how to change the world.

Who had come back apparently hearing not the voice of God, but of his divine opposition. Who now used that belief to persuade his followers that their time was coming, that a better world awaited them, one that they would be in charge of.

If they just obeyed him.

The Day of the Serpent—the day the devil himself would come to earth and take New York as his kingdom.

It was nonsense, a fantasy, of course. Saint John was a damaged man, but there was no way he believed in the devil. Spouting pseudo-Biblical claptrap was an easy way to elevate himself above his gang, and an easy way to keep control.

Because some people would believe any story if you told it in the right way.

But the Day of the Serpent? *That* was real. That was the day that Saint John would unleash his army in some kind of attack.

Hopper replaced the gun in the crate, fighting a wave of nausea and panic that began to boil somewhere deep inside him.

What was the plan? Where would they attack? Were the Vipers merely going to spill out of the warehouse, guns blazing?

No, that made no sense. Saint John was a planner. He'd been building up the gang and building up his arsenal slowly and carefully. Biding his time.

Readying his plan of attack.

And Hopper knew exactly where those plans were held.

He raced from the storage bays, heading for the stairs.

Heading up to Saint John's office.

Hopper proceeded quickly but not without caution, but found the place deserted. The search parties seemed to have all moved into the west side of the headquarters, Leroy spreading word of Hopper's false sighting, clearing the way to getting Lisa out.

He only hoped that Saint John had joined the rest of his gang, because if not, Hopper would have to scratch his plan of getting into the boss's office. As he approached, he decided his backup plan would be to simply get the hell out. He had more than enough information for Gallup's task force to make a move against the Vipers, not to mention whatever intel Lisa could add. True, he didn't know what the Day of the Serpent was, and he'd gotten no closer to establishing a concrete link between the Vipers and the card homicides, but Hopper just had to trust that that would all come out in the wash once Saint John and his gang were in federal custody.

But Hopper's luck held out. Saint John's office was empty.

Hopper moved inside. The table still had the warehouse map stretched out across it, next to it a set of draftsman's tools. Hopper took a moment to study the diagram, then quickly folded it and slid it under his jacket. The layout was sure to prove useful to the task force when they planned their raid.

Then he turned his attention to the wide file cabinet standing against the wall. It had six drawers, and all but the second from the top—which was empty—were locked. However, the drawers were not designed for security. Peering into the gap between the top drawer and the frame of the cabinet itself, Hopper could see the tooth of the flimsy lock mechanism.

He went back to the table, picked up a metal ruler that lay among the compasses, pencils, and set squares, and forced it into the gap above the drawer. Applying a little leverage, the lock assembly snapped, and Hopper yanked the drawer open, pulling it out far enough so he could stand beside it and look through the sheets layered inside.

They were blueprints, the traditional white lines on dark paper, crafted in meticulous detail. Hopper could make no sense of the diagrams shown, but searching the edge of the paper with his finger, he soon found the legend. He squinted as he tried to read the tiny text.

They were, apparently, plans for a turbine—a huge industrial unit from a power plant.

Frowning, Hopper leafed through the blueprints underneath. There were more of the same, and of similar devices—transformers and power systems. Underneath those were sheets of white paper, which looked, on the face of it, like street maps. It was only on closer inspection that Hopper realized they were circuit diagrams of something on a truly vast scale.

Hopper pulled out the sheets and dumped them all onto the table. Repeating his trick with the ruler, he opened the other drawers. There were architectural drawings and sheets taken from a ledger. Hopper didn't know what any of it was, and there was no time to start poring over it.

Were these the plans for the Day of the Serpent? He had no idea.

He had to keep looking.

First, he checked the big desk. The drawers were all empty, save for the one on the top right—the drawer Hopper had seen Saint John check earlier. Inside was a silver crucifix.

Hopper frowned, but then he remembered the engraving on Saint John's dog tag, identifying his religion as Catholic. Did Catholics keep crucifixes? Hopper wasn't sure, and he didn't know why it was in the drawer. But it wasn't important, and it certainly wasn't what he was looking for.

Next, he turned and opened the first door behind the desk—the file room that had been used as Lisa's makeshift prison cell. Stepping past the small round table, he cast an eye over the metal shelving, then froze.

Lined up along one shelf was a set of big black file boxes, each marked with a label Hopper had seen before.

U.S. DEPARTMENT OF DEFENSE
WITHDRAWAL FORBIDDEN

The files from Hoeler's secret apartment. They were all here.

Well, that was one mystery solved. Hopper didn't know if it was important, but it would certainly form part of his report to Gallup. He continued to search the shelves, looking for anything useful that might have provided a clue to Saint John's plan, but after a few moments he stood back, confusion clouding his mind.

All of the metal shelves were full, but Hopper couldn't make sense of the collection of books Saint John had gathered. There were large, fat hardcovers on psychology and psychiatry—academic textbooks, Hopper assumed. There were books on military history, and practical manuals on bushcraft. On another shelf was a motley collection of older tomes, each one a different size, some leather-bound with gilt page edges, others bound in what seemed to be plain cloth. The writing on the spines of several volumes was not in English; Hopper recognized the Latin, and made a guess at Greek for some others. The ones he could read gave him little clue as to the contents:

The Key of Solomon. The Calvacan Grimoire. The Word of the Eye.

Turning on his heel, Hopper scanned the rest of the shelves. More books, new and old. More files—these in binders, the spines labeled alphabetically below a printed sticker:

ROOKWOOD INSTITUTE

Hopper paused. That was where Lisa said she and Saint John had first met, but there was no time to investigate now. If the contents of Saint John's little library were important, fine, but he couldn't take anything with him, not now. He'd seen enough.

Time to leave.

That's when he heard movement from the office. Hopper stilled himself, then silently stepped backward until his back was pressed into the corner of the room by one of the metal shelves. He waited, listening, willing himself to become invisible—or, at least, for nobody to come into the file room.

He heard another door open, and close, and then quiet settled once more. Hopper counted in his head, and then moved cautiously to the door. There was no sound from beyond, so he risked looking around the doorjamb.

The office was empty. The paperwork he had piled onto the table was still there, untouched.

Stepping out into the office, Hopper thought about what he had heard, the sound of the other door. It wasn't the main office door—that was still open. It must have been the other one, the second door, leading to what he assumed was another file room.

Hopper slipped along the wall behind the desk, and tried the second door. It was unlocked.

The room beyond was as he had expected, the dimensions

identical to those of the first. Here, though, he was surprised to find the space occupied by a large freestanding closet.

Hopper opened it. Inside were a couple of empty coat hangers, and one from which hung a long, hooded black robe made of some cheap stiff cloth.

Hopper shook his head, aware of how time was slipping away from him. He closed the closet and went back into the office.

And heard a bang from somewhere over his head, like something very heavy had been dropped on the floor. Looking up, Hopper realized that the only thing above him was the warehouse roof itself, and as he stood in the middle of the office, he now heard more noises. People moving around over his head.

Lots of people.

He had to find out what was going on.

Hopper emerged onto the roof and flattened himself against the wall of the stairwell block, grateful for the easy cover it offered as he crabbed sideways until he could peer around the side to see what was going on.

The roof of the office block was a flat, square expanse that stood above the roof of the warehouse itself, which was a football-field-sized array of angles stretching out on Hopper's left. From up here, the lights of the Bronx shone brightly in the warm air of the summer night. The warehouse complex seemed to be the tallest structure around for several blocks, although ahead were the lights of apartment buildings. Taking a quick scan around, he saw that the sky behind him was a brighter blaze as the lights of Manhattan painted the scattering of clouds above in brilliant orange. Even from this distance, the glowing tower of the Empire State Building was clear, along with the other tall landmarks of Midtown; farther still, the red lights that topped the spire of one of the World Trade Center towers blinked on and off, on and off.

But Hopper had no time to enjoy the view. He turned to watch what was happening on the office roof, careful to keep himself out of sight behind the stairwell block.

The rooftop was filled with people—the Vipers, of course, although Hopper wasn't entirely sure he could be certain of that fact, given that every member was now wearing a long white robe, their heads covered with hoods. They were lined up in several straight rows, facing away from him.

Standing in front of his—what, congregation? Coven? Hopper had no idea what to call it—stood a man in a robe identical to the others, except it was black.

Saint John. He *was* facing Hopper, but while the rooftop was fairly well lit by the surrounding glow of the city, Hopper was fairly sure he was invisible in the shadow of the stairwell block.

Saint John had his arms raised, his fingers splayed as he addressed the gang.

"My brothers! Oh, my sisters! We gather here in the black shadow of our dark master and we give thanks to Him! Yes, we give our thanks, like we give our blood, and our life, and our souls to Him. Hear me!"

Saint John lifted his head. His face was lost in the shadow of his hood, but Hopper saw, even now, the light glinting from the silver aviator sunglasses he was still wearing.

"We stand here at the dawn of a new day. Of our day. The day of our *reckoning*. The day of our *awakening*. The day carved into the fabric of our souls from the moment we were born and lost to the darkness. Hear me! The day has come. The Day of the Serpent is now!"

The gang was silent. Saint John dropped his arms and dropped his head. Nobody moved, or spoke.

Then Saint John lifted his head again.

"I have your back," he said, almost too quietly for Hopper to hear. "And you have mine."

At this, the gang roared, throwing closed-fist salutes into the air as they repeated the familiar phrase. Saint John lifted his arms again, gesturing to his followers to increase their volume, their fervor.

The Vipers obliged. Hopper sank down onto his haunches, shaking his head.

"Hear me!" Saint John yelled over the chorus of the gang. "Hear me! We have but one more task! One more act before all will be ours, before the master of the night descends to bestow His dark blessing upon us. One final sacrifice, and the darkness shall come, the night, serpent black!"

Hopper jerked his head as he spotted movement out of the corner of his eye. He sank farther back into the shadows as two more white-robed Vipers appeared from the side of the roof, dragging with them a woman in a red dress, her dark hair flailing as she struggled to free herself.

Hopper felt his chest go tight, his breath leaving his lungs as he stopped himself from making any movement, no matter how small.

Lisa. They'd caught her.

The two men pulled her toward Saint John. Lisa gave it her all, but she was held firm. Dragged into position, she looked around, the expression of fear on her face making Hopper's blood run cold.

This is my fault. This is my fault. I should have gotten her out myself.

Saint John stepped up onto the low wall that ran around the edge of the roof. From somewhere he pulled out a silver object that glinted in his hand—the crucifix from the office drawer. He grabbed the stem of it and pulled, revealing the shaft of the cross was actually a blade, the scabbard now shining in his other hand.

Hopper swore under his breath. He scanned the rooftop,

his heart ticking along at approximately half the speed of light.

But it was hopeless. It was him against a hundred. There was nothing he could do.

Seeing the knife, Lisa cried out and pulled at the arms holding her again. As the two men fought to keep hold of her, the hood of one of them was thrown back.

It was Leroy.

Hopper felt the bile rise in his throat.

What have I done?

Lisa was pulled around until she was standing right in front of Saint John. He looked down at her from his position on the wall, his arms outstretched once more, the dagger in his right hand. He was talking, but Hopper couldn't hear it.

And then, Lisa stopped struggling. She stood tall, and as Saint John gestured, Leroy and the other man let go. Lisa's arms fell to her side. Saint John held his hand out to her and she took it, stepping up onto the wall beside the gang leader and turning around to face the others.

One of the acolytes handed a silver goblet to Saint John. The leader took it, then held it out to Lisa. Hopper heard the next word quite clearly.

"Drink."

Lisa took the goblet, almost without looking at it. She raised it to her lips and then—

She paused. She swayed a little. Saint John supported her back.

"The time is now," he said. "It is as it has been foreseen. You know that. You know what to do.

"Drink."

Hopper had to do something. He didn't know what was going on, and he didn't know what he could do, but there was no way in hell he could just stand by. He had to intervene. Even against these odds, even though it was hopeless, suicidal even.

He had to try. If nothing else, he had to try.

He adjusted his footing, falling into a crouch, ready to power out of his hiding place.

Then Lisa dropped the goblet. It clattered onto the rooftop.

Hopper moved forward, breaking his cover, his only advantage being the fact that the gang members were all—Saint John aside—looking the other way.

Saint John, and Lisa. As he stepped out from the stairwell block, she looked up—looked *at* him, he was sure of it.

And then she took a step backward and disappeared over the edge of the roof, her red dress billowing as gravity took over.

"No!" Hopper yelled. The gang turned around in surprise to look at him. At the head of the group, Saint John lifted his arms.

"The darkness has come! The Day of the Serpent has dawned!"

Behind him, the lights of the Bronx went out.

Hopper felt his breath catch in his throat. He looked around, the warehouse now surrounded by nothing but a black void in three directions. He turned toward the orange glow behind him, Manhattan, a glittering jewel in the night.

And then the lights began to go out there, too, starting at the top of the island. Blocks of color vanished, almost in a zigzag pattern, as the power failed, the wave of darkness sweeping down toward Midtown.

Hopper watched as the Empire State Building vanished. A moment later, the lights of the World Trade Center blinked out of existence.

New York City was caught in a massive blackout.

Hopper turned; the rooftop was now lit only by the moon. Standing on the edge of the roof, Saint John laughed, and then he pointed with both robed arms at Hopper.

"Get him!"

That was when Hopper felt a hand in his, pulling him back. He turned around.

Martha looked him in the eye.

"Quit dawdling, start running," she said.

Hopper obeyed.

CHAPTER FORTY

LIGHTS OUT IN BROOKLYN

"Anything?"

Delgado looked down the stepladder, angling the flashlight so as not to catch Diane full in the face. By her own head, the brownstone's fuse box was open, the ancient mess of wires, ceramic fuses, and switches exposed.

"Nope, looks okay to me, although I'm no expert," said Delgado. She closed the box and made her way down the ladder, which was being held by Diane's upstairs neighbor, Eric Van Sabben. Eric's wife, Esther, shone her own flashlight at Delgado's feet, providing some much needed visibility as she descended, while another light was thrown on the closed fuse box, this one from Ms. Schaefer, the older lady from the ground-floor apartment.

"I told you," she said, "it's like 1965 all over again. Power was out, oh, twelve hours at least. And it was winter, too. A cold one at that."

Returning to the ground, Delgado braced herself for another of Ms. Schaefer's reminiscences from the good old days. She'd only known the woman for a half hour, but already knew the history of not just the building but the whole neighborhood, including how it had coped with the last power outage a little over a decade earlier.

This time, however, Ms. Schaefer seemed to get the message. The group stood in the building's entrance hall, flashlights pointed at each other.

"I think she's right," said Delgado. "It's not just us." She moved to the front door and pulled it open. Outside the street was dark, save for the glow of a few more flashlights as other residents ventured out to investigate.

"I think I'll take a look," said Eric, taking the flashlight from his wife. "Not much else to do now, is there?" He looked at his wife, then at Delgado, as if either of them could make the power come back on so he could continue watching the Mets game. When neither of them said anything, he sighed. "I want to see how far it goes."

"Shea Stadium is a long walk," said Diane, folding her arms, a smile playing over her mouth. Eric glanced at her, then chuckled.

"I'm sorry," he said, his own grin growing in size. Then he looked at Delgado again, like he was waiting to be given permission.

Delgado realized that, in theory at least, she did hold *some* kind of authority, being a police officer. She nodded, and pointed to the door with her own flashlight.

"Okay, but be careful. It'll probably be darker than you think."

Eric smiled. "Don't worry, I'm not going to get mugged." At this, Esther gasped, and grabbed hold of her husband's arm.

"It's not mugging I'm worried about," said Delgado. "You're

more likely to trip and fall, or step down a hole or something. This is not a good time to break a leg, Eric."

Eric gave a salute with his flashlight. "Understood." He turned to the others. "I'll be as quick as I can, see what I can see." He gave his wife a kiss on the cheek. "Back soon," he said, and then he flicked on his light and headed out. Esther moved to the door and watched as he vanished into the darkness. Delgado watched her for a moment, then made a decision.

"Okay," she said, "how about we stick together, okay? We'll wait for Eric to come back, see what he's found out. Meantime I should make a few calls." She turned to Diane. "Are we okay to go back to your apartment?"

Diane nodded. "Of course. We have a battery radio somewhere, too. There might be something on the news."

"Great," said Delgado. Esther turned around; Delgado caught her eye. "Does that sound okay?"

Esther nodded.

"Ms. Schaefer? Would you prefer to wait in your own apartment?"

"Oh, heavens no, I want to hear what Eric has to say when he comes back."

"Okay, good."

"Just let me get a few things first," Ms. Schaefer said, turning and heading back to her apartment. "We can have a nice game of Monopoly by candlelight."

Delgado watched as the older woman disappeared through her door. When the coast was clear, she gave a big sigh.

"Okay, good," she said again.

Diane laughed, and patted Delgado on the shoulder. "Ms. Schaefer's fine, you'll like her."

"Just whatever you do," said Esther, "don't get her started on *American Graffiti*."

Delgado frowned. "*American Graffiti*? Like, the movie?"

Diane nodded. "Yes, and it's a *very* long story. Come on, let's see if we can find that radio."

CHAPTER FORTY-ONE

BLACKOUT

JULY 13, 1977
SOUTH BRONX, NEW YORK

Martha reached the stairwell first and swung herself through the door, pushing at Hopper's back as he passed her. She slammed the door shut, then jammed the barred opening mechanism with a crowbar, perhaps the very same one she had wielded against Hopper earlier.

"Come on," she said, heading down the stairs. Hopper followed, pushing every question save the obvious one out of his mind as he focused on making it down the stairs in one piece, his path lit only by weak shafts of moonlight that penetrated the darkness at irregular intervals through small, high windows set into the very top of the stairwell block.

"What the hell's going on?"

"Later. No time to yabber now. And don't break your neck on the stairs, either."

Hopper took this to be good advice. As they descended, the stairwell became a black hole. He could hear Martha ahead of him, but he was forced to slow his pace, feeling his way down with one hand on the rail and the other groping the darkness on the other side, his fingertips occasionally making contact with the wall.

Then light exploded into the stairwell as, below, Martha pushed open the bottom door. She looked up, waiting for Hopper to follow. He sped up, taking the stairs now two at a time, and went through the door as his apparent rescuer held it open.

They were back in the warehouse—not that Hopper could see any of it. He held his hand up to his face, shielding himself from the glare. He heard the steady rumble of the engine before he realized he was looking straight into the headlights of Leroy's decrepit station wagon. Martha was already behind the wheel.

Hopper needed no invitation. He ran for the passenger side and slid in even as the vehicle lurched on its worn suspension, Martha twisting the wheel as she spun the car around in reverse, the headlights now pointing for the warehouse exit. Hopper's door swung shut under its own weight as Martha shoved the column shift into gear, flooring the accelerator. The screech of tires echoed around the warehouse as the wagon sped toward the open doors and out into the night. Hopper grabbed the handle above his door and hung on as the car bounced over the rough road, the headlights playing over the walls of the alleyway. A few seconds later, the walls disappeared as they made it out onto the main road. Martha turned sharply, heading out of the industrial zone and toward the Bronx proper.

"Any sign?"

Hopper turned on the bench seat as the car bumped over another pothole. There was nothing behind them but the vague suggestion of the warehouse, what moonlight there was vanishing for now behind a cloud.

"I can't see anything," he said.

"Okay," said Martha. She pulled the wheel again, taking a corner with too much speed. The wagon bumped up onto the curb, and the engine spat loudly, then died. Martha jammed the brakes and the car slewed to a halt. She sat behind the wheel, her chest heaving, shaking her head.

"Piece. Of. Shit." She banged the wheel and swore again.

Hopper turned around to her.

"Now you can tell me what the hell is going on. What was that up on the roof, and why the hell are you helping me now? Last time we met, you wanted to kill me."

Martha looked sideways at him, not taking her hands from the wheel.

"Yeah, sorry about that," she said. "But I had to do something. Lincoln was going to blow your head off and I figured you were worth keeping around. But don't worry, I wasn't going to kill you. Maybe give you a little beating, that's all. But listen, that thing with the cops—you're still working, right?"

Hopper blinked. "What?"

"It was just a cover," Martha continued, "to get you in? Come on, I'm not stupid. Although maybe I was looking harder than the others. Pays to keep your eyes open in the Vipers. Been doing that a year now, so I guess I got used to it."

Hopper just looked at her. "What do you mean, you've been keeping your eyes open? You *are* a Viper, aren't you?"

"Yes and no," said Martha. "But look, I don't think we got time to get into it. We need to get the hell out and do it *now*."

With that, Martha twisted the key in the ignition. It took three attempts, but the car spluttered into life. She pumped the accelerator a couple of times, then, apparently satisfied, put the car into gear.

"Keep a look out behind," she said. "It won't take them long to get after us."

"You're right, it didn't."

Martha turned to face the rear, as Hopper already was. In

the distance, lights flashed as vehicles approached from a side alley.

The Vipers were in pursuit.

Hopper turned back around.

"Go. Now!"

Martha pressed the pedal and the car shot forward.

CHAPTER FORTY-TWO

THE CITY UPSIDE DOWN

JULY 13, 1977
SOUTH BRONX, NEW YORK

The darkness that had enveloped New York was a surprise to Hopper; the realization that, really, the night *was* black—*serpent black*, said a voice at the back of his mind—was disconcerting.

He had experienced this kind of darkness before, of course. Perhaps that was why it unsettled him—even after his experience on the warehouse rooftop, seeing Lisa Sargeson apparently jump to her death.

Because it was the kind of darkness you could only really experience out in the wilderness.

Or out in the jungle, hundreds of miles from civilization.

Hopper pushed those thoughts to the back of his mind, compartmentalizing in order to get through the current situation. The plan was simple: Get the hell away from the Vipers, somewhere safe. Then he could stop to figure out who Martha really was and why she was helping him. And then he needed to get to the authorities, get to Gallup. Whether Martha would help with that part, he didn't yet know. But one thing was for sure—she was just as interested in running from the Vipers as he was.

And then he needed to get home. He didn't know if the blackout extended as far as Brooklyn—and he hoped to hell it didn't—but he'd been away from Diane and Sara long enough.

Hopper adjusted his grip on the strap over his door, pushing the thoughts of his family out of his mind—for now, anyway—allowing himself to focus on the immediate task at hand. But it soon became clear that any plans he had were going to be far from easy to carry out.

The streets around the industrial area were clear of both people and traffic, and Martha piloted the station wagon through the grid of featureless streets, apparently very familiar with the layout, in an attempt to throw their pursuers off. And it seemed to have worked, because after the initial sighting of headlight glow, Hopper hadn't seen any sign of their being followed.

Then the darkness began to wash out in a yellow-orange glow, from somewhere up ahead. The color shifted in a haze that Hopper realized was smoke.

Martha turned out of the industrial zone and onto a main artery and slammed on the brakes, twisting the wheel to avoid plowing into a crowd of people in the middle of the street. Ahead, on the corner, a building was ablaze from floor to roof, the structure already reduced to a skeletal shell as the flame licked twenty, thirty feet into the air. Hopper could feel the heat from where they had stopped. Around them, people spread out across the width of the street, some carrying flashlights, everyone giving the burning building as wide a berth as possible.

Martha tooted the horn gently, and the crowd lazily began

to part around them. It seemed to Hopper that they were the only vehicle on the road, and he understood why.

The blackout had drawn everybody out onto the streets. It was still relatively early—about nine, according to his watch, and the night was hot and muggy. No power meant no lights, no TV, no AC—for those in this neighborhood lucky enough to have AC—and no fans.

But the people in the crowd, Hopper realized as the station wagon slowly crawled forward, weren't afraid or nervous. If anything, they seemed to be happy. Faces turned to them as they moved past, smiling, waving. Some people gave the car a thump on the hood and the roof, and, over the roar of the burning building, Hopper heard the crowd's chatter, punctuated by the occasional shout, the more frequent peal of laughter. Past the fire, the crowd thinned a little, and there was space now for people to sit on the curb or on parked cars, drinking from cans and bottles, the orange sparks of cigarettes dancing in the half-light.

Martha leaned over the wheel as she risked picking up speed, her eyes scanning the way ahead.

"Hell of a time for a street party," she whispered.

Hopper frowned, and turned to look out the rear again. From a distance of half a block, Hopper could now see the full size of the crowd, illuminated by the fire. It did, indeed, look like a street party.

The heavy thud made Hopper spin around. Martha swore and jerked the wheel, moving the wagon into the opposite lane. She swore again as someone moved into her path, forcing her back across the center line. As she swung past the pedestrian, he yelled something and there was another thud; he'd thrown what looked like half a brick against the driver's door.

Martha floored it, and the car lurched forward. Hopper looked out the rear window as the sound of breaking glass reached his ears. Behind them, the men who had thrown bricks at their car had now thrown them through the windows of a store. Hopper watched a mass of people, backlit by the glow of the fire farther up the street, make for the opening in the windows, pulling at the edges of the glass panes until the whole frontage collapsed. Several people ran away at this point, but other silhouettes ducked into the store.

"Looting's already started," said Hopper. "This is just going to get worse."

"The sooner we get out of here, the better."

But Hopper shook his head. "Get out of where? The whole city is blacked out. The lights don't come back on soon, New York is going to turn itself inside out."

"That was his plan," said Martha. "The Day of the Serpent. Cut the power, throw the whole city into chaos. Turn out the lights, people turn on each other. The city destroys itself. That was the plan, Hopper. Saint John wants to destroy New York. He's got his own army. With the power out, he's the goddamn king."

As they spoke, the street got crowded again, lit by more fires. The faces here were less friendly, and the crowd moved quickly, people darting left and right across the street, most carrying armfuls of clothing. Hopper glanced across Martha's side and saw a large clothing store, the double doors of which were smashed open, the sidewalk in front littered with abandoned clothing as people went in and dragged more out.

"Listen," said Hopper, leaning across to Martha. "I don't know what your story is, but yes, I'm still a cop, I'm still doing a job. I need to get to the authorities, and I'm going to assume that you'll help with that, otherwise you would have left me up on that roof. Am I right?"

As Martha focused on weaving a path ahead, she didn't speak, but she did nod in confirmation.

Then, lights from behind. Hopper looked over his shoulder and saw another car approaching, horn blaring as it swerved to avoid the people in the road.

"Vipers." Hopper turned back around. "We have to lose them."

Martha gestured out the window. "There are too many people here. We're not going to be able to get through."

Hopper was already scanning the way ahead. He pointed. "There."

Coming up was a large four-way intersection, looping around the corner of which was a line of cars, nose to tail, lights flashing and horns beeping as they got snarled in the jam. On the opposite side, the street was clear.

Martha took the clear road, the wagon once more enveloped in darkness as they escaped the glow of fires on the main drag. She slowed, leaning over the wheel as she looked out of the windshield.

"What's the matter?"

"Just trying to get my bearings," she said. Then her face was lit up as headlights appeared behind them and were reflected off the rearview, momentarily blinding Hopper. He ducked down and turned in his seat, only to see the Vipers' car hurtling down the street toward them.

"Come on!" said Hopper.

"This is as fast as this hunk of junk will go!"

The headlights of the pursuing car swept over them as the Vipers pulled alongside them, their newer vehicle roaring as they easily overtook the station wagon, a couple of its occupants leaning out the back window hollering at Martha and Hopper. Hopper saw Lincoln at the wheel, and they momentarily made eye contact. Then the vehicle shot forward, barreling through an intersection ahead and, once enough distance had been reached, swerved, swinging back into their lane and heading straight for the slower station wagon.

"*Goddammit!*"

Martha slammed on the brakes again. The tires protested but did little to stop their forward motion. Hopper braced himself for impact, not thinking Lincoln was crazy enough to ram them, but not willing to regret that assumption.

That was when a third vehicle appeared, coming toward the intersection from the street on Hopper's left. A dump truck, squat and gray, a solid mass of reinforced steel. Hopper saw it first, out of the corner of his eye, just in time to reach over and pull the wheel out of Martha's hands, sending the wagon into a sideways skid in an attempt to avoid joining the scene of the oncoming accident.

Hopper wasn't sure if Lincoln saw it coming, but in the last moments before the impact he thought maybe the Vipers turned to look at the approaching vehicle. As the gang's car reentered the intersection, the dump truck powered across its path, smashing into the passenger side. The impact slowed the truck, but not by much. As the station wagon skidded to a stop, rocking on its suspension and angled across the middle of the street, the dump truck veered only a little, dragging the Vipers' car across the intersection, virtually tearing the vehicle in two. Orange and white sparks flew in huge arcs from the roadway as the truck and car continued their journey, finally coming to a rest by the pedestrian crosswalk on the opposite curb.

Hopper sat up in the car, his ears ringing, while Martha curled herself into a tighter ball beside him. There was no movement from the Vipers—Hopper couldn't imagine anyone in their car surviving the accident—but from the raised, and perfectly intact, cab of the dump truck, two men stepped out, one pulling himself through the passenger-side window to climb onto the roof, the other swinging open the driver's side door and standing with one foot on the arch of the front wheel. As Hopper watched, the man standing on the roof raised both arms in the air and lifted his head, screaming at the heavens, while the driver jumped down onto the road to inspect the wreckage of the car. As he moved into the beam of the truck's twisted, but still functional, headlight, Hopper saw he was wearing a leather jacket with a patch on the back:

DREADNOUGHTS

Another gang. The pair must have stolen the dump truck to take it on a joy ride.

"Holy *shit*."

Hopper glanced at Martha, who was straightening herself out behind the wheel, her eyes fixed on the carnage at the corner.

"Yeah, that's about right," said Hopper. "Sorry I grabbed the wheel. I wasn't sure you saw the truck coming."

"We would have been killed if you hadn't," said Martha. Her hands fumbled with the wheel and shifter, her breath coming in ragged bursts. Hopper turned to her.

"You hurt?"

She shook her head.

"Okay, let's go, before they get interested in us, too."

Martha got the car into reverse, wincing as she ground the gears. Ahead, the driver of the dump truck looked in their direction, his form nothing more than a silhouette against the truck's headlamp, but a second later Martha had the car turned around and pointed down the dead side street. As they moved out of the intersection, Hopper kept watch behind, but nobody was following.

CHAPTER FORTY-THREE

HOW THE OTHER HALF LIVES

JULY 13, 1977
SOUTH BRONX, NEW YORK

Martha shook her head, leaning over the wheel again. They'd been traveling for all of fifteen minutes, the back streets relatively clear. It seemed like most people had gone out into the wide main avenues in the chaos. Hopper didn't blame them. Here, in the narrow streets between tall buildings, the darkness was almost like a physical presence, a thing alive, a serpent coiled around the city itself, squeezing, squeezing.

Hopper told himself to stop imagining things.

"We're going the wrong way," said Martha, slowing the car to a gentle stop in the middle of a residential block. "If we're going to reach the authorities, we need to head south, into Manhattan."

A moment later the idling engine spluttered to a stop again.

Hopper turned in his seat. "So why are you helping me?"

Martha sucked in her cheeks, and tapped the wheel with both hands before dropping them to her lap and twisting to face Hopper.

"Look, you're a cop, and where I come from, cops are bad news."

Hopper shook his head. "I don't get it."

Martha sighed. "What I mean is, can I trust you? I need to be able to trust you. I made a bet with myself, and right about now I'm hoping that bet was a winning one."

"You're right, I'm a cop. I am—I *was*—undercover. My job was to find out what Saint John was doing with the Vipers, what his plans were, and how to stop him. When I had all that, I was to take it back to a federal task force, and they'd move in. So, yes, you can trust me, but now I need to know I can trust *you*. Because I need to get my information to the authorities, fast, and I might need your help on that."

Martha nodded. "And you've got it. I know I waited too long, but maybe there's still a chance we can do this."

"Waited for what?"

"Look, I'm no cop," said Martha, "but I was just looking out for my brother—Leroy."

"*You* were looking out for *him*? He was trying to get you out. That's how I got involved in the first place. He came to the cops and asked for protection if we helped him."

Martha's jaw hung open. "*That's* where he went?" Then her astonishment turned into amusement, and she smiled. "Shit. But that's my little brother." She adjusted herself in her seat and shook her head, like she was considering this revelation again. Then she turned back to Hopper. "It took me years to find him— Listen, life at home was no piece of cake, and sometimes I don't blame him. The gangs, they made him promises, gave him a look at some other kind of life, and he took it. Our mom, she was real cutup. You know how old he was?"

Hopper said nothing.

"Eleven," said Martha. "That damn fool was *eleven* when he

started running with the Bronx Kings. I tried to help him then, and more than once, but it never took. Finally I lost touch completely—most of our family figured he was dead, gotten himself killed on some damn street corner, most likely. But not Mom. She never gave up on him. And neither did I. So eventually I told her I would go and find Leroy and bring him back, you know? So I quit my job, and I said goodbye to my mom, and then I went looking. By then he'd moved on from the Kings, was hanging with the Furies. Didn't take much to get in with them. Leroy spoke out against me. He was afraid I'd come to take him home—and of course he was right. But I'm his big sister and I knew how to play it and I knew if I was going to get him out then it was going to take a while, you know? He was in pretty deep, and I knew there was more to go before I could reach in and pull him out."

"So you stuck around, keeping an eye on him?"

"Damn right I did. I made a promise to our mom. You'd do the same thing, right? Wouldn't you?"

Hopper nodded.

"Right you would," said Martha, turning her gaze to the footwell. "And it was okay—we got talking, Leroy and me, I mean. He seemed less angry with me around, which I took to be a good thing. So we stuck it out together. Then the Vipers came along, and the Furies joined up with them, along with all the other gangs. Slits, Fixers, Crazy Jacks, the whole lot."

"And you went in with them?"

"Oh, trust me, I was looking for a way out, but that is something easier said than done. All I could do was keep us safe and keep my eyes open." She looked back up at Hopper. "And like I said, I'm hoping I made the right choice here with you. Because I need to get out, and I need to get Leroy out too. We need to go back home."

"You're not the only one," said Hopper. "We can help each other. You seem to know a lot about Saint John and the Vipers—and about whatever the hell is going on now."

Martha shrugged. "Some. More than others. I rose up in the Furies, and Saint John kept me around. So yeah, I know some."

"You know more than me, that's for sure," said Hopper. "We need to take as much intel to the feds as possible." He paused. "So you'll help?"

"Hell yes. If it gets Leroy home to his mom, I'll do anything." Martha looked at the row houses on either side of their stationary vehicle. "I don't suppose there's much chance of using a telephone?"

"Well, the telephone system is separate from the power grid," said Hopper. He turned in his seat. "There. There's a booth on the corner. See if you can get this thing going again."

Martha turned the key, and the car grumbled to life. She put it in reverse and it heaved backward, arrowing into the curb by the booth. Hopper got out, and as he walked around the car he kept thinking he saw movement out of the corner of his eye, shapes and shadows dancing along the rooftops of the row houses, but as he looked around, there was nothing to see. Just dark buildings against a lighter sky, the cloud cover now lit by more and more fires as the Bronx burned. In the distance he could hear the sirens of fire engines, but they sounded miles away. So far, he hadn't heard—and they hadn't seen—any police presence of any kind.

The telephone booth was relatively untouched by vandalism, which gave Hopper a cautious optimism. The telephone itself was in place, and appeared to be all in one piece.

It was, however, dead in his ear. He rattled the hook a few times, but it made no difference. It seemed the phones were out along with the power.

As he stepped out onto the sidewalk, he listened to the sirens and the honking of cars far away, and he thought he could hear something else. He stepped out into the middle of the street, scanning the houses.

"Any luck?"

Hopper glanced over his shoulder, and saw Martha standing beside the station wagon, one foot in the car as she leaned on the driver's door.

"No," he said, then looked around again. "Can you hear that?"

Behind him, the car door thunked shut and he heard Martha approach. He walked forward into a T-junction. Dead ahead was a small park ringed with trees, a paved path cutting across, curving around a dry fountain in the middle. On the other side of the park, on the parallel street, Hopper saw that the top level of the middle row house was lit. People moved in the light, and he heard tinny music.

"I guess the rich don't need to worry about having no power," said Martha. Hopper glanced at her, then looked around again. She was right, the area around the park did look relatively nice. The row houses were five levels, and some of them seemed to share a large, open veranda on the top level, with big French windows behind. It was on one of these verandas that the party seemed to be in full swing.

Martha clicked her tongue. "You think we can use their phone?"

Hopper shook his head. "Phones are out," he said, hooking a thumb over his shoulder at the booth on the corner. "What we really need is to find a cop and use their radio."

Martha laughed. "You seen any cops yet? I tell you, they're leaving the Bronx to burn." She paused. "What about a fire crew? They'd have a radio?"

"We could try, but I think they've got their hands pretty much full as it is."

A shrill whistle echoed around the street, like someone trying to hail a cab.

"That you, Frankie?" someone yelled from the veranda.

With a frown, Hopper moved forward, so he could at least get a better look past the trees. As he crossed the park, Martha alongside him, he saw about a dozen people on the veranda, talking, smoking and drinking. There was a table in the corner and a large battery-powered tape deck, from which came the sounds of Bruce Springsteen's "Born to Run."

"Not Frankie, sorry," Hopper called back. At this, some more of the party gathered at the veranda's rail, leaning out to look. Hopper couldn't make them out, backlit as they were by the lights from the French windows.

"Charles?" called a woman.

Hopper exchanged a look with Martha, then turned back to the party.

"Sorry, not Charles either."

"Well, for the love of *Mike*, you'd better have brought some more champagne."

As if to emphasize the woman's point, there was the sound of a cork popping. Someone laughed.

Then came another kind of *pop*—a gunshot, and close. Hopper and Martha instinctively ducked, while someone at the party screamed in fright, and the veranda went quiet, save for Bruce and the E Street Band.

Crouching, Hopper turned to Martha; then came another gunshot, then a third. He tapped her on the shoulder, and together they darted over to the cars parked at the curb, underneath the party house. Martha looked up over the trunk of a car, Hopper back at the house. The veranda was still lit, and someone was looking down over the rail at them.

"Get everyone inside," Hopper called up, as loud as he dared. "Shut off the music and the lights and stay indoors."

The shadow at the veranda didn't give an answer, but disappeared. A moment later the music stopped and the lights went out, followed by a clatter as the French windows were closed.

Hopper turned to Martha, who was still scanning the area.

"That sounded a little close for comfort," he said.

"I can't see anything," said Martha. "Sounded like it was maybe the next street."

"Come on, we need to get moving. You know where you are now?"

"Yep, I've got it. We good to go?"

Hopper stood slowly, checking around. There hadn't been any more gunshots, and nobody else was in the street.

"Okay, we're good. But move, quick."

Martha ran out from behind the car and crossed the park. Hopper did another check of the area, then followed. He reached the station wagon at the same time as Martha, the pair jumping in. Martha turned the wheel as she executed a three-point turn in the narrow street. The station wagon was so long that she was forced to pump the gas and push the front wheel up onto the sidewalk, and by the time they were facing the right direction, both front and rear tires on the left side of the car were on the curb. The engine stalled again.

There was a thud, the car sinking down on its springs before bouncing back up and rocking slightly from side to side. Beside him, Martha looked up, then yelped in fright as the ceiling above her head indented with another heavy thud, the car bouncing again as something else landed on the roof. There were two more thuds, the front windshield cracking loudly at the top, just in front of Hopper, as the roof was bent down farther.

Martha struggled with the gears as the car continued to rock, then looked up again and yelped in surprise. Hopper saw a pair of legs appear in front of the windshield as someone slid down it from the roof, coming to a rest on their knees on the hood. Immediately they spun around and flattened themselves against the windshield, their mouth gaping as they whooped and laughed.

There was more movement all around them as more men slid off the roof of the car, front, rear, sides. Hopper turned this way and that on the bench seat, then quickly slammed his hand down on the door lock on his side, before diving across Martha and doing the same on hers.

The car was surrounded, the men having apparently jumped from the veranda of the house under which the car had stopped. Hopper counted seven of them, and as they began to rock the car from side to side, he saw more coming on foot from farther up the street. Some of them carried makeshift weapons—baseball bats, and one even seemed to be holding a fire ax. They were all dressed in pale blue denim, like a uniform.

Another gang. It wasn't the Vipers, but Hopper didn't think that was going to make much difference to their chances of survival.

Martha twisted the keys in the ignition and the car roared to life, but when she pushed the accelerator, it spluttered and died again. She repeated this while Hopper could only watch the men around them, the car rocking like a ship lost at sea. All it would take was a little coordination, and the gang could flip the vehicle right over, with them still inside.

He raised his arms instinctively as the head of the fire ax carried by one of the newcomers was embedded in the windshield in front of him. The screen didn't shatter, but what cracks had already formed began to spider out across the glass. The gangster jumped onto the hood and heaved at the weapon. As it came free, he lost his balance and fell off the car, to the delight of his cohorts. His position was replaced by another gang member, who picked up the ax and swung a second time.

"Come on!" Hopper yelled, and grabbed a handful of Martha's baseball jacket as he swung himself over the top of the car's front bench seat, landing heavily in the rear, his legs flailing. He felt Martha grab him by the ankle, using his legs to pull herself into the back with him. She crashed onto the floor beside him, but he wasn't stopping. He crawled over the top of the rear passenger seat, until he was in the spacious open trunk. Martha quickly followed, and they crouched behind the seat as the gang, their full attention apparently on the front of the vehicle, began battering the windows with their baseball bats, while the man with the fire ax now worked on the hood.

Whether the gang even knew he and Martha were still inside, Hopper had no idea, but it was now or never. Looking out the rear, he saw the street was clear. He moved to the hatch, then turned his attention to the floor of the wagon, his fingernails tearing at the carpet as he levered it up, revealing an empty void where the spare wheel was supposed to sit. But he found what he was looking for: the tire iron sitting in its cradle on one side. As he pulled it free, Martha scooted past him and opened the rear hatch using the internal handle. With the escape route clear, she turned to Hopper.

He nodded ahead. "Go! I'll be right behind."

She turned and slid out of the car, and sprinted off down the street. Some of the gang finally saw them trying to escape; Hopper heard two men call out, the pair running around the side of the car to give chase.

Hopper jumped out, swinging the tire iron. His improvised club connected with both men, the pair dropping instantly, one out cold, the other rolling on the ground, clutching his face, blood already streaming between his fingers.

The others at the front saw the commotion, but by the time they got to their fallen comrades, Hopper was halfway down the street, arms pumping as he put as much distance between him and the gang as he could. Ahead, he saw Martha crouched by a parked car. He waved at her, and she set off again, Hopper on her tail.

They ran.

CHAPTER FORTY-FOUR

THE RIDERS FROM HELL

JULY 13, 1977
SOUTH BRONX, NEW YORK

They made better progress on foot—so good, in fact, that Hopper wished they'd ditched Leroy's station wagon earlier. The gang of carjackers had given up easily, chasing him and Martha only partway around the small park before giving up. When Hopper and Martha stopped to rest, gasping for air as they sat on a curb, she grinned at him. Hopper found himself returning the smile, sharing her sense of elation, but he knew they'd had a lucky escape. Had the carjackers been carrying guns, things might have ended very differently.

Recovered, they headed back toward the main thoroughfare—they needed to use a police radio to call down to Delgado and, hopefully, Special Agent Gallup, and Hopper reasoned they stood more of a chance of finding the cops out on the main streets rather than in the quieter areas. Martha agreed.

The problem was, there were no cops to be found. The larger streets were busy, as they had been farther uptown, but whatever good humor there had been had long gone. The power had been out for a few hours now, and, with no sign of the authorities, the citizens had split into factions, taking matters into their own hands. As they walked south, Hopper and Martha passed more stores either being looted or having long-since been cleared out, now nothing but empty husks surrounded by shattered glass and trash. They passed an old man sitting on a garden chair outside McCammon's Sporting Goods, shotgun leaning against his shoulder, pistol in one hand, while the grocery store next door was being dismantled, right down to the shelving units, by a line of people. As Hopper and Martha walked past, the man in the garden chair gave them a look and adjusted his grip on the pistol, the store behind him completely untouched, while a pair of youths wheeled an entire drinks refrigerator out of the grocery store on a two-wheeled trolley.

"The city is dying," said Martha, looking ahead with dead eyes as they continued their journey. "No power, extreme heat, and the place turns into a zoo."

Hopper said nothing. He just kept his eyes open, watching the destruction unfold, searching for any sign of the police.

There was none.

They stopped at the next intersection, taking their bearings and picking an alternate route as the street ahead was blocked with several cars, one of which was on its side, another on fire. In front of the wreck, one young man was arguing with a group of three others, a trio of women standing nearby, shouting. A moment later, the young man was on the ground, the others kicking his body while two of the women held the third one back.

The next street over looked like a bomb had hit it, but Hopper recognized the damage as old, just New York falling to pieces long before the power went out. Two wide buildings with boarded windows flanked an empty lot filled with weeds nearly as tall as he was. On the other side of the street, two men leaned against a chain-link fence, smoking.

Hopper picked up the pace, Martha matching him step for step.

At the corner ahead, they heard someone calling for help. It was a woman's voice, older, and it echoed around the streets, the direction it was coming from impossible to place. As they walked on, the voice got louder, then it got softer, then it stopped altogether.

Hopper gritted his teeth. He glanced at Martha, and saw the young woman staring ahead again, her expression blank.

She was right. The city was dying. Destroying itself.

Saint John's Day of the Serpent.

Hopper vowed to make the Vipers pay.

As they continued, heading to the main arterial route to Manhattan, the night was much brighter thanks to the fires that had steadily increased in number during their trek. A few blocks over, it seemed like a whole street was ablaze, and they saw the glow of fires all around, flickering in the darkness. What the Bronx was going to look like at daybreak, Hopper could only imagine.

"Do you think it's like this in Manhattan?"

Hopper glanced at Martha, pursing his lips. He thought of the towering skyscrapers, the tourist clichés of the Big Apple, and couldn't imagine them on fire. But Manhattan was a big island and the part that people thought of as New York City only occupied a relatively small part of it.

"I don't know," he said, and he was telling the truth. "We haven't seen any cops up here because I bet they're all down there, keeping the peace. There's a lot of rich people in the city."

"And a lot of poor people in the Bronx who are going to have nothing left, not after tonight."

The street began to get busy again, with more cars now as people tried to flee, although all were stuck in another traffic jam. That didn't stop the drivers from leaning on the horns. Hopper winced at the volume as they passed the worst of the snarl-up. Ahead, Hopper saw a group of people on motorbikes cutting across an intersection, dodging around stationary vehicles without any apparent difficulty.

If only we had bikes of our own, he thought. *We would have reached Manhattan hours ago.*

As they walked on, the sound of the motorbikes grew louder again, and a moment later one appeared from a side street and stopped. Hopper watched the rider as he seemed to look up toward them, then gunned the bike and went back the way he had come, the engine giving a high-pitched whine as he shot out of view.

Hopper slowed, then stopped. He was worn out, his tired mind playing tricks on him, but he had a very bad feeling growing somewhere inside him.

Martha stopped and turned around. "What is it?"

The whine of the motorcycles appeared as though out of nowhere. Martha spun around. Hopper followed her gaze as the rider reappeared, now followed by a group of six others, each of them on the same kind of light, tall motocross bike. The rider in front stood up on the foot bars, and gave a whoop.

"Hey, hey, if isn't Martha W. and her bang buddy from the cops! Hey, Martha W.! How's it hanging?"

The lead rider was City, and behind him his companions rode in slow circles, their laughter audible over the whine of the bikes.

Martha looked at Hopper. He just shook his head.

The Vipers had found them.

CHAPTER FORTY-FIVE

ERIC'S FIELD REPORT

JULY 13, 1977
BROOKLYN, NEW YORK

"So I said to George, look, I said, you want to make a picture that really means something to an audience, you make a picture that means something to *you*. And then he looked at me and he said, what do you mean? And then I looked at him and I said, listen, sonny, you know what the best time of your life was? When you were at school, that's when. And then you graduate and all your friends go away and then, well, *pfft*, that's it, show's over. So maybe make a film about that."

Delgado gave Diane a sideways glance, but Diane's expression was set as she tried to hold back a yawn. She gave a slight shake of the head.

This was not the first time they had heard this story that evening. The Monopoly set was still out on the dining table in front of them, but Delgado had grown quickly bored with it and had, despite the warning, decided to ask Ms. Schaefer about the forbidden subject.

Ms. Schaefer had been all too happy to oblige, and now, a couple of hours later, she had somehow managed to repeat the story four different ways, each a slightly different retelling, but always about how she had inspired some director named George Lucas to make his, according to her, "landmark film" when she had tutored him at USC. Delgado had no idea whether it was the truth, or just a fantasy conjured up by the eccentric older woman. Diane refused to be drawn out on the subject.

Perhaps another game of Monopoly by candlelight wasn't such a bad idea after all.

Esther stood over by the windows that looked down onto the street. She'd been there awhile, looking out for her husband's return. As Ms. Schaefer burbled on, Delgado checked her watch. She looked at Diane, but Diane shook her head. They'd had this conversation a few times already.

"You go out there," said Diane, "there's no way you'll find him. He could be anywhere. Then he'll come back here and you'll be the one who is missing."

She was right, of course. All they could do was wait. They knew that the city was caught in a blackout, but that was about as much as they had learned from the radio before the batteries had died. They'd spent a good half hour searching through each apartment for a set of spares, but none were to be found.

The only thing left to do was sit tight and wait.

Delgado had at least managed to get a call through to Gallup. She didn't know quite why she felt the need to report to him, but it seemed logical—she'd taken what she'd learned from her own little investigation to him, and he'd even shown a glimmer of interest, happy enough with the information to overlook the small matter of how she knew about Hopper's undercover operation in the first place.

An operation that Delgado wasn't a part of—and still wasn't, although she felt in the circumstances it was best to at least keep Gallup, or his agents, informed of her whereabouts during what had the potential to blow up into a citywide crisis.

Gallup had advised her to report to her own superiors at the NYPD, but as soon as she had gotten off the phone with him and tried calling up to the 65th, the line had died. Delgado had toyed with the idea of reporting to the nearest precinct instead, but discounted that idea quickly.

She'd made a promise to Hopper.

"He's back!"

Ms. Schaefer fell silent as Esther ran from the window and over to the apartment's front door. She flew through it, and Delgado could hear her feet thudding on the stairs as she ran down to the entrance hall. A few moments later, she and Eric returned to the apartment together.

Diane stood from the table.

"Jesus Christ, Eric, you were gone for hours! Where the hell have you been?"

Eric flicked off his flashlight and deposited it on the table. He pulled out a chair and sat down, and took a deep breath. Esther reached for his hand, and he took it.

"Oh, I've been all over," he said, shaking his head. "It's a circus out there. Lots of people, lots of cars. I've never seen anything like it." He looked up at his wife. "So I went over to Charles and June's place. They're fine, but Charles was going to take a look around himself. So we went out together. I'm sorry, I didn't realize I'd been gone so long. But we made it as far as Willoughby Avenue."

Eric stopped, and shook his head again.

The others glanced at each other. Then Delgado pulled out a chair and sat beside Eric.

"What is it?"

Eric looked at the detective. "I don't know what's going on, but something weird."

Diane leaned in. "Weird?"

He nodded. "On Willoughby, there's a building that still has power, or maybe a generator or something. It was all lit up." He lifted his hands and moved them in the air in front of him, like he was sculpting the story for them. "But there were all these people—I don't know, hundreds of them?" He shook his head. "I don't know. But they were all moving down there— they were marching. And they were all wearing the same kind of jacket, and they were all carrying rifles."

"The army," said Ms. Schaefer. "I knew it. I knew they'd come in to help out."

"No, no, this wasn't the army," said Eric. "Look, as soon as we realized, we came back as fast as we could." He leaned forward. "This was a *gang*. A big one, too. They all wore this patch on the back, a snake."

Delgado's heart kicked in her chest.

"A snake?"

"Right," said Eric.

Delgado slumped back in her chair. Esther squeezed her husband's hand as she looked at the detective.

"Does that mean anything? Do you know who they are?"

Delgado sat back up, ignoring, for the moment, that particular question.

"You said this was Willoughby? Do you remember where, exactly?"

"Oh, sure, sure," said Eric. "The building with power, it's a big place. Called the Rookwood Institute."

CHAPTER FORTY-SIX

ESCAPE TO DANGER

City brought his bike to a stop, leaning it at a sharp angle as he put one foot on the road. He grinned, twisting the handlebars, revving the bike constantly as he spoke.

"Damn, girl, we've been looking for you all *over*!" Hopper thought he could detect a faint southern twang in his voice. "Didn't your momma ever tell you not to go off with strange men, huh?"

Hopper felt Martha tense beside him. She'd been in the Vipers for a long time as she'd fought to look after her brother. She'd have gotten very close to the gang members, including the youth who called himself City.

Behind City, the other six bikers lined up in a row, revving their engines like their leader. One man on the end seemed a little overenthusiastic, the rear wheel of his bike kicking out from underneath him, tipping the bike sideways before he had a chance to correct.

Hopper didn't know much about motorcycles at all, but these were light, and tall, with long suspension rods. They were designed for rough terrain, to be ridden in a certain way. Their torque was high, the controls twitchy.

Hopper glanced sideways at Martha, catching her eye.

"When I say run," he whispered, his voice inaudible to City over the noise of his bike, "you run, okay?"

Martha frowned, but nodded, just a little.

"Whoa, hey now," said City, "you don't keep any of them secrets from your brothers now, Martha W. See, we gotta take you back to the Saint. I figure you can ride with me, you know what I'm saying? You're gonna have to hold on *real* tight now." He revved his bike again, once, twice, three times. Behind him, the others laughed and did the same.

"Run!"

Hopper darted to his right, heading toward the awning overhanging the sidewalk. Past the street ahead the fence posts of a city park gleamed in the dark, indicating a much larger space than the one they'd found earlier. Reaching the fence, he glanced behind, only to find Martha nowhere in sight.

"Shit!"

She'd run in another direction. Ahead, he saw three of the bikes peel off, tires skidding, as they tried to make a tight circle in order to start their pursuit, while the other three and City were already speeding down the middle of the street toward him.

Hopper ducked through the gate, nearly stumbling as the path began to slope down almost immediately. Ahead, the park stretched out into the darkness, a few worn and narrow paths winding a tortuous route between mature trees, the ground uneven and sharply sloping in places.

Hopper half ran, half slid down the embankment, using one

of the trees to arrest his momentum as he stopped to pick a direction. Already the whine of the bikes was close; he turned, and saw City and his three companions shoot through the gate, the bikes leaving the ground as, perhaps unintentionally, they jumped the slope and landed on the flat area of the park. One of the riders tipped sideways upon landing, but the others didn't wait for him to right himself. Spotting Hopper, City kicked the gears and lifted himself in the saddle, hollering in delight as he charged toward him.

Hopper ducked behind the tree as City went past and then doubled back, weaving from tree to tree as he attempted more tight turns, his companions having as much difficulty negotiating the terrain as he was. As Hopper had suspected, the motocross bikes were a real handful in inexperienced hands—fine for speeding down a paved street, but, while they were designed for just this kind of arena, for the Vipers the machines were awkward among the trees and slopes of the old park.

"Hopper!"

Hopper stopped by another tree, the lights from the motorbikes playing over the park around him as the Vipers righted themselves. Over on the other side of the park, Martha waved, her white jeans and white jacket clearly visible in the darkness. Then she ran forward, arms wheeling for balance as she negotiated the steep path. A moment later she was lit by more headlights as the other three Vipers appeared at the entrance, pausing to spot their quarry before revving once more and entering the park.

Martha reached Hopper just as City did, the gang leader lifting the front of his bike, the wheel spinning in the air at head height. Hopper dived in one direction, Martha in the other, then he scrambled to his feet, kicking up a cloud of dust from the parched ground. City got his bike turned around and pointed toward Hopper, the headlight turning the air into a choking brown haze.

The other Vipers yelled at each other, their wheels spinning as they charged toward Hopper and Martha. Hopper put a tree between him and his pursuers, and Martha did the same, the pair hugging the bark as the bikes shot past, filling the air with more dust and debris. Hopper turned, watching the headlights spin as the Vipers were forced to slide to a halt and manhandle their bikes back around to resume their chase. Lost in the cloud of dust, Hopper took the opportunity to change positions, moving to a different hiding place behind another tree. He leaned out and motioned Martha to stay back, but with the air full of dust, he wasn't sure if she could see him.

Bikes revving, City called out—not to the two fugitives, but to his fellow gang members. Then, engines whirring in quick bursts of power, the Vipers advanced, slower now, the wobbling headlights lighting up the dusty air.

It was as Hopper hoped—the Vipers had lost them. Unfamiliar with the motocross bikes, they'd had to concentrate just on staying upright, rather than on tracking their quarry, their tires tearing up the ground and providing even more cover for Hopper and Martha.

Hopper crouched on the ground, his hands feeling over the loose surface. There were plenty of pebbles and stones, but what he was really after was something much larger.

He found it. It was embedded in the ground, but came out quite freely. The rock was about the size of a baseball. It would do just fine.

As the bikes approached, Hopper hefted the stone, throwing it in a high arc, over the illuminated clouds of dust. It disappeared into the night, and a second later came down with a crash in some unseen bushes.

Immediately the headlights of the bikes turned, pointing in that direction. As one of the riders revved his engine, Hopper stepped out from behind the tree—he was now behind the last rider. As the Vipers in front cautiously rode toward where they'd heard the sound, Hopper grabbed the last man by the collar of his gang jacket.

Just that action was enough. The man's hand slipped on the handlebars, the bike skidding out from underneath him. Hopper jumped out of the way, releasing his grip on the man's jacket as the bike fell sideways, throwing the Viper clear. Wasting not a moment, Hopper fell onto the man's chest, knees first, driving the air from his lungs. He grabbed the man by the front of his T-shirt, yanked him up, and delivered a sucker punch. He felt the man's nose shift under the impact, then the warm splash of blood over his knuckles.

Standing, he stepped over the Viper and went to the bike, which was running at full revs as it lay, unattended, on its side. He righted it, took control of the throttle, then glanced back. Martha emerged from behind a nearby tree and got on the rear of the bike.

Hopper looked down, sorting the positions of the gear and brake pedals. Martha wrapped her arms around his middle and almost yelled in his ear.

"You sure you know how to work this thing?"

"It's been a while," said Hopper. While this particular motorcycle was alien to him, he'd ridden a few in his time. And once out of the park, riding the sensitive machine would be easy.

At least, that was the theory.

Martha tapped him on the shoulder. Up ahead, the lights of the other bikes swung around as City began to lead his group back toward them.

Hopper squeezed the accelerator, kicked the gear pedal, and hung on for dear life as the bike leaped forward. Figuring that sheer speed would keep them upright, he twisted the throttle and aimed for the park entrance; as they passed through the gate, he clipped his shoulder on the edge, sending them on a wobbling trajectory. Hopper swore and increased the throttle even more, and as soon as the bike's spinning tires hit the hard tarmac of the street, they got full traction, the sudden increase in speed surprising both himself and Martha, who shouted something in his ear.

But they were upright and still moving.

Hopper took that as a win.

Hopper pointed the bike west; then, with the Harlem River in sight, he turned and followed parallel to it, taking a narrow street that ran between empty, overgrown lots on the riverside and railway tracks on the other. Earlier, Hopper had piloted a random course across the grid of streets, the speed and agility of the bike allowing a clean getaway from the other Vipers. Now, here, in a straight line on a deserted street, the motorbike ate the miles with ease.

As they headed south, highways and feeder roads began to crisscross above them as several main routes converged on a bridge ahead, the streets now clogged with cars, horns blazing, lights flashing. Nothing was moving, but Hopper hoped that if they encountered any jams, the bike would see them through.

It was the University Heights Bridge they came to, the area in front of it a messy hash of junctions where several streets converged. Hopper slowed as he brought the bike up an on-ramp, skimming past stopped cars until he was forced to bring their journey to an end.

This was no ordinary traffic jam. The bridge was closed—more than that, it was barricaded, heavy portable fencing having been dragged across the street, closing it off to traffic, forcing the jammed cars around in a curve to direct them away from Manhattan. In the space beyond the fences, huge spotlights had been set up, with four generators the size of small vans purring by the side of the roadway.

And farther ahead still, where the bridge proper began, stood a row of mounted police. They stretched across the width of the bridge in both lanes, the cops clad in riot helmets with mesh visors down, long wooden batons held in hands protected by armored gloves. The horses—somewhat less protected than their riders—nodded and stamped in the warm night air.

"Finally, the authorities," said Hopper. "Hang on."

He squeezed the throttle and edged the motorbike along the row of stopped cars, then pivoted and slotted between a gap in the fencing. He headed straight for the row of mounted police.

"Stay where you are!"

Hopper slowed, turning the bike as he brought it to a halt. On the end of the row of police, one officer had a megaphone to his mouth. He brought his horse forward a little, the animal turning sideways in protest.

"Get off the bike and stay where you are!"

Martha swung herself off the back; Hopper checked over his shoulder, then kicked the stand down and got off himself. He and Martha exchanged a look, then Hopper walked forward.

"Stay where you are and keep your hands where I can see them!"

Hopper stopped and lifted his hands out to his sides. He had to give it a shot—technically he was a wanted man, but in the current chaos he reasoned there was more than a fair chance the cops guarding the bridge had enough to worry about without recognizing his name.

"My name is Detective Jim Hopper! I work at the 65th Precinct in Brooklyn, homicide!"

The mounted officer lowered his megaphone and moved closer to his companions, leaning forward as he spoke to the one closest, who then turned his horse and trotted back down the bridge. The rest of the cops adjusted their positions to fill the gap.

Hopper sighed and began to walk forward.

"Hopper, wait!"

He turned to look at Martha, then heard the hoofbeats behind him. Turning back to the front, he saw two of the mounted cops coming toward him.

He stopped and held his hands up.

"Listen to me! I'm a police officer! I need to radio back to my precinct! I have important information that needs to go to the federal authorities."

The two mounted cops began to circle Hopper, isolating him in the center of the bridge, forcing Martha to back away.

"Hands on your head! On your knees!"

Hopper looked up at the cop, but he couldn't see his face under the visor. The cop raised his long riot baton.

"Get on your knees!"

Hopper sighed and complied, locking his hands behind his head and lowering himself to the warm tarmac. So much for not knowing who he was.

The row of mounted police parted again, and a police cruiser appeared, lights strobing, followed by a larger black police van. The cruiser and van pulled up and several officers, wearing the standard street uniform of light blue short-sleeved shirt and dark pants, got out of both vehicles and ran over, some holding pistols, covering Hopper.

"Hey, get off of me!"

Hopper turned his head and saw that Martha was already in cuffs, two uniforms dragging her over toward the big van. As he turned back around, a fist connected with his jaw.

Hopper's world went sideways as he tipped to the ground. Dazed, but not out, he felt hot liquid on his face, and his mouth was filled with the taste of pennies. Then his face was pushed into the road as the cops dragged his wrists together and cuffed him before pulling him up.

Hopper's feet didn't touch the ground as they carried him to the van and dumped him in the back.

HOPPER'S CABIN
HAWKINS, INDIANA

The snow had stopped falling. That was something. Hopper looked out of the kitchen window as he washed his coffee mug. He must have drunk a gallon of the stuff.

Over in the den, El was lying on the couch, buried under a mound of blankets. Glancing over, Hopper could see the top of her curly hair over the arm of the couch. She hadn't moved in a while. It was late, and they'd taken another break from the story. El had probably fallen asleep. It was probably for the best. Hopper had been talking all afternoon and into the evening. He wasn't sure how much longer he could keep it up, although his voice felt fine.

They could carry on in the morning. And, in fact, he could just give her the edited highlights. Those few days in New York,

1977, were complicated, and, he thought, the story was really too much for her.

Wasn't it? Or was he doing her a disservice? She was smart. Okay, she wasn't like other kids her age, but she actually had been enjoying the story, listening with rapt attention. He was revealing a whole new world to her, of course, and showing himself in a completely different light.

He hoped it was a good one. He'd done his best, back then, but he didn't want to lie. Didn't want to make himself out to be someone he wasn't.

The story was dark and scary, even with the parts he had censored. But maybe that was okay. Kids liked to be scared—safely scared. But what could be safer than this? Hopper had made it out of New York City unscathed. He'd already established that Delgado was doing just fine.

There had been deaths, yes—and there were more to come.

Hopper sighed. Maybe he was overthinking this. Maybe he was underestimating El.

No, no maybe about it. Of course he was.

El stirred on the couch. Hopper returned to the den as El pulled herself up from under the blankets.

"What happened next?" she asked.

"I thought you'd fallen asleep!"

El shook her head as she adjusted herself on the couch, pulling one leg up underneath her. "Was Saint John like me?"

Hopper worked his jaw for a couple of moments. "Like . . . *you*?"

El nodded. "Special . . . different."

Hopper rubbed his chin. El's question was a good one—and she must have been mulling it over for a while, now. Given her own experience with Dr. Brenner and the MKUltra project, it was a logical conclusion to make.

And maybe one that wasn't so far off the truth.

"Well," said Hopper, "he couldn't move things with his

mind, like you. But yes, he was part of a project. A different kind of project, not like the one at Brenner's lab. But we're getting ahead of the story a little again." He sat next to her, resting a hand on her blanketed leg. "And I don't want you having nightmares, okay?"

El seemed to consider this very seriously, then she looked at Hopper and gave him a nod. She got herself comfortable on the couch, clearly awaiting the resumption of his story.

Hopper ruffled her hair and stood, stretching once again. Then he went over and sat in the armchair, leaned back, and locked his hands behind his head.

The adventure continued.

CHAPTER FORTY-SEVEN

COMPARING NOTES

JULY 13, 1977
NEW YORK

"See anything?"

Martha peered out of the back of the van, through the tiny square of mesh-reinforced glass that provided the only view of the outside world. She sighed, and shifted back onto the metal bench, one of two that ran the length of the van's interior, one on each side.

"Nope. No clue where we are."

Sitting opposite, Hopper tried to get himself more comfortable, but it was no use. His head throbbed along with his cheek and lip, which had been split by the cop's punch, and the inside of the transport van was cramped for a man of his size. He couldn't even sit fully on the metal bench, forced instead to half crouch on the edge, the sharp ninety-degree angle cutting painfully into his ass, and his hands cuffed behind him didn't make things any easier.

So far, their journey had been a start-stop affair. They'd sped off the bridge at a reasonable pace, then had stopped again, apparently at some other checkpoint. Through the rear window, Hopper had seen the looming shadows of more mounted police, and then the van had resumed the drive to who-knew-where.

Ten minutes later they had come to a swift stop, and remained stationary for another ten minutes before the journey resumed.

Ten minutes after that, the van had stopped again. That was at least a full half hour ago. The van was still running, and Hopper hadn't heard anyone get out of the cab at the front. Nor had anyone come around to the back to check on the prisoners.

"Do you think anyone is even going to listen to us?" asked Martha. "A gang member and a runaway cop?"

Hopper frowned. She had a point. "Well, we have to try. If I can get to someone in the task force, they know who I am."

Martha only raised an eyebrow. "The city is on fire. I don't think anybody is going to want to put us through to anyone." Martha slumped back against the wall of the van. "They'll throw us in a cell and we'll be processed along with everyone else they've mopped up. So, sure, they'll find out we're telling the truth. But probably not until sometime around Christmas."

Hopper ran his tongue along his teeth. She was right. The underfunded, overstretched police department would be operating well beyond its means in a crisis like this. The thought then occurred to him that there might not even be any holding cells available. Perhaps they were destined to stay in this van for a very, very long time.

Martha moved back to the window, pressing her nose against it as she tried to see what was happening outside.

Hopper shifted awkwardly again, and felt something dig into his chin. Glancing down, he saw a corner of the folded map of the Vipers' headquarters poking out from the collar of his jacket.

He looked up. "So tell me what you know about Saint John's plan."

Martha sat back down on her bench. "I don't know a lot. Saint John, he let a few people in on parts of it—me included—but he keeps most of it close to himself. But he's been building the Vipers for a couple of years at least—taking over other gangs, taking their territory as well as what they got. People, money, you name it."

"Guns," said Hopper.

"Oh yeah, he got guns all right. He did a few deals with some cartels, real heavy hitters from Colombia and Mexico, groups that had a slice of New York already. He knew how to work with them, and they got what he needed."

"What did he give them?"

Martha shrugged. "I don't know. Money, maybe. Routes into the city. I don't know. I figure he knew just what he was doing, though. He's a mastermind, you know what I mean? An expert—like, he knows how to work people, knows how to get hold of them, make them do what he wants them to do. Man, I've seen people die because he told them to."

Martha stopped, and sucked her cheeks in. Hopper nodded.

Lisa Sargeson. He'd seen her jump to her death—apparently on the orders of Saint John. He'd seen it with his own eyes, but he still didn't understand it.

And Martha had seen it too. She must have. She'd been up on that rooftop with him.

Hopper lowered his eyes, staring at the molded metal floor of the van. There were still connections he couldn't quite understand, pieces of the puzzle that still wouldn't quite fit; but he felt like they were close.

Of course, maybe close wasn't close enough.

"It's psychology," said Hopper.

"What?"

Hopper looked up. "Psychology. Saint John had a collection of books behind his office—textbooks, guidebooks. Like his own private research library. He told me that he was involved in some shady stuff, back in Vietnam. He said he was seconded for 'special duties.' What if those special duties were all about brainwashing?"

Martha narrowed her eyes. "What, is that stuff even real?"

Hopper shrugged, and shifted position on the bench. "I don't know. I never saw it myself, but I heard stories. But look, we've both seen what Saint John can do. He's got some kind of power, some kind of hold over people. That's where all that black magic mumbo jumbo comes from—he needed a hook, something strange, something most people wouldn't ever encounter."

"Yeah, well, Saint John was into all kinds of weird stuff."

Hopper cocked his head. "But he didn't sucker you in?"

Martha shrugged. "He might have tried, but like I said, I had my own agenda, you know what I mean? I stayed focused and did what I had to do to survive, and to keep Leroy safe."

"Except Saint John got to Leroy, didn't he? He might not have been able to convince you, but he convinced your brother."

Martha shook her head. "I thought I could keep him out of that—I mean, he was doing good. Or at least I thought he was doing good. I guess I was wrong."

"No, you weren't," said Hopper. "That's how I got into this. Your brother came to me, asking for help to get *you* out. He was fighting whatever hold Saint John had on him. And he almost succeeded."

"Yeah, well, sometimes almost ain't good enough, right? But yeah, I saw what he could do. I *know* what he can do."

"But like I said, it's just psychology. He knows how the human mind operates. He knows that if he can convince people—the right kind of people—that he was in touch with, I don't know, some other kind of power, that scares them. And fear is a powerful tool—maybe the most powerful one there is. He doesn't believe in any of it himself. He doesn't have to, so long as his followers do. He just reinforces it by getting the Vipers to dress up in robes once in a while, and by getting his followers to commit ritual killings."

"Ritual *what*?"

"Before we knew the Vipers were connected at all, I was investigating a series of murders with my partner. The killings were ritualized, but they had no meaning on their own, they were just part of Saint John's method of control."

Martha breathed out, long and slow.

"I don't know anything about that. No way, no how. You got to believe that."

Hopper nodded. "Oh, I do. But this plan, how much do you know? He's behind this blackout. He's got to be. He's killed the power to the city, but there has to be a reason for it."

Martha just shook her head.

That was when the back doors of the van were flung open. Hopper and Martha turned at the sound, squinting into the harsh glare of flashlights held by more police in heavy riot gear. As he and Martha were pulled out, Hopper saw that the officers were actually more military than police, their equipment more advanced, more protective. Out of the flashlight glare, he was able to read the two words stenciled in large yellow letters on the front of the men's bulletproof vests:

FEDERAL AGENT

Hopper looked around as the agents swarmed over the van. They were in a large open space; around them were tall buildings with flat sides, all dark. More spotlights and generators had been set up, but even so, it took Hopper a moment to realize he was standing in the middle of Times Square.

An agent gently pushed at Hopper, turning him around to

uncuff his wrists. As Hopper shook his hands, getting the circulation back into them, another agent approached at a jog. He was wearing a dark suit, over the top of which was slung a bulletproof vest.

"Detective Hopper," said Special Agent Gallup. "So glad you could attend the party. This way, please."

CHAPTER FORTY-EIGHT

THE FINAL BRIEFING

JULY 13, 1977
MANHATTAN, NEW YORK

The makeshift command center was a large white tent, occupying the width of Broadway as the street cut a diagonal through Times Square. The place was bustling with activity as Gallup led Hopper and Martha in, uniformed police and federal agents mixing with people in civilian clothes and others wearing work overalls and hard hats. This last group were studying plans laid out on large trestle tables. Hopper saw that a military field radio had been set up in one corner, and nearby a diesel generator hummed.

As they walked, Gallup filled them in on the situation.

The entire Con Edison power system was out, the company forced to shut down what little of the network had remained operational after the initial blackout in order to try and rebalance the load and find the fault, although some areas, including a section of Queens and the Rockaways, did have power, through sheer luck—connected not to Con Edison but to the Long Island Lighting Company supply.

Gallup drew Hopper and Martha over to one side, where a large vertical board had been erected and covered with an acetate sheet so people could write on it with marker pen, the board already nearly completely covered with information.

Gallup continued his summary of the situation, but now there was only one single thought looping around in Hopper's mind, quickly drowning out everything else.

He heard someone speak. He blinked, and the person spoke again.

"Detective Hopper?"

His reverie broken, Hopper looked at Special Agent Gallup.

"Look, I've done everything you want, and now you're going to help me, okay? No more of your bullshit. I need to get home," he said. "Diane, Sara—it's time I got back. This whole situation will be tearing Diane apart, and now if all the power is out, even down in Brooklyn."

Gallup stepped closer to Hopper, and put a hand on his arm. "They're fine. They're fine."

"I . . . what? What do you mean, they're fine?"

"Detective Delgado is with them."

"What? *Delgado*?"

Gallup nodded. "She came to us yesterday, presenting evidence that she'd been busy gathering while you were away. When we were done, she said she was heading straight down to your apartment, said she had a promise to keep. And lucky she did, too. I don't have anyone I can spare, now that the power's gone. She's still there—she checked in as soon as it went dark."

Hopper nearly choked on his laugh, the relief the most glorious, wonderful feeling he thought he had ever experienced. To know that his wife and child were safe in the middle of all this chaos . . .

"I need to go to them." Hopper looked at Gallup, then at Martha, then gestured to the board. "There's nothing I can do here. Martha knows more about what's going on than I do." At that, he unzipped his bomber jacket and pulled out the folded map of the Vipers' headquarters. "This will be useful. If the task force raids the Vipers now—"

Gallup held up a hand. "Easier said than done, Detective. The task force isn't ready. They're split all over the city, waiting for instructions they won't get."

"What do you mean, 'waiting'?"

"All radios are down," said Gallup. "With no power, no AM repeaters. Even if you could have gotten to a police radio, you wouldn't have been able to reach me. I only knew you were coming because a motorcycle cop came down to give an update on what was happening in the Bronx."

"The Bronx is turning into a war zone, is what is happening," said Martha.

"Trust me, I know that," said Gallup. "When the blackout hit—before the phones went down—all police were ordered to attend the precinct closest to where they live."

Hopper swore. "What? That's a terrible idea."

"You can't blame them for trying, Detective."

"But cops don't usually live near their own precincts, and certainly not up in the Bronx!" He turned to Martha. "That explains why we couldn't find any cops. There weren't any there."

"That's not quite true," said Gallup. "Those on shift would have been there."

"Not nearly enough to deal with what we saw," said Martha.

"In any event," said Gallup, "we're getting a backup radio network up and running." He gestured at the military communications equipment in the corner. "But we have to run it out to the task force teams before they can all link up. It'll take a little while, but we'll be able to move on the Vipers soon."

Hopper turned back to Gallup. "Okay. But look, I need to go. Now."

Gallup nodded. "Understood. I can debrief with Martha here, and I'll get a police bike organized for you."

Gallup turned and called to one of the uniforms nearby. Hopper watched, suddenly feeling . . .

Guilty?

All their work, all this time, the danger the city faced, Saint John doing who the hell knew what up in the Bronx, and now all he could think was . . .

Diane.

Sara.

Because while he had a duty to serve and protect the city, he had a duty to serve and protect his family, too.

And he'd done what he had intended to do, what he had been tasked with. Bring back information. And he had, in the form of Martha.

Gallup returned a few moments later, carrying a large military field telephone. "I take it you know how to work one of these?" he asked, handing it over.

Hopper took it. The thing weighed a ton, the long-distance two-way more or less unchanged since he had last used one back in Vietnam.

"I do, thanks," said Hopper.

"There's a bike waiting. Good luck."

CHAPTER FORTY-NINE

NO SLEEP TILL BROOKLYN

JULY 14, 1977
BROOKLYN, NEW YORK

It was midnight by the time Hopper got to his apartment. Gallup had requisitioned a large police motorcycle for him, a beast of a machine that Hopper was far more comfortable riding than the twitchy, unpredictable motocross bike. With siren and lights on full, he'd crossed Manhattan and into Brooklyn against the jammed traffic and through the crowded streets with few holdups. As he'd traveled, the situation seemed, as Hopper had suspected, far more stable in this part of the city. Thanks to the ad-libbed orders from the police chiefs, Manhattan and Brooklyn were now disproportionately well-staffed by cops—which was good news for the neighborhoods down here, but less so for the Bronx and other less affluent areas, where there were plenty of police precincts but too few staff to man them.

Hopper stopped on the sidewalk right by the stoop, kicking the stand down almost before he had turned off the engine. He hopped off and immediately got to work extracting the field radio from the bike's side cargo bag, then turned and ran with it up the stairs.

Hopper pushed the front door of the building open, even as someone was pushing back against him. Confused, Hopper kicked the door, forcing it in, then nearly tripped over something as he crossed the threshold. The building lobby was lit by candles, and looking down, Hopper saw a man sprawled on the floor.

"Jesus H. Christ!" the man yelled, getting himself up on an elbow; then he stopped. "Is that you, Jim?"

It was Eric Van Sabben. Hopper glanced at him, then made for the stairs.

"Ah, yeah, hi, Eric. Sorry!"

At the door to his apartment, Hopper hammered with his fist, not wanting to frighten the occupants by unlocking the door with his own key.

"Diane? It's me! Open up! I'm here, open up!"

A moment later he heard a scraping sound as something heavy was moved from behind the door. Then the chain was released. Then the lock was disengaged.

"Jim!"

Diane almost fell into Hopper, wrapping her arms around him, burying her face in his chest, her whole body shaking with sobs. Still holding the field radio, Hopper did his best to return the hug, pressing his face into the top of her head. He breathed her smell, long and deep.

"I'm here," he said, and he kept saying it until Diane's sobs began to fade. Eventually she pulled away and looked up into his eyes. He carefully drew her hair away from her face with a finger, and smiled, his own tears dropping, mingling with his wife's.

"Where's Sara?"

Diane stepped back into the apartment, Hopper following. As Diane moved to close the door, she pointed at the bulky object Hopper was carrying.

"What's that?"

Hopper moved to the kitchen counter and set it down. "Field radio," he said. "So I can call back to base. Sara?" Already he was heading for the hall leading to the bedrooms.

"She's asleep," said Diane, following behind. "Don't worry, she's fine. She was already in bed when the power went."

Hopper opened the door and entered Sara's bedroom. His daughter lay facedown, having kicked off the sheet. With no power there was no AC, and the room was warm.

He carefully sat on the edge of the bed. Sara's eyes flickered open, and for a moment she looked at her father. Then she was out again. Hopper sat and watched her, stroking her hair.

I'm home, I'm home, I'm home.

With a heavy sigh, he rubbed his face and gently stood. He took one more look at his sleeping daughter, then left the room. Out in the living room, Diane was lighting more candles before moving to the front door as a knock sounded. She let their neighbor, Eric, in. Hopper gave him a sheepish wave.

"Esther okay, Eric?"

Eric nodded. "Yeah, she went to bed. We've got Ms. Schaefer in our spare room, too. Do you think I should go wake them?"

Hopper held up a hand. "No, if they're okay, they're okay." Then he looked around the room.

"Where's Delgado?"

Diane and Eric exchanged a look. "That's what I was going to ask you," said Diane.

"What?"

Eric shook his head. "Didn't she find you?"

"Find me? Where?"

"At the Rookwood Institute."

———

It took a few minutes to get the field radio working. While Hopper tried to raise Gallup back at the Times Square command center, Diane quickly gave Eric a very potted summary of what her husband had been doing, or at least, thought Hopper as he half listened, as much as Delgado had told her.

Delgado, who now had gone off on her own, into who knew what.

Finally the field radio crackled into life, and the rest of the room fell silent.

"T-Seventy-Seventy Command, reading you, over."

Hopper sighed in relief, and pressed the speak button. "This is Detective Jim Hopper. Get me Special Agent Gallup, will you? Over."

"Roger."

The line went dead for a moment. Diane came and stood next to Hopper at the kitchen counter.

Then the radio clicked on.

"Hopper, you'll have to be quick. Over."

"Delgado isn't here," said Hopper into the mic. "She's gone to the Rookwood Institute. Over."

The radio fell silent; Hopper thought Gallup might have been relaying the information to Martha, as it wasn't until after he'd spoken that Hopper realized the agent might not know what the place is—or what it meant to Saint John.

Then again, did Martha?

Hopper glanced at his wife, then pressed the call button again.

"Do you need me to repeat, over?"

"Sorry, I was talking to Martha. We don't know what that means. Do you know the location? Over."

Hopper rubbed his face. He didn't have time to go into Saint John's history with the place, not now, and especially not over a bad radio connection.

"I do. Apparently the Vipers have been seen down here,

heading to the institute in one big convoy. The place still seems to have power. Over."

"And that was enough to send Delgado out there? Over."

"Rookwood is important to Saint John. Did Martha tell you about Lisa Sargeson? Over."

"That's affirmative. Over."

Hopper nodded to himself. "The Rookwood Institute is where Saint John met her for the first time, just before he was released from federal prison. I can explain that all later, but that's where this all started. If the Vipers are heading there, then Saint John will be leading them. Delgado thinks I'm still with them, so she went out to find me. Over."

"Okay, stay where you are. I'm sending as many agents down to you as possible. If what you say is correct, then we can take Saint John there—"

Hopper shook his head, thinking of the sheer firepower that the Vipers had at their disposal—firepower that was now coming to his neighborhood.

"Negative, negative!" he nearly yelled into the mic. "You come down here with agents, you'll start a war." He paused, then lifted the mic again, but before he could speak, the radio crackled again, louder this time, the speaker popping several times, as though a mic button was being depressed and released in rapid succession. Hopper looked at the mic in his hand, but the boxy device seemed to be working properly, the red light on the top indicating his own microphone was off.

"What is that?" asked Diane.

Hopper shrugged. "Trouble at the other end, I think."

"Hopper!"

The voice that squawked from the radio now wasn't Special Agent Gallup. Hopper squeezed his mic.

"Martha?"

There were a few more pops, then the mic at the other end was held open. Hopper heard some scuffling, and what seemed to be two people arguing. After a moment, the voices got louder.

"Get off of me!" This was Martha. The mic went dead again, then came to life. *"Yeah, okay, keep your shirt on, jeez. Hopper, you still there?"*

"I'm still here. What's happening? Over."

"I'm just borrowing the radio for a second."

"You heard what we said? Over."

"Yeah. Listen, if they're all going to the Rookwood, then Leroy will be there too. Ah . . . over."

Hopper shook his head, knowing exactly what was going to come next. "Martha, stay where you are. I can handle things at this end, and Gallup is on standby with his agents. Okay?"

"No way, Hopper. I'm coming down now. I need to get Leroy out before anything else happens, okay? And I'm not going to let you or Mr. Special Agent here stop me, okay?"

"Martha, wait! Martha?"

Hopper released the button. The radio fizzed, then popped again as Gallup came back on the air.

"You need to stay where you are too, Detective. We will handle this."

"Yeah, and you've done a great job so far. Over and out."

Hopper dropped the mic onto the kitchen counter, and flicked the main switch on the field radio. The device went dead. He looked up, and saw Diane and Eric watching him.

"I'm going after her."

Eric opened his mouth in surprise, but didn't speak. Hopper ignored him. All his attention was on Diane. She wasn't speaking either. She was waiting for something—waiting for a better reason, a better explanation.

All Hopper had was the truth.

He moved around the counter and reached out to Diane, but now she took a step back, her arms wrapped tightly around herself. She shook her head.

"Jim . . ."

"I'm sorry," he said. "Delgado might be in trouble, and I need to go help her and I need to stop what's happening. If I can do it peacefully, before the cavalry arrives, then I need to try."

Diane nodded. "Who's Martha?"

"She's someone trying to save her brother. And she's capable—if she's on the way too, then maybe, together, we can stop all this."

Diane looked at him for a few seconds, then she dropped her head.

"Just be careful, okay?" She looked up and smiled, weakly, her eyes already brimming with tears.

Hopper moved forward and hugged her again, and this time she didn't retreat. They swayed side to side as they embraced. Hopper looked over the top of her head at Eric, who was still standing in the middle of the room.

"Eric, look after my family for me."

Eric nodded.

Then Hopper broke off his embrace with Diane, and kissed her on the forehead.

"I'll be as fast as I can," he said, then left the apartment, and didn't dare look back.

CHAPTER FIFTY

INTO THE SERPENT'S NEST

The backstreets of Brooklyn were quiet and dark, the chaos and carnage of a city on fire feeling almost like a half-forgotten dream as Hopper stashed the police motorcycle in an empty lot and made it the rest of the way to the Rookwood Institute on foot. He knew what was happening in his head, of course, to start thinking like that. Adrenaline, exhaustion, hunger, thirst, not to mention the minor injuries he had sustained since escaping from the Vipers, were all starting to take their toll. He'd experienced it before, in Vietnam, so at least he could recognize that he wouldn't be able to keep this up much longer.

Finding the institute was not difficult. It was a huge building, a pile of Gothic columns and arches, somewhere between a church and a country mansion, that sat square at the end of a wide avenue, the focal point for the neighborhood.

It was also the only building for miles that had any lights on. All Hopper had to do was follow the brilliant white glow—and the Vipers, who marched in a steady stream, gathering in the street outside the institute. The gang must have come by vehicle—their headquarters was a *long* way uptown—but at some point they had all disembarked from whatever mode of transport carried them here and continued, like him, on foot. Hopper wasn't sure why, and he wasn't sure he cared, but there was something . . . disturbing about them now. As they marched, they didn't speak, they just walked—not in time, but in silence, save for their steady footfalls on the road.

Hopper lost count—there were certainly many more here than he had ever seen at the warehouse, but they were all wearing the leather vests with VIPERS emblazoned on the back. Each of them also had an AK-47 slung over their shoulder.

Saint John's private army, marching mindlessly toward . . . *What?*

Hopper had to get inside the institute. The Vipers, still arriving on foot, lined up outside the building and looked up at it, waiting patiently for, Hopper supposed, their master to address them. The scene reminded him of the rooftop meeting he had witnessed—the meeting that had led Lisa to her death.

Hopper pushed that memory aside. He watched the gang for a minute longer, then made his decision.

He wasn't going to wait for Martha. It was going to take her a while to get here, and that was assuming she'd even managed to persuade Gallup to lend her some transport. He really had no idea where she was or even *if* she was coming, so there was no point in dawdling. Besides, if she did arrive and see the assembled Vipers lined up outside the building, Hopper hoped she would defer to her common sense and stay the hell out.

Which was precisely what he wasn't going to do.

Hopper turned and jogged back down the deserted street. At the next intersection he turned, then turned again, and soon found himself watching the tail end of the Vipers' march, the last few stragglers spaced out fairly well as they headed toward their destination.

This street was lined with mature trees; using one as cover, Hopper watched, counting time and counting marchers, then swung himself out, hooking his elbow under the chin of the last man in the line and squeezing with all his might. The Viper struggled, but before he could call out, Hopper clamped his other hand over the man's mouth. He dragged him backward toward the curb and behind a parked car, twisting the man's body so the assault rifle over his shoulder didn't fall off and alert the others.

When he was sure the man was unconscious, Hopper released his grip, then slipped off the gangster's leather vest. He shed his own bomber jacket and put the Viper's colors on over his bloodstained yellow T-shirt.

Grabbing the gun, Hopper pulled it over his shoulder and jogged back down the street, following the others. Staying at the back, Hopper was virtually invisible as the gang members reached the institute and filed into ranks behind their compatriots. They all looked up at the building, alive with white light streaming from every window, and . . .

Waited.

Hopper peeled off the rear, using more parked cars as cover. He had to get into the building, and the front door was clearly out of the question. But the institute was a huge, rambling building that squatted on a block all of its own. Following the line of parked cars, and keeping down, out of sight, Hopper made it along the street, almost to the front of the building. From this angle, the bright lights of the institute cast a deep cone of shadow on either side of the place; despite being in clear view of the Vipers, Hopper took the risk, running across the street corner and vanishing into the darkness at the side of the building. He waited, pressed up against the brickwork, listening for something—*anything*.

He was in the clear. Turning to look up at the building, Hopper then moved along the dark street, looking for another way in.

He found his opportunity just a short while later. At the back of the building, the flat wall of the place turned inward, leading Hopper into a large rear yard, in which sat a Dumpster surrounded by bags of trash. There was a door nearby, nearly hidden by a low brick wall. The door was locked, but, bracing himself against the wall, Hopper kicked at the handle with the heel of his boot. Four heavy blows, and the door buckled, enough for Hopper to apply pressure with his shoulder and force it open.

Inside it was pitch dark. Hopper took a breath and stepped over the threshold.

His eyes adjusted quickly; the room he had entered was dark, but there was a light ahead, spilling out from underneath another closed door. Hopper moved, swiftly and silently, carefully turning the handle. It was unlocked. Hopper checked the corridor, then entered the building proper.

The hallway was wood-paneled and lit by large, ornate cast-iron lights that hung from the ceiling. The floor was shiny, polished linoleum tiles. After hours spent in a city caught in a blackout, being inside a building with power was somewhat unsettling, especially as he knew it was the only place for miles around that still had electricity. Hopper cocked his head, listening intently, and then he heard it: faint, but ever present, the rumble of a generator in operation, probably in a basement.

Hopper moved on, carefully placing one foot in front of the other, the AK-47 sitting comfortably—perhaps too comfortably—in his grip.

After a little while Hopper picked up the pace, because the Rookwood Institute seemed to be deserted. But unlike the Vipers' Bronx headquarters, this building was in perfect condition, the floors polished, the furniture in the disused offices neatly stacked to one side. It reminded him of the end of school back in Hawkins, oh, twenty-five years before, when the pupils helped the teachers move the classroom contents into a neat pile so the place could be cleaned over the summer break.

Hopper kept looking, not knowing where he was going, not willing to give up.

Delgado was here somewhere. So was Saint John. He knew it.

All he had to do was find them.

On the third floor, Hopper found a map: the layout of the building crafted in meticulous, beautiful detail in marquetry, framed on the wall next to the main stairs. Hopper didn't know what the place had been used for before the federal government acquired it, but he thanked the nineteenth-century craftsmen for their work as he scanned the layout, trying to devise a pattern to better conduct a search. After a moment, he gave up and decided to continue with his path. It was too late to start second-guessing his methods now.

Ahead was a set of double doors, inset with stained-glass panels. Behind the glass, the light seemed to move—not flickering, exactly, but there was . . . motion. Curious, Hopper moved up and glanced inside—then swore and yanked the door open, rushing inside.

It was a big, long room—perhaps a meeting room or lecture hall, although now devoid of any furniture—lit not by the old iron lamps but by hundreds of black wax candles placed around the floor.

In the center of the room was Delgado. She was flat on her back, her arms and legs spread as she lay in the center of a large five-pointed star, the symbol carved directly into the wooden floorboards beneath her. Around the star were more symbols, drawn this time in a bright red substance, like thick paint. Delgado's eyes were closed, but her chest rose and fell in steady breaths.

At the door, Hopper was frozen, taking in the room—staring at the man standing over Delgado's head.

Saint John.

He was wearing the black robe, but the hood was pulled back. The candlelight shimmered in the silvered lenses of his sunglasses.

"Welcome, oh brother mine."

Hopper felt the scream build inside him before he even opened his mouth. He lunged forward, forgetting the weapon in his hands as Saint John stood, hands clasped, smiling.

This, Hopper knew, he wanted to do with his bare hands.

And then his forward motion was brought to a quick stop as he was grabbed from behind, two sets of hands taking hold of his upper arms before exerting pressure downward, forcing him to his knees. Hopper hit the deck, looking up as the AK-47 was wrenched from him.

Leroy tossed the weapon to one side, then moved back and pushed down on Hopper's shoulder again. On the other side, another of his crew—Reuben—held him firm. Both men's eyes were glazed, their expressions blank.

Just like the others outside.

Saint John was in control.

Hopper turned, looking up as the gang leader stepped around the supine form of Delgado.

"What the hell is all this for, huh?" yelled Hopper. "What could you possibly be doing all this for?"

Saint John stopped in front of Hopper, then crouched down so he was eye-level with his prisoner. Hopper stared once more at his own reflection.

Saint John didn't speak.

Hopper shook his head.

"What is this mystical crap? You were a leader once, right? Back in Vietnam. You commanded men. You gave orders, you followed orders. There was nothing magical about it. Not then. Not now." Hopper nodded, indicating the bizarre way Saint John had staged the room. "All this doomsday shit about the devil coming to New York, the end of the world, the Day of the Serpent. It's all an act. You don't believe it, but you don't have to. You use it, seeding it in the minds of your followers, giving them something to fear, giving them a reason to serve you, because for them, you're the only way out. You're the only one standing between them and the devil. Right?"

Saint John tilted his head, but didn't speak.

"And you enjoy it too, don't you?" Hopper peered at the man's glasses, trying to see behind the lenses. "This gives you power. You feel strong, gathering the weak and the vulnerable into your cult. You're a manipulator—a mastermind, someone said. They're right, too. A master planner. A *leader*. Trust me, I get it. You've been planning this a long time. The blackout, I don't know how you did it, but it was a stroke of genius. The perfect flashpoint, the start of your Day of the Serpent."

Hopper glanced around Saint John. Delgado hadn't moved. The candles around them flickered, as though a small breeze swept through the room, although Hopper couldn't feel the air move a single molecule.

The tip of Saint John's tongue appeared between his front teeth, and then he nodded.

"Congratulations on your detective work, Hopper. We could really have been something, you and I."

"What is it for?" asked Hopper, his voice nothing but a whisper. "Just tell me, what are you doing all this for?"

Saint John stood, and then he laughed. He walked back over to Delgado and looked down at her, then turned back around to Hopper. He spread his arms, his black robe fanning out around him.

"You said it yourself. This is the Day of the Serpent, the appointed hour where the devil himself will take His throne." Saint John crouched back down in front of Hopper.

"He came to me, back then, when I was crawling through the mud, when I was killing because I was told. He came to me, and He gave me His plan, and He showed me the future. He told me how to prepare the way, how the rituals must be arranged."

Saint John stood again and moved back to Delgado, his back to Hopper.

"Five sacrifices to summon the veil of shadow over the Earth."

Hopper felt his pulse thud in his temple.

He'd gotten it wrong. All so very, very wrong.

Saint John wasn't just manipulating the Vipers. He believed every single word himself.

He *believed* it.

The gang leader reached into his robe, and pulled out a large white card. He turned around and showed it to Hopper.

A Zener card—homemade, like the other, the symbol on the front a hollow square. Then he knelt by Delgado, and placed the card over her heart.

Hopper counted the victims in his head.

Jonathan Schnetzer. Sam Barrett. Jacob Hoeler.

Lisa Sargeson.

And Rosario Delgado made five.

Summoning his energy, Hopper pushed against the two men holding him down, but it was no good. Tendons in his neck as taut as cables, Hopper gritted his teeth, heaving against Leroy and Reuben, while in front of him Saint John walked forward, taking something else from his robe.

Hopper saw a flash of something silver, and felt a hot electric sting in his neck.

And then he saw nothing else.

CHAPTER FIFTY-ONE

THE FINAL VICTIM

JULY 14, 1977
BROOKLYN, NEW YORK

Lights danced in the darkness. A fire, sparking in the distance, growing, burning, bright in a night of serpent black.

Hopper awoke with a cry and sat, gasping for breath, as he took in his surroundings.

He was still in the big meeting room. Delgado was still on the floor, at the center of the carved pentagram.

Hopper looked down, his brow creasing in confusion. He was sitting in a wooden chair, his hands clutching the arms, but he wasn't restrained. In front of him was a small round table, and on the other side an identical chair, in which sat Saint John. Between them, on the table, was a silver goblet filled with a dark liquid, and the silver crucifix-dagger, the blade unsheathed, the tip pointing at Saint John.

Hopper took a deep breath, and lifted his arm . . .

It didn't move. His breath catching in his throat, he tried again, tried to move his legs, but his limbs refused to obey. Chest heaving, he struggled against nothing at all, his fingers moving over the wood of the chair, but his arms not moving a single inch.

"What have you done to me?" he asked, looking up at Saint John. The gang leader's shoulders rose under his robe, then fell.

"Me? Nothing at all. What you do, you do to yourself."

Hopper tried to move again, this time succeeding in rocking the chair a little from side to side. He looked down, unable to understand how he was being held. Looking over one shoulder, then the other, he saw Leroy and Reuben standing impassively by the door, well out of reach.

"You were right."

Hopper turned back to face his captor. Saint John nodded.

"Vietnam. Now, that was hell, wasn't it, Jim?"

Hopper said nothing.

"The things we did out there," Saint John continued. "The things *I* did out there. I didn't volunteer, not at the start. No, they picked me out of my unit, said I was suitable, told me to report to a base they had hidden away somewhere deep in the jungle. They said I was doing a great service for my country, being there. Like I had a choice. Like I had a choice about anything."

Hopper breathed deeply through his nose, and nodded.

"Some kind of covert op? I heard stories about the CIA being out there, experimenting on soldiers, using drugs and all kinds of weird stuff. I didn't believe any of it at the time. You were part of that?"

"They used me as a guinea pig. Subject Zero, they called me. They told me they wanted to create a better kind of soldier. And I believed them. I thought I was doing my duty. I didn't understand any of it, not at first. But I didn't die. I think that surprised them at first. No matter what they did, what they tried, it didn't kill me. It killed the others, of course. But not me."

Hopper sighed. "I'm sorry."

Saint John gave another of his slow shrugs. "Don't be. I lived. I collaborated. In fact, I eventually joined the investigators, and I did to others what they had done to me. I helped them with the experiments, helped them refine the process." He smiled. "We did some good work. I learned a lot—about how the brain works." At this, he tapped his temple. "All we are is chemistry and electricity, you know that? The mind and the soul are illusions, side effects of a soup of neurotransmitters, hormones, chemical reactions, and nerve impulses. All of that happening right now, inside our skulls, making us who we are. Making us dream. Making us *believe.*" He dropped his hands before continuing. "Chemistry, you and I, just chemistry. Once you know how it works, you know how to work it, how to change it—or even control it. You use drugs. You use other things. Call it programming. Turn the mind into a machine, ready for instructions, commands, ready to do whatever the hell you want it to do."

Hopper shook his head. "I'm sorry."

"You already said that, and saying it again doesn't make you mean it any more than you did the first time."

Hopper glanced around the room. "What about this place? You were here, being rehabilitated? What happened?"

The corner of Saint John's mouth curled up in a smile. "What happened? You been listening at all? Vietnam happened. That's what. And then when they were finished trying to make me into a superman and when I was finished trying to make others into supermen they sent me home and told me to forget about everything. Told me it had never happened. Told me I had dreamed it. Imagined it. Called it a post-traumatic fantasy. But I knew it was true. I knew what I'd been through. You know how hard it is, when people don't listen? When, no matter how hard you try and make them, they just don't see what they're supposed to see?"

"How long were you inside?"

Saint John laughed. "Oh, I've always been inside. But it was here, at the Rookwood, that I found my salvation. Because it was here that I heard Him again. It had been years, but I knew I'd heard Him once, and that I would hear Him again. They didn't believe that either, so I learned to keep quiet. As soon as I was dragged through those doors, I heard His voice again. He reminded me of my path. He reminded me what had to be done. This was where my mind was unlocked—I didn't know it, but I had closed myself to the world. I had stopped listening to Him. But He'd been there all the time. With Lisa's help I heard His voice again. It's a shame she isn't here to see His plan come to glorious fruition, but she was always a part of it."

Saint John lifted his head and looked at the ceiling. He smiled, and Hopper watched his throat bob as he seemed to be hit by a wave of emotion.

"It is fitting that He told me to come here, to this place, for the final act."

"You need help," said Hopper. "I can get you that help. I'm like you, remember? I've been through it. I came back, and I struggled. But I got through it and I got strong again. You can be too. You just have to trust me. I can *help* you. I can help you fix this."

Saint John dropped his head, looking at Hopper now from over the top of his glasses. For the first time, Hopper had a glimpse of the man's naked eyes. They were clear, and brown, and . . . that was it. Because Saint John was just a man, like Hopper. The detective felt a strange feeling of disappointment.

Saint John was just a man.

"Fix this, yes," said Saint John, softly. "You know, they sent us over there, into a nightmare, and what for? For this? For America? For New York? New York is the American nightmare. A ruin, a wasteland. But He can fix it. He has shown me how to fix it."

Hopper's mind reeled as he took in the extent of Saint John's madness. He had been broken by his experiences in Vietnam, put through a world of pain not by the enemy, but by his own side. And then he'd returned only to find his home heading in the same direction.

Hopper understood—there, then, he hated himself for it, but . . . he understood. He'd come back from Vietnam wanting to fix things, change things. Control things.

And so had Johnathan Saint. Two veterans, trying to find a new path in life, a new place in the world.

How different their paths were.

"The boxes," said Hopper. "Those files—the ones at the warehouse. Jacob Hoeler had them stashed away. I stumbled on them, but they disappeared. That was you, right? Or one of the Vipers, anyway, you sent in to get them."

"Ah, Jacob, Jacob, Jacob," said Saint John. He steepled his fingers in front of his chest. "Those files were *mine*, Detective. A record of my work in the jungle. They said it never happened, but it was all there, wasn't it?"

"So Jacob got them for you? He was sent into the Vipers, but you found out who he was, who he worked for. Was that how it went? You found out who he worked for, and what you could use him for."

Saint John made a clicking noise with his tongue, like he was getting bored with the conversation. Hopper took the opportunity to pull again at his arms, but he still couldn't move.

"Jacob Hoeler worked for me, yes," said Saint John. "He was easy to corrupt to my will. He kept the authorities away, giving me the time to set my plans in motion. He had a certain level of access, and was able to leverage that to get my files. There was important work recorded there that I wanted to continue."

"But what? He managed to break free of your control, and tried to take them back? So you had him killed, under the guise of your rituals, and got the files back yourself?"

Saint John's head snapped up. "Have a care, Detective. This is no guise."

Hopper ignored him. "You had him killed, like you had Sam Barrett killed and Jonathan Schnetzer killed."

"James Hopper . . ."

"The support groups, that was your recruiting ground. You went looking for the vulnerable, the susceptible. People who are afraid. Because fear is the key, isn't it? If people are afraid, then you can control them."

"Enough!"

Hopper took a breath. "Listen to me, *Johnathan*, I can help you."

Saint John smiled. "Yes, you can help all of us."

Hopper frowned. Then Saint John gestured to the objects on the table between them.

"You will take the knife and you will kill your partner. Then you will drink from the goblet, and you will die. One victim for Him. One for myself."

"What?"

"You will do what is right. You will do as I command. You will find the path, and you will follow it, because you know it is the truth."

Hopper grimaced. He felt . . . strange. Not light-headed, exactly, but . . . disconnected.

"You want to take the knife. You want to kill her. You want to drink."

Hopper blinked, the room suddenly feeling like it was a thousand miles away, like he was looking down the wrong end of a telescope.

He wanted to take the knife. He wanted to kill. He wanted to drink. He wanted these things because they were right, because they were true. Because he wanted to. Because he wanted to—

He gasped, whooping in great lungfuls of air. He felt spittle on his chin. His hands clenched the arms of the chair, so hard his fingers hurt.

Saint John was speaking, but Hopper couldn't hear him, he just saw his lips move as the instructions continued.

I've been drugged. The sudden moment of clarity brought the room back into sharp focus, Saint John's voice suddenly loud.

Drugged. Whatever it was that he'd been stuck with—some cocktail of hypnotic agents, something from Saint John's time in Vietnam—was interfering with his brain chemistry, making him susceptible to suggestion, pliable to Saint John's commands.

Hopper concentrated. He needed to focus, to clear his mind, to try to resist—perhaps impossibly—the gang leader's suggestions. He began to recite the alphabet backward.

"Z . . ."

"Take the knife. Take the goblet. This is your truth."

"Y . . ."

"Kill the woman. Kill yourself. This is your truth."

"X . . ."

"You serve only He who is coming. This is your truth."

"W . . ."

"You know what you must do. You know what you want to do. This is your truth."

Hopper looked at Saint John. He licked his lips, and frowned.

"W . . . ?"

Then Hopper's head dropped to his chest, and he gave a big, ragged sigh.

"Check him."

Cold fingers on his neck, checking his pulse. Hands on his face, pulling his head around, pulling back his eyelids.

Hopper let them.

"He's too far gone. Give him something to bring him around a little. But measure the dose carefully."

Noise, somewhere behind him. Metallic . . . someone— Leroy?—fixing a new syringe, a new cocktail, something to counteract the original dose that Saint John had miscalculated.

Leroy moved behind Hopper, and pushed his head to one side. Hopper could feel the man's breath as he leaned in, picking the injection spot carefully.

That was when Hopper sprang into action. He jerked his elbow up, connecting with Leroy's throat. The gang member gasped and fell backward, dropping the syringe. Hopper swung out of the chair and, spinning around, grabbed the stumbling Leroy by the collar and dragged him forward, head-butting him. There was a crunch as Leroy's nose broke, and Hopper's own forehead exploded in pain.

Pain he needed, the surge of adrenaline waking him up, clearing his senses.

He spun around as Reuben ran for him, fists already swinging. Hopper avoided them easily, ducking to one side before delivering an uppercut into the man's abdomen. Reuben doubled over, falling sideways and flipping the round table over. The silver goblet flew into the air and fell on Reuben's head just as the gangster was scrambling up from the floor, the surprise of the impact sending him back down as the dark red contents of the goblet spilled over his face.

Saint John roared. He dived at Hopper, catching him around the neck, using his body weight to throw the detective on the ground. Hopper got his arms together and pushed up, trying to break the gang leader's hold, but Saint John was strong. They rolled on the floor, knocking over candles. Hopper pushed— Saint John pushed back, shoving Hopper against the unconscious Delgado. Saint John kicked out, trying to get purchase on the floor, the edge of his robe flying into more of the candles.

There was a soft *whump*, and his robe caught fire. He glanced down, distracted for just a second, and Hopper took the opportunity, bringing his feet up and kicking the gang leader off. Saint John fell backward, then spun on the floor, grabbing for his robe, trying to put the burning edge of it out.

Hopper moved forward, stumbling as a wave of dizziness struck him, the effects of the drugs threatening to take hold once more. Something sparked brilliant white in his vision; shaking his head to clear it, Hopper saw it was the silver dagger, lying on the floor by his hand.

He picked it up, just as Saint John dived at him again. Hopper turned and moved into his attacker, thrusting with the dagger. The blade bent, as though it was going to snap, then Hopper's hand slid forward as the knife shifted and the tip penetrated Saint John's robe at the shoulder, the hilt smacking into Hopper's knuckles as the blade sank all the way in.

Saint John yelled in pain, his strength suddenly sapped. He pulled away, rolling sideways as he hit the floor. He stayed down, one hand groping his shoulder, the other trying—failing—to push up from the floor.

Hopper turned, ready for the next attack, but none was forthcoming. Reuben was slumped against the door, gasping in great wheezing breaths as a white foam clogged his throat and spilled out from his mouth as the poison from the goblet took hold.

Leroy pushed himself up from the floor, his face a wash of blood that continued to flow from his shattered nose. Hopper fell into a crouch, one hand curled into a fist, the other open, ready for the attack.

Then Leroy began to laugh. Hopper tensed, bouncing on the balls of his feet, unsure quite what Leroy was about to do next, unwilling to make any kind of assumption.

That was when Leroy pulled the gun from the back of his pants. Hopper recognized it as a Colt M1911—the same model as his own gun, the one Lincoln had taken off him back at the warehouse.

It seemed that in his little scuffle with Martha, Leroy had picked the weapon up.

"Leroy, listen to me!" said Hopper. How deep was Saint John's programming? Had he dosed his minion up before coming to the Rookwood Institute? Hopper remembered Leroy's state back at the precinct, when he'd come in asking for help. He hadn't been coming down from a high; he'd been coming down from whatever it was that Saint John gave him.

How far gone was he now? Could Hopper even get through

to him? Or was Leroy blindly obeying the last orders of his master, as the rest of the Vipers were?

Hopper unclenched his fist and stood taller, spreading his hands in an unthreatening gesture.

"Leroy, come on now, man. I've got you. You just need to listen to my voice. Remember Martha. She's looking for you. She wants you to be safe. That's what we all want, right? To be safe, and to be free? I can help you. We can do that together. Don't think about anything else. Just focus on my voice. I can get you through this. Martha is waiting for us. We can both get out of here."

The gun in Leroy's hand began to shake. Hopper tensed, his eyes falling to the barrel. He took a step closer. He looked back at the young man.

"You can put the gun down. It's just me. You remember me, right? I tried to help you before. I can help you now. We can get out and we can go to your sister. Martha's outside. We can find her. She's waiting for you. You just need to put the gun down."

The shaking increased. Leroy's face twisted in agony, the muscles at the back of his jaw bunching as he struggled against his programming.

The gun arm went down.

Hopper took a breath, took another step forward.

"That's it, Leroy, I can help you. Just concentrate on the sound of my voice. I can get us through this."

Leroy shuddered.

He lifted the gun and took aim.

Hopper stopped right where he was, and raised his hands, shaking his head.

"Leroy, I can help you."

The gangster dropped his gun arm again; Hopper moved forward, but then Leroy cried out, his mental pain self-evident. He lifted the gun and squeezed the trigger.

Hopper was too late. He knocked Leroy's arm as the gun went off, the explosion of sound deadening the world, leaving nothing but a high-pitched whine in Hopper's ear. He felt a tugging on his upper left arm, and then a moment later it felt like his shoulder was on fire.

He'd been shot. How badly, he didn't know, but his arm still worked. For that he was grateful, as he continued to wrestle with Leroy.

Leroy's resistance quickly faded. Hopper had his gun arm by the wrist, and it only took one shake to make him drop the weapon. Hopper managed to throw his other elbow under Leroy's chin, the impact making Leroy's knees buckle. The young man grunted, then collapsed onto the floor.

Hopper fell to his knees, his hand clutching at his injured upper arm. His sleeve was soaked with blood, and the pain was a white-hot sear that flared as he rolled his shoulder.

He would live.

He got to his feet and spun around, other concerns on his mind.

Delgado.

In the struggle with Saint John, she had been shunted across the floor, and was now lying on her side, her hair perilously close to a couple of the black candles. Hopper ran over and fell to his knees, swiping the candles out of the way as he rolled Delgado onto her back. He checked her pulse and lowered his ear to her mouth, ready to administer CPR, but then she gave a groan, her eyes flickering open. She lifted her head, looked at Hopper, then sighed again, her head falling back onto the hard floor. She winced in pain, and gave a faint "ow."

Satisfied she was beginning to recover, Hopper looked over to Saint John. The gang leader was still lying on the floor, but had rolled onto his side. He was facing Hopper, one hand clutching the soaked mess of his robe at the shoulder. He was panting, and blood trickled from the corner of his mouth.

His glasses were gone, lost in the fight. He blinked as he looked at Hopper.

Hopper moved over, ready to push the gang leader onto his

back and apply pressure to his wound. The knife had been pulled out, and the injury was worse than Hopper had initially realized. The amount of blood suggested a major artery had been severed.

As he touched Saint John, the gang leader tried to push him away, but he had little strength.

"Hey, hey, settle down, I need to stop the bleeding."

Saint John didn't speak, but he did smile, and as Hopper rolled him over, he began to laugh.

Hopper found the hole in the robe and poked his fingers through, tearing the cloth open to expose the wound. Bright arterial blood was bubbling out of it like spring water.

"Sacrifice," Saint John managed to whisper. He looked at Hopper with his big brown eyes. "You . . . believe me . . . don't . . . you?"

Hopper didn't answer. His fingers slid around in the blood, trying to find a way to stanch the flow.

How was there so much blood?

Saint John closed his eyes. "Sometimes good men . . . good men do bad things. Sometimes . . . good men . . . have . . . no choice."

He lay still, his face pale, his blood soaking the robe and soaking Hopper and soaking into the pentagram carved with heavy, ragged strokes in the floor.

Hopper knelt beside him for a few moments, then pushed himself to his feet.

"Ah . . . Hopper?"

He turned as Delgado moved again on the floor. He went over to her and helped her sit up. She shook her head and leaned into his chest. He cradled her head in his bloodied hands.

They stayed like that until the agents arrived.

CHAPTER FIFTY-TWO

THE AFTERMATH OF TERROR

JULY 14, 1977
BROOKLYN, NEW YORK

After they'd patched up his shoulder—although it was only a graze, his arm ached like the bullet had gone right through it—Hopper sat on the tailgate of the ambulance and, with a wince, pulled the blanket around his shoulders just a little tighter. The night hadn't gotten any cooler, but he felt a chill from somewhere.

His imagination, most likely.

The area around the Rookwood Institute was packed with vehicles—ambulances, fire trucks, and at least a dozen police cruisers, their lights strobing the street in a maelstrom of blue and white that made Hopper's head spin. The drugs still hadn't quite worn off, and once again he felt a little disconnected, like he'd been sitting on the tailgate for a thousand years, and what had happened inside the Rookwood Institute had taken place in some kind of dream, long ago.

He slipped off the tailgate and got to his feet. He waited, making sure he really could stay upright, then walked over to the next ambulance. Inside, Delgado was sitting up on a stretcher, answering the rapid-fire questions from the attending paramedic as he inflated a blood pressure cuff strapped to the detective's upper arm. As Hopper appeared, she met his eyes and smiled, giving a small nod before sinking her head back into the pillow.

She was alive.

As was Leroy. Hopper moved to the next ambulance—here, the young man was laid out on the stretcher, a paramedic examining his pupils with a penlight while another filled out a checklist on a clipboard. Leroy lifted an arm, but the medic with the light pushed it back down; he was conscious, but still under the influence of whatever the hell Saint John had dosed him with.

But he was alive.

Hopper turned back to the street. Of the army of Vipers, only a handful remained, and they were all in police custody, sitting in the backs of cruisers, the uniforms already trying to get them to talk. The rest had apparently fled before the first federal agents—a small section of Gallup's task force—had even arrived.

As two police cruisers moved away from the curb, another vehicle appeared, a dark, unmarked car with a magnetic light flashing over the driver's side. It pulled up at an angle and the front doors flew open, Martha and Special Agent Gallup piling out. Hopper ditched the blanket and joined the pair in the middle of the street.

Martha looked him up and down. "Are you okay? What the hell happened?"

Hopper glanced down at himself, still soaked in Saint John's blood.

"I'm okay, I'm okay," he said. "I'm guessing you didn't find a way down here after all."

"Yeah, well, you can blame this fool for that." Martha threw a glare at Gallup. "Said he could give me a car, then damn well locked me in it!" Then she turned in a circle, looking around at the gathering of emergency vehicles. "Where's Leroy? Hopper, was he here?"

Hopper pointed to one of the ambulances. Martha took off, almost falling over her feet. She ducked into the ambulance, ignoring the surprise of the paramedics, and fell on Leroy as she hugged him. Hopper could just see Leroy lift his arms, embracing his sister weakly.

"It's over, Detective."

Hopper rubbed his face, and turned to Gallup. He took a deep breath, pulling himself together. His body ached and he felt so very, very tired.

Gallup patted him on the shoulder.

"It's over," he said. "Go home. Go to your family."

Dawn was breaking as Hopper ran up the stoop in front of his building, the lights of the police car he had been driven in beginning to be washed out by the brightening morning sun. Before he got to the top, the front door opened and Diane appeared, Sara cradled in her arms, the young girl sleeping with her head tucked under her mother's chin.

Hopper paused, two steps from the top. Diane laughed, a reaction to the intense relief she must have felt, her face wet with tears.

Hopper joined her, his own eyes streaming. He and his wife stood in the middle of the building's lobby and hugged. The pressure on Hopper's injured arm, trapped between their bodies, was painful, but Hopper happily ignored the discomfort.

Ensconced safely between them, Sara blinked awake, and lifted her head. She looked up at Diane, then at Hopper. She rubbed one eye with the back of her small hand.

"Is that you, Daddy?"

"It's me, darling, it's me." He kissed her cheek. "I'm home."

CHAPTER FIFTY-THREE

HEROES, JUST FOR ONE DAY

JULY 26, 1977
BROOKLYN, NEW YORK

"So, Cher, you sure you want to do this?"

"Shouldn't you be standing with your hands on your hips?"

"Jackass."

"Hey, wait a second?"

"Wait, what?"

"I'm Sonny. *You're* Cher."

"Why am I Cher?"

"What? Because Cher is a woman. I'm Sonny. You're Cher."

"Cher is a woman?"

"Are you telling me you don't know who Sonny and Cher are?"

"Should I know who they are?"

"You *have* to be kidding me. Please tell me you're kidding right now."

"Hey, don't blame me, I'm from Cuba."

"You're not from Cuba, you're from Queens. And you know who Sonny and Cher are."

"Question still stands."

"Question?"

"Are you sure you're ready for this? Because you know what's going to be waiting for us on the other side of this door, right?"

"Yeah, but . . ."

"So are you sure you want to do this?"

"You're telling me we have a choice?"

"Ah . . . well, put it that way."

"Maybe they haven't done anything."

"Actually, that wouldn't surprise me."

"It's not the captain's style, right? He's not into that."

"No, that's true."

"So maybe there's nothing. Maybe they haven't done anything."

"Right."

"Which means we can just go in."

"Right."

"You know what else that means, Detective Delgado?"

"What's that, Detective Hopper?"

"It means we're actually late for work."

Delgado looked up at her partner, her mouth hooked into a wicked grin.

"I think we're allowed to be. I mean, just this once, right? We've been through a lot. I was in the hospital, you know? They even kept me in overnight. Over*night*, Detective Hopper."

Hopper laughed. "I should have sent you flowers."

"I'm allergic," said Delgado. "How's the arm?"

Hopper lifted his left arm, which was still in a sling. "It still hurts. Quite a lot, too."

"One."

Hopper frowned. "One what?"

"I'm keeping count. You're allowed to say your arm hurts four times a day, and that's me being generous After that, you will see a somewhat less patient side to me, partner."

Hopper used his injured arm to give a salute. "Ow. Yes, ma'am."

That was when one of the double doors leading to the homicide bull pen was pushed open. Captain LaVorgna stood in the doorway, shaking his head.

"Are you two going to come in, or do you want an invitation from the mayor?"

"Only if it's from Bella Abzug," said Delgado.

"And only if it's engraved," said Hopper.

"You wish," said LaVorgna. "City can't afford shit like that. And you weren't in the hospital *that* long, Delgado. Besides, after all that went down, Cuomo has it all sewn up. Just you wait and see."

Delgado gave Hopper a frown.

"It's the heat, right? The captain's rigid adherence to dress code has finally boiled his brain? Or maybe it's from being cooped up in a tiny office with a perpetual cloud of cigarette smoke."

Hopper opened his mouth to say something, but the glare from LaVorgna suggested he keep it to himself.

The captain then stepped into the hallway, holding the door open. He gestured for the two detectives to step through.

Hopper and Delgado exchanged a look. Hopper couldn't resist cracking a grin; Delgado matched his expression, and led the way through.

The bull pen erupted in applause. Hopper followed Delgado in, the pair stopping as around them the other detectives all moved forward to make a semicircle, hailing the returned detectives. It wasn't just their shift, either—Sergeant Connelly's night crew had stayed behind to join the welcoming party.

Hopper felt a heavy hand slap him on the back. LaVorgna stepped between the two detectives, an arm around each of their shoulders.

"Okay, people, that's enough. Someone might hear and think we've actually solved a case." He dropped his arms as the applause died down, and stepped forward to address the assembled detectives. "Now, it's not often we have cause to celebrate quite like this, but the fact is that your two colleagues here have done good work. You might think that's faint praise, with what they've been through, but let me make myself clear. I expect each and every one of you to do your jobs. That's why you are here. That's why you work for me. So when I tell you that the work you have done is good, believe me, there is no higher level. Good work is what keeps this town safe. Good work will save us when nothing else will."

There was a murmur of laughter from the detectives, as well as a fair number of puzzled expressions, mostly from, Hopper noted, the night shift.

The captain turned around to face him and Delgado. "You've done good work, Detectives. And there's still good work left to be done, not to mention the report you're going to have to prepare for your trip down to Washington on Thursday. Special Agent Gallup already called to say he and his besuited friends are looking forward to a very long and very productive debrief with you two and Leroy and Martha."

Delgado raised an eyebrow. She glanced sideways at her partner.

"Long and productive?"

"Sounds like that'll be a fun day," said Hopper.

"So," said the captain, gesturing over toward their desks, "how about you get your asses in your chairs and get started?"

Then he grinned, and gave a single, loud clap.

"And there's drinks at Mahoney's tonight."

Hopper laughed. "Thanks, Captain, it's good to be back."

LaVorgna gave a nod and headed back to his office. As Hopper and Delgado made their way over to their shared desks, the other detectives moved in for handshakes and backslaps. Hopper acknowledged them all, but he felt the smile on his face fade by the time he was standing behind his chair. Delgado sat down at her own desk and stared at it with a frown. Then she looked at him.

"What's up?"

Hopper pursed his lips, then sat down. "Returning heroes, right?"

"Hey, don't let the captain's speech go to your head, Hop," his partner joked.

Hopper smiled, weakly. "I was a hero before, once. At least that's what they told me."

"They gave you a medal for it. That seems like proof enough to me."

"But," said Hopper, his eyes falling to his desk, "that's not why we do it, is it? The captain was right."

"Actually he was. We're here to do our job. And that's what we did."

Hopper stared at his desk. Delgado sighed and reached down, pulling open a drawer and pulling out a bottle of scotch. She placed it on the desk between them. Hopper looked at it, one eyebrow raised.

"They drink scotch in Cuba?"

"No, they drink scotch in Queens, jackass."

Delgado poured a measure into her coffee mug, and did the same for Hopper.

"To doing a good job," she said, raising her mug.

Hopper raised his.

"To doing a good job." He drained it in one gulp, then offered his mug to Delgado.

She laughed, and poured again.

"Drinking on the job, Hop. What would the captain say?"

Hopper smiled and lifted his arm. "Still hurts. Bad sprain, they said."

"Two."

Hopper lifted his mug. "I'll drink to that," he said.

HOPPER'S CABIN
HAWKINS, INDIANA

In Hopper's grandfather's cabin, silence reigned. Hopper himself sat in the armchair, El on the couch in front of him, the blankets still wrapped around her as she sat, watching something in the middle distance.

It was late—after midnight, in fact. But that was okay. They had no plans for the day. They could both have a big sleep-in.

But he wasn't sure he could get to sleep. Not just yet. And as he looked at El, he worried again that he'd gone too far.

"Ah, look," he began, and then he stopped as El looked up at him.

"Thanks," she said.

"I . . . Okay, sure, I guess." Hopper rubbed his face. "I just wanted to say I was sorry."

El sat up taller, giving him a quizzical look.

"For telling you that story, I mean. Maybe you're a little young for it."

"No," she said. "I learned . . . You helped people."

Hopper laughed, "Hey, thanks!"

"Why were you sad?"

Hopper looked at El, the laughter dying in his throat. "Sad?"

"You saved people," said El. "But . . ."

"I also watched people die."

"You were a hero." El tilted her head. "Heroes are good."

Hopper chuckled quietly. "That's true, but I think I spent most of the time just trying to get the hell out of trouble and stay alive. And look, kid, being a hero is all fine and dandy, but it's not why you do things. Nobody should want to be a hero. All you should want to do is the right thing. Heroism is not a job description. Being a cop is my job description. Being a cop is the right thing for me to do, so I do it—I do it now, I did it then. It was just my job, and I tried to do it well."

El nodded, then yawned. Hopper tried to resist yawning himself, but the face he pulled in his attempt made El laugh. Giving in, Hopper then stood and stretched.

"Okay, kid. Bed. Now. And you're allowed to sleep in, but not too late, okay? I don't want these late nights to become a habit."

El unraveled herself from the blankets and headed to her room. She stopped at the red table and picked up the Zener card, still sealed in its evidence bag. Hopper paused, watching his daughter as she looked at the card before placing it back in the New York file box and closing the lid.

Then she headed into her bedroom, the door closing behind her without being touched.

Hopper smiled, his hands on his hips. He was exhausted, but happy. Maybe El had learned something, something about his past, his old life, in a city far away, doing a job that was as rewarding as it was dangerous.

His old life.

Hopper lifted the New York file box and carried it back into the den. Kneeling down, he pushed the rug to one side and pulled up the trapdoor leading to the storage space. Reaching in, he felt for the light switch and flicked it, the small, cramped space weakly illuminated by the small bulb.

Hopper gently dropped the box into the empty space.

Then he turned off the light, closed the trapdoor, and went to bed.

BROOKLYN, NEW YORK

I t wasn't snowing, it was sleeting, and it was coming down in sheets that were being driven by a wickedly sharp wind that made the sub-forty-degree chill feel dangerously arctic, and the whole street outside was just an icy nightmare and—

And Hopper was loving every frozen minute of it. Because inside their apartment, inside the Brooklyn brownstone, it was warm and light and he had his family around him.

And it was Christmas.

Hopper loved Christmas.

He sat back in the armchair and closed his eyes, and when he opened them a moment later he found Diane staring at him from her position on the floor, where she was wrangling wrapped gifts from under the tree with Sara's able assistance. She had a large, flat, rectangular present in her hands now—*ah, yes, that one next, excellent, Sara's going to love it*—but with one eyebrow raised and her lips pursed, Hopper wasn't sure what the holdup was.

"Everything okay there, grandpa?" asked Diane.

Hopper opened his mouth, then closed it again. Sara laughed, and told Diane in no uncertain terms that Daddy was most certainly not Pops and to think otherwise made Mommy the silliest person in the street, if not the whole world.

"*Grandpa?*" Hopper finally managed. He glanced down at himself. "Is this your way of telling me this delightful sweater my delightful wife got me for Christmas makes me look mature and dignified?"

Diane laughed, their daughter joining in while attempting to reclothe her new doll, the first Christmas present she had opened. Beside her on the floor was gift number two, a large picture book, the cover proclaiming the wonders of outer space. Hopper was quite keen to take a look at that book himself, when he had a chance.

"No, it's not the sweater," said Diane. "But I'm glad you like it."

"Like it? I love it!"

"Good. But no, it was more the contented sigh and the closed eyes. Maybe I should have gotten you a pipe and slippers, too."

Hopper grinned. "If I sighed—and I'm not saying I did, hear me out here—but *if* I sighed, then it most certainly was contented." At that, he sat back again and closed his eyes, then wiggled his behind in an exaggerated way and clasped his hands across his middle. He pretended to snore, eliciting another gale of giggles from Sara.

The *whack* of the heavy present in Diane's hand brought Hopper back to life. He laughed and scooted forward, taking the gift and checking the card.

"Oh, hey, this is a special gift for Sara from her Mommy and Daddy! Come over here, kid. Come on!"

Sara bounced up from the floor and raced over to Hopper's

armchair, clambering onto his lap before reaching for the present. Diane stood and moved over to her husband's side, settling down on the side of his chair and draping an arm around Hopper's neck. Hopper glanced up and the couple exchanged a quick peck on the lips while Sara demolished the wrapping paper, revealing a large, hardcover book. On the front was an illustration of a young girl in a blue dress with blond hair peering into a mirror.

Sara turned to look up at her parents, her face a picture of delight. She recognized the girl on the front of the book, and immediately started flipping through the pages, searching out the other familiar illustrations she clearly knew were hidden within.

"Hey now, careful there, kid," said Hopper, gently taking hold of Sara's hands to guide her in a less frenzied pace. He adjusted the book in front of her and turned back to the title page.

"*Through the Looking-Glass, and What Alice Found There,*" he read, tracing the words with his finger.

"Alice!" Sara nearly shouted. "I love Alice so much, because she had tea with the queen and the cat and she fell down in that hole."

Diane stroked Sara's hair. "That's right, honey! And she has a whole other story. Daddy can start reading it to you tonight."

Sara twisted to look up at her dad. "Can I go to bed now so you can start reading?"

"You can't go to bed now, or you'll turn into a grandpa like your dad."

Sara laughed.

Diane leaned into Hopper. "You know, I'm not sure I ever read this book."

"Well, she loved the first one so much, didn't she? Actually, you did too, now I recall."

Diane squeezed Hopper's shoulder. "Maybe I can come listen, too."

Sara flipped the book over to show the back cover, then laid her arms across it and gripped the far edge with both hands.

"I think Daddy can start reading now. Because you can read books at any time of the day, not just bedtime."

Hopper pursed his lips.

"She's right, you know."

"Actually, she is," said Diane.

"Okay," said Hopper, sitting himself upright and dragging Sara back into his lap. "Gather round, gather round, it's time for a Christmas story." He paused. "Well, a story told on Christmas, not a Christmas story—"

"Daddy, come on!"

"Oh, tough crowd," said Hopper.

Then he opened the book, and with his child on his lap and his wife at his side, he began to read.

Acknowledgments

My thanks to editor extraordinaire Tom Hoeler, for his ceaseless hard work, endless enthusiasm, and superlative skills. Tom, Elizabeth Schaefer, and the whole team at Del Rey pulled out all the stops on this one, and I'm eternally grateful for being given the opportunity to work on such an exciting project—a project that wouldn't exist if it weren't for the imagination and vision of the Duffer brothers and Netflix, who created a whole universe and were gracious enough to let me play in it. My thanks also to Paul Dichter for his advice and insight.

Heartfelt thanks as always to my agent, Stacia Decker at Dunow, Carlson & Lerner. Thanks also to David M. Barnett, Bria LaVorgna, Cavan Scott, and Jen Williams for their support, and to Martin Simmonds for the wonderful art print of Eleven that hangs proudly on my office wall. Special thanks to Jason Fry and Greg Prince for the in-depth knowledge of baseball in 1977, and to Greg Young and Tom Meyers of *The Bowery Boys: New York City History* podcast for research assistance.

Being able to add to the mythology of a show like *Stranger Things* is a real honor, and it just wouldn't be the same if it wasn't for David Harbour and Millie Bobby Brown, who brought Jim Hopper and Eleven to such vivid on-screen life. I hope I've done your characters justice.

Finally, to my wife, Sandra, for infinite patience and love and encouragement when I needed it the most. This one is for you.

About the Author

ADAM CHRISTOPHER's debut novel, *Empire State*, was *SciFiNow*'s Book of the Year and a *Financial Times* Book of the Year. His other novels include *Seven Wonders*, *Hang Wire*, *The Burning Dark*, and the Ray Electromatic Mysteries series. A contributor to the internationally bestselling *Star Wars: From a Certain Point of View* fortieth-anniversary anthology, Christopher has also written the official tie-in novels for the hit CBS television show *Elementary* and the award-winning *Dishonored* videogame franchise and, with Chuck Wendig, wrote *The Shield* for Dark Circle/Archie Comics. Born in New Zealand, Christopher has lived in Great Britain since 2006.

adamchristopher.co.uk
Twitter: @ghostfinder

About the Type

This book was set in Aster, a typeface designed in 1958 by Francesco Simoncini (d. 1967). Aster is a round, legible face of even weight and was planned by the designer for the text setting of newspapers and books.